PRAISE FOR TALL BONES

FROM

'A striking first novel, a chilling in ... re bad thoughts and bad deeds ripp ... t'
Alison Fl

'A nuanced thriller that will haunt you long after you race through its pages'
***GRAZIA* Book of the Month**

'One of the most exciting debuts of the year'
SUNDAY EXPRESS

'Fast-paced and moving'
Natasha Cooper, *LITERARY REVIEW*

'Beautifully written and very moving ... an assured debut'
Laura Wilson, *GUARDIAN*

'Both menacing and haunting'
Geoffrey Wansell, *DAILY MAIL*

'Spellbinding and darkly beautiful... a stunning debut'
WOMEN & HOME

'Bleak and haunting'
Maxim Jakubowski, *CRIME TIME*

'The best kind of small-town crime novel... a dark and compulsive literary crime-drama that will stay with you'
CULTUREFLY

'Cleverly written, Anna Bailey's debut shines a light on the darker and more oppressive side of small-town society'
Sophie Morris, *INDEPENDENT*

'Bailey writes with perfect poise. She is destined for great things'
SAGA magazine

'Has all the elements of classic American crime'
I NEWSPAPER

'Vividly captures a simmering atmosphere of suspicion and repression'
IRISH INDEPENDENT

'A mix of the Salem witch trials meets *Gone Girl*, this is an eerie, timeless book'
WOMAN'S OWN

FROM AUTHORS:

'With *Tall Bones*, Anna Bailey bursts on to the scene with a wonderfully haunting debut. Small-town intrigue, exquisitely drawn'
JANE HARPER, author of *The Dry* and *The Lost Man*

'Irresistible, a compelling and nuanced psychological thriller suffused with small-town prejudice and dark family secrets'
PAULA HAWKINS, author of *The Girl on the Train*

'[The] portrait of small-town intrigue is scarily credible. Bailey understands that the dynamics that drive small-town relationships are the same the world over'
VAL McDERMID

'A clever, twisting debut, about the dark side of small-town America. It is packed with secrets like firecrackers ready to ignite'
FRANCINE TOON, author of *Pine*

'Anna Bailey writes like a dream about teenage love and lust, the terror of knowledge and the claustrophobia of families and of small towns'
EMMA FLINT, author of *Little Deaths*

'An intricate and compelling thriller, beautifully nuanced and wonderfully claustrophobic. Brilliant'
S. J. WATSON, author of *Before I Go to Sleep*

'As atmospheric as it gets. Anna writes beautifully'
RENEE KNIGHT, author of *Disclaimer*

'Extremely well written ... fantastic'
HARRIET TYCE, author of *Blood Orange*

'A terrific debut about guilt, secrets and complex family dynamics – Anna Bailey is definitely one to watch'
LUCY ATKINS, author of *Magpie Lane*

'Chilling and compulsive ... a dazzling debut'
KATE HAMER, author of *The Girl in the Red Coat*

'Smart and compassionate, full of poetry and rage'
TAMMY COHEN

'Brilliant! Could not put it down. It's utterly gripping and beautifully written'
KATIE FFORDE

'Simmering resentments and long-held prejudices boil over in this beautifully realised evocation of small-town America ... I loved it'
KATE RIORDAN, author of *The Heatwave*

'Gripping and so beautifully written, *Tall Bones* is spellbinding; dark and menacing, but also so full of love and hope'
CRESSIDA McLAUGHLIN

FROM READERS:

'The most beautifully written thriller I've read for a long time'

'A nuanced, literary thriller written with stunning attention to detail in such eloquent prose I savoured every word ... if I could give more than five stars I would'

'I loved this book from the very first line'

'An exceptionally well-crafted and engrossing novel. What really held me throughout though was the sheer emotional intelligence which brought the disparate characters to life and genuinely made me care for them'

'Raw, heart-wrenching and tender'

'I'm currently suffering a bit of a book hangover and I can't stop thinking about it. Absolutely gorgeous and utterly glorious. From the opening chapters this book had a hold over me and I savoured every moment I spent with it'

'This book had me spinning around, chasing my tail at every page turn'

'Gritty, haunting, and frighteningly plausible ... this is one story that will keep you hanging on its every word and take your breath away'

'Perfectly drawn characters ... A lyrical and beautiful style ... A fearless tackling of difficult subjects, realised with compassion, depth and humanity... These are all things that make *Tall Bones* a must-read'

'This book gave me *Twin Peaks* vibes along with *The Devil All the Time*'

'Read this if you like small towns, murder, and becoming so emotionally attached to characters that a part of you dies when you finish a book ... I'll be thinking about this book for a long time'

'I rarely give out 5 stars but this one deserved every one of them. When you find yourself reading passages out loud to the family, you know you are enjoying something special'

Tall Bones

Anna Bailey

PENGUIN BOOKS

TRANSWORLD PUBLISHERS
Penguin Random House, One Embassy Gardens,
8 Viaduct Gardens, London SW11 7BW
www.penguin.co.uk

Transworld is part of the Penguin Random House group of companies
whose addresses can be found at global.penguinrandomhouse.com

First published in Great Britain in 2021 by Doubleday
an imprint of Transworld Publishers
Penguin paperback edition published 2022

A CIP catalogue record for this book
is available from the British Library.

ISBN
9781529176452

Typeset in 10.14/14.20pt Giovanni Book by Jouve (UK), Milton Keynes.
Printed and bound in Great Britain by Clays Ltd, Elcograf S.p.A.

The authorized representative in the EEA is Penguin Random House Ireland,
Morrison Chambers, 32 Nassau Street, Dublin D02 YH68.

Penguin Random House is committed to a sustainable
future for our business, our readers and our planet. This book
is made from Forest Stewardship Council® certified paper.

For my mother, Jane

1

THE ROAR OF the bonfire is hard to distinguish from the sound of the trailer-park boys and the schoolgirls who holler and dance in the shadow of the Tall Bones. It is a small-town sort of night – the last that Whistling Ridge will see for many years to come, although nobody knows this yet – in the kind of town where coyotes chew on stray cigarette butts and packs of boys go howling at the moon.

Abigail Blake turns at the edge of the trees and smiles at Emma. This will be the memory of Abigail that stays with Emma long after the rest has been drunk away: long and pale as a moonbeam, flyaway red hairs curling gently in the damp air, hands buried deep in her sleeves, standing on the balls of her feet, like she might take off running at any moment.

'I'll be fine,' she says. Her eyes give her away, darting ahead into the forest. They are not long into September, but fall comes quicker in the mountains, and already the early night has stolen over the pines, their opaque shadows broken only by the beam of a single flashlight.

'But how are you going to get home?' There's a little dent in her brow, Emma thinks, just the right shape and size for the pad of her thumb.

'Em.' It's as if she has to remember to smile again. 'I'll just call a cab or something. I'll figure it out. Really, it's fine.' She looks at the light hovering among the trees and, behind it, the vague shape of a boy. Emma follows her gaze, but it's too dark to make him out properly.

'I don't think you should go.'

Abigail's grin looks so tight it must hurt. 'It's just fun, Em. Don't worry about it.'

Emma does worry about it. She isn't tall like Abigail, doesn't have the same gap between her thighs like all teenage girls want; the only thing her father ever gave her was his Latino complexion, and it has dogged her all the way through school; she isn't the kind of girl boys ask to go into the woods with them, so what would she know? But still she shakes her head as she peers into the darkness. 'I'll wait here for you.'

'No.' Abigail takes a deep breath and smiles firmly again. She smells of her strawberry Chapstick. 'Come on, Em, let me live a little, huh? I'll be fine. *Promise*.'

Abigail Blake is seventeen and, like all girls her age, she believes she's going to live for ever. Deep down, Emma believes it too, and that is why she leaves her friend there, where the stomped-down grass of the field meets the trees, and slouches back out past the Tall Bones to her car. The fire is still crackling away, its light snaking off the surface of those towering pale rocks. The partygoers cheer as they smash beer cans together and hurl them on to the fire, cooing with delight as the flames *whoosh* higher into the dark.

Emma doesn't look back. If she had, she might have seen Abigail hesitate, hand outstretched as if perhaps, in the end, she hadn't really expected Emma to leave.

There is another young man watching her from the other side of the bonfire. He has a wicked sort of gaze, which makes

Emma feel as if she's shivering even though she isn't. She has seen him around, lingering on the edge of town since springtime, but she knows him only by sight. A profile sharp enough to cut cocaine, dark hair brushing the collar of his worn-out leather jacket: there is something in the motion of his hips, the way he juts out his chin, that feels like he might have been a highwayman in a previous life. Evening rain has stripped back the heat of the day, and now his cigarette breath hovers in the cool air the way storm clouds do around mountain peaks. When she looks again, he is gone.

'Where have you been?' Dolly Blake stubs out her cigarette as her eldest son tries to close the front door quietly behind him.

'Nowhere.'

Noah emerges from the gloom of the hallway, and for a moment Dolly tenses, seeing in his lean, lanky shape that of her husband. From a distance they are often confused for one another – the same down-and-out plaid shirts, that same flash of red hair, same high-set shoulders, as if they're worried someone might peek over and see something they shouldn't. But although at twenty-two he is a man now, Noah's face retains the gentle edges of youth, which his father Samuel Blake exchanged a long time ago for a wiry beard and weathered skin from long hours spent hauling timber. Dolly breathes a sigh of relief.

'You're lucky your dad went to bed early,' she says. 'What did you do to your jeans? They're filthy.'

'None of your business.'

Above him on the wall hangs the large gemstone cross that Dolly's mother-in-law gave her as a wedding present nearly a quarter of a century ago. Behind it, Dolly knows, there is a hole where Samuel once punched through the plaster.

'Don't give me that attitude, young man,' she says, but she isn't looking at her son, she's looking at the cross. 'I don't care how old you are, when you live under this roof, you get yourself home on time, and you talk to your mother with more respect.'

'You never give Abi the third degree like this.' He steps around her with his long muddy legs, and beats a hard, familiar tattoo up the stairs to his room.

Dolly sighs and digs her nails into her scalp. She wishes he weren't the only one she can stand to lose her temper around, but she knows she has to lose it sometimes. Otherwise one day she might just burst.

Emma turns the car radio on, some late-night psychic, who says nothing of the events to come, so she drives away from Abigail without a second thought. Puddles on the county road flash yellow in her headlights, and the smell of wet tarmac coming through the air vents reminds her of wax crayons. She knows the route well, even at night. On either side steep banks are covered with conifers, leading up to dusty mountain peaks where the trees grow stumpy and fade out altogether as they approach the timberline.

After a mile, the tree line following the curve of the road breaks away. Pine bark beetles have infected the evergreens here, and huge patches of the woodland are grey and brittle. In the daylight, through their thin dead branches, she can glimpse the blackened remains of the old Winslow house, hollowed out by fire over a century ago. Usually she can look right through the empty windows all the way to the other side, and even though she knows she won't be able to see a thing in the dark, Emma glances at it as she drives by, just out of habit.

There is a light.

Something glimmers behind an old window frame. Emma slows the car, but the light swings suddenly, sharply, and is snuffed out.

She will tell the police this when they question her, eventually, plundering all the last precious details she has of Abigail.

The bonfire has been tamped down and now the blackened circle of its remains looks like somewhere a UFO might have come to land. The Tall Bones are silent silhouettes against a night sky silvered with moonlight. The partygoers have scattered back down the road towards Jerry Maddox's trailer park, or crammed into their friends' cars and driven home through the woods, so there is no one around to hear the gun when it goes off.

Tomorrow is Sunday, and the Blakes cannot yet imagine that they will sit in their usual lonely row of fold-up plastic chairs at church without Abigail beside them. Tomorrow is Sunday, and Emma is supposed to bleach Abigail's hair for her, because Abigail is tired of being ginger, even though she knows her parents will say she looks cheap. Tomorrow is Sunday, and Emma lies awake listening to the coyotes wail and wishes she were one of them. In the morning she will check her phone, void of any reassurance from Abigail that she made it safely home. Her eyes will return to that box of bleach, sitting unopened on the dresser, and somehow, she will know.

By the end of the week, Abigail's face will grin emptily from a hundred flyers tacked to telephone poles and church billboards, flapping in the Rocky Mountain breeze. Samuel Blake will go out into the forest with the police department, crying his daughter's name into the trees. Noah will scrub the stains on his jeans until his fingers are raw, and Emma will hide the box of bleach under her bed. Dolly, sucking on her cigarettes, will knead the flaky flesh of her scalp, and stare at the big cross hiding the hole in the wall, afraid that, now, all the wrong things will come out.

2

'HOLD STILL, JUDE.' Dolly catches her youngest son by the chin and keeps him in place while she dabs concealer over the bruise around his eye. He winces, but she only shakes her head and grips him tighter, forefinger and thumb pinching deep into the skin. 'Got no one to blame but yourself. You know what your dad's like if you wake him early.'

Samuel won't like the makeup. No boy of mine wears makeup, he'll say. At sixty-two he is old enough to be her father, and often that line seems blurred enough that Dolly will do what he says without question. But today will be different. He won't like the makeup, but he'll like it better than everyone at church staring and whispering behind their Bibles. No wonder the daughter's gone, they'll say, in a house like that. No wonder the daughter's dead.

Dead. She heard the word in Safeway the other day, muttered in the frozen-food aisle. Mr Wen from the liquor store and Carla Patterson, who taught Abigail in her sophomore year, said it softly under the hum of strip lighting and refrigerators, hoping perhaps that they wouldn't be heard. At least they had the good grace to look guilty when they saw Dolly round the corner with her empty shopping cart. She didn't say anything, as she so often doesn't, perhaps because she wasn't really sure how it made her feel.

Dead. It sounded like a stop at the end of a sentence. She imagined sending a telegram and replacing all the stops with 'dead': Abigail will be just fine dead Abigail will come back dead. By then it had been only a week since her daughter's vanishing, but time felt strange and long to Dolly, as if it were being stretched out like taffy on one of those old machines you sometimes saw in candy-store windows.

Two weeks exactly now, and Dolly has gone to the grocery store almost every day, just so she can rest her weight on the handle of a shopping cart and let it drag her along. Meandering through the aisles gives her something to do. She refuses to be like those women in movies who go stir crazy sitting at home waiting for the phone to ring. Time keeps on going, and so, she thinks, it can't be the end of the sentence yet.

In the bathroom, Jude sticks out his bottom lip, an action he has learned from his older brother, although in all other ways he and Noah are chalk and cheese. Ten years apart, Jude slight where Noah is all broad shoulders; dark-haired and unopinionated, and with a tendency towards neatness, where his brother has the dirt of this town embedded in the whorls of his fingerprints. And then, of course, there's Jude's leg. A shattered bone, struck too hard like white-hot metal on a blacksmith's anvil, all beat out of shape. No boy should have to walk with a stick at twelve.

Dolly applies another layer of concealer to her son's swollen eye socket but does not meet his gaze. Poor unplanned Jude. Jude, whom she tried to escape by sitting in scorching baths until the water turned cold and dirty, drinking two thirds of a bottle of gin from her husband's liquor cabinet before she threw up. A cruel trick of the Lord's, she'd thought back then, to bring another child into this house. She still wonders if she wasn't right.

'There,' Dolly says, taking a step back to assess her handiwork. The swelling will take a day or two to go down, but at least she's managed to neutralize the insolent red left by her husband's hand.

'Do I have to go?' Jude leans in closer to the grey-edged mirror, his fingers hovering around his eye, as though he wants desperately to touch the bruise and make sure it's still him underneath. 'I don't feel like church. Everyone will look at us.'

Of course they'll look at us, Dolly thinks. The remaining Blakes have spent the last two Sundays knocking back can after can of Lone Star, or wandering grocery-store aisles, or lying on the bed in the middle of the day listening to the rhythmic click of the ceiling fan. (Dolly doesn't know what Noah's been doing, but she's noticed him looking over his shoulder more than usual.) Yesterday, however, Pastor Lewis caught her pretending to read the ingredients on a bag of sliced bread. He announced that the First Baptist Church of Whistling Ridge would be holding a special service this Sunday so that the congregation could dedicate their prayers to Abigail and the Blake family, and everyone sure would love to see them there. Dolly was taken aback by how easily he could stand there and lie to her face like that, when they both knew exactly what the congregation thinks of them. But it was not a request, however many times he smiled and patted her on the arm.

We can pray or be prayed for, she thinks, and perhaps it is this sense of having to choose between active and passive that makes her so determined to go. She tries to explain this to Jude, but he just chews on his lip and looks sulkily at the floor.

'Maybe Abi ran away because she didn't want to go to church any more,' he says, his voice so thick with scorn that Dolly feels like she could smack him too. Instead, she turns away and fumbles for a cigarette in her pocket. Her hands itch with a want to break something – *so break yourself, not Jude. After all, if anyone's to blame here . . .*

'Abigail didn't run away,' she tells him, and he has to believe her because she is his mother. Abigail would never have just upped and left her like this, no matter what the police seem to think. But Dolly's fingers shake as she puts the cigarette to her lips, plugging her mouth from saying any more. If Abigail didn't run away, then what happened to her? She hears it again in the monosyllabic click of the lighter. *Dead.*

It's all her fault. That's what they're saying at school. The corridors smell like glue and cleaning products, and Emma presses herself deep into the corner of the girls' bathroom, trying to drown out the echo of their voices, knocking back the travel-sized whiskey bottles her mother keeps for trips they never take.

'Can you believe Emma Alvarez just left her there?'

'OhmyGod, do you think that's why she got taken?'

'She didn't get taken. She ran away with that gypsy boy.'

'She did not. I saw him at the diner last week.'

'Yeah, well, I heard she got eaten by coyotes.'

'I'd never leave *my* friend to get eaten by coyotes.'

Her mascara turns her tears black, and she rams her knuckles into her mouth so that nobody can hear her sobbing.

A week after the party at the Tall Bones, Principal Handel holds a special assembly in the gym, where she asks the students of the high school and middle school to keep Abigail in their thoughts and prayers, and to extend their support to her family and friends. Little Jude Blake chews on his lip and sinks into his shirt collar like he hopes nobody will notice him. Emma watches it all through heavy-lidded tipsy eyes and thinks, That's it. All two of us here. Abigail's family and friend. There's no one else who remembers the sight of grass stains on Abi's socks, sitting out on the old couch at the bottom of the Blakes' backyard through countless summers; or copying each other's homework and eating candy that turned their tongues blue. No one else who heard her say, when she was thirteen: 'I'm going to be an artist.' Emma had snorted and said, 'What, in Whistling Ridge?' and Abi had told her no way, she was going to catch a bus to Denver and never look back. This had seemed very impressive at the time. Abi was like something from a movie. She'd looked wide-eyed at Emma then, and added, 'You'll come with me, won't you?'

Now Emma downs another tiny bottle in the bathroom, and pukes when she gets home.

That night Emma dreams of a coyote pack screaming among the trees. She ploughs through them with her car and their blood gums up her tyres. Then she's bleaching Abigail's hair, and while their nostrils sting with the reek of ammonia, they sip on Samuel Blake's bourbon. *It burns, it burns*, Abigail keeps saying, or she's mouthing it, or the words just appear in Emma's head. Abi kisses her, spilling blood on to Emma's lips, down the front of her body, her chest, her arms, her *hands* . . .

When Emma wakes it is barely dawn. The mountains are dark and steaming with fresh September rain, and she can smell dried vomit in her nostrils from when she threw up earlier. Wrapping herself in her blanket, she sneaks to the bathroom and washes her hands, over and over, until they're so cold from the water she can hardly feel them. Melissa must hear the faucet because, wordless, she comes and puts her arms around her. When Emma finally stops shivering, they shuffle into Melissa's bed, and she strokes Emma's hair until they fall asleep – mother and daughter curved like some strange rune against the sheets. The next morning, Melissa pours away any remaining alcohol she can find, but they say nothing about it. Emma's grandmother liked to say that people in glass houses should not throw stones, and Melissa has been aged prematurely by the guilt of marrying a man who could not love her enough to stay, or so she says.

Before Abi's disappearance, before the drink, Emma never realized how many decisions she had to make just to get through the day. *Am I going to bother having breakfast? Should I drive to school, or get the bus? Who should I sit next to at lunch? Who is least likely to look at me like I'm gum on the underside of their desk?* But starting the day with a drink means there is only one decision to make: *Do I keep drinking?* Everything else just sort of falls into place after that. She knows her mother means well, but good intentions won't stop Emma crying in the girls' bathroom. Christmas break is still months away, and she's not sure she can make all the decisions that stretch between now and then.

She knows – she *knows* – it is worse if Abigail is dead. But people at school say she ran away and who could blame her, and that feels like a buck knife in Emma's stomach, tearing a big hole through her guts. Abi wouldn't just leave without saying anything. She wouldn't have caught a bus to Denver and not said a single word about it. You don't run out on a friendship of ten years like that, you just don't. But, then, would it be better if Abigail were dead?

In the morning, after her mother leaves for the clinic where she is the local GP, Emma doesn't go to school. She goes to Mr Wen's liquor store, stuffs a bottle of Jack Daniel's inside her coat. She's almost out of the door with it when she sees the young man with the leather jacket grinning at her from the parking lot, all brilliant teeth like he eats knives for breakfast. Something about him looks familiar, and this familiarity seems to take her by the scruff of the neck and tell her to sit up straight, so much so that she loses her grip on the bottle.

Mr Wen has a kind face, crinkled like a paper lantern, and he tells her he isn't going to press charges this time, although he does make her pay for the broken bottle. He takes it all in: her smudged mascara, her puffy eyes, her bitten-down nails, and says he hopes she'll feel better soon. She knows, without him needing to say, that he understands what it's like to be different in this country. That thought alone – that sense of fragile solidarity – makes her want to burst into tears all over again, and in the parking lot she braces herself against her car to steady her gasping breaths.

'Hey, you okay?'

When she looks up, the guy with the leather jacket is watching her. With his head cocked to one side, his hair lifting in the wind like feathers, he looks like a big crow. Emma swallows, and tries not to screw up her eyes too much when she nods.

'No ID.' She hates how small her voice sounds, carried away by the rumble of traffic on the main drag.

'I'll buy it for you,' he says, with an accent that sounds faintly Eastern European. 'You can drink with me.'

Emma runs a hand through her hair, and the greasy residue it leaves on her fingers makes her feel queasy. In a few years' time, college friends will tell her not to accept free drinks from men she doesn't know. Even now, her head rings with folkloric warnings: nothing is ever free, everything has its price. But right now there is nothing lovelier, she thinks, than light filtered through whiskey-brown glass, and if she puts a bottle in her hand, she can forget about the feeling of last night's bad dream.

She sniffs loudly. 'Okay. Sure.' Everything has its price, but she cannot yet imagine the real cost of this one bottle of whiskey. Neither of them can.

3

Then

The month before Abigail disappears, Noah and his sister go down to the river. He does not remember having asked Abigail to come with him, but she grabs her big movie-star sunglasses and follows him out of the house without a word.

They drive through acres of muggy August. Tourists sag under the trees, stopping to catch their breath, while kids roll in grass the colour of old men's teeth. Noah's AC is broken, which makes their lungs feel as if they're full of damp wool, but they don't dare roll down the windows in case the insects get in and they end up scratching themselves ragged. Abigail sits in silence, her face half obscured by her big glasses. Noah can't tell if she's looking at him or not.

He chooses a stretch of river outside of town on the south side, which is usually free of tourists because of the steep rock faces obscuring the picturesque views. Brother and sister scramble down the bank, pine needles poking into their bare feet, low branches whipping at their cheeks, and still they do not speak to one another. The heat feels arrogant, as if it's been here so long it can't imagine being pushed away by fall. In the shallows, they lie on their backs fully clothed, like they used to when they were kids, letting the water, still blissfully cold from the mountain springs, slip over their bodies. Hummingbirds, fat with nectar, zip back and forth overhead. From somewhere among the trees comes the creaky call of a blue jay. At last, Abigail says, 'You would have graduated college this year.'

Noah knows she's looking at him, but he keeps staring at the sky through the branches.

'Are you ever going to forgive us, Noah?'

You've grown too used to forgiveness, he wants to say. He is not God. He is not obliged to forgive her just because she's asked.

Instead he tells her, 'You'll be off to college yourself next year. Then you won't care what I think. You'll make new friends, see new places, forget I was ever mad at you at all.'

She is quiet for a moment, but he can guess what she's thinking. *I won't make new friends. We don't make new friends.*

When she speaks again, it sounds as if she's on the brink of laughing. 'Another year? I think I'll go crazy if I have to wait another year.' It's not a good sort of laughter. Noah shivers, and he knows it isn't just the chill of the river.

'No,' she says, 'of course you're still mad. I'd lose it if you cost me my one chance of getting out of here. I'd bash your head in.'

Noah sighs. 'What do you want from me, Abi?'

'I just want you to *do* something. You haven't even mentioned it in *four years,* and I can't stand it any more. If you're not going to forgive me, then maybe you should just bash my head in.'

'Abi . . .'

She stands up. Her summer dress is heavy with water and clings to the outline of her body. Noah has avoided her for so long, he hasn't noticed that his little sister has become a woman. He looks away quickly, and she laughs.

'I'm the only woman you've ever really seen, aren't I? Poor Noah.'

He sits up too fast and the water slides off his chest, like something solid. It reminds him of his baptism, when Pastor Lewis dunked him in the tank.

Abigail sneers. 'Poor, poor Noah. Couldn't get Chrissy Dukes to go to first base with you, couldn't get Sabrina McArthur to put out, couldn't even get Erin Broadstreet to hold your hand in the nativity play.'

'Shut up.'

She kicks water in his face. 'That's right, let it out.' Several birds take off from the trees, startled by her voice, their wings beating like fleeing footsteps. 'There's something wrong with you, isn't there?'

Noah's hair drips over his eyes and he can't see her, but he itches to cut that sneer out of her voice.

'You'd never have gone to college anyway, because you know there's something wrong with you. I remember, Noah. That's why you don't have any friends. That's why you can't keep a girlfriend. *That's why Mom and Dad don't love you.*'

'Shut *up*!'

He lunges at her blindly, knocking his cheekbone against her elbow, but the sudden pain feels good. They fall back into the water with a crash, and she struggles against him, but he's taller than her, stronger than her, and he holds her down. The seconds pass. The river bubbles over Abigail as though she were just another stone on its bed. It's the soothing noise that helps him steady his breathing again, helps him realize what he has done. He's holding her down by the shoulders, holding her head under the water. She is staring straight up at him, and her mouth is curled in the barest trace of a smile, but she doesn't move or blink.

For the briefest moment, Noah thinks she might be dead, and his mind races away to a future in which his shoes take up all the space in the hallway, and his college degree hangs on the wall instead of her dried-macaroni art. Their mom says goodnight to him first, and their father has no choice but to hold *his* hand when they pray before dinner. It's his day they ask about, his Steinbeck and Vonnegut strewn across the couch instead of Abi's magazines, his hair in the plughole. Of course Noah knows deep down that her absence will change none of those things, that the space their parents have made for her and do not have for their sons would quickly be filled with their grief, and he would fade into the background once again. He knows this and lets go, his hands poised in the air, as if in surrender, as if he is expecting to be caught.

But then she sits up, and paws the water from her eyes, taking huge breaths that make her whole body shudder, and relief floods through him. She looks at him, and he looks at her, and he understands: she is the only thing holding them all together.

On the way home they do not speak. They do not speak of that day ever again. Just sit making little puddles on the floor of Noah's truck as their bodies drip with baptismal waters.

Now

The First Baptist Church of Whistling Ridge looks like a recreational centre with a white fibreglass steeple tacked on the top. Noah knows this is how most churches around here look. But he also knows that on the east coast there are huge Gothic-style churches built from heavy stones, as grand as

God Himself. God should be made of stone, if He's made of anything, Noah thinks. In this country He is made of styrofoam, smells like tarmac and tastes like fries. God is a truck stop or a billboard. There would be no point in making Him out of stone, because stone is made to last. God is always being reshaped to fit.

As the Blakes pull into the church parking lot, they pass the big LED board out front where the schedule of worship is written up, like a special deal at a drive-through. Noah leans against the car and stares at the wonky black letters, while behind him his mother helps Jude out of the back seat, and his father spits in the grass. *Casual worship 9–11 a.m. every Sunday. Has anyone else died for your sins?*

Noah wonders.

There are more cars now, and the people emptying out of them take their time pouring long gazes over the Blake family. There is Samuel, a scarecrow GI Joe, with shadows of the Vietnam jungle in his grey eyes and hunched shoulders. There is Dolly, with her split-ended hair, nicotine-stained fingers, the heels on her best shoes worn down unevenly so she seems to lean like a tree that's been pulled by the wind. There is Noah, all denim and corduroy, could be Marlon Brando handsome if not for his chapped lips and crooked nose, the same haunted look as his father. There's little Jude with his old man's walk, his long hand-me-down flannel sleeves that hide so many secrets. But where is Abigail? That's what everyone wants to know, and they stare harder at the Blakes as they file past, hoping perhaps to bore right through them to the truth.

Noah knows that's why most of them have lingered out here. They buzz around the parking lot, shaking each other's hands or embracing, sticking to the concrete like so many flies. They exist in this strange purgatory where the Depression feels not so long ago, yet the present seems oddly far away. His sister's disappearance is just fresh roadkill to them.

The sudden howl of a motorcycle shreds the idleness of the crowd. Noah tenses and shoves his hands inside his pockets. Across the street in the Dairy Queen parking lot, Rat Lăcustă takes off his helmet and shakes out his wild black hair. He moves like a hooker whose rent is due, and he doesn't seem to care about the way his jacket rides up as he leans over his bike. There is something primal in the reaction to that strip of exposed skin. Teenage girls in their Sunday best bite their lips and glance at their mothers, who dare to watch the boy because they know it will get their husbands all riled up.

Even Dolly can't help cocking her head to one side and saying, molasses slow, 'Isn't that the young man from the trailer park? The gypsy?'

'He's Romanian, not Romani.' Noah busies himself scraping dry mud off the edge of his best shoes against the kerb. 'He just happens to live in an RV.'

'And you shouldn't say "gypsy",' Jude pipes up. 'It's a slur.'

Samuel snorts. 'Give me strength, boy.' He elbows Jude, who wobbles slightly under the contact. '*This* generation, eh? Honestly.'

Dolly narrows her eyes at her husband, as if to say: Not in public. Samuel just smiles and delivers a short, sharp kick to the back of her ankles. Noah sees his mother stumble, watches the pink shame rising in her cheeks as she scans the church parking lot, afraid that someone will have noticed. But the truth is that, just for a moment, everyone has forgotten about the Blake family. At least the Blakes are of the town, of the church, of the faith. Rat – with his tight jeans and the smooth, dark laterals of his unfamiliar accent – is a stranger. He is a bullet that has entered the town and not yet left an exit wound. People have still to decide where he fits, or how they will shape themselves around him, or if they will do so at all.

Noah is vaguely aware of his father saying, 'Come on, we're going in,' but he's still staring across the street. He feels like he's been doused in gasoline and he's shivering from it, the kind of shivers that make your spine arch and your toes curl. Rat props a cigarette between his lips and grins right at him, like they both know some private thing that nobody else knows.

4

HUNTER MADDOX SLOWS the car, squinting through the rain on the windshield as they pull into the trailer park owned by his father. It used to be a burial ground, centuries ago when the Maddox family first came to Colorado. Now there are rows of squat trailer homes with dusty drapes and peeling tarp roofs. They seem to shrink against the grass, as if the fierce mountain winds have beaten them into the soft earth. On days like today, when the rain comes down in sheets and swells the mountain springs, the ground still gives up bones and arrowheads. On those days the trailer-park people stay indoors.

It surprises Hunter, then, to see a familiar figure picking her way through the mud. He shakes his head, muttering, 'There she goes again.'

Beside him, his father Jerry does not look up from his phone. 'Where who goes?'

'Emma Alvarez. She's going to the gypsy's RV again.'

Emma's jeans are spattered with dirt and she keeps stumbling. It could just be the ground, slick with rainwater, but Hunter's seen her with that same glassy-eyed look at school too. He's spent enough afternoons baked under the bleachers to recognize intoxication when he sees it. He feels a twinge of guilt and has to look away.

'Well,' says his father, 'however Melissa Alvarez-Jones-whatever wants to raise her half-breed kid is no business of ours.' Jerry is a broad-shouldered man with a square jaw and a military-grade haircut, who takes up space without apology and always wears his top two buttons undone. Hunter knows there is plenty of his father in his own face, and he is of an age where he isn't sure if he likes that any more.

Jerry glances up at him at last. 'You had a look at those latest brochures your mom ordered?'

Hunter pouts at the wiper blades sweeping across the windshield. 'Yeah,' he lies.

'College is just around the corner, you know. Plenty of good places for basketball. Have you looked at North Carolina?'

'Sure. Whatever.'

'No, not *whatever*, young man. If you don't get your act together soon, you're going to end up wasting your life like that Romanian boy, moping around some dump like this.' Jerry frowns. 'Most kids would be a little more grateful, you know, with me and your mom still helping you out, after what you've done.'

Hunter grips the steering wheel tight until he can see his knucklebones white under his skin. He watches Emma knock as she reaches the RV, watches the way she pushes her rain-soaked hair back from her face.

After what I've done.

He bites his lip. 'Yeah, Dad, I'm real grateful.'

You have no idea what I've done.

Rat sits on a mound of Byzantine-coloured quilts, strumming his grandmother's guitar. The grey headache light coming through the RV window winks off the wolf fang he wears through his left earlobe. Emma hesitates in the doorway, rain dripping down her sleeves and on to the chipped plastic flooring. Incense burning on the kitchen counter lends a hazy kind of quality to the air.

'You're back.'

Emma fiddles with the hem of her jacket. 'You don't mind?'

He places his grandmother's guitar reverently to one side. 'Well, don't just stand there, *drăguță*. You're getting water on my floor.'

'Oh.' Emma takes another step inside. 'Sorry.'

She takes off her jacket, the denim heavy with damp, but she doesn't know where to put it, or where to put herself, so she just stands there, water trickling down her neck.

Rat shakes his head and gives her his idle Cupid's bow grin. 'Bad morning?' He gets to his feet and heads to the kitchenette, already reaching for the cupboard where Emma knows he keeps the liquor. She watches his T-shirt rise up as he roots around, revealing a few inked petals of a tattoo that disappears below his waistline.

'Someday I'll get my hands on some decent *pălincă* for you,' he says, 'but for now we'll have to settle for good old No. 7.'

She doesn't even see the bottle, just feels him press the weight of it into her hand. Tilting her head back to let the whiskey run over her tongue, the cool rim of the glass pressed to her lips, it's the best kiss she's had all her life.

'You want to talk about it?'

No. It was nothing.

She takes another swig of Jack Daniel's.

Just something stupid that happened this morning – a joke she'd remembered, and without thinking she had reached for her phone to text Abigail. When she'd realized what she was doing, it took her a while to tune out the sound of her own breathing again.

She misses the wispy hairs at the back of Abi's neck that never stayed up in her ponytail, the particular way the rubber peeled on the bottom of her sneakers, her strawberry smell – but she wonders when these little details will fade into some larger sense of absence. Just missing Abigail altogether. Already this lack of her feels too familiar, but perhaps that's because Emma started missing her before she was even gone. Lately, Abigail had been speaking in the future tense – a place that, even now, Emma does not know how to get to.

At least when she drinks, time seems to loosen its hold over her. When she drinks, Emma feels that maybe she could be a day closer to . . . what? It's been two weeks now, and Abigail is still gone.

I just want to live a little. That was what Abigail had said.

Emma flops back into the nest of throws and quilts. The shadows of the rain rolling down the windowpanes make it feel as if the whole RV is melting around them. Rat perches beside her and they pass the bottle back and forth between them. Emma's head feels large and heavy, and she wonders if she'll ever be able to get it to stand back up again, or if she even cares. She gazes up at the ceiling: a mosaic of eclectic nonsense, some of which Rat points out to her; other parts he discreetly ignores. There are sections of maps, almost entirely Europe, and some have towns and cities ringed in coloured pencil. The twinkle in his grandmother's eyes and the heavy slope of his father's brow are preserved for ever in various photographs. Postcards of the Colosseum, stony English villages, and Romanian castles with their Gothic towers intersect with yellowing pages of classic novels, torn out and staked to the ceiling like dead butterflies.

'Who are you?' Emma asks him.

'I'm like you, *drăguță*.' He runs a finger around the rim of the bottle. 'I'm on the outside.'

She considers this for a moment. 'Is that why you let me drink with you?'

'So many questions.'

'I saw you, you know. That night at the Tall Bones.'

Rat's so close she can feel the warmth of him in the air between them, can smell the trace of cigarette smoke and incense that clings to his clothes. The thing she remembers most about her father is his legs, walking past her, always past her, and it occurs to her now, nestled against this warm, musty body, that this is the closest she has ever really been to a man. In the silence, she hears her heartbeat keeping time with the rain clamouring on the metal roof.

At last Rat says, 'I know.'

The taste of alcohol on her tongue makes Emma bold. 'And we're just never going to talk about it?'

He sighs, fishing a battered pack of Marlboros from the pocket of his jeans. 'It's not for me to talk about.'

'What's that supposed to mean?' Emma watches him light up a cigarette like they're having any old conversation. 'You know' – she leans on her elbow, jabbing a finger at him – 'you've got no family, no friends, no job, as far as anyone can tell. Nobody knows anything about you except what they've heard from someone else. And you're only, what, twenty-five? Twenty-six? You don't think you're going to turn heads in a place like this? You just happen to show up here and then a few months later my best friend goes missing, and you don't think people are going to ask questions?'

Rat drags lazily on his Marlboro, the light glinting off the rings on his fingers.

'I think,' Emma says, 'that maybe you should have some answers ready, just in case things get ugly.'

'Do things usually get ugly around here?'

'I've seen it get bad for some people.' In the back of her

mind she catches glimpses of her father again, of burly brown arms and fresh bruises, of blood on broken glass. 'It's like you said, we're on the outside.'

Rat sighs and shuffles around to face her. He takes hold of her shoulders in both hands, and for one terrifying moment she thinks he's about to start shaking her, but instead he leans forward and presses a kiss to her forehead.

There's nothing romantic about it – it feels almost parental – but it makes her catch her breath.

'I like you,' he says, very matter-of-fact. 'But let's get something straight: if we're going to do this, if you're going to keep coming here, then the questions have to stop. You have to stop, or I'll cut you off, you understand? I'm allowed my secrets, *drăguță*, just like you have yours.'

Emma watches his pale throat bobbing as he takes a long swallow from the bottle. When he's finished, he wipes his mouth with the back of his hand and gives the whiskey back to her.

'I don't have any secrets.' She thinks she could get cut just meeting his gaze.

'Yes, you do.'

He reaches for his grandmother's guitar once more, as if he has to fill the silence left by all the things they haven't said.

5

SHERIFF GAINS LOOKS as though he's been carved from wood and then left out in the rain. He is not an old man – Jude knows he is barely forty – but he smells like the forest, all pine resin and woodsmoke, and somehow that makes him seem ancient. Standing in the Blakes' living room, he flips through his notebook with his bear-trap-mangled hand, and picks at the scab of Abigail's absence.

'Now, you said before that you didn't know she was planning on going to the Tall Bones.' His vowels have a nasal Kansas drag, and maybe that's why God made him so tall, Jude thinks. So that he could stand in the middle of some great cornfield and still see over the top. 'Are you boys absolutely sure about that?'

Jude glances at Noah, but his brother just shrugs, two fingers buried in the pages of Thomas Mann to mark his place, as if to reassure himself that he can return to that world any time. Noah shakes his head, so Jude does the same.

'Abigail doesn't normally go to parties,' Noah adds. 'Sir.'

From his balding armchair, Samuel Blake snorts loudly. 'Haven't we already been over this, Chief?'

Gains's face gives nothing away, but he ignores Samuel, talking gently to Jude and Noah instead. 'I know last week you were all in a state of shock, and sometimes it can be difficult to remember the details. We're just following up, in case there's anything new that's come to you in the last few days. For instance . . .' he turns over another page in his notebook '. . . do you know if she was meeting anyone at the party?'

'She's friends with that little Mexican brat,' says Samuel. 'Always following Abi around. She's the one you ought to be questioning, not my boys.'

Jude watches his mother nibble at her fingernails. She is staring at a framed square of embroidery on the mantelpiece that reads: *Proverbs 14:25: A true witness delivereth souls, but a deceitful witness speaketh lies.*

'That'd be Emma Alvarez, would it?' says Gains.

'Who else? Ain't too many Mexicans in Whistling Ridge.'

Jude's face feels heavy. It's been only a day, and the bruise around his eye shows no sign of fading, but he wishes his mother had let him go to school all the same. As lonely as school can be for Jude Blake, son of a drunk, anywhere is better than this house.

His mother didn't have time to daub him with concealer before Gains knocked on the door, but her hasty explanation of 'He fell down the stairs, would you believe!' seems to pass, even though it's the standard excuse. One of the accompanying deputies even laughed, and why wouldn't he? Falling down the stairs. It's the sort of thing that only happens in cartoons.

'I've already spoken to Miss Alvarez,' says Gains. 'She said Abigail went into the woods with a boy, but she's not too clear about who it was. Would you know anything about that? Has Abigail been seeing someone?'

He looks at them all in turn: Jude and Noah together on the couch, Samuel slouched in his chair, Dolly propped up in the doorway, every now and then casting her eyes towards the hall and the big gemstone cross.

Overhead Jude can hear the floorboards creaking as officers search Abigail's room for the second time. Every so often he forgets it's them and his heart picks up at the familiar sound of someone moving around in his sister's space. Then he remembers, and his fingernails leave little crescents in the meat of his palms.

'Seeing someone?' Samuel sits up straighter. 'Our Abi? The hell she has.'

Dolly frowns. 'I think what my husband's trying to say is that Abigail is a little young to have a boyfriend.'

'I know what I'm trying to say, woman. Abi's a good girl, a *God-fearing girl*, doesn't go messing around with boys.'

'Mr Blake,' says Gains, 'your daughter is almost eighteen.'

'What's that got to do with it?' Samuel narrows his eyes, but the sheriff turns his attention to Dolly.

'Are any of your daughter's things missing? I know we had a look at her room before, but I expect you have a better sense of her belongings than we do. Anything you've noticed in the last couple of weeks? Any of her clothes gone, perhaps?'

'What's this?' Dolly stares at him. 'Why would any of Abigail's clothes be missing?'

Jude watches the sheriff rub the stumps of his fingers on his disfigured hand.

'Well, now, in cases like these, kids of this age . . . it's possible that Abigail left town of her own accord.'

'Not a chance,' says Samuel. 'I hope to hell that's not the best you've got, Gains.'

Jude hopes it is. He hopes that, if she has to be gone, then Abigail has just run away. The two of them used to watch cop shows on her computer, so he knows what they say: after seventy-two hours the chances of finding a missing person alive go way down. In two weeks there are 336 hours. Jude knows this because he looked it up. He also looked up how long it takes for a dead body to decay. The website he found had a timeline, so now he knows that in 336 hours – if she really is dead – his sister's internal organs will have begun to rot, her body will have bloated and foam will have leaked from her mouth and nose. In a few more weeks, her nails and teeth will fall out. In a month, she will begin to turn into liquid. Jude desperately wants to know if this is all some lie spread by the internet, but he doesn't have the heart to ask his mother.

Footsteps on the stairs seem to give the whole living room the excuse they need to let go of a collective breath. A deputy with a big moustache appears at the door beside Dolly, wearing latex gloves, brandishing a beat-up notebook.

'We found the girl's diary, sir,' he announces.

Jude doesn't like the hint of a smile curling under that moustache, or the way he called Abigail 'the girl', as if this is all some game at which they have managed to beat her.

'But Abigail doesn't have a diary.' Dolly's eyes dart from Gains to her husband.

Wincing, Jude hauls himself up on his stick and hobbles over to try to comfort his mother. She does not look at him, but she grips his hand so tight it starts to hurt. Samuel gives the slightest roll of his eyes and mutters something under his breath. The deputy doesn't even look at them as he brushes past, handing the notebook to Gains. 'Found it jammed between the slats in the bed frame,' he says. 'Thought it might be an old one but there are dates from this summer.'

Out of the corner of his eye, Jude sees his brother's jaw clench.

The sheriff nods, already leafing through the dog-eared pages. Jude has never seen the book before.

'Some of the pages have been torn out here,' says Gains. 'And again, later on. Looks like they would have been the last entries. Know anything about that?'

Samuel scratches at the whiskers on his chin. 'Teenagers get mad, tear shit up all the time.'

'Any reason why your daughter might be particularly angry, Mr Blake?'

'No,' Dolly answers instead. Jude feels her wedding ring pressing its shape into his knuckles. 'Abi has always been a happy girl.'

He sees her glance at the embroidery on the mantelpiece again. *A deceitful witness . . .*

'Well, then.' Gains tucks the notebook under his arm. 'I'll hang on to this for the time being, if you folks don't mind. You let me know if those missing pages turn up.'

Samuel doesn't get up to show Gains and the other officers out, but Noah at least does them the courtesy of accompanying them to the door, followed by Jude and his mother. Perhaps, in his own sulky way, he understands it will go easier for them if they can at least pretend to be a normal family.

Halfway out of the door, however, Gains turns back. 'One last thing, Mrs Blake. We found a shell casing up near the Tall Bones, 9mm semi-automatic by the look of it.'

He pauses, like he's expecting something, but Dolly seems confused.

'A gun? My daughter doesn't know how to use a gun.'

She sounds so convincing, Jude almost believes her.

'You don't have a handgun on the property? Perhaps your husband, or your son here.' Gains gestures to Noah, who tenses all over again.

Dolly juts out her chin. 'No, we certainly do not.'

'Our dad has an old rifle,' Jude offers. 'It's a souvenir from 'Nam, but he keeps it locked up.'

'Very wise.' Gains nods. 'Ah, well. I'm just covering my bases, Mrs Blake.' He puts on his hat, which is shaped too much like a cowboy hat for Jude to take him seriously any more. 'Soon as we hear anything, you'll be the first to know.'

The moment they close the door on Gains, Noah is already reaching for his boots and shrugging into his big corduroy jacket.

Dolly stares at him. 'Where do you think you're going?'

'Out.'

'Just like you were *out* the night your sister disappeared? Where do you keep running off to, Noah? Don't think we haven't noticed.'

'Mom, I'm twenty-two, I can go out if I want.'

Jude looks pleadingly at them both, willing them, as hard as he can, not to fight. Not now. Not today, when Abigail's teeth and nails could be falling out.

Noah reaches for the door handle. 'What do you even want me here for, Mom? What fun family activity did you have planned?'

Their mother's little shoulders sag slightly. Don't talk to her like that, Jude wants to say. *Don't talk to her like Dad does*. But he wants Noah to be friends with him again, like he was when they were younger, like he was *before*, so he says nothing.

'I thought we could pray for Abi,' Dolly says hopefully.

Noah is looking at the shoes piled up under the coat rack – Abigail's cowgirl boots, Abigail's sandals, Abigail's real leather brogues that she wears to church. His face grows harder the longer he stares, and Jude thinks he looks like their father. 'Do whatever you want,' he mutters, and slams the door on his way out.

Back in the living room, their mother sighs as she braces herself against the mantelpiece, eyeing the embroidery once again. *A true witness delivereth souls.* It was something Abi made at Sunday School. Jude settles back on to the couch and closes his eyes, blocking out the stitching. He has indeed witnessed something, but it will be many days before he realizes what it means.

6

Then

'Why don't you go back to Mexico like your dad?'

In some ways, it is almost a relief. All through school Emma has whittled herself down, shaving off the thick dark hair on her arms until her skin is chafed and scabby, coating her face in foundation just a shade too light, puking up meals in the hope of shedding the weight on her thighs, trying to reshape herself into something they might find less objectionable, but it has never made any difference. Standing in her junior prom dress on this May evening, the hair that Abigail tenderly curled for her coming undone in the crowded heat of the school gym, it is both a punch to the gut and a weight off her shoulders to finally hear them come out and say it: *this* is why they have always hated her.

'Dalton Lewis, what the hell did you just say?' Abigail steps up beside her, and Emma almost feels as if she's watching the scene unfold from outside her body. She must look very small, hunched inwards trying to make her arms look skinnier, while Abigail towers next to her, straight and stiff as a preacher's finger.

'Relax, Ginger, I wasn't talking to you.' Dalton Lewis, the pastor's son, leans back on his heels, a grin stretching his big face like someone put two fishhooks in the corners of his mouth. 'You girls got your period or something?' Behind him, Cole Weaver and Bryce Long snicker.

Emma looks around for a teacher or a chaperone, but the gym is a sea of sweaty faces and crushed plastic cups. She catches sight of the Orozco twins in their matching white dresses, like a pair of stone pillars, and she begs them with her eyes: Please say something. But she already knows they will stick their noses in the air and whisper something in Spanish, a language they know she cannot speak because her white mother never taught her.

Her own dress is damp under the armpits already, and suddenly she's worried that they can see. The clammy feeling makes her stomach turn over. She puts a hand on Abigail's arm. 'Come on, let's just go.'

'Yeah, that's right,' Dalton sneers. 'What time does the last bus out of town leave? You might just make it.'

'I think it goes at eight,' says blunt-faced Beau Dukes, helpfully.

Dalton ignores him, leaning in closer to Emma as he whispers, 'My daddy knows *all sorts* about what happened to your daddy.'

His breath smells like hot tarmac, and now she definitely thinks she's going to hurl. It must show in her face, because Dalton straightens up, his cloak of friends gathering tighter around him. 'What's the matter, Brownie?' he whines, and that's when Abigail throws her drink in his face.

By the time any of the teachers notice ('Oh, fruit punch,' laments Carla Paterson, 'your mom will have a hell of a time getting those stains out, Dalton'), Emma and Abigail are already running down the hall, fingers intertwined.

They are breathless with laughter and adrenalin and an urge to cry so hard they might pop their eyeballs out of their sockets.

Out in the parking lot, catching their breath against the cool metal of Emma's car, they hold each other very close, and in that moment, Emma thinks she loves Abigail more than anything in the world. Not because she threw punch all over Dalton Lewis (although she will recount this story many times to Melissa in the days to come), but because even here, where there is no audience to impress, Abigail lets her sob against her shoulder. She says nothing as Emma's mascara leaves ugly tracks like black veins all over her prom dress. She has never said a word, over the years, whenever Emma has come to curl against her. Just rubs Emma's bare arms and kisses the top of her head, leaving sweet notes of strawberry lip balm in her hair.

'Hey,' someone says, and Emma jerks up, almost hitting Abigail's chin. The boy standing by the car looks like a model from a 1940s German propaganda poster, fair-haired, jaw like a brick. For a moment she's afraid he might be one of Dalton's friends, but as he moves closer, she recognizes him and she can smell the joint he's been smoking. Beside her, she feels Abigail stiffen.

'You looking for something, Hunter?'

He shrugs. 'Saw you guys running out. You okay?' This he directs at Abigail, who, in the greasy light of the parking lot, looks like she's the one about to throw up.

Emma sniffs, squeezing her friend's hand. 'We're fine, aren't we, Abi?'

'Let's go,' Abigail says suddenly. 'Come on, Em, let's get out of here.' Then, almost as an afterthought, she adds: 'Jeez, Hunter, we don't want to buy any weed.'

*

They drive out to the Tall Bones. The night is coming down faster now, and in the deep shadows of those towering rocks, the two girls slip off their shoes and dig their toes into the cool grass. Abigail plays Fleetwood Mac through the whispery speakers in her phone, and they dance in and out of the stones like a pair of witches, stretching their necks towards the sky as they each try to yell 'FUCK' the loudest.

'We really don't know anything about them,' Emma says, when they're lying side by side in the middle of the Tall Bones.

There are six in total: a circle of white rocks, about twelve feet tall, etched with generations of teenage graffiti, ice damage, and grooves where moose have rubbed the velvet off their antlers. Nobody knows who put them there. As far as Emma's aware, nobody's ever thought to find out. She often wonders how far down they go, how much of them is sitting there buried under the earth. Later she will think, in that respect, that the Tall Bones remind her a little of Abigail.

Abi spreads her arms out in the grass, like she's being made love to. 'Maybe the old families know. The ones who've been here for ever.'

'Like the Lewises, or the Maddoxes.' Emma rolls on to her side and grins. 'You should ask your friend Hunter.'

'He's not my friend.' Abigail starts scratching her arm. 'You're my friend. You're the only good person, Em.'

'What are you talking about? I wish I was like you – turning boys down, throwing drinks in their faces. You're living.'

Abigail scratches harder. 'You don't want to be like me, Em. Trust me.'

Easy for you to say, Emma thinks. Nobody called Abigail names at her junior prom. Nobody told her to leave town. Abigail gets to wear makeup that suits her skin tone. Abigail gets boys walking all the way across the parking lot to ask if she's okay. Her father is the town drunk and she still gets more respect than the daughter of a doctor. Don't tell me I don't want that, Emma thinks. *I bet you'd still rather be you than me.*

When Abigail gets in, she finds Noah slumped on the couch, half lying, half sitting, and the angle of his body is so odd that for a moment she imagines something terrible has happened, that their father has done this to him. But then he looks up from his book, eyeing her streaky makeup, and says, 'Halloween's not till October,' and she lets herself breathe again.

'Oh, good, you're here. I brought something back for you.' She pulls her hand out of her clutch bag, middle finger extended.

Noah blinks at her.

'Whole thing was kind of bleak, actually,' she admits, not quite ready for their interaction to be over.

'Shocking.'

'Saw your old girlfriend, though.' When his face doesn't change, she adds, 'Sabrina McArthur? She was chaperoning.'

'Ah,' he says, as if just now remembering the only girl he's ever dated. 'How the mighty have fallen.'

Abigail nods. 'Are Mom and Dad still up?'

'Dad went to bed early, said he had a headache. Mom's out back having a smoke.'

'You're reading in here by yourself then, huh?'

'I guess.'

'*Leaves of Grass*,' she says, tilting her head so she can see the cover. 'Is that good?'

'Sure. It's okay.'

Abigail nods again. 'Well, goodnight.'

'Night.'

She pauses in the doorway, glancing back over her shoulder.

It's the first time he's said goodnight to her in four years. She lingers in the living room for a moment, hoping he'll look up again and she'll see forgiveness in his face, not just the broken shape of his nose. Eventually, on her way to the stairs, she averts her eyes from the gemstone cross on the wall.

In her room she doesn't bother to turn on the light, preferring the privacy of the dark, how it keeps her from seeing her reflection in the mirror as she undresses. She hasn't looked in the mirror for some time. Not since it happened.

Peeling off her prom dress, she wrinkles her nose at the stale smell of herself, but she is too tired to shower now, too tired to do anything, except burrow into her bed. Her eyes are still ringed with black liner that will smudge during the night and make her look bruised come morning. She yawns and stretches herself out; there's something different about the motion, these days, as if her bones don't quite fill out her skin the way they used to.

'Dear Lord Jesus, I know that I'm a sinner, and I ask for Your forgiveness,' she recites dully in the dark.

At Sunday School they used to say you should pray for provision, pardon and protection, and to end all your prayers focusing on God's glory. Abigail won't admit this to anyone else – perhaps because it appeases her parents to think otherwise, perhaps because she is ashamed to have got it all so wrong – but she's not sure she really believes in God's glory any more. He can't be that glorious, if He just sat back and watched what happened to her. She doesn't know what to say to God now. There's no point in asking for provision, pardon or protection. It's all too little too late.

With a sigh, she gives up on prayer, and rolls over to check her phone: a text from Emma saying *Love you, goodnight,* and one from her mom saying she hopes she's having fun at the prom. It occurs to her then, squinting in the brightness of her phone screen, that there is someone whose pardon she could ask for.

Hey. Weird night.

Her fingers are sluggish as her body yearns for sleep, and she can only just about keep her eyes focused, but eventually she manages to type roughly what she wants.

Seriously, Hunter, I'm sorry for running off like that. I just don't think we should be seen together right now. My parents would kill me.

7

Now

On the west side of town, where the concrete is crumbling and the strange shapes of empty shopping carts lie strewn about with their legs in the air, there's an old truck-stop bar. To the summer tourists it's the Riverside Roadhouse, not that any tourists ever go there: the river was diverted long ago. Now even the building looks dried up, its flesh-coloured paint cracking around greasy tinted windows. There's a notice board outside, plastered with flyers that rustle like dead leaves, advertising concerts and open-mic nights that took place a decade ago. For two weeks now Abigail's face has fluttered among them, under the words 'HAVE YOU SEEN ME?'

Noah thinks this place feels like the inside of someone's mouth. It seems to be made up entirely of dark corners, where men wearing flannel and too much denim cuss as they spill their drinks, and leathery women roll cigarettes with bright press-on nails. Shot glasses clink and Merle Haggard strums through the overhead speakers in his lonesome way. Noah moves carefully, aware that he is out of place here, afraid of leaving some imprint of himself as he makes his way to the booth in the back.

'Why did you pick literally the worst place in town?'

He drops into a seat that reeks with a history of cigarette smoke. Across the table, Rat Lăcustă fingers his wolf fang earring and grins.

'Your text said *incognito* – which I had to look up, by the way, so thank you for that.' The dim lighting catches the amber in one of his rings as he gestures idly at the bar. 'I don't know any of these people, and I assume none of them go to your Bible class.' He shrugs. 'Incognito. You want something to drink?'

'No . . .'

'You sure? I might get a daiquiri.'

Noah doesn't think this is the sort of place that serves daiquiris.

'Are you going to tell me what this is about, Blake?' Rat watches him from under the dark fan of his eyelashes, tapping a finger against his mouth, like he wishes he had something to smoke. 'Don't get me wrong, I love our chats, but I have a friend waiting on me.' The dim light picks out his high cheekbones when he smiles, and Noah feels like he's secretly laughing at him.

'Just shut up and listen, will you?' He stuffs his hands into his pockets and tries to focus on the faux-wood grain of the seatback. 'The police were just at my house. They said they found a shell casing up at the Tall Bones. From a gun.'

'Yeah, I know what a shell casing is, Blake.'

'You're not *listening*.'

Rat rests his elbows on the table and steeples his fingers together. 'I am listening, Blake. I just don't think you need to lose your head over this. There were a lot of people up by the Tall Bones that night.'

Noah can see the delicate blue veins in the exposed skin of Rat's wrists. He clenches his fists in his pockets.

'But I wasn't *supposed* to be there. I wasn't invited to Hunter Maddox's dumb party. If the police find out I was up there, they're going to come back with more questions, and if my *parents* find out I was there—'

'Then make something up. You're a good liar.'

'Jesus, you know what? Do whatever the hell you want. I was just giving you a heads-up, but I'm done with this now, okay? I'm done.'

Rat laughs faintly. 'You know your problem, Blake? You're repressed.'

Noah feels a twinge of heat across his shoulders. The image of the gemstone cross in the hallway comes back to him without warning, and behind it, the hole in the crumbling plaster that could just as easily have been a hole in his head.

'I'm not *repressed*,' he says.

'It's not your fault. All Americans are.'

Noah can feel the grit in the seams of his pockets getting up under his fingernails. He shifts in his seat so that he's not facing Rat directly. 'Look, the police are obviously combing the woods,' he says, addressing Rat's shoulder. 'Aren't you afraid what else they might find?'

That afternoon is the grey kind, where the clouds are so low it feels as if the sun has disappeared for ever. After school, Emma joins Rat on the roof of his RV, shooting cheap bourbon and listening to the pines creaking in the wind. It's peaceful in the way it reminds her a bit of Abigail, that time they stole her father's whiskey and spent the afternoon in Emma's backyard daring each other to drink just a little more. Abi could shoot it better than her then, like maybe she'd had more practice, and perhaps she had, being Samuel Blake's daughter, although Emma figures she could give her a run for her money now. That had only been back in the spring, but already it feels like it happened to another person.

What had they talked about, wrinkling their noses and laughing at the bitterness in their mouths? Something normal – parents, brothers, crushes, all things that Abigail seemed to have in abundance compared to Emma, and back then she'd been happy to share the details. Emma hasn't had a conversation like that since, not even with Abi.

As if she had voiced that last thought aloud, Rat asks: 'Do you like boys, Miss Alvarez?'

Emma nods slowly. 'Sure.' He's looking at her with his eyes half closed, his mouth just a little open, like everything he does has to scream *Fuck me*, and Emma begins to sway slightly, unsure if she's getting drunk on the liquor or the boy. She gets the feeling he might be making fun of her, so she laughs and adds, 'Do you?'

Rat gulps back another mouthful of Wild Turkey. 'Who am I going to like? People round here are all too busy getting their rocks off to Jesus. Or they're strung out on legal highs like it's going out of fashion.'

Emma snorts. 'You mean like Hunter Maddox?'

'You know he collects my rent in person?' Rat shakes his head and hands her the bottle. 'Like him and his daddy can't trust me to pay it myself? *Bulangiu*.'

She remembers what Rat said yesterday about asking questions, so she says nothing about how he gets his money. But she knows there's an old cookie tin in the same cupboard where he keeps their drinks, and more than once she's seen him take out a handful of bills, crumpled soft and smelling sweetly of methadone, like the boys from the basketball team.

The wind makes furrows in the grass, the sound like something solid pressing around them. Emma pulls her denim jacket tighter and rests her drowsy weight on Rat's shoulder. 'I never liked him anyway,' she says. 'Hunter, I mean.'

'No?'

'No.' She mutters it around the mouth of the bottle, and the word echoes like it's trapped inside – the same word Abigail snapped at her before heading into the trees that night.

'He used to deal weed when we were juniors. Got hold of it from dispensaries somehow and sold it on at school at a profit. I mean, I don't care, but then he'd have all these parties in the woods, and people said . . .' Emma squints into the trees that border the trailer park, then suddenly she sits up straight.

'It was his party, at the Tall Bones. That's what everyone said: it was Hunter's party.'

'So?'

'So, I never saw him.'

Rat is staring off into the trees as well, toying with the rings on his fingers, his pretty mouth turned down at the corners. 'Didn't you say your friend went into the woods with some guy?'

It was dark, and the boy's face had been hidden by the branches. It could have been anyone, she thinks, but that doesn't mean it couldn't have been Hunter.

'We should go back up there.'

'And do what, Scooby Doo? Look for clues?' Rat laughs sharply.

He doesn't understand. It's not as if she wanted to leave Abigail behind – and Emma almost hates her, hates her a little bit for not getting in the car that night, for leaving her like this – but that doesn't make Abi any less missing. *It's still my fault, even if it isn't,* she thinks, reaching for the bottle again. She never inherited her father's Catholicism, so she's never been one to ask for absolution, but she imagines it now: finding some clue among the pines – strands of his hair, the end of a discarded joint – and walking into the sheriff's station, head held high, to say, *Hunter Maddox knows what happened to her. It was his fault*, and that sure feels better than God or bourbon.

'I don't know,' she says. 'Maybe.'

But Rat isn't laughing any more. He reaches over and swipes the bottle from her, leaning back to tip the dregs into his mouth. Perhaps it's the suggestion of strength in his hands, or the alcohol simmering in her bloodstream, or the rakish angle of his throat, but Emma feels something like desire uncurl in the pit of her stomach. Even when he tosses the bottle over his shoulder, and she hears it shatter on the ground below, she just sits there and lets him lean in, his breath warm against her cheek, as he says, 'Stay out of the woods, *drăguță*.'

8

Then

It is April, before the disappearance, and the snow is finally retreating up the mountainsides, revealing banks of crisp blue columbines and rough patches of colourless grass. The days are balmy, but there's a tang in the air come evening, drifting in from the depths of the forest like a warning. The pine pollen will be heavy this year, everyone says. They stockpile anti-allergens and decongestives as if they're prepping for biological warfare.

Hunter Maddox, walking into town from basketball practice, rounds the corner and sees two girls up ahead of him, dappled in green spring light. Abigail Blake brushes her fingers through the low-hanging leaves of a mountain ash, scattering blossom that falls like a fresh layer of snow on Emma Alvarez's bare brown arms. Hunter watches them nudging against one another, laughing quietly. Sometimes they walk so close together it looks as though they're holding hands.

He follows the girls all the way to Hickory Lane without wondering why. They keep walking, and so does he, as if they're pulling him along on some invisible thread. From the top of the lane he can't see the Blakes' house, only the scrubby, empty land bought up by a property developer, curving gently away with the slope of the mountain. In the months to come, Abigail will tell him how she hates that house; how, sometimes, she feels like her family are the only people in the world.

The girls hug goodbye as they part ways: Emma heading towards the cluster of modern housing on the north-west side of town, and Abigail traipsing slowly along the track towards her lonely home. Hunter stands at the top of the lane, concealed by the row of hackberry trees that borders the road, and watches her getting smaller as she puts more distance between them. With a sigh, he turns to leave, but her sudden movement catches his eye. She has left the track now and is bending down in the grass, the shape of her like some strange, pale letter written on the dark landscape. He watches her take off her shoes and make an arc in the air with each leg, one at a time, as if exploring the space she is allowed to take up. Hunter takes a deep, slow breath, because he never thought something so simple – so unintended to arouse – could make him feel like this.

Then, without warning, Abigail takes off, sprinting over the uneven ground, her long hair trailing behind her like the tail of some portentous comet. Come fall, come the absence of her, Hunter will stand at the top of Hickory Lane again, and wonder if she had not been planning to run all along.

Now

The Maddoxes live in a big wooden lodge just off Elkstone Bend, densely hemmed in by trees, a couple of miles from the Tall Bones. Andie Maddox is from east Texas: Sheriff Gains can hear it in the whispery way she says *ah* instead of

I. 'Can *ah* get y'all some sweet tea?' she says, as he and Deputy Saidi take a seat across from Jerry Maddox and his son.

'No, thank you, ma'am.'

Jerry Maddox asks, 'Any news about that poor girl?'

'Poor girl,' his wife echoes. 'How are the family holding up?'

Well, now, there's a question. 'They're very concerned, of course,' says Gains, because that's what he's expected to say, just as that's what Andie was expected to ask. 'Very concerned.'

There is a TV about the length of a man's arm span on the wall behind, and young Hunter Maddox cranes his neck to continue watching a muted Broncos game over Gains's shoulder.

'So, now, what can we help you with, Eli?' Jerry is half looking at the TV as well.

'Do you keep any firearms on the property, Mr Maddox?' It's been a long time since he cared to call him Jerry.

'Hm? Oh, firearms, sure. We've got the Weatherby, the Finnlight, couple of Rugers, and, Andie, do we still have your dad's old Marlin? Now *that* was a deer-hunting gun, that's for sure.'

Deputy Saidi gives a low whistle. 'My old man had one of those back in the day. Landed my first doe with it. Beautiful machine. They don't make them like they used to.'

Gains knows that isn't true – Farid Saidi's father was a prison guard in Algeria, and the only does he ever shot were johns – but he keeps quiet, lets Saidi have his story. That sort of thing is important to men like Jerry Maddox.

'Amen,' says Jerry. 'I tell you, that Finnlight gets hot enough you could fry an egg on it.'

Gains leans forward. 'What about a 9mm semi-automatic, Mr Maddox? Do you own one of those?'

Jerry scratches the back of his head. 'Ah,' he says slowly, 'no, nothing like that.'

Hunter isn't looking at the TV any more. Gains tries to catch his eye, but the boy is staring rigidly out of the window.

'What about you, Hunter?' he asks. 'You ever see a gun like that?'

'Now, Eli.' Jerry glances quickly at his son. 'What's this all about?'

'We found a shell casing this morning,' says Saidi, 'belonging to a 9mm.'

Jerry frowns. 'You think this has something to do with that missing girl?'

'There's no way of knowing what time the gun was fired,' says Gains, 'but we do know that somebody recently discharged a firearm in the same stretch of woods as a teenage girl went missing – the same woods that border both the Tall Bones and your property. It would be of great help to our investigation if you and your family could think back, try to remember if you saw or heard anything that might help us pinpoint when the gun was fired.'

'Well, of course, Eli,' says Jerry. 'We'll have a think for you, but I'm sure if any of us saw or heard anybody firing a gun, well, we'd have remembered it, wouldn't we, hon?'

'Certainly,' says Andie. 'We'd remember a thing like that. But, Chief, you know, there's all kinds of guns up in these woods most times of the year, what with hunting and the like. Couldn't it just be something like that?'

'A 9mm's no deer-hunting gun, hon. Probably just some kids messing around.' Jerry glances at his son again. 'Anyway, Eli, you want to know what I think? I reckon that girl probably hopped on a bus and high-tailed it out of here. You know what those Blakes are like.'

Gains thinks back to the Blake family in their cold living room, mugs and whiskey tumblers and even an old paintbox strewn about as ashtrays, the torn-out pages of Abigail's diary. 'You're probably right,' he says. You couldn't blame a girl for wanting to get out of a place like that. 'Just covering my bases.'

After the sheriff leaves, Hunter is subjected to a stiff hug from his mother, who digs her chin into his shoulder as she says, 'I didn't like that, Jerry. I didn't like that at all.'

'I know, hon.' His father makes the same sort of wheezing sound as an old school bus pulling into a stop. 'And since when has Eli let some Muslim fella in the department? What this country's coming to . . .'

'Oh, I know, honey, but you did fine. At least they were only asking about some gun.'

Hunter shakes his mother off and heads for the door.

'Don't you slouch away with that look on your face, young man,' she says. 'Not after what you've put us through this year. You're the one who's going to be in trouble if the police start poking around up here.'

He thinks his father looks almost sympathetic then. 'It's your future on the line, Hunter. That's what really matters – state play-offs, college, real opportunities. The missing girl is a tragedy, of course, but when all is said and done, she was a Blake. I mean, what can you expect? There's something not right about that family. Something unclean about those kids, for all their daddy cries Amen. Your little . . . problem shouldn't be dragged into it.'

Andie nods wearily, and Hunter has to bite his knuckles to keep from telling his mother what he saw that night – how, standing at the edge of the road by the old Winslow ruins, he saw his own father come creeping through the trees.

9

Then

Today, Pastor Lewis announces, he will be talking about *the homosexual*. Noah is only seven years old, and does not know who the homosexual is, but Pastor Lewis clearly doesn't like him because he calls him 'arrogant' and 'heartless' and, worst of all, a 'God-hater'.

The pastor is not a very tall man or, rather, he looks as though he should be, but God got bored of making him half-way down, so he has an elongated torso carried around by two short legs. In spite of this, he has always seemed huge to Noah. He gives his sermons from a raised platform at the front of the congregation, and now, brandishing his red-letter New King James as he mounts his podium, he's already beginning to tremble with the thrill of holding everybody's attention. Noah listens intently, hoping to get some idea of what the homosexual has done to make everyone so mad, but the more the pastor talks the less he understands.

'The liberal society that we live in preaches that there is nothing wrong with same-sex relationships; your children and grandchildren are being taught this on TV, and I have to ask, my brothers, how have we gotten here? The answer is that most Christians do not understand how God views homosexuality, or when they do, they do not have the backbone to stand up and show His love to those who are struggling.'

Noah listens with his hands in his pockets and thinks it is a very strange thing to say. Backbone is something his father talks about a lot, and he knows it's very difficult to love his father. According to Samuel Blake, Noah does not have much of a backbone either. He wonders if that's why he finds it so difficult to love God too.

Pastor Lewis has a lot to say about the homosexual. Everyone has to look at some quotes from Romans and Leviticus that Mrs Lewis has photocopied for them. Noah's father underlines a few things, so he does the same. The pastor also reads them a passage from Genesis about Sodom and Gomorrah. Noah likes that one better because God blows up an entire city, and that's kind of exciting, but he's still not sure what it has to do with anything. So Sodom was a city full of boys, big deal. He'd rather live with boys than whiny Abigail, or his mother with her smoky smell that makes him feel sick. Boys, on the other hand, smell sort of salty, the kind of salt that makes your lips swell when you've eaten too many potato chips, which is probably why Noah always feels so aware of his mouth when he's around them.

'See now,' Pastor Lewis is waving his Bible frantically, 'why would someone even begin to think that God gives credence to people who follow this lifestyle? A lifestyle that is so clearly not in line with His teachings. Must we now accept adulterers into our churches? What about thieves and drunkards? What about murderers? Yet because of the pressure on society from this particular group, the world deems homosexuals to be acceptable. Because to deny them is to be called a homophobe or worse, and, oh, we could not bear to be disliked because we dared to stand up for God! We could not bear to be laughed at by our children or goaded by strangers on the news! But in our cowardice, we have allowed mankind to step in and have the *gall* to try to tell God how things need to be run.'

By now Pastor Lewis is quite red in the face, and the joints in his fingers have gone white from gripping his Bible so hard. He takes a swig of water from a plastic bottle beside the podium, like a rock star pausing between songs.

'But there is hope. That hope is in repentance and turning to Jesus Christ for cleansing. As Christians our job is not to condemn, but to pray for the souls of these misguided individuals. It is our duty to show them the way to the forgiveness and deliverance that is in Jesus Christ. Do we dare take up this responsibility? My brothers, my sisters, *do we dare*?' He punctuates the last three words with a jab of his finger at the congregation. Then he smiles, nods, and says, 'Thank you very much, ladies and gentlemen.'

One day, Noah will read on some colourful corner of the internet that being in the closet is like having someone constantly tapping you on the arm. At first it's just annoying. Then it becomes unbearable. In the end it's all you can think about. For the rest of his life, he will look back on that Sunday as the very first tap.

On their way out of the church, Samuel cuffs his son round the back of the head and says, 'I hope you were paying attention.'

Noah waits until his father is walking ahead of him, and then sticks out his tongue. Of course he was paying attention. He's always paying attention. Years from now, he will see something not meant for his attention at all, but much like Pastor Lewis's sermon, he won't understand its significance until it's too late.

Now

'Dolly, if I've told you once, I've told you a hundred times . . .'

Standing in Abigail's bedroom, Dolly can hear her husband coming up the stairs. She feels cornered by the sound of his voice, but she cannot bear to walk away from all the things her daughter has touched. Not yet.

'You don't put the frying pans in the dishwasher. The coating's come right off them. I'm not buying new ones, Dolly. I don't have money to throw away.'

Why don't you do the dishes for once, then? She runs a hand over the surface of Abigail's desk, dismayed to find it furred with dust. Already things are beginning to change.

'What's the matter with you that you can't remember that, huh, Dolly? *Dolly?* Hey, you up here?'

She doesn't answer. Instead she kneels beside Abigail's bed where her daughter's shape is still gently pressed into the bedding, a few of her red hairs still clinging to the comforter. It is a strange semblance of prayer – her kneeling there with her hands clasped together, the rough carpet making static with her pantyhose. *Is this my punishment?* She raises her eyes to the ceiling, feeling like some child who still thinks God lives in the sky. *Are you punishing me because we don't talk like we used to?*

'What are you doing in here, Dolly?'

She starts at the sound of Samuel's voice and turns to see him sloping through the door. All of a sudden, there doesn't seem to be enough room for both of them.

'You praying?' Her husband leans against the desk, his cracked-dry hands knocking over a cup full of pencils that rattle to the floor. Dolly swallows. She can't explain it, but somehow she feels that if they leave the room exactly as it is, they might wake up one day to find Abigail still asleep under the covers, filling out that shape in the bed that belongs to her.

She can't remember the last thing she said to her daughter, or even the last time she really saw her. She just recalls Abigail's vague presence moving down the stairs and out of the door to catch a ride with Emma Alvarez, and Dolly must have said something like, *Don't be home later than nine,* or *Keep your phone turned on*. It definitely wasn't *I love you*.

'You praying for little Abi?' Samuel asks, and now Dolly wonders why she ever liked the lowdown sound of that Louisiana drawl. 'Or you praying for yourself?'

She stretches her neck, easing the tension, then gets to her feet. 'I'm just praying, Sam. It's nothing.'

'Prayer ain't ever nothing, Dolly. Of all the women in the world, the Lord's making some time to listen to you, even after everything you've done. That ain't nothing.'

'All right, then. Maybe I was praying for Abi. What's wrong with that?'

'Nothing wrong with it.' Samuel shakes his head, smiling slightly at his knuckles as he clenches and unclenches his fist. 'It's quiet without her, don't you think? She was always singing, humming something or other. I've been missing it.'

Dolly doesn't know what to say to that. She reaches out to touch Samuel's shoulder, because she thinks that's what he wants from her, but he snatches up her hand, squeezing her fingers until she fears he might snap them.

'Maybe you ought to pray for a bit of backbone, Dolly.' His voice is steady. 'Pray for the backbone to do what needs to be done. I have spoken with the Lord, and I know why He's taken Abigail from us. We have allowed sin in this house. Get that whimpering look off your face – you know exactly what I'm talking about.' He clenches her hand tighter still, and she has to suck on her tongue to keep from making a sound.

'The boy, with all his sneaking out, I know what he's up to. He's doing it again, Dolly. We've neglected our duty. We have to show him the way to repentance through Jesus Christ. Cast out the sin, and then God will bring Abi back to us.'

After Samuel has left, Dolly crouches beside her daughter's bed again and rests her cheek against the covers. The fabric is cool, bordering on damp, but it still smells of her, of hair spray and artificial strawberries and the something else that has always reminded Dolly a little of freshly baked bread. Downstairs she can hear the rattle of her husband slamming the dishwasher door. She rubs her sore hand and thinks, If God really did take my girl away, it's because He knows anywhere is better than here.

10

WHISTLING RIDGE CAN barely keep its eyes open. In the Aurora diner, at the junction of 17th and Main, Emma and her mother blow idly on their second coffee of the morning, looking out over the main drag. The tourist season has finally come to an end and the last of the pop-up summer businesses are shutting up shop, having plundered the town for all it's worth. Drifts of dead leaves line the sides of the roads, punctuated by telephone poles and chipped public benches. Above it all, the mountains rise up solid and white, sharpening the wind as it funnels down the slopes into town. It's the same view Emma's been staring at since before she can remember, only something feels different, unattainable, like returning to a conversation with old friends who all have their own in-jokes now.

'I think some time out from school might do you good,' Melissa says, quietly so that no one else in the diner will overhear. 'Some time away from all this drama, just for a couple of weeks. What do you think?'

Emma nods and takes a sip of her coffee. She doesn't really know what she thinks. They finally had a talk about the drinking, after her mom found her kneeling over the toilet, retching up the last of the Wild Turkey. Melissa held back her hair and spoke softly, saying it was all going to be okay, but then Emma had stood on the landing afterwards, and listened to her mother gasping as though she was trying not to cry. She didn't mean to listen for as long as she did, but she knew that when she moved the floorboards would give her away, and she didn't want to embarrass her mother.

At the same time, she hated Melissa for crying. It's not like Emma got drunk to hurt her. It wasn't about her: it was about control. The only control Emma has is over this angry little body of hers, and screwing it up for a while feels like power, the way a mad king might slaughter his people, just to prove he can.

Can you believe Emma Alvarez just left her there?

She hasn't told her mother about befriending Rat: this grown-up boy who lets her drink his whiskey. Instead Emma made up some story about a girl at school with a fake ID, which will keep Melissa distracted for a while. Rat is hers, and not for anyone else just yet. Sometimes she feels as if he only exists at the trailer park, and she is the only person who can see him. He was funny about her wanting to investigate the woods, but maybe he was just looking out for her; she thinks she understands that now. As he will understand too, the next time she talks to him, why she has to do this, and together they'll prove it was Hunter Maddox out there in the woods, and Emma won't have to drink cheap bourbon ever again.

She smiles into her coffee, and her mother seems to take this as a good sign.

'I've been saving up my vacation days. I thought maybe I could take some time off with you. We could drive over to the national park. We used to do that all the time when you were little, do you remember?'

Emma has only a vague memory of a long road under a blue sky, surrounded by white on all sides, but then those trips weren't really about her anyway. They were so that her parents could sit together in the front of the car and marvel at the wilderness rushing past their windows, glowing side by side in the surety of that 'us against the world' feeling that kept them together for as long as it did.

But Emma knows her mother doesn't want to hear that. Melissa no more wants to talk about Miguel Alvarez than she wants to talk about her daughter's drinking. They are reminders of a road not taken, of her own sense of guilt at a choice she made a long time ago. Emma knows guilt now, recognizes it in the cracked skin on her mother's hands, in the deflated shape of her body lying in bed past her alarm, in the sobbing she tries so hard not to let her daughter hear. So instead Emma says, 'Yeah, Mom, sounds good.'

A police car pulls into the parking lot outside the window, and Sheriff Gains emerges, turning up the collar of his jacket and holding his Stetson to his head as the wind assaults him.

Melissa sits up a little straighter, muttering into her coffee mug, 'Well, look who it is.'

Gains's jaw is dark with stubble, but Emma remembers that he was clean-shaven when he interviewed her the week before last. He'd put his hand on her shoulder – the hand with three fingers missing – and said: 'I know this must be a hell of a time for you.' Now, in the parking lot, he props a cigarette between the stumps of those same fingers and uses his other hand to shield it from the wind. He smokes quickly, hungrily, like it's a thing of need rather than an aesthetic point (not like Rat), and Emma thinks, He is what a man ought to be.

Melissa puts down her cup and begins winding her scarf around her neck. 'Come on. We can go out through the other door.'

'Are you avoiding the cops?'

Melissa makes a low humming sound as she shuffles into her big parka. 'Of course I'm not.' She pauses, one arm in the air as she prepares to shake it through her coat sleeve. 'I just don't think he's . . . Oh, Em, I'm trapped. Pull my arm through, will you?'

Emma obliges, still unsure what her mother has to be so nervous about. She is wary of Gains in her own way – the way young women are always wary of older men, the way women of colour are wary of police – but he is sort of slow and gentle, like a river. His big dark eyes remind her of a donkey's, and donkeys always have such sad faces. The sight of the stumpy fingers on his hand opens up some deep well of fondness within her that she doesn't quite understand. But Melissa's anxiety is tangible, something in the air that Emma can't help but inhale, so she finds that she, too, is casting hasty glances out of the window as Gains finishes off his cigarette and flicks the butt away.

'Mom, why don't you like Sheriff Gains?'

Melissa tucks her thick yellow hair up under her hat. 'I don't have an opinion of him.'

'You didn't, like, *hook up* with him, did you?' Emma wrinkles her nose. 'Mom, that's gross.'

'Not so *loud*, Em.' Melissa looks around, but the diner is mostly empty. Just big Mo Dukes counting change at the bar, and his daughter Chrissy wiping down tables, working around an unfamiliar couple in anoraks and hiking boots.

Melissa squares her shoulders, dignity spared for the moment. 'No, Em. Certainly not. I just don't trust him, is all.'

They head for the other door, the one that leads out on to the little cobbled promenade running alongside the river.

'How come?' asks Emma.

'How come what?'

'How come you don't trust him?'

Melissa pulls her coat closer around her throat as they turn into the wind. 'Doctor–patient confidentiality. Forget I said anything.'

Then

One day in July, the summer before Abigail vanishes, Melissa is watching the main drag from the clinic break room, trying to catch a little breeze from the open window. The bohemian clothing store on the corner is having a sale – lots of knock-off Native American jewellery, and T-shirts with the town's elevation printed across a big marijuana leaf along with the slogan 'This whole town is high'. Yellow streamers from one of its promotional banners have come loose and now roll down the street, like bright tumbleweed. Melissa sighs. Summer drags, she thinks, but it's better than fall, when the kids bring animal bones out of the woods, and the valley feels like a mouth full of blood and rainwater, poised on the brink of a question it knows she cannot answer: *What are you still doing here?*

An eighteen-wheeler pulls up at the crossroads, stacked high with logs from the lumber mill. The driver's hairy arm lolls out of the window, his fingers tapping idly on the door to the tune on the radio, which declares that everybody is in love.

Folded up between Melissa's loyalty cards and crumpled dollar bills is her husband's smiling face – smiling because it was their runaway wedding day, and how simple it had all seemed back then. Just pack a bag and hit the road. Drive through the night until daylight emerges with the moon still caught in its teeth, and suddenly you're in another town, another world, where your parents can't find you and tear the love of your life right out of your arms. *Oh, Miguel.* The ache in her chest is too familiar. *Can we ever forgive each other?*

She pulls her hair back into a ponytail, tugging hard at the roots to distract herself. She's about to turn away from the window when something catches her eye. Abigail Blake, wandering expressionless along the sidewalk, bends down to pluck the tumbleweed of yellow streamers from the road. As she does so, Sheriff Gains walks right into her. Melissa watches their mouths move, each laughing slightly, apologizing to the other, and as Abigail turns to go, Gains puts his hand on the small of her back.

11

Now

If they had met in the wintertime, Noah thinks, things might have been different. By first snow, everyone is already starting to unravel, all wind-bitten and tired. It's hard to think of anyone erotically when they're bundled up in layers of scarves, thermals and fleece jackets. It's hard to think of yourself in any way at all, when your clothes are soaked through with melted snow, and your hands are pink and raw. In the winter, people just put their heads down and try to keep going until spring. If it had happened in the winter, Noah is certain it wouldn't have happened at all.

But summer nights are sensual. They are slow and easy and so very private. You can act out desire among the trees, behind barns, in the shadows, and only the stars will be watching. Night is made for unspeakable longings. Night is made for not speaking at all, but for furtive glances under streetlamps on dusty back roads, for the scent of a lover's hair, for fingers brushing past fingers in the darkness.

Now Rat and Noah stand in the remains of the old Winslow property, rooting through the ferns and moss-kissed debris, trying to undo the summer.

Noah sweeps an assortment of candles – which have melted together to form an unnameable colour – into a trash bag, then pauses for a moment to knuckle the small of his back. The Winslow house is the kind of place that seems like it has always been in ruins. Storms and ivy have got in through the skeleton roof and torn away great chunks of the walls. Blackened support beams that must have fallen inward during the fire now reach into the open air, while wildflowers spring from the crumbling mortar where some nineteenth-century housewife might once have trained roses.

Rat straightens up too, bored of deflating an old air mattress. 'This is the dumbest thing I've ever done.'

Noah sighs, pushing his hair back out of his eyes. 'I doubt that.'

'No, you're right. One time, when I lived in England, I pissed in the school's air vents to get back at my PE teacher. Took them a whole week to get rid of the smell.' He grins and retrieves his pack of Marlboros from his jacket pocket. 'But this is a pretty close second.'

'I told you, there are cops in these woods now. We can't leave all this shit lying around.' Noah stretches his arms up over his head until he hears his shoulders pop. 'How come you were so mad at your PE teacher?'

'He wanted me to cut my hair. Said he'd make me play netball with the girls if I didn't.'

'That's not so bad.'

'You would say that, Mr High School Basketball Team.'

For a moment, things are almost like they used to be, and Noah offers him half a smile. 'That was for one year and then they dropped me. I was going to be an English major, though. UCLA. Even you're a little impressed by that.'

'Sure am. I didn't know the Bible counted as literature. So what are you still doing in this dump?'

As if on cue, the sun slips behind a wall of thick white cloud and the Winslow house suddenly grows gloomy. Noah clears his throat. 'Family stuff.'

Rat leans against a charred wall and lights a cigarette, taking a long, slow drag. 'Do you think we'd have carried on coming up here if your sister hadn't gone missing?'

Noah frowns, but Rat just waves him away.

'You can drop the act, Blake. You told me they found a shell casing in the woods, and your first thought was someone might find out we were fucking, not whether your sister might have been shot.'

'That's not true.' Noah can feel his sister's absence like a stone in his chest, as though all the things he's never said to her are piling up inside him now. He keeps thinking back to that day at the river – how, climbing back into his truck, she had put her hand on his shoulder and he had let her. What might they have said to each other, if the drive home had been just a little longer? Now, it seems, they are out of time.

Noah sniffs, and crouches back down to scrape old wax off the lichen-spotted hearth with his fingernails. He tries to breathe steadily, but the air is thick with the smell of cigarettes.

Rat says, 'If you say so. You just seem more concerned about those damn candles than about your sister.'

'You don't know this town like I do. If people find out about this, it'll be bad for you too.'

They finish packing the summer away in silence, until the sky begins to simmer with the first signs of sunset. The evening is sweet and damp with the prospect of rain; Noah notices the way Rat's hair is starting to curl from the moisture in the air.

'That's that, I guess.' Rat looks around, nodding to himself.

'I guess.' Noah, leaning against the old chimney stack, chews his lip and says, 'See you round.'

They stand there, looking at one another in the raw evening light, only half listening to the rattling aspens and the crows calling overhead. Rat's eyes wander over Noah's face like he's trying to memorize it.

'In Europe, I'd kiss you on the cheek to say goodbye.'

'Don't.' Noah rubs his nose and feels its crooked outline. 'It's not worth it.'

'Maybe it's worth it to me.'

Noah wants to touch the places where the light falls on him – his hair, his cheekbones, the tips of his ears – but the distance is too far, and there is so much more between them than just the curling ferns and charcoal timbers of the Winslow ruin. He feels it again, that tapping on his arm, and he wants to say something, he really does, but he also feels the places where the bruises were, hears his father's voice in his head, sees the hole in the wall behind the cross. When bad things happen people turn their faces upwards and ask, *Why? Why?* but Noah already knows. His father's fist was the right hand of God that night he put the hole in the plaster, and God said unto him: I didn't raise no faggot.

'Blake, are you okay?'

Rat takes a step towards him. Noah slams his own hand hard against the musty stone behind him, and something drops out of the chimney.

Later, when the Blake family holds hands around the dinner table to give thanks to the Almighty for their microwaved lasagne leftovers, Dolly opens one eye and looks at her elder son. Perhaps to make sure he is still there. At some point in the last ten years, these features he now wears have assembled themselves into a final arrangement, and she feels late in noticing this. He has been this person for some time, yet she has been none the wiser.

But there is something else, and it feels as though some hard little ball in her chest has suddenly dropped to her stomach, as she realizes it is fear she sees in her son's face. And that same night, as Emma Alvarez lies awake listening to the coyotes howl, missing the taste of whiskey; as Jude dreams of his sister decomposing; as Samuel remembers how he once cradled a dead woman among black trees and soldiers' voices, Dolly Blake lies in bed feeling flattened by the weight of her own guilt.

On the other side of town, Rat Lăcustă strums his grandmother's guitar, and stares at the bag that fell out of the Winslow chimney.

12

'THERE WAS ALWAYS something odd about them, though,' says Ann Traxler, as she snips off Debbie Weaver's split ends. 'And now the girl's disappeared – well, you can't help but wonder.'

Emma pretends to be engrossed in her magazine, but she can see their reflections at the edge of her vision, and so far they haven't thought to moderate their voices for her.

Eleanor Lewis, sitting with her foil highlights under a heat lamp, gives a sage nod. 'Always something off. The father for one thing – oh, Debbie, tell us about that awful birthday party.'

Debbie, whose youngest son Cole once called Emma 'the daughter of a no-good wetback', slings one massive leg over the other, gearing up for the long haul. She smiles at them both in the mirror, pleased at having been given the floor by the pastor's wife.

'It was back when Luke was in the youth league with the son – what's his name? Noah?'

'Don't even get me started on him,' says Eleanor.

'Well, he invited Luke to some birthday thing over at their house once – and this was *before*, you know, so how was I to know any different?'

'Of course.'

'So I go to pick Luke up at the end of the afternoon, and he starts crying in the car, says Samuel Blake told them about how one time he shot a woman in the back while she was running away.'

'You're kidding,' says Ann.

'It was in some place called Sơn Tịnh, I think. Vietnam. He just gunned her right down. Naturally, Luke never wanted to go back there.'

Emma had heard rumours, the way you always do in a small town, and Abigail had often told her about how Samuel used to scare friends away, but she had never mentioned any dead woman.

The haircut had been Melissa's idea: 'You could do with some pampering,' she'd said. But then she'd had to duck back into the clinic, leaving Emma in a gown with a towel around her shoulders, completely on the periphery of Ann Traxler's attention. It suits Emma just fine, though, now that they're really getting to the meat of things. Even Melissa has avoided mentioning Abigail to her face, and she had begun to feel as if Abi was just one long dream in the coma of her youth. But these women couldn't care less about Emma's feelings, and it feels good to hear the familiar names spoken aloud again.

'That's the other thing, of course,' says Ann. 'You've got to wonder why Dolly married him in the first place, that Samuel. He's so much older, after all, and he comes with all that baggage.'

'She was pregnant, that's what I heard,' Debbie puts in.

Ann raises her eyebrows. 'You think he got her knocked up? That's why she married him?'

'Not Dolly. The woman he shot, she was pregnant. That's what Luke said.'

Eleanor Lewis frowns. 'He's a dreadful man. Comes to

church smelling of beer and thinks that just because he says "Amen" the loudest, that makes it all right. Besides,' she adds, lowering her voice, 'I've seen his children's knees, all rubbed raw, and the younger boy once told me that sometimes he makes them get down to pray on the gravel in their driveway.' She shakes her head. 'Now, I'm a Christian woman and that kind of thing's their own business, but it's just the wrong shade of devout for me.'

Emma doesn't much care what they think about Samuel. Or even Dolly, for that matter. Dolly just makes her feel worse. The other day, they ran into her at Safeway, and she was stooped over her shopping cart, following it around rather than pushing it. She stared at Emma the whole time, barely seeming to register Melissa, and Emma knew she was picturing Abigail standing next to her.

'No, I'm afraid I don't have much sympathy for Dolly Blake,' Eleanor continues. 'Women like that are so dramatic. She used to be on the church committee, and you could see her lazy attempts at covering up the marks on her arms and face. It made everyone uncomfortable.'

Ann rolls her eyes. 'It's the internet and all that, it's created a bad culture. People think they've got to share everything.'

'Exactly.' Eleanor points at her. 'And if it was really so terrible, she'd just leave him.'

'Is that why you let her go in the end?' Debbie asks. 'I always thought her hymn choices were real nice. She brought a bit of east-coast class.'

'She looked down her nose at us, is what she did,' says Ann.

'I let her go because she stopped showing up. After that whole strange business a few years ago – you remember?'

'Oh, yes.' Debbie nods. 'The business with the son. That *was* strange.'

'Well, that's what I mean,' says Ann. 'Now the daughter's disappeared, you can't help but wonder.'

She looks down at Debbie's hair, but as she does, she catches Emma's eye in the mirror. 'Oh, you want a glass of water, hon?'

Eleanor peers at her over Debbie's shoulder, her little rose-bud mouth creasing along familiar lines as she scrunches it up in disapproval. Debbie blinks with bovine slowness and waves a chubby hand in Emma's direction.

'You just ignore us, sweetie,' she says, forcing out a little giggle, like trapped wind. 'Just a bunch of old chickens clucking away.'

On the way home, Emma asks if they can drive past the Blakes' place, and Melissa reaches across the car and rubs her shoulder, before taking the turn off on to Hickory Lane.

With pale drapes drawn over every window, the house looks almost blind. Yet Jesus watches from the porch, His plastic face a little melted from the heat of summer, wailing silently for their sins. An angel crouches in the branches of the blue spruce that pushes against the second storey, its hands glued together in prayer. An elk skull on the fence post, one antler broken, fixes its hollow stare on Emma and her mother, and she feels that, if it could talk, it would tell them to turn the car around and drive away.

None of the family cars – Samuel's rusted pick-up, Dolly's little hatchback, or Noah's truck with the engine like a bone saw – are parked in the driveway. *He makes them get down to pray on the gravel* . . . Picking little stones out of the cuts in Abigail's knees, rubbing anti-bacterial cream into the grazes to stave off infection, squeezing Abi gently around the shoulders as she mumbled about wickedness – Emma remembers these things just as well as she remembers the two of them boiling deer bones to get them clean for art projects, or wearing matching dresses, or sprinting through Emma's backyard with grassy feet, shivering and reeking of chlorine from the neighbour's pool.

'Jesus,' says Melissa, 'I forgot what a dump this place is.'

Emma nods. 'Yeah, we can go if you want. I don't know, I just wanted to see it.'

'Of course.' Melissa looks over her shoulder as she puts the car into reverse. 'I can't believe I ever used to let you come play here. Feels like for ever ago.'

Eleanor Lewis's words come back to her now. *That whole strange business a few years ago – you remember?* Four years, Emma thinks, that's how long it's been since she was last inside the Blakes' house.

Oh, yes. The business with the son. That was strange.

For days Noah didn't come to school. Chrissy Dukes said he hadn't shown up for work at the Aurora diner either, nor had anyone seen him in church, although a few people had spotted Dolly crying in the parking lot. At first Abigail said that Noah had hurt himself playing basketball, but Noah had dropped off the basketball team when he was a sophomore, and this was in his senior year. Abi got all weird and squirrelly when Emma tried to dig deeper. Then, during a fraught encounter in the chips-and-dips aisle, Dolly had hastily explained to Melissa that Noah was depressed because he didn't get into any of the colleges he'd picked, and no doubt this was the story she spread at church as well. But Emma was the one friend Samuel hadn't managed to scare away. She knew Noah's parents: they didn't *believe* in kids getting depressed. Said it was all just a scheme to sell them medication they didn't need. So one day Emma called by to see Abigail, and that was when she saw Noah with his face all bashed in. After that she wasn't allowed to come over to the house any more. Nobody was – until the day, four years later, when Sheriff Gains arrived to tell the Blakes their daughter had disappeared.

Emma watches the house getting smaller in the rear-view mirror, and she thinks about Noah with his black and purple face, and Abi with the stones in her knees, and all the secrets that ordinary people carry around with them, and she hears Ann Traxler's voice again: *You can't help but wonder.*

13

THE PROBLEM WITH Abigail is that she's artistic. (Jude refuses to think of his sister in anything other than the present tense, even though she has been missing for 432 hours now.) He's been mulling this over for some time, and now, leaning against the shopping cart while his brother deliberates over fajita spices, he thinks he has finally figured it out. Abigail is artistic, and that's why Noah has always hated her. He hated her even *before*.

Their mother was artistic, a long time ago. Jude has a vague memory of her showing them how to make little figures out of modelling clay when they were younger and cooing over Abi's attempts the most. It's hard to imagine his mother being creative now, but perhaps that's why she always seemed to pay Abigail more attention.

'Hey, Limpy, do you want smoky barbecue or roasted tomato?'

Jude is glad to have his brother ask him about something, even if it's only seasoning. 'Barbecue,' he says, and Noah tosses it into the cart.

Abi is good with pencils and charcoal, but she isn't much good at anything else at school, so Dolly recycles Noah's old English essays for Abigail to hand in as homework. 'Don't look like that, Noah. It's not hurting anyone, is it?' Then, when Abi's grades come back top, their father says things like, 'That's my girl,' and sticks her report card up on the refrigerator. He never says things like that to Noah. So, Jude decides, even if what happened – was it really four years ago now? – had never happened, his brother would still have hated their sister anyway.

Samuel Blake never says, 'That's my boy,' to Jude either, but then Jude does not expect it. He is the piece of punctuation at the end of his siblings: Noah, Abigail, *Jude*. A small name, telling him how much space he's allowed to take up. *An accident*, his father called him once. His mother did not disagree. So Jude talks quietly, tucks his elbows in and gives whatever he can, the way Jesus taught him. His parents are like the elk that sometimes come down the mountain and eat the berries in their backyard – you have to be patient with them, and eventually, sometimes, they will let you pet their muzzles. They probably don't care much about berries, his parents, but he can give them patience. He will give it to them until he has given away enough of himself that he is the right size to fit into their lives.

And what about Noah? What does Noah need?

'Hey, wait with the cart, will you?' It's not really a question, and his brother takes off around the corner of the spice aisle, disappearing before Jude can reply.

Slowly, he hobbles to the end, leaning on the shopping cart handlebar for support, and peers around an early display of Halloween ornaments. His brother is talking to the Romanian boy, who has six cans of ravioli in his basket and nothing else, so it's hard for Jude not to feel a little bit sorry for him. Noah's movements are very jagged, jerking away when the other boy tries to reach out to him. At last Noah says, loud enough for Jude to hear, 'I said I don't want anything to do with it. I don't want anything to do with *you*.'

'But the money, Blake! You could finally get out of here, *we* could—'

'Just stay the hell away from me.'

Noah takes off in the other direction, not slowing even when his sleeve catches on a deal sign and rips down half the display, so he doesn't see what Jude sees: the Romanian boy standing there, arms hugging his chest, just staring at the space where Noah was.

Jude retreats back to the spices and seasonings, and thinks, Not again, Noah. Not again.

Emma stares at the bag: a little clear Ziploc of white powder, nestled in the remains of an old Safeway carrier. 'You need to take this to the police. Where the hell did you even get it?'

'Fell out of the chimney,' says Rat, 'at the Winslow ruin.'

'That creepy place up by the Tall Bones?'

'I'm not going to the police.' He leans against the sink, giving her that cocky half-moon grin. 'With a business opportunity like this?'

'But this is cocaine, Rat. Literal cocaine.'

'Twenty grams. More or less.'

'So, what, you're a drug dealer? Is that it?'

She thinks about the tin of cash in the cupboard – the cash he's no doubt been using to pay for their liquor – and suddenly she has a desperate need to be held by her mother, to be as far away from here as possible, away from this bag of coke and Rat's sharp edges. The feeling arrives so fiercely that she begins to cry.

Outside the clouds have grown dark, but only a little rain comes, like a leak in the sky, a weak tapping on the metal roof.

'Hey,' Rat says softly. 'Don't be frightened. Please don't.'

She rubs her eyes with the back of her hand, remembering

too late about her makeup, and now, standing in front of him with mascara smeared across her cheeks, she just wants to cry all over again.

'I'm not a drug dealer, Emma.' For a second, he worries his lower lip between his teeth in a way that reminds her of Noah Blake. 'Not since I came to America.'

'Is that supposed to make me feel better? That's why you didn't want me poking around, isn't it?'

'I told you, I *found* this, at the Winslow ruin.'

Emma takes a shallow breath in and lets a long breath out. It could be true, what he's saying. God, she longs for things to be simple again, to be simple herself, smothering giggles with Abigail as they sipped Samuel Blake's bourbon, like that was the worst thing either of them had ever done.

'But . . .' Emma rubs her eyes again, and her fingers come away all smudged with black. 'Are you still going to sell it, though?'

'We can make a little money, *drăguță*, you and me. I'll buy you whatever you like – Jack Daniel's, Russian Standard, French-fucking-champagne – you name it.'

'We? What do you mean "we"? Don't involve me in this.'

Rat scratches the underside of his jaw. 'I'll help you with Hunter Maddox.'

It's such an obvious play that it feels like a slap. Emma wants to be mad at him, to slap him right back on principle, but she also wants to prove Hunter's place in all this. More than anything else, she just wants to find out what happened to the only real friend she's ever had, and somewhere behind all that she wants for it not to be her fault, and God, Jesus, can you believe that Emma Alvarez just left her there? Can you *believe*? Emma knows it's not real but she can hear the coyotes howling again, and there are too many images crowding around her head: Abi in her prom dress dancing at the Tall

Bones, Abi in the moonlight about to turn into the trees, Abi with grass on the soles of her feet, with blood on her knees, with a smile on her face, scratching and scratching at her skin, and Emma can feel the weight of all their years together, the love and the boredom and the madness of it, caving in on her like she's being buried alive and her lungs are full of dirt.

'Emma—'

The next thing she knows, she's on the floor, shuddering with such awful, empty sobs that Rat puts his arms around her and holds her until she stops shaking. She makes strange sounds then, sad sounds as she buries her face in the crook of his neck where he is warm and heady with the smell of incense. Later, looking back, she thinks perhaps she'd hoped he might smell like her father.

'I won't let anything happen to you,' he says, as if he doesn't consider himself an event.

14

Much of his past now seems like some vague dark blur at the back of his mind. Samuel has drunk enough to make it that way. But sometimes he can still feel his parents' kitchen linoleum, hard and cold under his knees, as he picked the remains of a turkey dinner out of the garbage. 'You think my cooking's trash?' his mother yelled. 'Then you can *eat it* out of the trash.' The meat was lukewarm and slimy with the remains of yesterday's dog food. Even now his throat seizes at the thought of it.

The skin on the back of his right hand is tight and pale, and he is happy to let folks assume it was something that happened during the war. He'd rather they didn't know that his mother had walked in on him touching himself, aged eleven, and pressed his hand down under her clothes iron. 'Don't you ever do that,' she said. 'You make God mad when you do that.' When he'd cried, she'd shoved him against the sideboard and gone to swallow Valium alone in her bedroom with the drapes closed. It was not lost on him, even as a child, how the things that made God mad usually pissed off his mother as well.

That was the first lesson Constance Blake taught him: how easily you can blur the line between the Lord's wishes and your own. The second lesson was about sex. Constance did not approve of sex, so neither did God, which made things difficult for Samuel because he wanted to have it.

Georgia Lafitte was the housemaid's daughter, and she was sixteen when Samuel was on the cusp of manhood. He can still remember it: out on the veranda of the Blakes' crumbling old plantation manor, cicadas in chorus in the background, her little moans as the sun dipped behind the trees. The Spanish moss swayed in the cooling air. He didn't realize his mother was home until she came out to call him for dinner.

She wouldn't even let Georgia gather up her clothes. Samuel recalls the girl running across the lawn half naked, her hair a tangled mess from where Constance had gripped her by the scalp and torn her away from him. Mrs Lafitte was fired the following day. Samuel was informed that his attitude needed correcting, and two weeks later he found himself on a navy vessel bound for Da Nang.

At first it hadn't seemed like much of a punishment. Samuel had never had many friends at school, and suddenly here he was, part of a brotherhood, and better still, he was thousands of miles away from his mother. Despite the sweat and the rain and the danger lurking in every shadow, it felt as if he had finally been given room to breathe.

But he thinks now: It's strange the things we turn to in our darkest moments. And when he was crawling over bodies, holding a dead man's hand, watching a face – peeled clean off – just floating by in a stream of mud, there were times when he had wished for his mother.

Guilt is a hard body to bury, no matter how many times you might claim God forgives you. You let some things fester long enough, they grow teeth and claws and crawl their way back to the surface again.

Samuel gets these spasms sometimes now. His arms shoot

out and he makes this sudden, awkward noise as though someone has just walked up behind him and dug their fingers into his lower back. Then Dolly says, 'Oh, Sam,' and people think she's being kind.

He remembers it had happened once in church, right in the middle of Pastor Lewis's sermon, and afterwards Dolly had apologized *for him*. Little Dalton Lewis, peering out from behind his father's legs, wanted to know how come he'd made that noise, how come? And Dolly had said, 'He was in the war,' and Dalton thought she meant World War Two. Kids these days don't even know, he thinks, and if they do, they don't care. It's all the same to them, sitting on their phones, ignoring the world.

It's the fear in their eyes that he can't stand. Whenever people look at him, afraid, he sees a different face, one he would rather forget. 'Dolly,' he says, 'all you do is make me feel like shit,' and he teaches her with feints and lunges how to keep her face straight, how to keep the fear away. He has seen too much fear in women's eyes.

Except Abigail's.

Abi looks him straight in the eye – has done ever since she was born – not like the first son, or the second. When the noises come out, she just looks at him and says, 'Daddy, pass the mayonnaise, will you please?' or 'Anyway, as I was saying . . .' and then continues as if nothing ever happened.

Abigail was his gift from God, while Noah – sweaty-handed, lip-chewing, bookish Noah – was a trial. By the time he was old enough to walk, Constance Blake was phoning twice a week, asking when she could come up to Colorado and meet her first grandchild. Her husband, Samuel's own father, had passed away the year before, and this, Constance claimed, had been some kind of wake-up call. She was eating better, spending more time with other women in the community, and she was taking this new medication that helped stabilize her moods. But Samuel was having none of it. All that Valium she'd swallowed when he was growing up never seemed to do her any good, why should these pills be any different? It was all the same bullshit with a different price tag slapped on. Besides, Noah would only disappoint her, and that, in turn, would reflect poorly on Samuel.

'He swooned, Dolly,' Samuel remembers saying once. 'There's no other word for it. He bit his tongue when the ball hit him, and then he *swooned*. Can't even stand the taste of blood in his mouth, what kind of a man's he going to be?'

And Dolly had just looked at him and said, 'He's three,' like that was sufficient.

Later, Samuel told his son, 'You're letting God down.'

But Abi, he really prayed for Abi. He wasn't expecting a daughter, but when he took her out with his old M-16 rifle and she shot up a row of empty Lone Star cans at twenty paces, bullets pinging in the hot air, like lightning bugs, he knew this was the child, this was the one to be made in his image. He had been given a chance to do things right this time.

Afterwards, Abi had collected all the shell casings and Samuel had made them into a bracelet for her. He made a bunch of jewellery for her over the years, although Dolly would not allow her to wear any of it to school. Poor taste, she said. But now, when he goes up to Abigail's bedroom, chasing Dolly away because she's filling it with too much of her miserable cigarette stench, he sits down on the bedspread in the gentle silence that his daughter so often provided him, and he finds one of the shell casings tucked under her pillow.

Sometimes he hears his mother speaking through him. God forgive me, he'll say, but it isn't so much a request as a statement. If he repeats it often enough, everyone will believe it. But Abigail, wherever she is now, chose to keep this small memento of their time together. As though she, at least, forgives him.

Jude looks up from his homework to see his father standing in his bedroom doorway.

'Get your shoes,' he says. 'We're going out to pray.'

The night air smells like winter, smoky and sodden. Standing in the driveway, Jude pulls his scarf tighter around his throat as he looks up at the clear sky, and thinks that if stars were grains of salt, out here it would look as though God had knocked over the shaker.

His mother helps him get down on one knee. The other leg, already beginning to ache from the cold, sticks out at a stiff angle, and he holds on to his cane to steady himself. Then she and Noah kneel on either side of him in a half-circle, which they wait for Samuel to complete. The gravel digs into his shin through his jeans, and when he looks at his mother and brother, dimly lit by the orange glow shining out from behind the drapes, they too are tightening their mouths so as not to wince. It's been a while since his father asked them to do this. Jude wonders why he's chosen tonight.

His father's Bible is the potent King James Version, bound in black leather with gold edging the pages, and a tattered blue ribbon that he uses to mark his place. Even now Jude can see the tail of it fluttering in the chill breeze, but this evening there are also several scraps of paper marking pages, and Jude swallows. Tonight, it seems, God and his father have a lot to say.

'Psalm 5:5: *The foolish shall not stand in thy sight, thou hatest all workers of iniquity.*' Samuel's voice sounds like it's been dragged over a dry riverbed. 'We are told plainly that our Lord hates those who stand before Him in arrogance.'

Dolly clasps and unclasps her hands, once, twice, three times. Jude knows she probably wants a cigarette, but it's more than that: she keeps folding her lips together and looking hurriedly from Noah to the ground to her husband. *I thought this was going to be about Abi.*

'As it says in the Book of Revelation, all *immoral persons* will be put into the lake that burns with fire and brimstone.'

Samuel looks at each of them in turn, his gaze lingering a moment longer than any of them would like. Jude makes a conscious effort not to flinch, and the sting from the stones digging into his knee begins to make his eyes water. He keeps his head down, hoping his father won't think he's crying.

'I tell you what awaits these immoral persons: it is the fiery lake with no one but the devil himself for company for time everlasting. We are all sinners, oh, yes, truly we are all clad in sinner's coats, but we have found redemption through the love of Jesus Christ. Amen!' He barks those last two syllables, and the family echoes them back to him in a low murmur. 'And yet there are those who turn their faces away from the love of the Lord, who continue to stand before Him in arrogance, despite the threat of pain and torment, and it is these immoral persons who are the greatest affront to God because they reject His offer of redemption.'

He takes a deep breath in through his nose and lets it emerge from his mouth in a cloud of steam, as though instead of Samuel Blake, a demon is crouching with them in the driveway.

Slowly, he gets to his feet and begins to circle around them. 'It brings me no joy to tell you that there is one such person in this family, and that for their wickedness, we are all being punished.' Jude feels the back of his neck prickle as his father passes behind him. 'The false tongues of the Sheriff's Department would have us believe that Abigail ran away, but the truth is that God Himself took her to sit under the watchful care of His angels until we have driven out the sin from this house. Then, and only then, will He send her home to us.'

Suddenly he jabs a finger at Dolly. 'You want your daughter back?'

Looking at her now, Jude can see that her face is shiny with tears, although he had not heard her crying. He never does. Even the slight action of nodding seems to tire her out.

'You,' says Samuel, and Jude is alarmed to find his father now pointing at him. 'Do you want your sister back?'

He hesitates, but Samuel's heavy stare seems to be pushing him harder against the stones, and eventually he nods too.

His father reaches for his Bible again, reading slowly as he comes to stand behind Noah. 'Leviticus, 20:13: *If a man also lie with mankind, as he lieth with a woman, both of them have committed an abomination; . . . Their blood shall be upon them.'* At this he puts his boot against Noah's back and knocks him to the ground, then stands with one foot on his son's head, pressing the side of his face into the gravel. Dolly claps her hands to her mouth, whimpers into her palms, but does not move. Jude tries to stand, but loses his balance, and has to grasp at his stick to keep him upright. Noah scrabbles at the stones around him, choking in the dirt.

'You've brought this on yourself, boy,' says Samuel, voice like a buck knife, as he holds his son down. 'The ways I teach you are the ways of the Lord, and yet still you reject Him.' He takes a sharp breath and wets his lips, watching Noah struggling beneath him. 'Swear on the Lord our God that you will renounce this immoral lifestyle and seek redemption and forgiveness in Jesus Christ.'

Jude knows he should do something, but this all feels too familiar, and the twinge in his aching leg tells him: Keep your mouth shut, or he'll break the other one.

Dolly shifts like she's about to stand up. 'Sam—'

'Stay down, woman, or you'll feel the back of my hand. We are about God's work here.' Samuel grinds his boot harder against Noah's cheek. 'I said swear it.'

Noah groans, his mouth half full of grit.

'Swear it!'

Slowly, painfully, Noah nods.

Jude watches a smile split his father's face. 'Corinthians,' he says, and the triumph in his voice lends a golden edge to his words. *'Know ye not that the unrighteous shall not inherit the kingdom of God? Be not deceived: no abusers of themselves with mankind shall inherit His kingdom.'* He pulls out his hip flask and pours the contents over his son. *'And such were some of you: but ye are washed, but ye are sanctified, but ye are justified in the name of the Lord Jesus, and by the Spirit of our God.* Amen.'

Then, still smiling, Samuel tosses the flask into the dirt by Noah's head, and without even glancing at the others he turns and walks back into the house.

15

'WHERE ARE YOU going? It's getting dark.'

Melissa reaches the foot of the stairs and sees her daughter shuffling into her sneakers, phone in one hand, jacket in the other.

Emma tosses her hair. 'Mom, it's barely seven.' She's wearing a shade of lipstick that Melissa's never seen before.

'Are you meeting someone? Em, you're not going to meet that girl, are you – the one who bought you the liquor last time?'

Emma blinks at her for a moment, her face totally blank. Then: 'Oh. No, I'm not friends with her any more.'

What to do when your teenager lies to you. Melissa looked it up the night she found Emma retching over the toilet, and now she finds herself running through the website's top tips all over again. *Number one: stay calm.* Well, sure, but what about something practical? *Number two: let them know you're there for them.* Yesterday she took Emma to the hairdresser, and then they had doughnuts and lemonade at Aurora, and Melissa bought her some glittery nail polish on the way home. She's taken her out of school and avoided confronting her even though she knows both their hearts are breaking, but Emma just keeps smiling this empty smile at her, saying, 'Sounds good, Mom,' and smelling of breath mints and too much deodorant.

Number three: keep some perspective, it's not about you.

'Well, that's good, Em. But, you know, I really don't feel comfortable about you going out alone at night right now, not when the police still haven't . . . Well, you know.'

'Look, Mom, I won't be gone long, and I'll text you. But it's cool. I'm just meeting a friend.'

Melissa looks at the lipstick again. 'Oh.'

Emma glances at her feet, perhaps hoping that her mother won't catch her little smile. The sight of it makes Melissa's chest ache for her sweet girl whose untested youth is still so full of hope.

'What is he like? I'm assuming it's a he.' Melissa clears her throat.

Emma is still grinning privately at her shoes. 'He's real nice, Mom.'

Melissa knows the time is approaching when she will have to tell her daughter the truth: that deep down, most men are mediocre. Most people are, really, but men are allowed to grow up thinking the world is their oyster in a way that women cannot. Then they get to be forty and they wonder why it hasn't happened for them yet, and if there's a woman in their way, well, that's tough for her.

'Just be careful, won't you? Sometimes boys can . . . Well, they always want someone else to blame.'

'Is that what Dad did?' Emma asks.

Number four: model honesty in your own behaviour.

'No, Em. Your dad had to leave because . . .' Melissa sighs. Emma is looking over her shoulder through the window in the door: she doesn't really want the answer to this question now because she has somewhere else to be. But before she leaves, Emma reaches out and rubs her mother's shoulder.

'It's okay, Mom,' she says. 'I know.'

And Melissa squeezes her daughter's hand and thinks, No, you don't know. I hope you never do.

Emma checks her phone again. 'He's late.'

Rat leans back against the cool rock of one of the Tall Bones and lights a cigarette. Behind them, the moon climbs out of the forest, struggling over the tangle of bare branches that snag at its edges.

'He'll be here.'

When she'd called Rat the night before to ask what his big plan was, he'd said, 'Nothing big about it, *drăguță*. I've got twenty grams of coke to shift, you've got questions you want answering, so . . .' She could practically hear the shrug in his pause, like that was the sort of sentence people said all the time. 'We kill two birds with one stone. You told me yourself that Hunter Maddox is in the business of buying and selling, so we hit him up, let him know there's merchandise to be had. We get him somewhere private, get the money, and then we ask him what he knows.'

'That's terrible. We just ask him?'

'Real life isn't like *CSI*, *drăguță*. The only things we're likely to find if we go poking around in the woods are bird bones and pine needles. Sometimes the best approach is the simplest.'

'But what if he won't talk?'

Rat's impatience had crackled through the static. 'Then we remind him that he's now in possession of an illegal substance, and if he doesn't play ball then the Whistling Ridge Sheriff's Department is going to get an anonymous tip, all right? Just trust me, Emma. I know what I'm doing.'

A stiff breeze makes the forest rattle. When Emma was a child, it always seemed so full of promise, like you could taste adventure on the air. She and Abigail used to run away to the woods when they were younger, mix potions out of pine dust and crystallized sap, holler at the mountains, like the primeval bellowing of elk, to scare away the ghosts, and then traipse home, their bare feet stained red from the dirt. But Emma is older now, and when she looks into the trees, she thinks of coyote teeth, and cold limbs laid out against the dark earth, and she wonders, Is this what it means to grow up? To realize that magic and ghosts aren't real, and that the true danger in all those stories was always the real things, the wolves and the woods?

No. The danger was always the people.

'Hey,' says Rat, staring at his cigarette, 'what do you know about Noah Blake?'

'Noah?' Emma shrugs. He's Abi's big brother, so she's known him for ever, but he was always too grown up to hang out with them. Best of Creedence Clearwater Revival CDs, black coffee, muddy boots, that's what she remembers of Noah. Would much rather read about fictional people than spend time with real ones.

'He's kind of weird.'

'What's his story?'

'Why do you care?'

'Maybe I want to make some friends, *drăguță*. You can't keep me all to yourself.'

Emma grins. 'Well, who says I want you?'

The wind picks up again and a shiver takes hold of her. Rat shrugs off his jacket and hangs it over her shoulders. It is lined with the heat of him and she burrows into it, trying not to think about what he just said. He watches her with a smile.

Emma pulls out her phone again. 'He's twenty minutes late. What if he's figured something's up?'

The rumble of an engine makes them turn in time to see headlights licking the trees as a car pulls in at the edge of the field. Then the bulky figure of Hunter Maddox clambers out of the driver's side and strides across the grass towards them.

Rat says, 'Speak of the devil.'

'What's she doing here?'

Emma tucks as much of herself as she can into Rat's jacket, as Hunter runs his eyes over her.

'You didn't say anything about other people.'

'Did you bring the money?' Rat asks.

Hunter lingers on Emma a moment longer, and in the glare of his flashlight he seems painted with a darker, harsher brush. 'Yeah,' he says at last. 'All cash, like you said.'

Rat nods. '*Drăguță*.'

Emma clears her throat, not wanting to look at either of them particularly, as she reaches into her sweater to retrieve the old Safeway bag full of coke. Earlier, Rat had suggested she stuff it into her bra, and at the time the thought of him seeing her breasts made her toes curl enough to want to do it. Only he didn't see anything of her, just turned around and looked at some poem stuck to the wall. Now, handing Hunter Maddox a bag of cocaine that's been squashed between her tits all evening, she feels like the butt of some joke that all the boys in the world are in on.

Hunter raises his eyebrows. 'So that's why you brought her, huh?'

Rat doesn't say anything, and Emma wishes the ground would split open and swallow her. The shot of vodka the two of them took before leaving the RV has mostly worn off, and now, even with Rat's jacket, she feels cold and groggy.

'Let's just get it over with,' she says. 'Do you want the stuff or not?'

'All right, don't get your panties in a twist.' Hunter unwraps the Safeway bag, but then he just stands there blinking in the torchlight. 'Hey, come on, what the hell is this?'

Rat puffs smoke into the cold evening. 'It's twenty grams of powder, my friend. Like we said.'

'Yeah, but this is . . . Where did you get this?'

'That's my business.'

'But *how* did you—?'

'It's cocaine, Maddox.' Rat sounds bored now. 'I'm not going to tell you how I got it. You want it, then great. We'll take the money and be on our way. If not, you can quit wasting my time.'

Emma thinks Hunter looks sad as he dips one finger into the Ziploc and then sticks it into his mouth, rubbing at his gums.

'No, I'll take it. Here.' He pulls an envelope out of his Letterman jacket and hands it to Rat.

'Five hundred. Attaboy.'

Hunter wraps the coke back up and tucks it carefully inside his jacket.

'Hey, Maddox, don't disappear on us just yet. My friend here wants a word.'

A sudden buzzing makes them all start. Rat grimaces and pulls his phone out of his back pocket. 'Talk among yourselves, would you?' He tucks it between chin and shoulder as he turns away. 'Hey, hey, slow down, I can't . . . They did what? Are you okay? . . . Yeah, I know. Can you drive? . . . Uh-huh. Good . . . No, not there, it's too cold. Just meet me at my place. I'm already on my way.'

'Hey,' Emma hisses, 'what do you mean you're already on your way? You can't leave me.'

There's a nervous energy about him that she's never seen before, a sort of kinetic hum. 'Listen, a friend of mine's in trouble, I have to go.'

'What friend?'

'Just a friend.'

'You can't leave me with *him*.' She gestures over her shoulder to Hunter, now apparently focused on digging the toe of his sneaker into the dirt. 'What about getting him to talk?'

'Ah.' Rat can't seem to stand still, his body swaying towards the pines where, earlier, they parked his motorcycle. Scrunching up his eyes for a moment, he says, 'God, this is . . . phenomenal timing.'

'You're *not* leaving me. Why can't you drive me back?'

'Listen, you'll be fine. You'll be okay.' Glancing towards the motorcycle again, he sounds more as if he's trying to convince himself. 'Maddox is too much of a chicken shit to murder anyone by himself anyway.'

'Are you serious?'

'Look, he knows I'm leaving you with him. If he did anything it would be too obvious. It'll be fine, I promise. I'll call you, okay?' Rat flicks away his cigarette butt and the darkness quickly swallows any trace of the tiny light. 'You can keep the jacket.'

'But—'

'Look, I'm sorry, Emma, I *have to go*.'

She feels gooseflesh prickling her arms and shoulders as she watches his fierce stride back across the field towards his motorcycle. Just for a moment, it's not him, but Abigail Blake disappearing into those trees.

'How am I supposed to get home?'

Somewhere in the darkness she can hear the river rushing, punctuated by the rhythmic chirp of frogs. Then abruptly, from the depths of the woods, far off in the other direction, comes the cry of a single coyote. Emma shudders.

Hunter Maddox catches her in the beam of his flashlight, and nods to his car. 'Hey, *señorita*, you need a ride?'

Even with his hand on Beth Farmer's heavy breasts in the back seat of her stuffy car, Dalton Lewis, the pastor's son, can't help but notice the three figures grouped in the shadows of the Tall Bones. From this distance it's difficult to tell who they are. They have only one flashlight between them, and whoever's holding it never focuses the beam on anyone's face.

One of them hands something to the other. The person with the flashlight uses it to examine what he's been given – reaches into the bag, then puts his finger into his mouth, and Dalton thinks, *Oh.* Then, at last, something else is handed over in return.

Beth Farmer moans into his ear, and he thinks perhaps it sounds a little forced, but he's too busy watching the strange transaction play out to really care.

One of the figures takes a phone call – he can see the light of the screen – then walks away from the group. It's only when Dalton hears the rumble of the motorcycle that he realizes who it was.

16

Then

In a motel in Longmont, Colorado, eighteen years before her daughter walks into the forest and never walks out again, Dolly watches the sun coming up over the mountains on the horizon. The silhouette of the Rockies looks like some great wave rising above the landscape, and she cannot help feeling that at any moment it will come crashing down and devour her. She has already made up her mind that it is what she deserves.

Her breakfast tastes vaguely yellow, and the shower has such lousy water pressure it feels as though she's being gently peed on. Afterwards, Dolly climbs into her car and begins the long drive back into the mountains, back to Whistling Ridge.

All alone on the gravel driveway of Hickory Lane, she stands for a moment, suitcase in hand, preparing herself. It is still early enough that there is mist rising from the grass, like ghosts stalking in the front yard, and last night's rain has brought all the scents to the surface. She can taste the iron in the soil, the prospect of snow in the air, can smell the old shreds of meat on the buck skeleton Samuel has been drying in the shed. Is this God? she thinks, because at this time she still has her own sense of belief. *Is this how God speaks to us?* The thought that He is with her allows her to open the front door and go inside.

The whole house feels like a slab of old butter that has formed a rind around its edges. A staleness in the air tells her that, since she left yesterday afternoon, nothing has been washed, including the people. She leaves her suitcase in the hall, moving carefully as though she is visiting a crime scene. On the couch in the living room there is an empty pizza box, darkened by patches of grease, and there are several crushed beer cans on the floor. A stain on the carpet in the corner smells faintly of urine.

'Samuel?' She stands on the stairs and listens. 'Noah?'

The smell persists into her son's room, and when she calls again, she hears a muffled thump from inside the closet.

'Oh, God, Noah.'

Someone has put a chair against the door so that it cannot be opened from the inside. When she pulls it back, Dolly sees that her son's little hands are red and swollen. She does not want to imagine how long he must have hammered on that door. Her chest hurts, as if she is somehow trying to absorb his pain, and she surprises herself with a sudden desire to put her arms around him. But he reeks of urine – his own, she will discover – so she turns the comfort of her body away. Noah, only four, just stands there, wearing the same clothes she dressed him in the day before.

'What happened?' Dolly kneels down in front of him. 'Where's Daddy?'

Noah stares intently at his red hands and starts sucking on his lower lip.

'Hey, look at me. Did Daddy put you in there?'

'I was crying too loud.'

'And where is he now?'

Noah sighs, as if this is obvious. 'Daddy's gone. Like you.'

Dolly has felt guilty ever since she woke up on those dime-store cotton bedsheets this morning. Felt guilty the whole hour she drove home through the trees in silence, and by now it has become a dull ache in the back of her head. But blaming yourself is one thing, she thinks. The realization that her son blames her too, the confirmation that this really is all her fault, makes her feel like an eggshell, suddenly stamped on. And, as is so often the case, she cannot confront that thought.

She stands up, looking down at her little son in his soiled clothes with his trembling hands, and all she can say is, 'Come on, then, we'd better clean you up. You smell disgusting.'

Now

Noah waits in the truck with the engine silent, the lights off, and avoids catching his own eye in the rear-view mirror. He doesn't want to see what he looks like. If it's anywhere near as bad as he feels, then it will only make things worse.

The trailer park is a loose patchwork of orange and yellow squares – late-night lights against the black backdrop of the mountainside. Noah watches an elderly woman in the nearest window wrap her drawstring lips around a cigarette, her shoulders sagging on the exhale. He wonders if she is alone here, if she has always been alone. Are there children somewhere, and do they miss her? Does she miss them? Would she have stood by and watched their father push their faces into the dirt?

The snarl of Rat's motorcycle makes Noah sit up straight. He wipes his eyes and nose on his sleeve before slipping quietly out of the truck and padding across the grass to the

RV. The wind brushes against him and he stumbles. He could cry at how fragile he feels, and when Rat gathers him into his arms and closes the door behind him, he thinks he might cave in under the contact, like a rotten peach.

'I didn't know who else to call.'

'Dragul meu,' Rat whispers against his neck, rubbing circles between his shoulder-blades. Noah doesn't want to ask him what that means. Something about the way he says it, so tenderly – he doesn't think he could bear it.

For a little while Noah just lets Rat hold him. Rat is shorter than him by a good few inches, and Noah has to curl his neck and shoulders down, but it's worth the ache just to press his face into Rat's hair, to breathe in the smell that reminds him of summer, of smoke rings, tightly coiled ferns, and kisses in places he never knew people kissed one another.

Rat sits him down on his pile of quilts and washes the cuts on his face with warm water and neat vodka. It makes Noah wince, but it's the good sort of pain: a little exorcism. Sometimes Rat speaks in English, other times in his mother tongue. Sometimes he doesn't speak at all, but his hands are always gentle, the metal of his rings cool against Noah's skin where it feels hot and swollen. It's the gentleness of it that makes him start crying, as if, until now, he'd forgotten what it was like to be touched without violence.

'Hey now,' Rat says softly, 'it's okay.'

'It's just . . . my mom, man, it's not even my dad.' He wipes his eyes furiously with the heel of his hand. 'I don't know what's wrong with her. I mean, what is it? It's like she *blames* me for something, so she just lets Dad do whatever he wants. But then it's like she hates me for making her feel guilty about it, so she . . . she just . . . *Fuck.*'

He glances at Rat, his breath coming in short gasps as if he's trying to suck in all the air in the room.

'And you know the worst thing? I don't even hate her. That would be so much easier, if I could just hate her like I hate my dad, but . . . God, it's like, despite everything, there's still this young, hopeful, *stupid* part of me that keeps reaching out for my mom, hoping she'll be there, and she never is, man. She never is. Sometimes, I want to feel like I can ask her to just put her arms around me, or something. I want that to be okay. For me to ask. But I look at her, and it's like sitting outside a house with all the lights on when you know you don't live there any more.'

He takes another deep, shaky breath. His throat still throbs as if he's been retching, but the feeling of Rat's hand on his back steadies him.

'You know it's all bullshit, right?' Rat says. 'The stuff your dad said.'

Noah sniffs. It's not like he lives in a vacuum. He has the internet; he knows how the world's shaping up, these days. It's not as though he even wants to believe in *God* any more. But sometimes he thinks he catches a glimpse of Him, some elongated silhouette, creeping from tree to tree, or standing in the bedroom doorway at the edge of his vision. And if He's there, if Noah can't stop believing in *Him*, then doesn't he have to believe in the rest of what the preacher says too?

He blinks hard, trying not to let his eyes well up again. 'Sorry.' It comes out as a whisper, but he feels too exhausted to try for anything louder. 'I don't even know what I'm saying. I'm sorry. You don't want to hear about all this, you're not . . . I'm just some guy you—'

Rat leans over and kisses him, and their noses are at the wrong angle, and Noah's mouth is swollen and salty, and their teeth bump against each other, drawing just a little blood from the softness of their lips so that everything tastes like rust, but the fragility of the moment seems to demand the certainty of iron, of hard contact, and so, Noah thinks, it's the best kiss he's ever had.

The heat of so many grown men in one room has left a slight layer of condensation on the windows and the Formica desks of the Sunday school. Pastor Lewis shuffles the papers in front of him, then leans back in his seat at the head of the table, massaging the bridge of his nose.

'Last order of business, then. A few of the ladies feel there ought to be some sort of curfew for the kids until this unpleasant business with the missing Blake girl has been cleared up.'

Jerry Maddox, seated at the pastor's right hand, watches the rest of the guys fidget in their plastic chairs. The room feels too warm and sleepy, and the Whistling Ridge Men's Church Committee seems to be operating on a lag, as always, unsure of what they want until Jerry or the pastor gives it to them.

'I think that's a fine idea, Ed,' he says. 'Nobody under eighteen out after dark, how's that sound? We can tell Gains.'

One-eyed Bill Tucker nods, and corn-fed Drew Farmer snorts and rests his jowls on his hands. Mo Dukes, however, with fresh grease stains on his shirt from working the fry station at the Aurora diner all day, puts his fingers together and frowns. 'That's all right for some, but my Beau sees a tutor every Monday and Wednesday. Is he going to get rounded up by a deputy just for walking home? And what about basketball practice? They've got state play-offs to prep for.'

'The play-offs are important to all of us,' says Jerry. 'My son is shooting guard. I know what's at stake.' *He* knows, although he sometimes wonders if Hunter has any idea. The boy isn't exactly what you'd call academically minded. A supposed commitment to varsity sports is going to have to be the selling point of any of his college application letters.

Jerry turns to Mo again. 'Your boy can't play if he's dead in a ditch somewhere, can he?'

It's the same thing every month, Jerry thinks. What's this town coming to that even the men need their hands held through the simplest decisions?

Pastor Lewis sighs, but if he's tired, it's probably the weariness of having to deal with these people for the past hour. 'We can ask at the school about moving practice to lunch period,' he says. 'As for your son, Mo, perhaps you should consider tutoring him at home from now on.'

'Better to be safe than sorry, Mo,' Jerry adds, and Pastor Lewis nods approvingly. Mo Dukes narrows his eyes at both of them and does not stay to shake hands afterwards.

'Speaking of that whole bad business,' says Bill Tucker, stretching his shoulders back. 'They any closer to finding out what happened to the Blake girl?'

It's only Bill Tucker, Drew Farmer and him left now, the rest having filed out hastily into the cool of the night. Drew and Bill, they're good old boys, Jerry thinks, the kind of backbone this town needs in today's confused world.

'You know, I wouldn't blame the girl if she just plain ran out on that family. Pretty little thing like her could probably find work anywhere, if you know what I mean.'

Bill Tucker shakes his head, but he grins wide enough for Jerry to see his dark metal fillings. Drew Farmer's jowls wobble as he laughs, 'You want to watch yourself, Jer. Next they'll be saying you're not *politically correct*.'

'All I'm saying is these girls today, they sure look eighteen. I bet she's probably greasing a pole somewhere down in Denver by now.'

They wave goodbye in the church parking lot. Somewhere

in the distance, music is playing on a car stereo, fading as the car moves further away, but the beat makes Jerry pause on the way to his truck.

There had been music in the air that night. A soft June night, a gentle darkness relieved by the fairy lights strung between the trailers, and Abigail Blake had turned and looked at him. Not so far away, the Romanian boy was strumming his guitar, but she had turned her face up towards Jerry and he could see the freckles patterned on her nose. She smelt of strawberries and cheap liquor, and quietly she said, 'Thank you.'

17

She didn't say no. She doesn't see how she could have. Night has its own sort of terrain, where the rules of the day don't always apply, and Emma has read enough news headlines, heard enough horror stories to know what happens to girls alone at night when they turn down boys like Hunter Maddox. So when he asks, she gets into his car.

They drive without speaking for a little while, as if they have an understanding, and Hunter hums quietly. She never thought of him as the sort of person who would hum while driving.

At last he says, 'You got any plans for college?'

Emma stares at her dark reflection and runs a hand through her hair, wondering when she last took a proper shower. She's been relying heavily on deodorant because she can spray it on to mask the smell of whiskey, but suddenly it feels as if she's been running her body on fumes. Maybe he won't be interested if I'm greasy and stink of Rat's cigarettes, she thinks.

'My parents are really hung up on me going somewhere out of state.' Hunter glances at her. 'I said sure, California or something, you know? But they don't want me going anywhere they've got legalized weed. Said it'll mess me up. Like this town doesn't do a good enough job of that already.'

Emma watches the point in the road where the headlights

fade out and imagines that they're driving into some huge black throat.

Hunter drums his fingers on the steering wheel. 'So what are you doing hanging out with Rat Lăcustă?'

'What do you care?'

'Oh, she speaks!' He grins at her. 'I don't know, you just seem like a nice girl. Too nice for a weasel like that.'

'Rat's not a weasel, he's my friend.'

'Right.' He laughs. 'I can promise you he's not.'

Nobody like Hunter Maddox has ever called her a nice girl. She can't figure him out. She accepted the ride because she had no other option, but there is something about him – perhaps it's the way he talks about his parents, or his dreams of going away – that reminds her a little of Abigail. Which in turn reminds her of why she'd wanted to talk to him in the first place. Abi needs her, and if Rat won't help her, she'll just have to do this on her own.

Emma glances at him, fiddling with the zipper on her jacket. 'I need to use the bathroom.'

'Oh, well – you want to swing by my place? It's two minutes away.'

'Sure, if you're offering.' She tries not to sound too eager. Whatever happened between them, something of Abi is still clinging to him, and Emma wants it back.

There are lights on in the downstairs windows, but Emma doesn't see anyone as Hunter ushers her quietly through his parents' hallway.

'You'll have to use the upstairs bathroom,' he says, pointing to the stairs. 'Mom's having the downstairs one converted into some kind of tiny art studio.' Emma wrinkles her nose and Hunter nods. 'Yeah, I don't know. It's the second door on the right when you get up there.'

In the bathroom, Emma makes a show of closing the door loudly and turning on the faucet. Then slowly, so as not to agitate the hinges, she unlatches the door, and creeps out on to the landing. If Hunter is keeping anything that could lead her to Abigail, his bedroom seems like the best place to look. She opens an office, an airing closet, and an unsettled guest room with a cold smell before she finds what she's looking for.

Hunter's room smells faintly of matches and the floorboards are littered with cigarette papers and filters, among stiff socks, basketball kit and various USB cables. Emma doesn't dare use the overhead light, but switches on the torch on her phone, and that's when she sees the Polaroids. The walls, bare wood in the traditional cabin style, are plastered with little faces. She recognizes some of them from school – Bryce Long and Beau Dukes from the basketball team with cigarettes hanging out of their mouths, trailer-park beauty queen Shana Tyson shaking out her big Afro hair, Beth Farmer grinning next to her on the hood of some car, the gangly Weaver brothers with bloody knuckles. Her breath hitches when she sees Rat. The flat Polaroid doesn't do justice to his bone structure, but it's him all right. Photographed from the side, flowers in his hair, blowing hazy smoke rings into the night – a handgun resting in his lap.

A noise from downstairs makes her jump, and she takes a moment to steady her breathing again. The photo of Rat doesn't matter, she tells herself. Rat doesn't matter, not right now. It's not his secrets she came for.

She runs her eyes over the rest of the photos, scanning them for any trace of Abigail, thinking, I would know her shoulder, her hand, the edge of her jaw. But she can't find even a scrap, and another sound from the floor below makes her heart rate pick up, until she is sure she can feel the throbbing right down in the ends of her fingers. She checks her phone: six minutes she's been up here. Excusable, but then that can seem like longer when you're waiting for someone. Hunter might decide any minute to come looking for her. Taking one deep breath and then another, she squeezes her wrist, as if she can stop her heart racing just by holding her pulse.

She turns away from the Polaroids, shining her light over the spilling closet, the cluttered desk, the duvet bunched up like some big animal asleep on the bed – not sure what she's looking for exactly, but clinging to the hope that she will know it when she sees it. The moon casts strange shadows through the blinds, painting the room in bands of black and blue, and leading her eye across the floor to the little table beside the bed.

It is here, down on her knees among the tissues and tobacco crumbs, that she opens the single drawer and sees Abigail's Polaroid face smiling back.

Emma is just coming back down the stairs when Hunter's parents walk in. His mother says, 'You didn't tell us you were bringing a girlfriend over,' but his father points shamelessly at Emma, and his mom quiets.

'What are you doing here, young lady?' He juts his big chin in Emma's direction, and Hunter thinks, God, no, don't do this here, not now, not to *her*.

'She was just using the bathroom,' says Hunter. 'I said she could.'

'I'd have thought better of you, Hunter, letting some stranger into our house.' Andie Maddox looks Emma up and down, taking in the shade of lipstick that doesn't quite match her skin tone, how she seems too small in the man's jacket she's wearing. 'You have to be so careful who you let into your home.'

'Mom.'

Emma is staring very hard at the empty patch of floor between Hunter and his parents.

Sarcastically, Jerry says, 'Does she even speak English?'

'Yeah,' Emma replies, and Hunter can hear the tremor in her voice as she turns to him. 'Thanks for letting me piss in your house.' Then she walks quickly down the last few stairs, across the hallway and out of the front door without another word.

His mother presses a hand to her forehead at the sound of the door closing and lets out a loud sigh. 'Hunter, honey, please don't look at me like that.'

'Jesus Christ, Mom.'

'Don't take that tone with your mother.' Jerry cuffs him round the back of the head. 'After the crap you pulled this summer, you haven't earned the *right* to be disappointed in your parents.'

'Are you ever going to let me live this down?'

'Drugs, Hunter!' His mother waves her hands as if she's trying to illustrate what that means. 'Marijuana is one thing, but this summer you brought cocaine into this house. Cocaine! We gave everything we had to raising you right, getting you ready for college, for *life*, and then you just go and throw it all back in our faces by bringing home hard drugs, like none of it meant anything to you. This family has a reputation to uphold, Hunter, so I'm *sorry* if we've hurt your feelings because we didn't like your little Mexican friend, but what you're feeling now is nothing – *nothing* – compared to what you've put us through.'

Hunter chews the inside of his cheek. 'Dad,' he says. 'What did you do with the coke?'

'What?'

'You told me you got rid of it. What did you do with it?'

His father snorts. 'So you can go dig it up again? I don't think so.'

'Well, somebody already found it, so you obviously didn't bury it deep enough.'

'Somebody found it?' His mother rakes her hair back, pulling until the roots are stark against her scalp. 'Jesus, Jerry.'

His father squares his shoulders. 'He's just screwing around, Andie. Don't listen to him. It's not possible.'

'Oh, because you hid it so well? You know, Dad, maybe if you didn't want anyone to find it, you shouldn't have stashed it in the place Rat Lăcustă takes people to fuck.'

His mother twitches. 'Language, Hunter, for heaven's sakes.'

'How do you know where I . . . ?' Jerry stares at him but he doesn't look angry any more.

It's only a small comfort to realize that's what his father was doing, burying the coke, when Hunter glimpsed him between the trees that night. If he figures I saw him that night, Hunter thinks, then he'll know I was out in the woods too, and he'll want to know why.

'Hunter, don't close up on us now, we have to talk about this.' His father's big face seems softer all of a sudden, void of its usual tension. 'You've got a bright future, son. There's no need to lose it over some mistake like drugs. But if there's something else, we can help you, Hunter. You just have to talk to us.'

He can see his father reaching for this tenuous moment as if it will suture the hole Hunter has torn in his parents' summer, but he knows – has known right from the moment he stepped through the door, the night that Abigail Blake disappeared – there is nothing he can say to fix what he's done.

18

Once, in school, Emma had to look at some photographs of what different kinds of tears looked like under a microscope. Most were bizarre amoeba-like images, but tears of grief were like the bird's eye view of a bombed-out city. A sparse, abandoned landscape. That, she thinks, is how she feels now.

There's no sidewalk on the road that heads down from the Maddoxes' property into town so she keeps close to the edge of the trees, using the torch on her phone to light the way. It's about thirteen miles, and she knows eventually she will have to call her mother to drive her home, but for now she just wants to walk, to feel the wind in her hair, the certainty of the cold against her skin.

It's as if she has to lay out in front of her everything that's happened tonight, pick up every event physically, to get a sense of the shape and weight of it, of all the nuances, before she can decide how she feels about it. First there was Rat, ditching her like a bad prom date, then reappearing in a Polaroid on Hunter's wall. The only clear thing she can figure out about him now is that he is none of the things she thought he was, just the spaces in between.

Then there's the other photo: Abigail, her long hair caught up in the breeze, the bright greens and yellows of summer roaring in the background, a daisy tucked behind her ear. Hunter keeps that in his bedside drawer. He *sleeps* next to it. Did Abi know? What does it mean?

Somewhere overhead an owl hoots, and Emma glances over her shoulder at the black road stretching behind her. Ahead it is just the same. She stands there for a moment, listening to the *crack* of wood against wood as the wind shakes the aspens, and she wishes she could turn into a tree, and stay right here shouting at the sky the way they do.

Actually, if she's wishing for things, she wishes she had shouted at the Maddoxes instead. She can get mad about it *now*, replaying Andie Maddox's southern drawl, and Jerry's sarcastic 'Does she even speak English?' tossed at her as carelessly as if he were flicking away a cigarette butt. She can conjure all the fury she needs *now*, until her head feels like it's about to burst. *Now* she wants to dash her knuckles against a tree trunk just to get the anger out. But standing there in the hallway she had simply felt tired. A deep sort of exhaustion that seemed to pile down on top of her, so that looking at her life was like looking at this long black road – the same murky view whether she looked backwards or ahead.

Actually, if she's wishing for things, she wishes she had a full bottle of Jack.

She's been walking for about an hour, give or take, when the low rumble of a car makes her turn. She squints into the headlights just as the police siren squawks once, the emergency lights momentarily painting her in red and blue.

Sheriff Gains steps out of the car, flashlight angled so it doesn't shine directly in her face. His breath mists in the air as he says, 'Emma Alvarez, is that you? What are you doing all the way out here?'

*

Hey. Weird night.

And then: *Seriously, Hunter, I'm sorry for running off like that. I just don't think we should be seen together right now. My parents would kill me.*

Lying in the cool dark of his room, Hunter squints at his phone screen. They're not the last messages Abigail sent him, but he doesn't want to look at those right now. These were the ones that made him do something dumb, something he almost let slip tonight, if his parents hadn't been so hung up about the coke.

Everything seems to have slowed down in Abigail's absence. It's as if the town is expecting her back, and they can't bear to do anything worthwhile until she's here. But things were different on that promising cusp between spring and summer. That May, Hunter and anyone who mattered to him were finishing their penultimate year of school. It was a liminal time, crammed with fake IDs and hazy music and tasting each other's saliva. People were about to turn eighteen and everybody wanted to be lovers.

Junior prom, the same night Abigail told him to get lost in the parking lot, Hunter had driven up the mountain with a box of edibles and a bunch of the kids from his father's trailer park who were too frayed at the edges to get dressed up for a school dance. They had sat in the trees, bare legs dangling, their faces hidden by the branches, looking down at the lights of the town in the valley below. That was the night he had watched Rat Lăcustă, in a pair of white fringed cowboy boots, shoot a Budweiser bottle off a tree branch. Hunter heard applause in the shatter of the glass, and there was something in the ferocity of it that made him feel hot from the inside out. Shana Tyson had made Rat a crown of wildflowers and Hunter had taken a photograph of him, which he would later forget about. Then he'd got Abi's text message.

Rat said, 'What's eating you, Maddox?'

Hunter, high as the moon, had told him he was in love.

'Yeah, that'll do it. You want to go for a drive?'

There were candles at the Winslow house. He remembers laughing about that: *Candles in the woods, it's like witchcraft.* And it was, a little. Rat had flowers in his hair and flowers inked on his hip – Romanian dog roses, he said, to remind him of home – and Hunter had traced the pattern with clumsy fingers, while Rat slid his hand down his pants.

In bed, now, Hunter rolls over and buries his head under his pillow. It's really not a big deal, he thinks. *Everybody's a little that way, these days, aren't they?* He was just mad about Abi, and Rat was mad about *someone*, that much was clear from the gunshot and the hard friction of his hand. Clearly not a big deal to Rat either: he'd barely looked at him when Hunter handed him the money for the coke and their fingers touched. It's just a sick joke that his dad should have hidden it at the Winslow ruin, and that Rat was the one to find it.

'God,' he whispers aloud, and hopes nobody will answer.

Perhaps Rat was high enough that night that he's forgotten. He certainly doesn't seem to remember what happened afterwards. He doesn't know what Hunter stole.

Hunter sighs and rolls back over, staring at the dim patterns of the wood grain on the ceiling. There's nothing for it, he thinks.

He climbs out of bed, pulls on his sweatpants and sneakers, and grabs the flashlight from the desk. In the closet there's an old duffel bag, heavy on one side with the weight of something he wishes to God now he'd never laid eyes on. He slings the bag over his shoulder before heading out into the night.

From his house, it's about twenty minutes to Winslow on foot. He doesn't dare risk his parents hearing the car, but it's easy enough if he follows the river that runs almost in a straight line between both properties. A gentle rain patters on the dense foliage as he makes his way through the trees, pine needles crunching underfoot, the duffel bumping against his back. The cocaine he dumps in the river, as much for his parents' sake as his own. He should never have bought it in the first place, should never have driven all the way down to Boulder for it, but his priorities had been different then. His heart had sunk when Emma handed him the bag and he'd seen what was inside, but he'd had no choice except to buy it back. At least now he's in control of things again. Every last granule of evidence has to go.

Then there's the other thing.

The Winslow ruin looks worse at night – just a jagged shadow with nothing but his flashlight to pick out the crumbling black stone. The candles are gone, he notes, scrambling over a window ledge and into the bed of damp ferns within. The place is as abandoned as it should be, which suits his needs. He makes a point of not looking at the spot where Rat had leaned him up against the stonework. With a heavy rock in his hand, he hacks at the hard ground, and feels his fingers snagging on twigs and debris, grit collecting under his fingernails, but he keeps digging until the hole is deep enough to bury what he's brought. The clouds are smudgy from the rain, and there is no moon to illuminate what he drops into the hole and covers over again, stamping down the dirt so that it looks as flat as the surrounding earth.

A raccoon clambers along a branch overhead, black eyes momentarily blazing in the beam of the flashlight: the only witness as Hunter slings the empty bag back over his shoulder and makes his way home.

The reflection of the headlights on the bedroom wall looks like two giant eyes, and Melissa hears the slow putter of an engine coming to a stop outside. She crawls across the bed and pulls the curtain back. Just a little. It is almost nine thirty, and she knows she has every right to wonder who has kept her daughter out so late at a time like this, but she doesn't like the thought of being caught spying. At once she's glad of her own caution, because a cop car is parked there on the street outside her house.

Step number five of *What to do when your teenager lies to you* was about confronting your child honestly, not trying to catch them in a lie, because that in itself is dishonest and will encourage the same behaviour in them. Melissa thinks whoever wrote that article clearly didn't have a teenager. They probably weren't even a parent, or they would understand, wouldn't be so condescending. She imagines that, tomorrow, when she's sitting across from her daughter at breakfast, and Emma lies about how she made it home tonight, Melissa will *know* it is a lie and, through all her frustration, that there will be a little chink of glee.

Eventually, Emma gets out of the car and so does Sheriff Gains. They stand together under the streetlamp for a moment longer, heavy breath visible in the cold air, until he puts his hand on her back and steers her towards the driveway.

Melissa jerks back from the window. She knows they can't hear her from out on the street, but still she seals her hand over her mouth to keep herself from saying: Not my daughter too.

19

Even now – perhaps especially now – Dolly thinks often about how she'd made up her mind to leave Samuel right from their wedding day. For one thing, he screwed up their vows. She still flinches at the memory of standing there in front of all her friends and family, and him calling her *Darlene*, as if that could in any way be what Dolly was short for. She even confronted him about it afterwards, feeling so righteous in her indignation that she was certain he'd apologize. Instead, he'd simply groaned and said, 'I sure hope this isn't what the rest of the marriage is going to be like.'

It would have been impossible to leave him straight after the wedding, of course. Everyone would have shaken their head and said, 'I told you so,' like they were so wise for commenting on what she had known all along: Samuel Blake was going to be a lousy husband. If she had chosen him hoping for a good life partner then she might have been more disappointed, but young Dolly Hopkins had gotten married to prove a point, to prove she could make her own decisions, and as soon as her parents started treating her like an adult, she would make her excuses and leave. That had been the plan, at least.

Sometimes at night, when she hears Samuel's car pull into

the drive, hears him cussing as he drops his keys, pictures him staggering to the front door, bourbon-drunk, she wishes he had taken a bend in the road too sharply. She imagines him slamming on the brakes, heaving the steering wheel, but it's no good: the car goes skidding over the side of the mountain. Other times, like when he gives her a little kick in the back of the ankles, she wishes those Vietcong had just beaten him to death with their rifle butts.

In that sticky summer of 1992 when Dolly first met Samuel, she was fresh out of college, visiting friends in Shreveport, and he was already thirty-eight. The shabbiness of his solitary life excited her. He had his own apartment in the Riverfront neighbourhood, where she would let him pin her down and thrust into her, confusing sweat for arousal. After they were married, however, he had moved her into his parents' house on the pretext of them having more room there. Really, Dolly knew, it was because Constance Blake, Samuel's mother, had ordered it.

Constance always criticized Dolly for the way she did her laundry. You were supposed to snap the clothes when you were folding them, she'd say. *Get a real good snap when you shake them out. Otherwise they'll just crease again in the drawers.* Dolly didn't care if Samuel's clothing got creased, but Constance did. Constance worried a lot about her son. Dolly could tell that Samuel worried a lot about his mother too (her timid husband, Jason, was almost invisible and no longer slept in the same room as her), but still mother and son were unable to say two nice words to each other.

One Sunday after church – the Baptist church now, which somehow felt both lackadaisical and too serious to Dolly, who had been brought up sleepily Anglican – Constance asked, 'Has he ever hit you?'

Dolly was quite taken aback, although less by the content

of the question than by the fact that her mother-in-law had asked her something about herself. No, she said politely, Samuel had never hit her. But Constance had just sniffed and given the shirt she was folding a good hard snap.

Later that evening, after more sangria than she would ever admit to, Constance said, 'It's like standing on the beach and there's this great wave building out at sea, and you can see it coming towards you, getting bigger and louder, and you know it's going to suck you right down but you can't look away. That's what it's like with Samuel. Ever since he came back.'

Looking back, Dolly wishes she'd paid Constance more attention. At the time she'd disliked her mother-in-law as a matter of principle: Constance made Samuel even twitchier than usual, and always left it to Dolly to calm him down. But the mutual distrust between mother and son should have been a red flag, if only Dolly had wanted to see it. In those days she'd thought she understood. She knew about women who were beaten by their husbands, and she had vowed never to let that sort of thing happen to her. Stupid girl, she thinks now, as she presses her face into the pillow – as if *that sort of thing* is ever something that women *allow*.

Several months into the marriage, she made up her mind to go through with her plan. She'd had a letter from her mother just days before, saying she was going to phone her at the end of the week to discuss something, and Dolly had gleefully imagined her saying, 'I'm sorry we didn't take you seriously before, Dolores. If you want to be a sculptor then of course we'll support you. Please come home.' She would put up some resistance, of course, to make sure her parents were grateful to have her back, but she would go. She would.

But when Mrs Hopkins phoned, she wanted to know when Dolly was thinking of coming up for Thanksgiving.

'We can't come on the Monday, Mom. Sam's got work.'

'Oh, well, honey, I wasn't thinking of Samuel. We thought it'd just be you. I'll have to check with your father.'

'Sam's my husband, Mom,' she said, her Ss hissing down the line all the way from Louisiana to New Hampshire. 'You can't invite me and not him.' It wasn't fair. Her mother would have been insulted if someone had invited her over but said Dad couldn't come. 'You'll have both of us or neither.' She had slammed the receiver down so hard it cracked the plastic. It wasn't as if she even wanted Samuel to come to her family Thanksgiving. He was picky about food, he never made conversation, and he always got a headache. But she'd married him, hadn't she?, and people had to respect that. It was the lack of respect that got her so riled up, and she hated feeling as though she had to ask for it, as if she were just a child stomping her foot.

Those were the days when she carried a little white-hot ball of fury deep in her chest wherever she went and knew it could flare up at any moment. She wonders what happened to that little ball of anger. Melted now, all slumped out of shape, like the figurines she used to make from colourless dental wax, forgotten in the summer heat by her mother, trampled by her father.

Yes, the anger felt good, just for that moment, when she'd slammed down the receiver. But after that, when the cracks began appearing in her own life, there was no escape plan. She couldn't very well go crawling back to her parents. What would they think of her, after she'd made such a fuss? They would never take her seriously again.

She'd barely been married a year when Dolly discovered she was pregnant. Samuel didn't say much when she told him, but a few days later he informed her that he'd taken a new job with a logging firm up in Colorado, and that it would pay better. That, Dolly told her friends, was his way of showing he cared. It was the last time she spoke to any of them.

Whistling Ridge was named after the winds that came down from the mountains, and Dolly thought it sounded very romantic. Perhaps it was this that helped her take up her role as modern-day New Frontier Wife with such vigour. For that too-short while, she had relished the task of cooking dinner, or setting the table, or doing her husband's laundry. These were the sorts of things that happened in a *family*. In her proud round belly, she was shaping this family, sculpting this new little person as if he were one of her wax figures – forgetting, in the process, that she had not made anything of her own since before she and Samuel were married.

Perhaps Samuel could have helped around the house a bit more, she conceded. Maybe he could have picked up the groceries once in a while, instead of waiting until he was home from work, sprawled out on the couch with brisket on a tray in his lap, saying, 'Oh, we're out of barbecue sauce. Run down to the store and get some more, will you?'

That first time, when she'd been only a few months along, she'd felt the familiar ball of anger in her chest, and had snapped, 'Why don't you get it yourself? God knows you never do anything for me.' Samuel hadn't answered her at first, but his eyelids had started twitching, and he raised his arms up around himself, his fingers stiff and claw-like, while his mouth opened so wide she thought it might rip his face in half. The air in the living room suddenly seemed pulled taut, and Dolly felt herself rise up on the balls of her feet, as if some primal instinct was telling her to run. Then Samuel began to scream. It wasn't like anything she'd ever heard come out of a human being before. He listed to one side and fell off the couch, and before she could stop him, he was on all fours, just wailing like some animal on fire. After that, she did as she was told.

Sometimes, in the brief moments of vulnerability between waking and sunrise when he allowed her to hold him, he would talk in mumbled half-sentences about Vietnam. About rivers of mud and crawling over bodies of men he knew. Dolly felt sorry for Samuel then, although now she can see she confused that feeling with love. She was vaguely certain, however, that the screaming wasn't just something he'd brought back with him from the war. He would get agitated any time his mother called, and while Dolly lied and told Constance he was at work, he'd stalk into the bedroom and knock things off the shelves. Dolly would clutch her belly, then, and send a silent prayer up to God: Please don't let my baby be like *him*.

But when he was born, Noah Isaac Blake wouldn't stop crying. Dolly was convinced this was abnormal, even for a baby. She tried everything that the books suggested, but Noah just kept on screaming – and she felt, with a certainty she could not fully comprehend, that he was screaming at her in particular. Samuel started drinking, and then he would scream at her too.

'Can't you shut that little bastard up for one minute?' He would slam the flat of his hand down on the table when he said this, making the gravy leap off his dinner plate. 'I'm at work all day, and this is what I have to come home to? I hate that noise, Dolly, I really do.'

I, on the other hand, just love it, Dolly thought.

The worst thing was that she really wanted to love it. From the moment the midwife placed Noah in her arms, and he looked up at her, eyes wide open, like he couldn't wait to get started with life, she had thought that here, finally, was a friend. An ally. They were going to look after each other. *You and me against the world, kid*. But all he did was cry and throw up and do all the regular crap that babies do, which just made Samuel angrier – as if it was her fault his son hadn't come out of the womb a fully formed all-American brat that he could take hunting or shoot beer cans with. An unnameable sense of loss overtook Dolly whenever she looked at her squalling son, and she started smoking just to have something to do with her hands, which should have been holding her baby.

And, of course, now any plans to escape had receded. Everything had changed. She had a baby. What was she going to do? Pack him into her suitcase? Once – in fact it was the first time that Samuel kicked her in the back of the ankles, when they had to leave church early because Noah wouldn't stop wailing – Dolly had locked herself in the bathroom, and stuffed a towel into her mouth so that she wouldn't have to hear herself say, *I wish I'd never had the goddamn baby*. If it wasn't for Noah, she told herself, she'd be worlds away from Samuel Blake by now.

That was when she started to imagine her husband getting so drunk he would drive himself off the road. Or perhaps be crushed by a falling tree at work. Or electrocuted by his bathroom razor in the morning. She used to lie in the cool indigo of pre-dawn, staring at the dark, solid shape of him snoring in bed beside her, and think: One day I am going to leave you. I am. I *am*.

She did try. More than once she'd started packing a bag while Samuel was at work. One night, she even managed to get all the way to Longmont, when Noah was still small, and booked herself into a motel before the gravity of her situation really sank in. 'How do you do this?' she'd asked a man at the bar, who'd told her he was leaving his wife. 'How do you decide which parts of your life you want to keep and which parts you want to leave behind for ever?' He'd said when it got real bad, you just took anything you couldn't replace. Dolly thought about Noah crying, and Samuel turning up the volume on the TV so he wouldn't have to hear it, and she drove home the following morning.

She told him some story about Debbie Weaver having a breakdown, and that was why she'd been gone all night. He was not very understanding.

After that, whenever the urge to escape rose in her again, she would get down on her knees and try to reason it out with God. Always she came to the same conclusion: she was being unreasonable. Samuel had his demons, but then who wouldn't, after everything he'd been through? Although what he had been through, she wasn't quite sure – all she had were his occasional mutterings, and a vague concept of the Vietnam War as something dark and ugly in the national consciousness. Still, a good wife would be more supportive. And what did she have to complain about, really? Sure, he yelled sometimes, got a little crazy, drank himself to Heaven and back, a slap here and there, a kick in the back of the ankles, but at least he never beat her black and blue. That was something, wasn't it? Some women had it worse. He never beat any of them badly until the night he put his fist through the wall, the night everything went wrong.

She knows they all still carry bits of that night with them, and for all her singing around the house, Abigail is no exception.

And now her daughter has vanished. Maybe she has done the one thing Dolly never could.

20

It has been three weeks since Abigail Blake disappeared, and the sheriff's deputies are wading through black water, turning over the riverbed. Only a few days before, about a mile upstream, where the banks are steeper and the water flows faster, they had found the shell casing. Now the calls of the crows nesting in the pines sound like human voices, and the deputies keep glancing at one another, unsure whether the person standing beside them was speaking or not. They bury their hands in the grooves of withered bulrushes, trailing their sleeves over moss-covered rocks, trying not to lose their concentration. Finally, one of them sticks her hand in the air, and calls out, 'Hey, Chief, I think we've got something over here!'

Gains makes his way down to the edge of the water with Deputy Saidi in tow. Deputy Moore, submerged up to her knees, holds out something stained and shapeless.

'I think it's a cardigan, sir,' says Moore, as she drops it into Saidi's evidence bag.

Gains nods. The waterlogged wool is still pale in patches, hinting at some original colour, but for the most part the fabric is scrunched up and torn, blotted with a brownish red. It is hard to say how long it's been in the water, but there is still the slight whiff of copper about it that makes Gains grit his teeth.

'Come on,' he says, starting back towards the car. 'We'd better go tell them.'

'Yes.' Dolly Blake reaches for the evidence bag, smoothing her thumbs over the creases in the clear plastic. 'That's Abigail's cardigan, I'm sure of it.'

'Is that blood?' Samuel asks, gesturing to the cardigan. It's a Friday morning and he is not at the mill. Gains doesn't mention this, but he does note the Lone Star cans lying crushed around the foot of his armchair.

'We'll have to send it to the lab in Denver to be sure, but it's a possibility, considering we found it not far from where we found the shell casing.'

'So what are you saying?' Dolly glares at him, raw-faced. 'Are you telling us . . . Is she dead? Is that it?'

'I'm not in a position to confirm or deny that right now, Mrs Blake. I'm sorry.'

Dolly doesn't show him to the door this time, but Gains is surprised to find Samuel following as he makes his way out.

'Eli,' Samuel says, his voice low. 'If that . . .' He drags his hand down over his face. 'If that is Abigail's blood, I mean, do you think there's any chance she could have survived?'

Gains rubs the stumps of his missing fingers. He does not care to be cornered by this hard man. 'I meant what I said back there. Without a body, it wouldn't do any good to speculate at this point.'

'Come on, Eli, we're talking about my daughter. I need to know.'

'Samuel, I'm sorry, there are just too many factors here: whereabouts she took the bullet, her competency with first aid, whether or not the shooter followed her. And that's all supposing this is even her blood. I mean, okay, sure,' he holds up his hands, as if trying to contain something large, 'if this *is* her blood, but it was only a grazing wound, if she knew how to apply pressure and clean it up proper, then it's *possible* she could have walked away from this. But this is a teenage girl we're talking about: if she was shot then it's much more likely she just panicked.'

Samuel nods slowly. 'All right,' he says at last, turning back towards the living-room door. 'I would prefer it, in future, if you didn't bother my wife with this kind of thing until you're certain. She has problems with . . .' He twirls his finger around in a circle by his temple. 'If Abigail really is dead, Eli, you just tell us that. Don't mess around with bits and pieces here and there.'

Eli Gains has never had to tell anybody their child is dead before, but tonight he will practise saying it in front of his bathroom mirror.

'Just where in hell were you last night?' Melissa shakes her head at her daughter, who is slouched against the kitchen counter eating dry cereal straight out of the box. 'I can't have you running off and not telling me where you are or when you're coming home. A girl has disappeared. It isn't safe out there at the moment.'

An image of her husband, his lip bust open, his eyes black and swollen as overripe plums, flickers briefly in her mind. She can almost hear him, spitting blood as he says: *When has it ever been safe here?*

'I'm sorry, Mom.' Emma sounds tired. She looks it too, with her hair unbrushed and last night's eyeliner still smeared around her eyes. Melissa wants to put her arms around her, to believe she really means it, but perhaps that has always been her problem, with her daughter, with her husband, even with God – she can never really bring herself to believe all the way.

'I don't want to see you in Sheriff Gains's car again.' She holds up a hand to silence Emma before she can open her mouth. 'I don't expect you'll tell me why he was driving you home last night, but I want you to promise me you won't let yourself be alone with him.'

'My ride fell through. He was just being nice. What's the problem with that?'

'This isn't supposed to be a one-to-one ratio, Em. There's supposed to be someone else here who can help me steer you in the right direction, but there isn't, there's just me, so when I tell you I want you to do something, I need you to work with me, okay?'

'Mom, you're being weird. What is it with you and the sheriff?' Emma puts the cereal box down. 'Did he . . . do something to you?'

'No.' Melissa rubs her arms, feeling the raised skin there. 'Not to me.'

'Mom? What're you talking about, do you know something? Is this about Abi?'

Melissa squeezes her eyes shut for a moment. Why did she say that? It just slipped out, but she can't afford to let things slip out, not at a time like this. 'It's nothing, Em. Forget I said anything.'

'It's not nothing, you're clearly upset, so what happened? Did Sheriff Gains do something to Abi? You have to tell me.'

'I said it's nothing, Em. Come on.' She clears her throat. 'Did you see those books I left on the table? I asked Principal Handel what the senior English class was doing this year. I know you're taking some time out, but you need to keep up with the reading if you want to graduate on time.'

She's not sure if Emma's really hearing her, as she watches

her across the kitchen with that black-eyed stare. *She knows you know something.* Knowing is too strong a word, perhaps. But Melissa does remember Abigail standing in the doorway at the clinic, twisting a coil of long red hair around her finger, a faint gleam of sweat on her pale forehead. It was early April then, and there were still patches of snow on the ground. The toe of Abigail's sock was visible through a hole in the end of her sneaker. 'Please, Melissa,' she'd said. Her cheeks were pink from the cold, but one had that sore kind of look, as though she'd been slapped. 'You're the only one who can help me.'

It had bothered Melissa at the time, not being sure. But then July had rolled around, and she'd seen Gains put his hand on Abigail's back. Now the story about what happened to that poor girl seems to change from week to week, depending on what the sheriff says.

Jude needs to get away, just for a little while. He limps down to the bus stop and catches the shuttle that takes tourists up to the national park. It's mostly empty at this time of year, and if there is conversation on board, he doesn't really hear it. He stares out of the window and thinks about his mother, how he came home from school to find her sitting in Abigail's room, doing up the buttons on one of Abi's old cardigans. He digs his fingers into his palms, trying to still the shaking thing that has started to grow inside him. In a sudden panic, Jude asks the driver to let him off.

They had only been driving for twenty minutes or so, and Jude remembers seeing the sign for the Maddoxes' trailer park a little while back, so he decides to cut across the forest and head in that direction. At some point he will have to call his mother to come and collect him, but he tells himself this will be okay. I will walk to the trailer park, he thinks, and by the time I get there, Mom will be okay again.

Jude walks with his head down, paying attention to where he puts his stick so that it doesn't sink too deep into the soft earth. When he eventually looks up, the Winslow ruin is looming ahead of him. He gives a small sigh of relief, glad to find that he has been walking in the right direction, but then he stops at the sound of voices coming from within the black, broken walls.

'Or else by stealth in some wood for trial, or back of a rock in the open air . . . But just possibly with you on a high hill . . .'

That is his brother's voice, although he has never heard Noah talk like that before.

'Or possibly with you sailing at sea, or on the beach of the sea or some quiet island, Here to put your lips upon mine I . . . I permit you.'

Jude limps to the side of the house, peering through the ferns and the missing bricks, and sure enough there is the Romanian boy leaning against the stonework, his whole body like some giant question mark. And there is his brother, with his grazed face and his hair askew, holding a dog-eared book close to his chest. But the way he stands straight-backed with his chin in the air – it reminds Jude of the Noah from years ago, before the hole in the wall. It seems like an act of rebellion now, the way his brother is standing. Proud, almost. Then he takes the Romanian boy by the waist like he owns the space between them, and it has been a long time since Jude saw that kind of certainty in him.

He is not watching *them*, he is watching his brother, but it quickly becomes apparent that he shouldn't be doing either. The Romanian boy gets down on his knees. Jude feels sweat forming over himself so completely that he can sense it in the strangest places, like the backs of his knees. He adjusts his grip on his stick, preparing to push away from the wall, but then something catches his eye and he cannot look away.

Noah unbuckles his belt and slides it out of the loops of his jeans in one quick, sharp motion, and Jude feels sick. He has seen somebody do that before.

Noah arches his back and makes an oddly primal sound, and Jude has heard a sound like that before too.

21

Then

Right at the tail end of August, when the rattlers are still bathing on the hot asphalt, Noah is working the register at the Aurora diner, and in walk four throwbacks to the Whistling Ridge High School basketball team.

Ethan McArthur looks fine in his army fatigues, a little filed down around the edges now, but he still has that bookish air to him that Noah always liked. He waves at Noah while the others cram into the nearest booth – lanky Luke Weaver, back from pissing away his sports scholarship in Arizona; Jaden Tucker with arms that could pop a man's head like summer balsam; and Austin Traxler, who has managed to grow a beard.

'Hey, man, long time no see.' Ethan smiles as Noah approaches the table to take their order. His teeth are very white, like he's had something done to them. Noah smiles back with his mouth closed.

'Didn't realize you were still working here, or we'd have invited you.'

No, you wouldn't.

Austin Traxler adjusts his thick-framed hipster glasses and

makes a show of looking at the menu. 'What would you recommend, my good waiter?'

'The waffles are okay, I guess.'

The others snigger and Noah chews on his lip.

'With such a glowing recommendation I can hardly refuse!' Austin declares, in a faux-transatlantic accent. 'Waffles it is, my good man. Waffles all around.'

Noah takes his time laying out their cutlery. He makes himself as close to invisible as he can while still being near them, and even though he tells himself he doesn't care, that it doesn't make any difference because what's done is done, he wants to hear them talk about college, to press on that bruise.

'How's Denver, then?' Ethan asks.

'Oh, you know,' says Jaden. 'I'm thinking about staying down there.'

'Jessica and I are looking for a roommate,' says Austin, 'if you don't mind Boulder.'

Luke snorts. 'Boulder's for hippies and snowflakes.'

'You don't think you'll move back home, then?'

'Hell no.' Jaden glances at Noah. 'I wouldn't want to be stuck here for the rest of my life.'

Noah retreats to the counter and rests his chin on his hands, watching the teenagers outside sprawled on the benches, like lizards in the heat. In a week or so they will start a new year of school, or pack up and head off to college, and he will still be here in this diner. He thinks, Low-hanging fruit, Jaden.

The bell over the door goes and there's a tangible shift in energy as Rat strolls in, leather jacket slung over one shoulder, a cigarette propped behind his ear. Chrissy Dukes, refilling the napkin dispensers, gives him a dirty look but then pulls her blouse a little lower around her cleavage when she thinks no one's watching. The boys in the booth regard him with a wolfish sort of wariness, uncertain how they should react to his arrogant gait.

'Hey, Blake,' Rat says, elbows on the countertop. 'You know what I want.'

Noah stares at him, his heart beating like a little bird trapped in his chest.

Rat grins. 'Caramel frappuccino? Like usual?'

'Oh.' Noah wonders how he can stand to wear his jeans so tight in this weather.

He loathes making anything with caramel because he always gets the syrup all over his hands. He's told Rat as much, but the guy still comes in every week and orders the same damn thing.

'I hate the way you call it *carmel*. It's ca-ra-mel,' Rat said once, real slow as if Noah was dumb. 'But I like it when you lick it off your fingers. Makes me want to read you poetry.'

Noah ducks behind the espresso machine and hopes – *prays* – Rat won't say anything like that in front of the basketball alumni. Maybe I am dumb, he thinks, but at least I have a sense of self-preservation.

'I'm telling you,' says Luke Weaver, loud enough that they can hear at the counter, 'that trailer park is full of gypsies and queers.'

Jaden Tucker sighs. 'Man, this whole country's full of gypsies and queers.'

Noah feels that tapping sensation on his arm again. He knows he should say something – he wants to say something: these boys aren't Samuel Blake, after all – but he feels like a fraud. Like maybe he's just pretending this whole gay thing, and wouldn't it be awful if he made a big song and dance about it now, only to snap out of it later? It's not worth it, not in a town like this.

When he glances at the counter again, Rat is gone.

Luke drums his fingernails on the plastic tabletop as Noah sets down his plate of waffles. 'Hey, you guys want to hear a joke? What does LGBT stand for? 'Let God Burn Them.' Get it? A preacher in Phoenix told me that one.'

Jaden snorts and Austin grins into his drink. Noah chews his lip again.

'Come on, man,' says Ethan. 'That's just stupid.'

'Oh, excuse me, did I offend you?'

Ethan rolls his eyes. 'I thought college was supposed to make you smarter.'

Noah swallows and thinks about the beginnings of Rat's disgusting frappuccino, congealing in a lonely cup behind the counter. He wishes he didn't stink of milk and bacon grease. He looks at these four boys he used to know and feels as though he hasn't washed for days.

'It was just a joke.' Luke looks at the others for commiseration. 'Everybody's so sensitive, these days.'

Noah tells Chrissy he has a migraine and leaves work early. It's been a long time since he was home alone in the afternoon, and it makes the house seem unfamiliar, a little dangerous even. He cranks up the AC and flops down on the couch with an ice pack over his face.

The sunlight makes everything pale and bright behind his eyelids. He didn't use to feel like this. Four years ago he had a bit of backbone, as his father would say. Before the night Samuel Blake put that hole in the wall, Noah might have said something to those boys at the diner. But if the doubts keep at you long enough, he figures, you come around to this way of thinking: that unhappiness is a terminal illness. Maybe you'll manage another year, another five, another ten. But eventually everything will get too heavy, and you'll swallow some painkillers, take the bathroom scissors to your ulnar artery, and lie back listening to the water running over. Something like that. You'll succumb to it like you would a cancer. Until then, you'll keep thinking, What's the point? What's the point of saving your money, of moving out of your parents' house, going to college? You're going to die anyway.

Something taps at the window and he starts, opening his eyes to see the blue spruce brushing against the glass in the sluggish summer breeze. Squatting in the branches, the angel he once made in 'shop class bobs with the moving tree, but its eyes stay fixed on him. Somehow, although he cannot explain why, he has the sense that if he were to look up now, the dark shape of God would be standing in the doorway, watching him.

And suddenly the memory comes to him. He swears he hasn't been thinking about that first time, but the very effort of not thinking about it makes it seem sweeter now, like he's been starving himself and he finally gets to eat. It was the last Sunday in April when Noah first saw him, parking his motorcycle at the Dairy Queen across the street. Rat had called out, 'Hey, church boy, where you going?' and stuck his tongue between his teeth when he grinned. Rat had been there the following Sunday, and the one after that, and Noah always kept his head down as he slouched across the church parking lot, only allowing himself to look up once he was settled in his truck and his parents were safely distant in theirs. Then one morning he had found a battered copy of Walt Whitman's *Leaves of Grass* tucked between his wiper blades. Rat was absent but somehow Noah knew he was the one who'd placed it there. 'You don't even like Whitman,' Noah had said to him, weeks later.

And Rat replied, 'But you knew what it meant.'

The angel sways in the tree. When Noah finally turns to

look at the doorway, it's empty, but he can hear footsteps in the hall.

Carefully, he gets up and pads to the living-room door, peering through the gap between the wood and the hinges. He'd thought his father was still at the mill, but Samuel Blake is taking down the big gemstone cross and laying it carefully on the floor, his hands touching the colourful stones with such tenderness it makes Noah ache.

The hole in the wall seems bigger than he remembers it. Noah can taste the memory of blood in his mouth. He watches his father take something from his pocket and place it gently inside the hole, before covering it with the cross again.

22

Now

Samuel pulls into the driveway with blood on his tyres – some shapeless dead animal in the road back from Boulder that had already been driven over too many times for him to tell what it was. He sees the light he left on earlier in Abigail's room. For a minute he just wants to sit there and pretend, but then he hears Dolly drop something in the kitchen, probably denting the linoleum while she's at it, and the abruptness of the sound makes him jump.

These support meetings he goes to, down in Boulder, they're no good. He can admit that, now Abi is no longer here. She was getting to be as bad as her brother these last four years, not looking at him properly when he spoke, still mad about the hole in the plaster. But he had been willing to make an effort for Abi.

It wasn't so bad in the beginning. Sure, these veterans' groups were mostly all *me me me*: people just wanted to talk about themselves, and they resented the moment when they had to stop and let somebody else take the floor. But Samuel felt it was a relief, sometimes, not to talk. There was some small measure of comfort in worrying about someone else for a little while, but more than that, there was validation.

One man, whose skin was all shiny with burn tissue down the side of his face and neck, said, 'We did what we had to do, out in the jungle. We did what we had to in order to get through it.' But in a sense, he was wrong, Samuel thought. Saying they'd got through it implied that somehow they'd come out the other side.

Her name was Hoa, and she'd lived above what he supposed must have counted for a bar in Sơn Tịnh. At first he would pay her to take him upstairs to her sweaty little room and ride him deep into her itchy pallet mattress, but after the third time she said she didn't want his money. She just wanted him.

Of course, that wasn't strictly true. What she wanted was America, but he would have given it to her anyway, back then: no woman had ever spoken to him the way she did. If only she hadn't spoken quite so much. If only she hadn't told him – that night when they were leaning up against the warm metal of the jeep, while inside the men were clinking their glasses together and hollering – that she was carrying his child.

It was as if Constance Blake was suddenly there in the jungle with them. Something like fear gripped him by the shoulders and shook him hard, and all he can remember thinking is, What the hell is Mom going to say?

Constance would never know, in the end. No one would – except for a handful of boys at Noah's eighth birthday party, who just so happened to catch Samuel Blake when, drunk and surrounded by children, he was suddenly reminded of a child he might have had. Most of the men in his squad who saw it happen – who saw Hoa take off running towards the trees as Samuel drew his rifle – would most likely be dead by now.

Hoa had once told him that her name meant 'like a flower', and sometimes, still, he wonders if there are flowers growing there now, in the spot where she fell.

Samuel never talks about Hoa or Sơn Tịnh at the veterans' meetings. Men talk about sins just as bad, but he can never bring himself to say his out loud. He doesn't like the thought of how the men might look at him afterwards. Not with judgement, but he pities some of them, the things they've had to live with, and he refuses to be pitied in return.

He considered quitting back in January. It was a hell of a drive down to Boulder with the mountain roads all iced up, but Abi was just starting to give him the time of day again, so he bought a new set of snow chains. He was almost proud of himself then, felt like he was turning himself around for his little girl, but that was when the guy running the support group went and jumped off the St Vrain bridge. Samuel had to laugh at that, the support-group manager jumping, but then they got some young fella in to replace him. Had served two tours in Iraq, *whoop-dee-doo*. Brought in a whole load of new members, and that was when things got bad.

These children – from a different war, a different time – were not his brothers. They wore unfamiliar faces, spoke in terms he didn't understand about places he didn't know, and they, in turn, did not know what Vietnam was. Oh, sure, they had a peripheral understanding. Some of them had even learned about it in history class – *history* class, like it was goddamn Ancient Rome or something. But to them it was just this thing that had happened in another time to other people. In the end, in a way he couldn't really articulate, he hated them.

He won't go to the meetings any more, he tells himself now, sitting in the car in the dark. The light may be on in Abigail's bedroom, but she is gone, so who cares if he keeps going or not? Dolly doesn't care. She probably thinks he holes up in a bar every Friday evening anyway.

'Father, we are coping with an empty seat at our table. Be with the one we are without tonight, and help us to trust in Your timing, purpose, and great love for us all. We pray for Your blessing upon Abigail Eden Blake and the space in between now and when we see her next. Until then, may this food bless our bodies and give us strength to endure what lies ahead. In Jesus's name, Amen.'

After Samuel lets go of his eldest son's hand, he wipes his palm on the leg of his pants.

'This is real good, Mom,' says Jude.

Dolly nods, prodding at the casserole with her fork. 'I didn't make it. Melissa brought it round.'

Samuel grunts and pops the tab on his can of beer. Melissa Alvarez-Jones is the sort of person he can imagine saying, 'Sorry for your loss,' at funerals, and 'No good crying over spilled milk.'

'You know I don't like that family,' he says, thinking: Nothing good ever comes of mixing races.

Dolly's face is pale and slack. 'She was just being nice.'

Sorry for your loss.

Samuel's too tired to argue, so he turns to a topic he knows nobody will backchat him about. 'Face's looking better, Noah. Your mom fix that up for you?'

His son pokes at his casserole and doesn't look at him, although little Jude gives his brother a strange sideways glance.

'You do it yourself?' If Samuel sounds impressed it's because he is, a little. The swelling has gone down considerably since the night before and the grazes are scabbing nicely. If he can patch up a face, perhaps the boy isn't a total lost cause after all.

Noah swallows visibly.

'Who did it for you?' Samuel asks. 'Come on now, who cleaned you up?'

Noah touches the tips of his fingers to his cheek, and Samuel thinks, just for a moment, that he sees a flicker of a smile. He opens his mouth, but just then Jude puts his glass down – too loudly, too suddenly – and Samuel starts, his elbow knocking over his can.

There's a smug *glug, glug, glug* as his beer leaks over the tablecloth. Dolly says, 'Oh, Sam,' and he feels like an old man who's wet himself in public.

Emma wraps her hands around her mug. The coffee's still too hot, but her fingers are so cold she doesn't mind burning them a little. For a Saturday morning, the Aurora diner is oddly empty, but still rich with the scent of coffee and a greasy sort of aftertaste that Emma can feel in the roof of her mouth. At the counter, Noah Blake nods his acknowledgement of her and Melissa in their spot by the window. The whole right side of his face is covered with little cuts, the way Abigail's knees used to be.

Abigail. Emma tightens her grip on her coffee mug, even though it's starting to sear her fingertips now. Her mother knows something about Abigail, some secret that, even now, Emma isn't allowed to be a part of. Abi knew all her secrets, yet it seems she'd been keeping back something of herself. Something it was fine to tell Emma's mom about, apparently, but not Emma.

'It's kind of nice, you know, you being off school,' Melissa says. 'We don't see so much of each other these days, do we?

Even over the summer, it was rammed at the clinic, and you were off out with Abi.'

Actually, Emma thinks, that wasn't entirely true. She'd barely seen Abi during the summer, and had spent most of the time binge-watching TV shows or walking alone in the woods. But there was one afternoon when she and Abigail had driven over to the national park, hiked one of the smaller trails around Wild Basin, and Abi had said, 'I've just been tired a lot lately, that's all.' She had certainly looked it, her eyes all puffy, makeup crusting over too many popped zits on her chin.

'Your dad been keeping you all up again?' Emma asked. They had stopped to rest on a huge boulder beside an idle stream, taking off their shoes to ease their blisters and stretching out on the sun-hot stone.

'I don't want to talk about my dad.' Abigail was scratching at her arm again. 'My parents don't understand anything. They're so stupid it makes me crazy sometimes.'

Emma watched her digging her nails into her skin. 'Are you okay?'

'Yeah. I'm just in a mood, Em. I'm sick of my dumb parents. They're not like your mom. She gets it.'

At the time, Emma hadn't thought to ask what it was, exactly, that her mother got. She'd been too busy enjoying the fact that Abigail thought her mom was cool, which meant that, by proxy, so was she. She had scrambled down into the stream, cupping the cold water in her hands and splashing it over Abigail, who had stopped scratching long enough to laugh and shimmy down to splash her back. The conversation had been forgotten in favour of just being girls again, but it comes back to Emma now, as if she were standing in that stream again, and when she hears her mother say, *It was rammed at the clinic*, something clicks.

'Mom, that thing you mentioned yesterday, about Abi? Was it a medical thing?'

Melissa frowns. 'I didn't say anything about Abi. I thought we'd agreed to leave this alone.'

'Did she come to see you at the clinic? Did she have a problem?'

'Em, come on. You know I can't tell you that.'

'So she did?'

Her mother looks into her coffee mug, like she's going to find the answer there. 'I didn't say that.'

Emma leans forward, lowering her voice: 'Does it have anything to do with Sheriff Gains?' As soon as she's said it, she feels something cold settle over her. 'Oh, Mom. Did he hurt her?' She searches her mother's face for some reassurance, but Melissa is looking out of the window at the squat adobe building of her clinic across the street.

'He was funny with her,' she says at last. 'That's all I know. I saw him talking to her once and he was funny with her.'

'Jesus, Mom. You have to tell someone, if that's really what you think.'

Melissa shakes her head. 'Who can I tell? And besides, Emma, I don't know what I think. There was just something odd about the way he was with her, that's all.' She looks over her shoulder quickly to where Noah Blake is wiping down the counter. 'You mustn't repeat any of this to anyone.'

Emma feels guilty, now, for being privately mad at Abigail. Oh, Abi. *Why didn't you tell me?* Melissa didn't deny it, didn't say: No, it was some other reason that Abi came to see me. But Sheriff Gains? Perhaps it's those sad donkey eyes of his, but Emma can't really believe it. Abi wasn't interested in older men – she was barely interested in boys, period, or her parents would have given her hell for it – so she would never have hung around trying to get attention from a man like Gains.

No. Emma taps her foot under the table. If anyone hurt Abigail, wasn't it more likely to be the boy who's sleeping next to a photograph of her every night? You hear about these guys, she thinks, guys who obsess over girls they can't have, and they work themselves up so bad that one day they show up at school and shoot them. Happens all the time, these days. She still can't get around it – Hunter sleeping next to that Polaroid. It makes her shudder. But if he had forced himself on Abigail – God, if he had, then he'd be afraid she might tell someone, wouldn't he? And if he found out she'd gone to see a doctor, then that would definitely put him on edge. Maybe enough to want to silence her for good.

When Sheriff Gains enters, he does so through the back door that Melissa once used to avoid him, so it's too late for that now. He makes a beeline for their table, and despite her suspicions about Hunter, Emma still finds herself crossing her legs as he approaches.

'Both Ms Alvarezes.' He takes off his Stetson and tucks it under his arm. 'My lucky day.'

Melissa becomes fascinated with the contents of her coffee mug again. 'Do you need something?'

Under the table, Emma feels her mother's leg bounce.

'Actually, Emma, it's you I was hoping to speak to.' He retrieves his notepad from his breast pocket and thumbs through it. 'Here we go – Emma, when you were first questioned a couple of weeks back, you said something to one of my deputies about seeing a strange light in the woods. You remember saying that?'

'Sure. It was over by the Winslow house. As I was driving home.'

'You have any idea what that might have been?'

'It looked sort of like a flashlight.' She adds, 'More towards the place where the Maddoxes live than the Tall Bones.' She shifts a little in her chair, as if she can sit on the memory of the Maddox house and squash it.

From the corner of her eye, she sees her mother glance at her. Gains nods slowly.

'Is this about what happened Thursday night between you and the Maddoxes?' Gains asks.

Emma taps her fingernail against the handle of her mug and shakes her head. 'No. But is there any news? About the investigation?'

Gains rubs the stumps of his missing fingers. 'You know I can't really talk about that.'

'But there is something.' Melissa looks at his twitching hands. 'Clearly there's something. Emma has a right to know. Abigail's her best friend.'

Gains eyes them both carefully, then lowers his shoulders. 'Look, it's nothing definite, but one of my deputies found a cardigan in the river, not far from the Tall Bones. Her mother says it's hers, but the blood—'

'The blood?' Emma can feel her hands growing clammy. 'What blood? Is it Abi's?'

'We're still waiting to hear back.'

'Oh my God.'

'We can't jump to any conclusions.'

'But she could still be out there – why are you wasting your time here? It's been three weeks! You should be out in the woods looking for her.'

'Em.' Her mother reaches across and puts a hand gently on her arm. A family two tables over is looking at them.

Gains shakes his head. 'Emma, we've *been* looking. We must have combed every inch of those woods these last three weeks. All we can do now is wait for the DNA results from Denver and follow up on any leads in the meantime.' He sighs. 'Listen, I'll look into your Winslow thing myself.

But I don't want you going up there, trying to figure this out on your own. In fact, Melissa, I'd appreciate it if you'd make sure she stays out of the woods altogether. Church committee's even asking me to enforce some sort of curfew, but then I suppose they're right this time. Got to keep an eye on our children until we figure out what happened to that poor girl.'

Emma doesn't like the way he's speaking about Abi in the past tense. She says this to her mother, but Melissa seems preoccupied as she watches the back door swing closed behind Gains.

'Wait here a moment, Em,' she says.

Outside on the little promenade behind the diner, with the river frantic from recent rain, Melissa has to raise her voice to be heard.

'What did you think you were doing?'

Gains stops, and he has the gall, she thinks, to look genuinely confused.

'Something the matter, Ms Alvarez?'

'I know the sort of man you are, getting too close to teenage girls. You stay away from Emma.'

'Hey.' He holds his hands up as if he's guilty, or mocking her with the idea of it. 'I have to question any witnesses. I can't *not* do my job.'

'You know that's not what I'm talking about. What were you doing driving Emma home the other night? You should have called me. I'd have come and got her.'

'I was just helping your daughter out.'

'The same way you helped out my husband all those years ago?'

Gains snorts and shakes his head. 'Well, maybe we could have done something about that if Miguel had stuck around to testify. Strange how he just disappeared like that, don't you think?'

She stares at him. Fear manifests as an ache under her breastbone. And when he tips his hat, saying, 'Be seeing you, Ms Alvarez,' she does not follow him.

23

Then

THE NIGHT SAMUEL Blake punched the hole through the wall was the same night he threw Jude down the stairs. Jude was only eight at the time, but he remembers it all very clearly. You don't forget a thing like that.

Noah had just walked through the door. It was a humid night in the middle of the summer, the threat of a thunderstorm hung in the air, and he had come home from seeing his girlfriend, Sabrina McArthur (come home from breaking up with her, Jude would later learn). Jude was a child but he thought his brother, standing there at the bottom of the stairs, seemed very grown-up. Especially when Noah looked their father dead in the eye and said, 'I'm going to study English at the University of California Los Angeles,' and even though he didn't say it, Jude heard, *And I'm not coming back*.

Noah was not grown-up then, of course. He was only eighteen, and the bones in his nose still sat straight.

What it all came down to – as it still does, even now – was Abigail. She had gone into Noah's room to use his computer while he was out, and she had seen pictures she was not supposed to see. Afterwards, when Noah would hardly speak to them and they had only each other, she told Jude about those pictures.

'I've never seen a man's thing standing straight up like that,' she said.

Jude had to admit he hadn't either, and then he felt like Abigail, at thirteen, was very grown-up as well, because she knew something about boys that he did not.

Abigail was upset by the pictures. She explained this to Jude later as well. In her rush to get out of Noah's room, she had knocked over his desk chair, which had roused their father, who was sleeping off a pack of Lone Star in the bedroom next door. There was no hiding it from him then. He did not say anything for a while, just went and stood on the stairs, staring at the front door.

When Noah came in and curled his lip at him, said he was going to the University of California Los Angeles, their father had said, 'The hell you are. I know what goes on in goddamn California, and let me tell you something, son, that is not the freedom I thought I was fighting for when I—'

'Oh, screw your war stories, Dad. Screw Vietnam. It was a million years ago, no one cares any more.'

Their father had levelled a finger at him. 'You say that again, you little faggot, and I'll—'

'No one. Gives. A. Good. God. Damn.'

Their mother stood on the landing, one arm around Abigail. Jude was standing next to them and watched her put her hand over her mouth when Noah said those things, as if somehow she knew what happened next would be as bad as it was. That night was the first time that Jude could remember her ever trying to hold their father back, and, really, it was the last time as well.

He got very quiet, their father did. Very quiet while the

veins in his arms and neck grew big and horrible, and then suddenly he just started screaming.

Jude has hung on to that sound ever since. He unpacks it in his mind sometimes and plays it over again when things get difficult, just to remind himself that he has been through worse. They all have. But the thing that slammed their mother's face into the banister, the thing that picked Jude up by his shirtfront and hurled him down the stairs, that thing was not their father. Jude – the only one of them who will cling to God right up until the end – thinks it was the devil himself that night, howling on the stairs.

Abigail did not cry. She never cried at the things their father said or did, and when he threw Jude down the stairs, she just pressed herself against the wall as if she wanted to make herself as small as possible. Jude, on the other hand, couldn't stop crying, not when his shin bone was poking through his pants leg all sharp and bloody. His father came loping down the stairs like some huge creature, and would probably have dashed Jude's head against the wall if Noah hadn't tackled him when he did.

Jude likes to imagine that his brother said something heroic, like 'Don't you touch him!' It would have made them feel better, him and Abi, in the years to follow, if they had been able to pretend that Noah really did like them still. But Jude knows his brother probably didn't say anything at all.

He gave as good as he got that night, poor Noah. Almost. But Samuel Blake had never beaten them with so much rage before, and it was as if he had been saving it up since the day they'd choppered him out of Saigon. He beat the shape right out of Noah's face, and probably would have killed him if Abigail hadn't screamed at him to stop.

'Daddy, don't! Please don't!'

Instead he had punched right through the wall next to Noah's head.

Noah wasn't seen around town for some time after that – except by Emma Alvarez, who glimpsed him on the landing, black with bruises, his nose held together by a couple of Band-Aids. He told people afterwards that he'd broken it playing basketball. Emma was not allowed at the house again.

Their mother put on lots of makeup and held Jude's hand in the ambulance on the way to the hospital over in Estes Park, but she didn't speak, except to tell the doctors he'd fallen out of the blue spruce in their front yard. It took her a long time to start talking to any of them again.

A few days later, she had dug out the gemstone cross that Grandma had given her on her wedding day and used it to cover the hole in the wall. She said, 'They'll take you away if anyone finds out.' Jude had only a vague sense of who 'they' were, but he knew he didn't want them to take him.

Jude would later learn that his parents paid his medical bill with the only substantial money they had to hand. Noah had to write and tell UCLA that he would not be accepting their offer. *Financial issues*, he explained.

Jude remembers standing with his sister in Noah's doorway as he pressed send on the email, and Abigail's eyes were all red and wet when she said, 'I'm sorry, Noah, I'm so sorry, I didn't think—'

Silently their brother got up and closed the door in her face.

24

Three nights Dolly stayed up trying to figure out what in hell she should do next. Three nights, since Samuel had broken her son's leg and put his fist through the wall. She had been to visit Jude in hospital every day. Not because she wanted to, but because the long drive from Whistling Ridge to Estes Park, the roads clogged with tourist traffic, felt like penance. As did the awful antiseptic smell of the children's ward, and the muggy heat of the car as she waited for the AC to kick in.

She spent the third night curled in on herself like a dying insect, eyes squeezed shut, begging God to tell her what to do next. She promised Him everything she had to offer: she'd volunteer for more mission trips, she'd get the kids involved with the give-back schemes, she'd try to help Noah with his sexual confusion, she'd quit smoking, she'd call her parents, she'd stop wearing lace panties . . . All night she prayed, wondering if His answer would come as a voice inside her head, or a white light, or an angel with many eyes and a burning sword, who would speak to her in a language she did not recognize but would understand all the same. Dolly waited, her limbs stiff from lying in the same position for so many hours, her face still tender from the shiner Samuel had given her. In the end, hollowed out by her long, sleepless vigil, she felt as if God was the one who had hit her instead.

'Dolly.' Pastor Lewis stood up when he saw her. 'What can I do for you?' He gave her a brilliant smile, and she thought: Thank you, God. This is going to be okay. This man is going to help me.

'It's about . . . well, it's about Samuel.'

'Come sit down,' he said, clearing some space for her on his little office couch. 'Why don't you tell me all about it?'

Dolly folded her hands neatly in her lap and hoped the pastor wouldn't see the cigarette stains on her fingernails. 'He's been hitting my sons.' She had to pause then, surprised at having actually said it. Somehow she didn't think she'd be able to say it, not after all this time.

'Go on,' he replied.

'He . . .' Dolly cleared her throat. Her mouth felt very dry. 'Three nights ago, he just lost it. I mean, you've never seen anything like this, Ed, it was . . .' She kneaded her forehead. 'Jude's in the hospital, Samuel pushed him down the stairs. And Noah, I mean I know he shouldn't have been . . . But that was no excuse.' She rubbed her eyes with the heel of her hand.

'That's very troubling to hear, Dolly. The Bible makes it very clear that when a man punishes his children it should be with the sole purpose of teaching them a lesson and instilling respect.' Pastor Lewis held up his hands as if he was expecting to receive something. *'Fathers, do not provoke your children to wrath, but bring them up in the training and admonition of the Lord.* Ephesians,' he added. 'It sounds to me like Samuel has lost sight of the duty that the Lord has laid out for him. I would recommend you direct him to me so that I can discuss the matter with him.'

'Well, sure, but what should I do? Should I call the police?'

Pastor Lewis scratched the little cleft in his chin. 'State law protects a man's right to punish his children in whatever way he sees fit.'

'Yes, but—'

'Dolly, I really think you should refer your husband to me. He may have lost his way, which is unsurprising for a man who's had his faith tested in the ways that Samuel has. The best thing you can do for him is pray that he finds his way back to the right path. You just leave the rest to me and the man upstairs.'

Dolly couldn't believe what she was hearing. *He threw my boy down the stairs!* She rubbed furiously at the makeup on the bridge of her nose. 'It wasn't just the boys. He hit me first.'

'Ah, now that's a different matter altogether, Dolly, and one that we can figure out together, I'm certain.'

'Yes.' She took a deep, grateful breath. 'Thank you.'

'Think back now, what did you do to make Samuel so angry?'

The question felt like a thump in the sternum. 'Excuse me?'

'You know, what did you do that ticked him off to start with?'

'I didn't do anything. He just lost it, like I said.'

'Dolly.' Pastor Lewis cocked his head to one side and smiled strangely at her. 'It sounds to me like you need to go away and pray on this. Then, when you've figured out how the argument started, you'll know how to avoid it in future. Do you see what I mean?'

'But . . .' she stared at him '. . . but he *punched* me.'

'Dolly, your husband has been through a lot. Things you and I can't even imagine. I'm sure you knew this when you married him, but there are bound to be times when he needs *you* to help him be the man that God intended. How can he lead the house without the support of his wife? I don't know where I'd be without Eleanor sometimes. Pray on it, Dolly. When you figure it out, you'll understand why he hit you.'

Eleanor Lewis, setting up the microphone stand for the following day's sermon, watched Dolly Blake leaving her husband's office. Dolly moved slowly along the wall as though she couldn't stand up by herself. Apparently unaware that she was being watched, she sat down suddenly, heavily, on a chair in the far corner and began to cry – the loud, ugly sort of sound that people only made when they thought nobody could hear them.

Eleanor rolled her eyes and raised the mic stand a little. Dolly Blake was hardly the first woman to fall out of love with a husband, she thought. There was no need to parade it around quite so dramatically. Imagine if everyone did that. Some things were to be endured, just as Christ endured his stack of splinters.

Now

The trailer park feels empty. On a Sunday morning, most folks are at church, but standing between the rusty swings and the double-wide is a thin man wearing only overalls. If he's cold he doesn't show it, but it makes Emma pull her jacket tighter around herself.

'I'm looking for Shana Tyson,' she says.

The man's face betrays no expression at all, but he never takes his eyes off her as he hooks a bird feeder to the awning of his trailer. Emma isn't sure what kind of birds he's expecting to feed round here. She has never seen any wildlife at the trailer park, except maybe the crows that congregate on the telephone wires, or the dead things people sometimes bring home to eat.

'Shana!' he calls suddenly, and a pretty girl pokes her head out of the trailer.

'What is it, Daddy?'

'Someone here to see you.'

Emma clears her throat, bobbing a little on the balls of her feet like maybe she might just turn and walk away. This was a dumb idea. Maybe.

But Shana Tyson smiles at her. 'Emma, right? I know you, you're Rat's friend.'

'Sometimes.'

Shana laughs. 'Yeah, he's a "sometimes" sort of guy.' She jabs her thumb at the door. 'You want to come in? That's okay, right, Daddy?'

Her father blinks slowly at her. 'Whatever you want, Princess.'

She kisses him on the cheek before they go inside, and before she shuts the door, Emma thinks she sees him smile.

The Tysons' place is nothing like Rat's on the inside. They have a proper couch, albeit a tiny one, a cuckoo clock on the wall and matching crockery stacked in the drying rack. These are real people, Emma thinks, not just a collection of junk. She frowns out of the window at Rat's RV across the lot.

'Sorry if my dad scared you there.'

Emma looks up. 'No, it's fine.'

Shana leans beside her at the window, running a hand through her thick hair while she watches the bent figure of her father pulling up weeds from the border fence. 'He's not been the same since he came back. He was in Iraq, you know.'

Emma did not know. She doesn't know much at all about the trailer-park people.

'There's lots of guys like him,' Shana says. 'Ghost-men,

Mom used to call them. Just wandering around like they don't really know who they are any more. Respect the troops, they tell you, but only when they're dying for you. It's like they get punished for living on afterwards.' She sighs and straightens up. 'Are you looking for Rat? I think he went out. His bike's not there.'

'Actually, I was looking for you.' She remembers Shana's face beaming from one of the Polaroids on Hunter's wall. 'I wanted to ask you something. If that's okay.'

'Oh, sure, what's up?'

'It's about Hunter Maddox. You know him?'

'Oh, that guy.' Shana laughs. 'I mean, he knows how to throw a party, I'll give him that, but he's a little wacky.' She mimes toking on a joint. 'Way too much of this, if you know what I mean. Surprised he hasn't been kicked off the basketball team.'

Emma grins. She likes Shana, she's decided.

'Why do you want to know about Hunter?'

'I think he might have known my friend.'

Shana's face drops. 'Wait, that Blake girl? You think Hunter might know something?'

'Maybe. I'm not sure. Is he ever, like, aggressive towards you? You know, sexually?'

'Nuh-uh, not Hunter. Some of those boys from the team can get pretty handsy sometimes, but he's not like that. He's real nice to girls.'

'Oh.'

'His daddy, though. He comes around sometimes, big Jerry, says he's just checking up on things, but he'll say some real weird stuff. Like, last week he said I had "filled out in all the right places". You know, that kind of thing. Daddy can't stand Jerry, but no one ever hassles him about it because he owns everything. Plus, he's friends with the pastor.'

Shana puts her hand on Emma's arm suddenly. 'I'm sorry about your friend. Abigail was a nice girl. A little weird, you know, but she was okay.'

Emma swallows. Why do people keep talking about her in the past tense, as if they've already given up on her? 'Did you know Abi too?'

Shana shrugs. 'Not well, but she used to come to Hunter's parties sometimes. Up here in the woods. And she'd take whatever anyone would give her, pills and stuff. I always felt sorry for her. You see people like that, there's always something they're trying to escape from.'

The word *pills* slaps Emma like cold water. 'No, Abi doesn't do drugs. She isn't like that.'

Shana folds her lips together and squeezes Emma's arm. 'Oh, honey.'

'No, she's my best friend, I know her.'

'Did you?'

25

'America is at war,' Pastor Lewis declares. 'This country is embroiled in a war on drugs, and we, my good brothers and sisters, are on the front line.'

It's cold in the church. The heaters aren't working, although they still groan like they're trying to gear themselves up for it, so the congregation sits in their coats and jackets, seeming a rather pathetic little mass as they huddle closer together under the pastor's gaze. Noah rubs his eyes, flinching as his knuckles press too hard against his still-sore cheekbone. Beside him, his mother is chewing her nails in her fingerless gloves. Every now and then she turns her head to scan the crowd as though she's looking for someone, or perhaps is worried she's being looked at. The slight pressure against Noah's right shoulder tells him Jude is seeking some warmth, and he is cold enough too that he does not push his brother away.

'Our society's problem with drugs is as old as civilization itself. Drugs make a user a slave to sensation, but they are false prophets, a chemical religion.' Pastor Lewis is wearing a white scarf that Noah can tell must have been expensive because he has gone to the trouble of keeping it very clean. He climbs down from his podium and begins pacing in front of the congregation, slow measured strides, but he never takes his eyes off them, never even seems to blink.

'The thing that shocks me most, my brothers, my sisters, the thing that shocks me most is how young the seeds of addiction can be planted. I was looking over some of these websites they got now, and some said as young as thirteen years of age, some said twelve. Some said that addict mothers can give birth to babies that already have an addiction to heroin. Newborn *babies*. Well, that got me thinking. We can direct our anger at the dealers and the pushers, but the addicts? They deserve our compassion. What is it I'm always telling you? Love the sinner, hate the sin? And those who have been coerced in a moment of weakness into consuming addictive substances, they are more in need of our love than our blame.'

A few rows in front, Noah sees Andie Maddox put her arm around her son and squeeze his shoulder.

'What this tells me is that these young people, who fall so easily under the influence of drugs, have a need in their life they want to be filled. A spiritual need. They must have something to believe in, something to turn to. The worst thing that can happen to a person is to have no belief in anything. The heart of this country's drug problem is a *spiritual vacuum*.

'Of course, it's natural to want to blame someone for all this horror in our society. It's quite natural to want to have something to direct your anger towards. We've all heard the old adage about the Lord and His mysterious ways – but believe me when I say the devil's ways are *always* clear. And if you want to have somebody to blame in the here and now, there is someone in this very town who is about the devil's work.'

Hunter Maddox sits up on his tailbone, his mother's arm slipping from his back.

'My son brought me some troubling news this Thursday

gone. He told me he had witnessed a drug deal occurring right here in Whistling Ridge, and who was behind it but that strutting little gypsy?'

Something turns sideways in Noah's throat. Out of the corner of his eye, he can see Jude looking at him. The congregation shifts, uncrossing their legs, murmuring like wind in the grass.

'My brothers, I ask you, what right does this stranger have to come into our town and intoxicate our children?'

'Hear, hear!' says Jerry Maddox.

Noah suddenly feels too tall among the bobbing heads of the congregation, and he sinks down into his seat, clenching and unclenching his fists, until Jude reaches over and takes his brother's hand. For the first time in a long while, Noah lets him.

'In John 8:7, Jesus says *He who is without sin among you, let him cast the first stone,* and we are all sinners, let us not in our anger forget that. It is the Lord who punishes sinners, but it is our job to recognize when God is seeking to work through our actions. In cases like this, my brothers, the Bible makes it clear. When Jesus found those money lenders in the temple, what did He do? When He found people in His Father's house – in God's own house – hawking and bartering as if this holy place was no more than a common market, my brothers, my sisters, what did He do? I tell you what He did. Jesus walked into that den of thieves and He tipped over their tables, He poured away their coins! He struck a blow for those of us who prioritize the spiritual life over earthly gains, and so, like Jesus, we must not be afraid to strike out against ungodliness when we witness it.'

Pastor Lewis climbs back on to his little platform, and there is a smile in his eyes if not on his lips when he says, 'These are uncertain times, but one thing I guarantee you:

those who corrupt the innocent will be punished with blood and fire.'

'I never liked this place,' says Deputy Saidi. 'Creeps me out.'

Standing in the ruins of the old Winslow house, with moss hanging from the charcoal roof timbers, and wind whistling through the cracks in the mortar, Gains has to agree.

'You really think there's something up here?' Saidi asks, rooting through the ferns with a pair of latex gloves.

Gains hooks his thumbs through his belt loops and sets his jaw. It's hard to imagine there being much of anything up here. 'Initial statement says Emma Alvarez mentioned activity here the night of the incident, but we failed to follow up at the time. Just got to cover our bases.'

'Gives us something to do until that cardigan comes back, at least.' Saidi sighs, leaning over on one side to stretch. 'You not in church today then, Chief?'

'Just as you see it. Can't say I'm much of a churchgoer – you?'

Saidi snorts. 'You think there's a mosque in Whistling Ridge?'

Overhead the sky is a heavy blanket of white, hinting at the snow already settling higher in the mountains as September bleeds into October. Today, Gains realizes, it is three weeks exactly since Abigail was reported missing. He had really wanted it to be true, that she'd just split, and he wouldn't have blamed her, with a family like that. But since they pulled that cardigan out of the river, he's been fighting this growing sense that he was wrong, and that they have now missed their chance of finding her.

'Hey, Chief,' says Saidi, suddenly, crouching in the dirt, 'this ground look a little uneven to you?'

*

Noah is unbuckling his seatbelt and launching himself out of the door before he's even killed the engine, taking off across the trailer park, oblivious to the mud churned up by his feet, spattering his Sunday best.

'Hey, Rat, open up!'

The heavy feeling of an approaching storm has seeped into the air, and Noah pulls his blazer tighter with one hand, resolving to bloody the knuckles on the other until he gets an answer.

When Rat opens the door, there's a curler in the front of his hair and a cigarette between his lips, like some trailer-park pin-up.

'You're not coming in here with those muddy shoes,' he says, grinning as he flicks the stub of his cigarette at Noah.

'Fine, whatever.' Noah rakes a hand through his hair, which is damp at the roots with sweat. 'Listen, you've got to get out of here, you're in trouble.'

'Trouble's my business, baby.'

'Seriously, can you just stop that for one second? That bastard Dalton Lewis saw you the other night, at the Tall Bones. Told his dad you were dealing drugs and now the whole town's in a frenzy about it.'

Rat leans out of the doorway and looks around. 'Okay, maybe you should come inside after all.'

Noah has always liked the RV. It's like some offshoot of Rat and that feels important. He remembers stepping in here one sultry summer afternoon, seeing the pages of poetry tacked to the walls, and, suddenly, knowing that Rat liked Bukowski felt more jarringly intimate than the fact they were about to have sex. Now he says, 'Guess it won't be hard for you to leave. You can just drive off in this thing.'

Rat makes a face. 'What makes you think I'm going anywhere? Bunch of Bible-thumping hillbillies don't scare me.'

'Well, they should. One of them's my father.'

He notices now that Rat is wearing one of the old flannel shirts that he left here months ago, and his feet are bare. Noah's knees feel weak.

'I don't think I can protect you if you stay. Not from my dad.'

'I don't need you to protect me, Blake. I do just fine on my own. Always have, but . . .' Gently he touches Noah's gravel-scored cheek. 'If I go, will you come with me?'

A heavy knock at the door pulls them apart. Rat goes to open it, still with the curler in his hair, still with no socks on, and he looks so small all of a sudden as Jerry Maddox and Sheriff Gains crowd the doorway.

'Rat Lăcustă?' Gains asks, although it isn't really a question. Noah doesn't know where to put himself as the two men peer into the RV.

Rat crosses his arms. 'Can I help you?'

Jerry says, 'It's his, all right. I make all the tenants show me their gun licences and I remember that one – 9mm semi-automatic. Goddamn gypsy criminal.'

Noah bites his lip and moves to stand behind Rat. 'Hey, what's this about?'

'This doesn't concern you, Mr Blake.' Gains holds up a clear bag with a handgun inside. 'Mr Lăcustă, is this your firearm?'

For the first time in all the months Noah has known him, Rat has nothing to say. He just stares at the gun and nods strangely, like his head isn't properly connected to his body.

'Hey, Rat, what are they talking about? You don't own a gun.'

Through the gap between their shoulders, Noah can see the storm clouds gathering along the skyline.

'Mr Lăcustă,' says Gains, 'you're going to need to come with us.'

26

THERE IS JUST a little icy rain as Emma picks her way over to the RV from the Tysons' trailer. Outside, there are too many footprints and she wonders who has been here. Even under layers of sweater and scarf and jacket, she shivers when she sees the door ajar, and somehow, even as she knocks, she knows that Rat won't answer. It seems wrong to go inside when he's not there.

'Emma?'

To her surprise, it is Noah Blake who pushes the door open, slowly, as if he's afraid who might be on the other side. He has always seemed afraid of something, she thinks.

'Where's Rat?' she asks. It had been strange, being up here at the park without seeing him. She didn't like all this bad feeling between them, lingering like those black clouds on the horizon, so she figured she'd look in on him, try to fix whatever had snapped when he took off the other night.

Noah shrugs his high shoulders, disrupting the clean pressed Sunday-School shape of him in his button-up shirt. His red hair looks like the aftermath of a slap against the dirty white of the RV, and it feels like one too, the way it reminds her of Abigail.

'Noah, where is he?'

'Rat's gone,' he says. 'The police took him in.'

She listens as he tells her about what Dalton Lewis saw at the Tall Bones, about the sermon, and the way people got all stirred up. When he mentions the gun, and the shell casing they found in the woods, she remembers the Polaroid on Hunter's wall, Rat with flowers in his hair and a handgun in his lap.

'Do they think he shot Abi? They think *he* did it?'

It feels wrong being in the RV without Rat. Outside the rain is heavier now, rolling down the windows in heavy, drumming sheets, and a burst of lightning flashes veins across the sky. There is a bottle open on the countertop. Noah takes a long swig, clearly not his first, and grimaces.

'Peach schnapps,' he says. 'Who drinks this shit, huh?'

Emma stares at the bottle in his hand.

'You want some?'

'I shouldn't . . .'

'Go on, I don't care.' He presses the bottle against her chest. 'Saves me from drinking alone.'

She tips her head back and takes a long, grateful swallow, and she's missed it, the warm way the alcohol spreads through her body, like so many hands catching her, as if to say *It's all right now, we've got you,* but the sickly aftertaste catches up with her. 'Peach schnapps, my ass. I've never had any peach that tastes like that.'

'He didn't do it, you know,' Noah says suddenly. 'What you said . . . Rat didn't shoot Abi.'

Emma doesn't know how to answer that. She sits down heavily on Rat's pile of quilts and takes another long drink, then wipes her mouth with her hand, the way boys do, because a little bit of her is still in awe of Noah Blake, Abigail's big brother. A little bit of her still remembers Abi's fierce need to impress him.

'Look,' she says, 'whoever you think Rat is, he isn't. I don't think I've got one straight answer out of him the whole time I've known him.'

'You been up here drinking his liquor a lot, then?'

'Sometimes.' Emma looks at the peeling label on the bottle. 'Not a lot.'

'He didn't do it.' Noah is staring hard at the rain on the windowpanes. 'He's not like everyone says he is. He's a good person.'

'Who sells drugs and buys alcohol for minors and keeps a secret gun he never told us about, sure. He was at the Tall Bones the night Abi disappeared. Did he tell you that?'

'Why don't you climb down off of that high horse if you're going to keep drinking what he paid for?'

'This is the guy who might have shot your sister, Noah. Why the hell are you defending him?'

'Because he didn't *do it*.'

It occurs to Emma that she'd had a similar conversation with Hunter Maddox not so long ago, the night he drove her to his house. *He's my friend*, she'd said, and Hunter had laughed like he felt sorry for her.

'You sound pretty sure about that,' she says, not unkindly, because she feels a little sorry for Noah too.

He crosses his arms tightly. 'Yeah, well. I was with him, wasn't I?'

'Like . . . *with him* with him?'

'Oh, come on. Don't act like Abi never told you.'

The way he looks at her then, she can see him as he was four years ago: standing on the stairs with his face all split and bruised, everything swollen out of proportion so that he looked like a surrealist painting, and she can hear Abigail saying, *Daddy says you can't come over to the house any more.*

'Hell, Noah. I had no idea.'

'Well, goddamn. Guess she was about as proud of what happened as I was, then.' Noah takes another swig from the bottle. 'I can't believe she never told you that.'

It seems there's a lot that Abi never told her.

The lumber mill is still on Sundays. The rich scent of timber still saturates the air, but without the smoke rising from the chimney stack, the thrum of moving bodies, or the constant snarl of machinery, it feels unfamiliar to Hunter.

His father shuts the top drawer of his desk when he spots him in the office doorway. 'What're you doing here?'

'Came to see the king in his court.'

Jerry stands up, one hand still held over the seam of the drawer. 'You should be at home. You're still grounded until tomorrow.'

'Did you get Rat Lăcustă arrested?'

'Is that what this is about? I don't have time to talk about that waster. Believe it or not, Hunter, some of us have jobs to do.'

'Rat didn't do anything.'

'That's not what Ed Lewis says, and I'll believe a man of God over some damn gypsy any day. Besides, what do you think his gun was doing up in the woods? You think he just happened to leave it there by accident and never went back to find it?'

Hunter stuffs his hands into the pockets of his Letterman jacket. 'Someone could have stolen it.'

'Well, that'd be very convenient for him, I'm sure, but it really doesn't change anything. It's not like any of those cheap trailer kids are going to come forward to save him.' Jerry rearranges some papers on the desk. 'Now, how about those brochures your mom got, Hunter? Have you taken a look yet? Time's running out, you know.'

'How can you even think about stuff like that when there's a girl missing?'

'Hunter, you've got a bright future ahead of you. There's no reason why you shouldn't get into a decent college, if you can just knock this drugs thing on the head. Your mom and I, well, we don't want to see you end up like Noah Blake, waiting tables for the rest of your life because you flunked out.' Jerry scratches the back of his head. 'The Blakes are that kind of people, son. I saw the way that girl hung around the trailer park. She was exactly the same. You're best just putting her out of your mind. She was asking for trouble.'

Hunter hates him. Hates the big bulk of him and how it takes up so much room in this little office, in this little town. 'What if *I* stole it?'

'What?'

'What if I'd stolen Rat's gun? Should I come forward?'

'What the hell are you talking about? Tell me you didn't steal that gun.'

'What should I do, Dad? What's the proper Christian thing to do?'

Jerry grips his son by the arm and marches him out of the office, all the way across the main saw room, and out to his car. 'Get in,' he says, thrusting Hunter forward so that he stumbles. 'I said get in. I'm taking you home. What the hell's wrong with you? What kind of college do you think will take you if you go around stealing people's firearms? And what about me and your mom? How do you think this makes us look? I will not let you flush your future down the drain over some delinquent, do you hear me? I'm not letting you out of my sight until that boy's been charged, and he will be, Hunter. You heard what Ed Lewis said this morning: we're ready to cast out the evil in this town. Blood and fire. You can bet everything you've got on that.'

Gains leans back against the desk and crosses his arms. 'You speak very good English, Mr Lăcustă. You pick all that up in America?'

The kid's a strange one, he thinks. Laughs like a buzz-saw even though he's got a bag full of evidence sitting right across from him and he's not even wearing shoes.

'We had Cartoon Network in Romania,' Rat says, like he's sucking on something sour.

'Is that right? And you learned it all watching *Powerpuff Girls*, did you? Now that is impressive.'

'Why does it matter where I learned English? I thought you wanted to ask me about the gun.'

'Son, we don't get a lot of strangers settling in Whistling Ridge, but this spring you roll into town and a short while later your gun turns out to be a match for the shell casing we found at the scene of a young girl's disappearance. Nobody knows anything about you. That makes people nervous, you understand? Folks are going to find something to pin on you one way or another. That's just how it works around here. But see, me, I don't think you have much of a motive to shoot Abigail Blake, whether the gun's yours or not, and I'm willing to run with that, so help me out. Who are you, kid? What're you doing here?'

Rat toys absently with the wolf fang dangling from his earlobe. 'My parents lived under Ceauşescu. You can play Good Cop all you want but I know about police.'

Gains sighs. 'Well, that's a start, I guess.'

Rat's fingers relocate to the tabletop, drumming in a restless way that Gains recognizes.

'Look, kid, the sooner you start being upfront with me, the

sooner you can get out of here, and the sooner we can both have a smoke.'

The whole room feels like the underside of a bandage, and the prospect of nicotine seems to do the trick.

'I learned English in England.' Rat doesn't look at Gains but stares at the wood grain on the table, tracing it with a bitten-down thumbnail. 'I used to live there. For a while.'

'How did you end up in America?'

'I just did, *la naiba*. It's all we ever heard about growing up – America this, America that. Figured it was worth a look, to see if it lived up to the hype.'

'And does it?'

'It's about what I expected, sure. Full of little men who think they're the real shit because they talk above a certain decibel and carry a gun.' Rat looks up at him from under his eyelashes. 'Scenery's not bad, though.'

'You carry a gun, Mr Lăcustă.'

'Well, there you go. Just trying to fit in.'

'Tell me about the gun.' Gains circles around the desk so that he can sit opposite him. 'When we picked you up, you told us it had been stolen. If that's the case, why didn't you report it missing?'

'I don't know, stuff came up, I got distracted. There's a lot of distractions up here. And, like I said, I don't set too much store by law enforcement.'

'You have any idea who could have taken it?'

Rat shrugs. 'One of the kids from the trailer park, probably. It was way back in May. We all used to hang out together then, shoot bottles and get high and stuff. Listen,' he digs his nails into the tabletop, 'I didn't shoot Abigail Blake. I didn't even know the girl.'

'You know her brother, though. He was up at your RV when we came to bring you in.'

Rat just stares at him with those cut-glass eyes that make Gains feel like someone's pouring cold water down the back of his shirt.

'Well, look.' He rubs the stump of one of his fingers. 'Can you at least tell me where you were the night Miss Blake disappeared, the night of that particular party?'

'No.'

'Jesus, kid. Temperature's getting pretty hot around here – people have a lot of questions about what happened to that girl, and as far as they're concerned, you're as good an answer as any. Do yourself a favour and be honest with me.'

'I *am* being honest. I can't tell you where I was.'

'Come on, what do you mean you *can't*?'

Rat leans back in his chair, stretches one arm back behind him, and then shrugs at the sheriff. 'It's not my secret to tell.'

At first Jude thinks Abigail's room looks the same. Things are a little messy but in a way that feels familiar, like his sister might still walk in at any moment and pick her hairband up off the floor or throw her sweater over the back of her chair. But the longer he sits there on the bed, the more he can see how much everything has begun to change. Three weeks she's been gone – 504 hours. By now her teeth could be falling out. Her room, too, is gradually coming apart. Pencils have rolled off the desk and disappeared; her books are covered with dust; everything is cold and faintly clammy to the touch. Jude can't bear it.

He knows what his mother believes: that if they leave the room just as it is, they'll keep Abigail with them. But a room needs life, or the dust will settle and settle until it buries his sister completely. So Jude moves her hairbrush, plumps her pillow, rearranges the clothes in her closet. It isn't much, but it's enough to make him feel she's still alive, as if perhaps he'll walk past her open door later, see all these little changes and think: Abi is home.

He still isn't sure about what he saw in the woods, between his brother and the Romanian boy. Or, rather, Jude knows what he saw, he just isn't sure what it means. The sound Noah made, the way he took off his belt – it reminded Jude of something else, something from months ago, which hadn't seemed so strange then, but now . . . He doesn't know much about sex, so he doesn't know how to explain it, but this is probably one of those things where, if he had a normal mother, he would ask her about it. He will look for a sign instead, he decides. Just like Pastor Lewis said: *It is our job to recognize when God is seeking to work through our actions.* If what he saw really was what he thinks it was, then God will find a way to tell him. God will give Jude the words to tell his mother.

In the bottom of Abigail's closet is a shoebox, and Jude already knows he's going to open it, even as he tells himself not to. The girl in the Polaroids looks like his sister, has her same bright red hair, that pointy face, those long limbs, but he has never seen his sister laugh like that, has never seen her look so *wild*. He sifts through photographs of Abigail dancing, head tossed back and hands in the air, of her arms around trailer-park kids, her bare legs splashing through the river while she beams at the photographer.

And then, at the bottom of the pile, there she is with a cigarette between her lips, wearing some green-and-black Letterman jacket that is too long for her in the sleeves. Standing next to her is the Romanian boy, and he has his arm around her shoulders.

27

Dolly Blake, standing in the police-station lobby, can't remember the last time her husband wanted to hold her hand. But then this afternoon he said, 'Dolly, they're saying the cops got the guy, they got the gypsy boy that took Abi,' and now here he is, rubbing his thumb against her knuckles, like this is something they always do. And here she is, waiting for him to stop.

'We want to see him,' Samuel tells the deputy at the front desk. She's a young woman with a rather austere face but clearly not the personality to match, because she shrinks away as Samuel leans towards her.

'We want to see the son of a bitch who shot our daughter.'

'Please, sir, nobody has been formally charged. No one's even been arrested.'

'Well, then, get on it. We want to see the boy you're holding, don't we, Dolly?'

Dolly nods once. She doesn't really know what she feels. They told her Abigail was a missing person and now people are saying she was shot, and all Dolly wants to do is shake somebody by the shoulders until they give her an answer – the right answer: is her daughter dead or not? Is this finally the end of the sentence?

She hears a door opening around the corner of the adjoining corridor, and the approaching footsteps sound far too loud to Dolly, who hasn't had a cigarette all day because 'It will set off one of my migraines, woman.' She squeezes Samuel's hand because her fingers are restless, but he must take that to mean something else, because he says, 'My wife wants to see who shot her baby girl,' calling her *my wife* like he's proud of it.

'Sir, I'm sorry,' says the clerk, 'but we don't . . .'

Dolly doesn't hear the rest and Samuel probably doesn't either, because around the corner comes Sheriff Gains, a little pink in the face, with the Romanian boy, who is wearing a curler in his hair and no shoes. Walking between them, shoulders hunched and lip well chewed, is their very own Noah.

'What the hell is this?'

Samuel lets go of Dolly's hand at once, and somehow, although she can't say why, she gets the sense he is embarrassed at Noah having seen such an intimate gesture between them.

'Gains, you're letting that little gypsy go? What in God's name is going on here?'

Gains raises his eyebrows, as if the entire concept of what's going on is too large for him to look at properly. 'I've no reason to continue holding Mr Lăcustă.'

'That's not what I heard.' Samuel sucks on the inside of his cheek, making one side of his face look especially gaunt. 'I had it from Jerry Maddox himself. This kid did away with my baby girl.'

'I'd appreciate it if you'd lower your voice, Mr Blake.'

Gains rolls his shoulders back and Dolly wants to thump him. It's all very well and good if you want to play the big man here, she thinks, but I'm the one who'll have to deal with the fallout of you pissing off my husband.

'Lower my— What the hell does that matter? You're letting the boy who took my daughter just walk out of here!'

Dolly glances at Samuel, who is flaring his nostrils as he breathes, and then she tries to catch Noah's eye, but he is staring pointedly at the police-station carpet. The Romanian boy, she realizes, hasn't taken his eyes off Noah the whole time. It almost hurts to see that now. Nobody has ever looked at her that way.

When Gains replies, 'Sir, your son has provided him with an alibi,' Dolly has a sinking feeling she knows exactly what he means.

Emma has almost finished the bottle by the time Rat gets home. She watches him from the window as he walks barefoot through the chain-link shadows cast by the sinking sun. The storm has left things feeling rusted around the edges, and the news about Noah Blake didn't help.

'So, you're sleeping with him,' she says, dropsy on her vowels.

Rat closes the door and leans against the table, like a ship taking on water.

'You're a real son of a bitch.'

'*Drăguţă—*'

'No.' She shakes her head. 'No, you don't get to call me that, don't act like I mean something to you. It was him, wasn't it? That night you left me at the Tall Bones with Hunter . . . you went to meet *him*?'

'You've seen the mess his dad made of his face. I had to go.'

'Yeah, well, the Maddoxes made a mess of me.'

'Emma—'

'You were supposed to help me figure out what happened to Abigail, and maybe she doesn't matter to you, but she is the only friend who's ever mattered to me, so you don't get to dismiss her like she's not worthy of your time.'

His whole face stiffens, and for a moment she can see the age between them.

'You know,' he says, 'I was glad when I saw your car out on the road. I wanted to thank you. Noah told me you were the one who encouraged him to come give his statement and get me out of there.'

'That was half a bottle ago, when I still loved you.'

There is no incense burning in the RV and suddenly Emma can smell the lack of it – a sort of coldness, mingled with artificial peaches and the earthy smell of mud caked to the bottom of Rat's bare feet.

He sinks into the seat beside the table. 'I never asked you to love me.'

From the window, Emma can see a group gathering outside, a mix of fraying flannel, faded blue jeans, and creased blouses and blazers. They're talking loud enough that she can hear the general buzz of their voices, but not so that she can make out any particular word. She recognizes one of the men as Shana Tyson's hollowed-out father.

'I think I'm going to leave,' she says, heaving herself to her feet. 'I would like to go home.'

'I don't think you should be driving, *drăguță*. You've had a lot to—'

'I said *don't* call me that. Jesus, you think you can get away with anything because you're *pretty*, and the worst thing is you just have. You've gotten off scot free.'

She sways as she tries to pass him, and he puts out a hand to steady her, but the metallic thud of something striking the side of the RV makes him pull back.

Outside the voices are louder now. Rat peers around the edge of the window, then ducks down sharply, motioning for Emma to do the same, just as a rock sends splinters of glass spilling across the floor.

Outside someone yells, 'You son of a bitch, you goddamn son of a bitch!'

'Selling drugs to our children, murdering that girl!'

'Come out, you gypsy bastard!'

Something shatters against the other side of the door, and Emma feels a scream threatening in her throat, but Rat clamps his hand over her mouth and pulls her under the table.

'I've got you, it's okay. It's going to be okay.'

He wraps his arms around her until she stops shaking, and they lie scrunched up together in the gathering dark while the people of Whistling Ridge cast all their stones.

28

Noah's father is waiting for him in the driveway as his truck pulls up to the house. He shuts off the engine, and for a while they just stare at one another, Noah imagining he can see the sparks coming off Samuel, like he's a frayed piece of electrical wire. He knows the longer he leaves it, the more inevitable it becomes. It'll be like cracking a stiff knuckle, he tells himself: uncomfortable, but best to get it over with.

In the end, it isn't much like that at all. Samuel smacks him with the back of his hand, and Noah feels the imprint of his father's wedding ring right on his jawbone. He staggers a little and sucks his fist to keep from making any sound.

Samuel shakes his head. 'I hope you know you've humiliated this family.'

After that, Noah moves about the house awkwardly, listening to his mother rustling grocery bags downstairs, the monotonous thud of his father chopping wood outside, the faint melody from Jude's headphones, and the steady silence of Abigail's empty room. They take up all the space and he is unsure of where to put himself.

In his own bedroom, Noah gets the familiar sense that God is looking over his shoulder.

I hope you know you've humiliated this family.

Noah wants to wring His neck: You asshole, don't you think I've tried?

When he was fifteen, Noah made up a wife for himself. In the Bible, Noah's wife was nameless, but he had been told at Sunday School that she was called Naamah so that was what he called this imaginary woman. In his head she looked a bit like the mother from *The Waltons*, because his parents watched a lot of that at the time, and Naamah was very kind, always calling him 'honey', like they did on TV. Sometimes, if he'd had a rough day at school, he would talk to his wife. 'Honey, you'll never believe the day I had,' he'd say, and he would imagine her replying, 'Honey, you're doing just fine.' He kept Naamah alive for three months, watering her like a flower with all the things he learned about marriage from watching his parents. Naturally, one day, she left him.

After that he just prayed. In a brutal cycle, he would go to what he believed were secret corners of the internet to look at pictures of men, and then afterwards he'd pray, like he was tied to a mast in a storm, trapped in each prayer, hammering his fists on the walls of it. He prayed until he was bloody. At sixteen, he broke down weeping in church when Pastor Lewis – *Pastor Lewis,* of all people – touched him gently on the bare skin of his forearm, and the pastor took it as a sign of something holy. Noah was so afraid as he stood there, catching his tears in his hands, that everyone could see he was a fraud.

'What should I have done?' he says now, staring down God. 'Just lied? Did you want me to lie and let them arrest an innocent man for something he didn't do? That's a sin too. That's a worse sin than love.'

Standing at the top of the stairs, his mother tells him he must eat dinner in his room tonight. 'Your father doesn't want you at the table.'

'*Mom*.'

'I'm sorry, Noah.'

No, you're not, he almost says.

'Just be grateful he hasn't—' She comes into his room and reaches out like she's going to touch his jaw, still pink and tender, and he leans towards her hand, some younger part of him hoping that perhaps, this time, she will hold on to him. But at the last moment she pulls away. 'Just be grateful.'

When she has gone, Jude appears in the doorway.

'Hey, Noah.'

'What? Have you come to piss all over me too?'

His brother clutches a Polaroid photograph in his hand. 'I need to show you something.'

'Well, save it.' Noah shoulders him out of the room, not stopping even as he hears Jude stumble against his cane.

He slams the door, and while his brother raps on the wood, saying, 'Come on, please, you need to see this,' Noah puts his pillow over his head and thinks, Naamah, honey, you won't believe the day I've had.

Then

It is the first evening of June, that odd cusp between seasons when the landscape feels briefly energized before the long lethargy of summer. The sun hangs on the horizon for over an hour, as if regretting that it has to set at all, but when it does, the music starts and the fairy lights come on, bright cobwebs strung between the trailers.

Shana's father is down in town for some church thing, so tonight they all crowd into the Tysons' double-wide. Shana mixes cocktails with cheap juice and even cheaper vodka, courtesy of Rat, who plays an acoustic cover of 'Sympathy For

The Devil' on his grandmother's guitar, while the Weaver brothers pull Beth Farmer's hair, and Bryce Long snorts a long line of methadone off the coffee table.

'All right, man, easy,' Hunter says, nudging Bryce's shoulder. 'Slow down or we'll run out before the night even gets going.' He glances at Abigail, perched on the edge of the couch, hugging her knees against her chest. 'You okay?'

She presses her lips together and nods.

An hour or so later, he finds her and Bryce in the Tysons' tiny bathroom, doing a line off the rim of the sink.

'Hey, man, come on. You're getting through my whole stash.'

'It's cool, Hunter.' Bryce waves him away. 'I'll pay you back. Don't worry about it.'

'Yeah, but . . .' He looks at Abigail, and her face is pink and puffy, like she's been crying.

Rat appears at his shoulder, narrowing his eyes at Bryce. 'You shouldn't be giving that to her, *pizda*. Can't you see she's drunk?'

Bryce sneers at him. 'Chill, comrade, she's fine. You're fine, aren't you?'

Abigail smiles, but it's too wide and weird, and when she tries to stand up, she wobbles and falls over. Rat is there in an instant, gathering her up, but she struggles and pushes back against his chest.

'Get your hands off me,' she slurs. 'I don't even want to think about where they've been.'

Rat unhands her roughly and she staggers against the sink. 'You know,' he says, his voice suddenly hard, 'your brother's right. You can be a real bitch.'

Abigail opens her mouth, but all she can seem to do is stare at him. Then she elbows Bryce and Hunter out of the way and storms back across the living room towards the door.

Bryce rubs his hand over his face. 'Jeez, you guys are killing the vibe.' He pushes past them, but when Hunter goes to follow him, he feels a hand on his arm.

'Hey, Maddox.' Rat's face has gone slack. He sounds tired and distant now, all the fight gone out of him. 'You want to fuck or something?'

'No! Are you crazy, man? What are you on? Keep your voice down.'

Rat sighs and lets his head fall back against the wall, and Hunter can see the ring of white powder crusted around his nostril.

'She shouldn't have said that, you know. About me. And the way she looked at me . . . She shouldn't have done that.'

'Yeah, I know, man, I know. I'll go talk to her.' Hunter claps him awkwardly on the shoulder. It seems like the heterosexual thing to do. 'Drink some water, yeah?'

Rat shrugs and squints at the stains on the plastic floor. 'Hey, Hunter?'

'Yeah?'

'People round here are going to get what's coming to them. You'll see.'

The air is brisk as Hunter steps out of the trailer into the night. Shana's little fairy lights give the park a hazy glow. He takes a moment just to breathe, soaking up the scent of pine trees and cheap liquor, while the breeze cools the sweat on his face. The faint sound of music makes the horizon seem broader. Out there, there is something else, beyond all this: there are people enjoying the company of one another.

All of a sudden, the sound of his father's voice brings him back to the present. 'You want to watch yourself,' Jerry is saying. 'Some of these trailer-park kids can be a little rough.' He is using a gentler tone than Hunter is used to, so he knows at once that his father isn't speaking to him.

Creeping to the edge of the Tysons' double-wide, he presses himself close to the clapboards, feeling the damp earth under his socks, and peers around the corner. They are standing barely two feet apart, his father with his hand on Abigail's shoulder, she holding a clear plastic cup of water, as she smiles – a real smile this time – and says, 'Thank you, Mr Maddox.'

'Don't mention it, sweetheart,' he says. 'I'd hate to see anything happen to a nice girl like you.'

29

Now

THE SUN MAKES a cameo appearance through low milky clouds, as Emma turns off on to Elkstone Bend, towards the Maddox house.

Last night was bad. She thought her mother was drunk when she got home, but it turns out there's some kind of state people can get into when they're really pissed off that is just as wretched. Melissa had never really yelled at her before, not like that.

'You can't keep disappearing, Emma. I was *this close* to phoning the police!'

'I just went to see a friend.'

'Oh, which friend, Emma? Which friend? Because it sure as hell wasn't Abi. And, Christ, are you really drunk again? After everything we talked about? You're ruining your body, Emma. Ruining it. When you're older and you've got liver damage and shaky hands and rotten teeth, you'll hate what you've done to yourself!'

What difference will that make? Emma had thought. I already hate myself.

'Are you trying to punish me because your dad's not

here? You have no idea how hard it is being your mother sometimes.'

They had said things they didn't mean then. They had said some things they did mean, too. When it was done, Emma listened for a long time for the familiar sounds of her mother moving about in her own room, but in the morning, when she was sneaking out, she passed her curled up on the couch with her makeup still on.

Hunter is sitting outside on the front steps, cleaning mud off his sneakers before school when Emma pulls up. She is still carrying the anger from arguing with her mother, but it has honed the manic unhappiness of yesterday's drinking, and now she feels fierce and constructive.

'Were you giving Abigail drugs?'

Hunter flicks a chunk of dried dirt from the tread of his shoes. 'What makes you say that?'

'You took her to all those parties. Up here. You gave her drugs.'

'You're way off.'

'Shana Tyson told me.'

'Oh, well, then, what are you waiting for?' He holds out his wrists. 'Better cuff me.'

'Is this a joke to you?'

'You're the one being dumb about it. I'd never do anything to hurt Abi.' He works another hunk of mud free with his fingernail. 'We were friends.'

'Friends? With you?'

'Sure, why not? You weren't the only one allowed to know her.'

You didn't know her, Emma thinks. Neither she nor Abigail had many friends: Abi would never have been so selfish as to keep someone from Emma like that or, worse, to replace her.

'I don't believe you.'

'Believe whatever you like, I don't care. But I didn't give her any drugs. She just . . . took them sometimes. From other people.'

'She wouldn't do that.'

Hunter is looking at her the same way Shana Tyson did. *Oh, honey.* A stiff breeze sets the aspen leaves clamouring but Emma feels too hot in her winter jacket.

'No, you – you *did* something to her. And then you found out she told my mom, so you lured her into the woods and—'

'Jesus, is that what you think of me?'

'I don't . . . no, I . . .' She's been thinking it all this time, so she doesn't understand why it's hard to say it now. 'But why take her into the woods, that night at the Tall Bones? I know it was you.'

'I didn't take her anywhere. She just came with me.' He looks down at his sneakers. 'She wanted me to give her some coke. She didn't want you to see.'

'No, Abi wasn't like that, I've known her my whole life.'

'She wasn't a very happy person, Emma. I'm sorry. But she talked about you all the time. She loved you, man, she just didn't want you to see that side to her.'

Emma digs the heels of her hands into her eyes and tries to concentrate on the pressure instead of the questions multiplying in her head: Abigail, Abi, who the hell are you? What was going so wrong that you couldn't tell me? What were you trying to hide?

'Hey,' says Hunter, 'you okay? Maybe you should sit down.'

She does, because she doesn't know what else to do. The stone is cool underneath her, sobering.

Abigail had seen the stretch marks on Emma's thighs, had watched the kids at school lay bare all her insecurities with comments about her size or shape or race, had listened to her sobbing down the phone about her loneliness. Abigail had wanted to know everything about Emma, had pulled it out of her, like loose threads, and there was a time when she gave pieces of herself back in exchange. Emma let Abigail know her. Isn't that what love is? But had she really understood Abi so little in return? It hits her now: Abigail's distance over the summer, always scratching at her skin, the way she had looked so worn out all the time, how Hunter had seemed almost friendly with her that night at junior prom. God, how had she not seen it?

Beside her, Hunter retrieves a cigarette from his pocket. 'You mind?'

Emma shakes her head.

'My parents would kill me if they knew. State play-offs this, college that, blah blah blah.'

Sometimes Emma wishes she knew how to smoke. Maybe she'd do that instead of drinking.

'Hey, can I ask, what were you doing talking to Shana anyway? Didn't know you two were friends.'

'We're not.' Emma stares at the lichen growing on the stonework. I only have one friend, she thinks, and now I don't even know who she is any more. 'I was asking her about you.'

Hunter laughs slightly. 'And what did good old Shana have to say?'

'She didn't believe me when I said I thought you'd done something to Abi. She said you were nice, that's all. Not like your dad. She doesn't like him very much.'

'Yeah, well, she can join the club. Bastard thinks he can get away with anything just because he owns half the town and he's friends with the pastor.' He sucks on his cigarette, eyes narrowed as he looks off into the trees. 'It's been, like, three weeks. Did you know that? Three whole weeks since Abi . . .'

'Yeah, I know.'

'Oh, hey, do you want to see something?' He retrieves an envelope from inside his jacket. 'I lent my camera to Beth Farmer that night and she's finally given me the pictures she took. Here's you and Abi, look.'

Their faces have the ethereal quality that the flash on film cameras often lends, and Abigail's pupils are red, making her look like some kind of demon, but it's them all right. Emma remembers Beth taking the photo – *Smile, girls,* she'd said, and Abigail had put her arm around Emma's shoulders and kissed her on the cheek. It had felt very special at the time, but looking at the picture now, it seems like the sort of thing you might do to a child. Patronizing. Emma kind of hates Abi a little bit for it. Kind of hates Hunter, too, for showing her the photo and ruining the memory.

'You can keep it, if you want,' he says.

'No, thanks.'

They sit there on the cold step a while longer – neither apparently ready to say anything more to the other yet – until Hunter's cigarette burns right down to his fingers, and he curses and throws it away. Beside him, Emma is very quiet, just staring at the photograph of her and Abigail. Then, all of a sudden, she holds up the picture and says, 'Was Abi wearing that cardigan when you two went into the woods?'

Hunter squints at the Polaroid. 'I don't know, it doesn't jump out at me.' And I would know, he thinks. He remembers the rest of the night with awful clarity.

'Are you sure?'

'Well, I mean, maybe. She could have been wearing it. Why does it matter? It's just a sweater.'

'Sheriff Gains said they found a cardigan a few days ago, in the river by the Tall Bones. He said it was all bloody.'

Hunter wishes now that he had another cigarette, but that was his last.

'Did you see anyone else that night in the woods?' Emma asks.

'You're really pushy, aren't you?'

'I care about Abi. I thought you said you did too.'

'Yeah, all right.' Hunter pushes his hair out of his face again. 'I mean, there were a lot of people at the party, you know?'

'Yeah, but when you and Abi went off to . . .' she makes a face '. . . get high, or whatever, did you see anyone then, in the forest? Anyone who shouldn't have been there?'

Hunter squeezes his eyes shut for a moment. *Anyone who shouldn't have been there*. I'm the one who wasn't where I was supposed to be, he thinks.

But the cardigan, that shouldn't have been there either. She *was* wearing it, wasn't she, when it happened? He remembers that look on her face – almost a smile – as the dark stain spread out into the cheap, pale wool. *Christ, Abi*. But if she was wearing it then, how did it end up downriver? It could have come off of its own accord, snagged on something perhaps, but all the same, he can't help thinking: Dead girls don't take off their clothes.

'What is it?' Emma asks. 'You looked like you were going to say something then.'

Hunter glances over his shoulder at the dark windows of his parents' house. 'There was someone else,' he says quietly. 'I saw my dad in the woods.'

Burying that bag of coke at the Winslow house, so it turned out, but Jerry could easily have flushed it down the toilet instead, so what was he doing out there? The track where Hunter spotted him leads to all sorts of forest trails. He recalls that evening in June, the way his father put his hand on Abigail's shoulder behind the Tysons' trailer, the way he looked at her, even as she walked away. Jerry Maddox would have taken her clothes off then, if he could.

He chews his thumbnail to keep his hands and mouth occupied. It makes him squirm to think what his father might have witnessed. But, worse now, he wonders: what else might his father have done?

30

SPEAK OF THE devil and he shall appear, Emma thinks, on her way back down the mountain, as she spots Jerry Maddox hammering a sign into the dead grass outside the trailer park. In large, handwritten letters it reads: 'AMERICANS ONLY'. For a moment she can hear the shouting again, feel Rat's arms around her as the two of them huddled under the table, while photographs and paperbacks rained down around them, light-bulbs shattered and candles toppled, spilling hardened wax along the floor. It is the memory of the pulse in his wrist, quick and terrified, as someone yelled, *Go back to your own country*, that makes her stop the car.

'Hey!' She winds the window all the way down and leans out. 'Hey, you can't do this.'

'You're on my property.'

'This isn't legal.'

'It's my land, I can do whatever I want, young lady, including shooting you for trespassing, so start that engine back up and get on out of here.' Jerry jerks his thumb down the road in the direction of town. 'And you leave my son alone while you're at it.'

As she ducks back in, Emma mutters, 'Is that what you said to Abi too?'

'What?'

She looks up to see him towering over her. He has dead eyes, she thinks, shark-like, as he places a hand on the roof of her car and leans in.

'You shouldn't go accusing people of things like that. Might get someone into real trouble someday.'

He is staring at her, not like he was the other night, when his wife was standing there beside him. This is different: it makes her feel as though she's only wearing underwear. Sharks feed in a frenzy, and she can feel something a little frenzied about him, something disruptive in the air between them. Is this the way he looked at Abigail? Maybe Hunter was on to something there.

Emma swallows. Her mouth is dry, her voice quiet: 'Leave me alone.'

Jerry straightens up. 'No, you leave *me* alone, young lady. And you keep your mouth shut about things you know nothing about.' He shakes his head, light bouncing off the patches where his hair has thinned. 'As bad as your daddy, you are, and just look where that got him.'

That hits her like a bucket of cold water. 'My dad?' She stares at him. 'What do you mean?'

But Jerry delivers a sudden kick to the side of her car that makes her jump in her seat.

'I told you, get out of here. Can't you read the sign? "Americans *only*" – go on, get!'

Emma watches her mother's chest in its uneven rise and fall, and wonders if Melissa is dreaming. She almost doesn't want to wake her. Her mother smells of hand soap and faintly of onion, and Emma clings to the familiarity of that, unsure if she will be allowed to after she has said what she needs to say.

Melissa's pale hair is splayed out across the pillow, but in the late-morning light gently filtering through the blinds, Emma can see there is more grey around the temples than there used to be. It shocks her a little, this obvious sign of ageing. She has always felt that her mother's age was something reliable, that she would always be roughly forty years old, that she always had been. That feeling isn't helped by the fact that she knows nothing about her mother's life before she came into it. But then, she thinks, that's the whole problem, isn't it?

'Em, is that you?' Melissa rolls over, slowly opening her eyes. 'God, did I fall asleep?'

'It's okay, you always sleep in late in the fall.' Emma says it like she's proud of knowing this detail, which she is – proud of knowing something private about her mother. She will keep all of these little facts like treasures, she decides, when Melissa is mad at her, which she inevitably will be.

'You've got that face on, Em. Are you okay?'

'I need to ask you something. About Dad.'

'You know I don't like . . .' Melissa sits up, pushing her hair back off her face. 'I prefer not to talk about him, you know that.'

Emma swallows, taking a deep breath of her mother's soap-and-onion scent. 'He didn't just leave, did he? Something happened to him.'

'Oh, he left all right.'

Emma has one memory, and even that is only fragments: the angle of her father's shoulder, the light from the streetlamp outside the open door, the blood on his hands.

'I remember him yelling at you the night he left.'

Melissa worries the duvet between her fingers.

'Please, Mom, this is important. Do you know where Dad is now? It's just, Jerry Maddox made it sound like—'

'Jerry Maddox? What have you been talking to him for? You keep away from that man, Em. He's as rotten as they come.'

'You're always telling me to keep away from people, but you won't tell me why. Did he do something to Dad? Did Sheriff Gains?'

'Emma, that's *enough*.' There's a tearing sound, and loose threads of cotton come away in her mother's hand. 'I said I don't want to talk about it. Christ, why can't you respect that?'

Quietly, Emma says, 'I do respect you, Mom,' because she knows that's what her mother really meant.

'You're poking your nose in somewhere you don't want to go, trust me.' Melissa shakes her head, wiping her cheek with the back of her hand. 'Your father left. Just leave it at that. For your own sake.'

'But he's my *dad*.'

'Oh, yes,' Melissa laughs faintly, 'and what a good job he's done, helping me raise you. Goddamn father of the year, that's Miguel. Em, he wouldn't even know you if he passed you on the street.'

'Mom—'

'For Christ's sake, Emma, just *leave it*.'

Hunter phones her during lunch. 'I got your number from Shana.' His voice is husky, like he's been smoking, and she can hear the distant sound of chatter echoing under the bleachers. 'Are you okay?'

'Yeah.' Emma sits cross-legged on her bed. 'Why wouldn't I be?'

'My dad got back before I left for school and he was *pissed*. Said you snuck up on him at the trailer park and started making accusations.'

'Oh.'

'Did you?'

'What? No. I mean, I might have mentioned something about Abi, but it was nothing. Seriously. He's the one who put up that sign. Have you seen it?'

'I saw him draw it himself.'

'That's kind of lame.'

Hunter laughs, which seems to surprise them both.

Don't get too comfortable, she reminds herself. Even if he was telling the truth about Abi, even if he didn't force himself on her, he still let her get off her face on cocaine. What sort of a friend does that? And, besides, he's one of *them*. The memory of prom night still makes her face warm with shame. Pastor Lewis's son and the other boys from the basketball team, the way they circled her in the school gym, the things they said . . . That's the world Hunter Maddox comes from. She mustn't forget that.

'Hey,' he says, and the soft uncertainty in his voice makes her want to ignore everything she's just told herself. 'Were you for real about that cardigan thing?'

'Of course I was. Sheriff Gains told me they found it in the river. Were you for real about seeing your dad that night?' She wraps a piece of her hair around her finger until the skin turns white.

'Yeah, I did see him. He told me he went to the Winslow house, but . . . I don't know, now I'm not so sure.'

The same place I saw the light, she thinks. 'Maybe you can find out. Does he have somewhere he might keep stuff he wouldn't want anyone else to see?'

'Not really. I mean . . . Oh, dude, his office at the mill. When I was there the other day he was being all shady about his desk.'

'Do you think you can get into it?' Hunter is quiet again for a moment and Emma winces. 'Sorry. I'm getting carried away. This is all kind of crazy.'

After a moment he says, 'You know I saw them together? Abi and my dad? At the trailer park back in the summer.'

'What do you mean "together"?'

'They were just talking, but it was weird. He was weird.' Hunter groans. 'This is all such a mess. That coke you and Rat found, it was mine to begin with.'

What surprises Emma most is how little this comes as a shock. After all she's heard in the last few days, she isn't sure what to think about anybody in Whistling Ridge any more.

'I can't get into that right now,' says Hunter, 'but my dad buried the coke at Winslow – at least, that's what he said. He made out like that's why he was in the woods the night Abi disappeared, but I can't stop thinking about the way he was with her. Something's off.'

Down the line, Emma hears the school bell signalling the end of lunch break. Hunter says, 'The mill's always empty on Sundays. If I go next weekend, after it gets dark, it should be fine. You want to come with me?'

'What – break into your dad's office?'

'Might make you feel better about his dumb sign.'

Through the open bedroom door, Emma can see her mother lying in bed with her back to her. Earlier she got up, showered, dressed, made a bit of late breakfast, but then she had moved around like a ghost, following, trance-like, some route through the house that only she understood. Then she had gone back to bed – still wearing her socks, her makeup, her earrings, and Emma thought that was as bad as seeing her naked.

'Sure,' she tells Hunter. 'Not like I'm doing much around here anyway.'

'Cool. Well, we should go in my car – that way it won't look weird. I'll pick you up at six next Sunday. But keep it to yourself, okay?

'Okay.'

'Hey, Emma?'

'Yeah?'

'I'm sorry about my dad.'

Emma flops back on to the bed and screws up her face. It's much harder to hate him when he talks like that. Is this why Abi chose to confide in him? But look where that got her, Emma thinks. *I mustn't make the same mistake.*

31

On Sunday, as church is getting out, Samuel grips his eldest son by the arm and says, 'Wait here.'

The people filing past pretend not to look at them, these rough-cut men standing together by the door. Noah makes a point of not looking at his father either – keeping the tender side of his face directed at the wall so that nobody can see – so he doesn't know Samuel is staring at him. Doesn't know that when Samuel pictures himself, he is always Noah's age, looks just like him, and then it comes as a shock to see his reflection and realize that he is practically an old man. *My son has all my youth and he's frittering it away.* Samuel thinks that sometimes, but then other days he reckons he never had any youth to speak of. Shot a woman in the back when he was only eighteen. How do you stay young after that?

When everyone has gone and there is only the wind blowing armfuls of dead leaves through the parking lot, Samuel says, 'I didn't want it to come to this.'

Noah simply chews his lip, like he always does.

'You're going to give yourself an ulcer, boy, stop that.' Samuel shakes his head. 'Some of the things I saw over in 'Nam . . . I understand shame, don't think I don't. The Lord understands shame. *He will not suffer you to be tempted above that you are able;*

but will with the temptation also make a way to escape, that you may be able to bear it. There is no condemnation for those who truly walk in the light of Jesus Christ, just you remember that. But as a rule, boy, you don't shit where you eat. This is my place of worship. I didn't want it to come to this.'

Noah says, 'Yes, sir.'

'But after what you pulled at the sheriff's station last week, after your little publicity stunt with that gypsy boy, I don't see as we've got much of a choice.'

We have to be seen to be doing something about it, he thinks, otherwise what kind of a father would I be?

'You listen to Pastor Lewis now. He'll know how to help you. Remember your Isaiah: *For the Lord God will help me; therefore shall I not be confounded: therefore have I set my face like a flint, and I know that I shall not be ashamed.*'

Noah puts his hands into his pockets.

'Go on, then,' says Samuel. 'I'm going over to O'Shannon's. Text me when you're done – I'll come pick you up.'

'Yes, sir.'

Samuel thinks his son sounds tired.

'Noah.' Pastor Lewis smiles at him. 'Come on in and sit down.'

The heating in the church hall still hasn't been fixed, but here in the pastor's office there is a small electric fan heater whirring away, and Noah feels too hot in his thick corduroy jacket and scarf. He takes a seat on the little plastic chair – a child's chair from the Sunday school – and watches the pastor steeple his fingers together over his desk.

'So, your father told me over the phone a little about what's been going on with you. I should tell you, whenever I go to conferences and meet with others in my line of work, it's evident that this sort of thing is becoming much more common, these days. You shouldn't place all the blame on yourself,

Noah. The society we live in celebrates – even encourages – homosexual behaviour, and you poor kids have got it coming at you twenty-four-seven, left and right, with your social media and TV shows. It's not surprising there's so much confusion among young people today.'

Noah shifts on the tiny chair, trying to get some air into his jacket. It feels as if he's being slow-cooked.

Pastor Lewis is still smiling at him. 'I've known you since you were born. I know you're a good kid. You don't want to go worrying your parents, do you? You don't want to give them this kind of stress when they're busy dealing with what's happened to your sister.'

'No, sir.' Noah thinks, What do you know about what's happened to my sister?

'That's good to hear, young man. That's good to hear. Now, your father said you were interested in some of the therapy options that our church has to offer?'

'Therapy?' In the stuffy office, Noah can feel sweat sticking his clothes to the contours of his body. This isn't how it was supposed to go. He'd overheard his parents talking, knew his father was angling to take him to the pastor, so Noah had stayed up most of the night revising quotes from Leviticus, Romans and Revelation, learning like some awful nursery rhyme every argument Pastor Lewis might make and every one of Jesus's own words that he could use in rebuttal. He'd had it all figured out (and, hell, he wished he'd done it sooner, because Jesus sure had a lot to say about love, and Noah had even begun to feel, if not better, then at least *less bad*), but now he realizes he and the pastor have been reading from two separate scripts long before Noah ever walked into his office.

'You look worried there, son. Did your father not talk this through with you?' Pastor Lewis nods sagely. 'I understand if you're concerned: honesty between family members is important, but you must understand that through your actions *you* have been dishonest. Not just with your family but also with yourself.' He smiles again. 'Your father only wants what's best for you, to help you see the love of God and Jesus Christ.'

Noah can't believe what he's hearing. 'My father?' He sticks his neck out, tilting his face up so the pastor can see him clearly, and points to the healing scabs on his cheek. 'My father did this.' Turning the other way, he shows Pastor Lewis the bruise on his jaw from the previous week. 'And this. And it's not the first time either. My brother walks in here every week on his busted leg and you've never said a word about that. Now my sister is missing and you – you want to talk about God's love? Well, where is it? Because hell knows we've never seen any of it.'

Pastor Lewis's smile has gone. '*As a father shows compassion to his children, so the Lord shows compassion to those who fear Him*. He reserves His love for the God-fearing, Noah. It seems to me you are no longer one of them.'

Can it really be love if God has to threaten you for it first? Noah thinks of the way, months ago now, he had asked Rat if he could kiss him, standing in the Winslow ruins with the sunlight coming through the trees. And Rat had smiled – a real smile, not that cocky thing he does with his tongue between his teeth to get people's attention – and stood up on the balls of his feet to kiss him first. There had been no bargaining, no intimidation, none of God's usual tricks. That was love, and Rat had never demanded he grew some backbone to receive it either.

'No,' Noah says.

Pastor Lewis blinks at him. 'Excuse me?'

'I . . .' He can feel himself hovering slightly above the chair, not standing, but no longer sitting either, like he can't quite decide where he wants to be. 'If I want fear I'll go to my father. I'm done with the fear of God.'

'Then, son, I'm afraid to say,' Pastor Lewis spreads his hands out in the air in the same lackadaisical way Noah sometimes does when he has to tell customers at the diner that they're all out of bagels, 'you're broken.'

Noah stares at him. None of the passages he memorized last night prepared him for that.

'As it is written in the First Epistle of John, *If we confess our sins, He is faithful and just to forgive us our sins and to cleanse us from all unrighteousness.* But God can't show you forgiveness, Noah, if you don't show Him you understand what you did wrong.'

'I told you, I don't want His forgiveness. And Jesus said—'

'Jesus isn't saying this, I am. You can only be fixed if you want to be, so until you want to be, you're broken. And this church has got no more use for you than your daddy does.'

'Melissa.'

'Dolly.'

'What – did you come to bring me another casserole?'

There's something about the way she says it that makes Melissa leave a good few feet between them as she follows Dolly through to the kitchen. She reeks of cigarettes; Melissa has to breathe through her mouth.

'You can just leave it on the side there.' Dolly gestures to the countertop with her elbow, already preoccupied with lighting up a Dunhill.

'Actually, I didn't bring anything.'

Melissa holds up her empty hands, and Dolly just nods mechanically, talking around a mouthful of smoke. 'You'll have to excuse me. I've had other things on my mind lately.'

'How are you holding up?'

'How do you think? Nobody will tell me anything. Police won't even tell me if the blood on my daughter's cardigan belonged to her or not. They must have heard back by now.'

Oh, yes, the poor girl's cardigan. 'These things can take time, Dolly. Especially if it had to go all the way to Denver. I expect they have a lot more of this kind of stuff to deal with down there.'

'You mean murder?' Dolly shakes her head. 'They just don't care, that's all. They hardly cared when she first went missing, got it into their heads that she'd just run off. Now they won't give me any kind of answer.' She leans against the edge of the table, looking Melissa up and down. 'What do you want, then?'

'Well, actually, do you mind if I sit down?'

'Samuel will be back soon, just so you know.'

Melissa feels as though that is supposed to frighten her, but she takes a seat at the table anyway, too tired to be afraid or upright. She watches Dolly staring out of the kitchen window, the glass clouded around the edges with ineffable grime. Back in the days when Melissa used to bring Emma over to play, this house always felt like the sort of place that stuck to you and wouldn't come off. There were always tiles missing by the back door, the plaster bubbling up behind the sink. But it seems worse now – perhaps because a child is missing, or perhaps because Dolly Blake feels like a stranger where once she had been a friend.

'Do your kids ever lie to you?' Melissa asks.

'Does yours ever tell the truth?'

Melissa smiles, because she thinks that might be a joke. 'That bad, huh?'

'Didn't invite you in so you could sit and judge me.'

'I wasn't—'

'God, you have no idea.' Dolly tilts her head back, eyes half closed, yellow fingernails tapping a faint rhythm on the countertop. 'I'm not a bad mother, you know.'

'I never said you were.'

'You're not a bad mother either. Sometimes I think all mothers worry they're doing it wrong, but then I think about my own mom and I . . .' She straightens up, as straight as a crooked tree like her can grow. 'You're lucky you've only got the one kid. Sometimes I wish I only had one.'

'Oh.'

Dolly's mouth trembles and she sucks hard on her cigarette. 'It's not that I don't love them, I'm just not good at being a parent and it pisses me off. I was only ever good with Abi, maybe because she's a girl . . . Sam can't stand those boys, and he can't stand me for having them.' Her voice comes out thin. 'My baby girl. She's gone now.' Dolly covers her face as it reddens.

Melissa gets up and rubs her shoulder. 'It's all right, hey, it's all right.'

'No, you don't understand. You think you're so good and that you can make me good by coming round here and being *kind*, but you don't know what I've done.'

'People make mistakes, Dolly, it's all right.'

'No, not like this. Not like I did.'

Melissa puts her arm around her and Dolly slumps against her side.

'I don't think I'm good, you know,' Melissa says, after a while. 'You said I think I'm so good, but I don't, Dolly.'

'You are, Mel, you're a good woman. Not like me. Sometimes I feel like I'm all rotten on the inside, like if you pressed on me too hard my skin would just . . .' She makes a shrinking gesture with her free hand. 'And I'd be all grey and mouldy underneath.'

I know, Melissa wants to say. I know exactly what you mean because that is guilt and I feel it too.

'Dolly, I did something terrible once.'

Why have I come here? Melissa wonders. Maybe she simply missed her friend. It's not been easy watching Samuel shorten her leash over the years, restricting who can come over to the house, how much money Dolly can spend, whom she's allowed to meet up with and when. *Sam really needs me at home*, Dolly used to tell her, until eventually Melissa got tired of trying.

Or perhaps, deep down, what she really wants is for this other woman's sorrow to break open a chink of light in her own. 'You've lost your daughter,' she says. 'I'm afraid I'm losing mine too.'

Dolly looks up. 'Has something happened to Emma?'

'She asked me about her father the other day.' *God, I could have handled that better.* 'Ever since then, she just keeps looking past me, you know, like she isn't really seeing me. Like she's seeing somebody else.'

Melissa stares out of the window now, at the wilderness encroaching on the Blakes' backyard, at the animal bones hung from the trees, at the dead leaves collecting in the hollows. Emma used to play here. There will always be a part of Emma in this house, and she realizes that is why she came.

'I'm worried Emma's going to find out what really happened.'

Melissa thinks she would have been relieved then, for Dolly to ask, to draw the past out of her, like venom from a snakebite. But Dolly doesn't seem to hear. She is picking at her scalp, dandruff drifting down on to the front of her sweater, and she sounds distracted when she says, 'I did something terrible once too. And I think maybe that's why Abigail is gone.'

32

'ELEANOR!'

Dolly hears Ann Traxler's reedy voice from the aisle next to the frozen foods and she lets her shopping cart roll to a stop.

'Eleanor, is it true about the Blake boy?'

'Really, Ann. That was a private conversation between my husband and one of his parishioners.'

Since Melissa's visit this afternoon, Dolly has been on edge, and she thinks if the pastor's wife were standing in front of her now, she might just run her over with her cart.

'But he told you, didn't he?' says Ann. 'Maggie Tucker says it's all over the sheriff's station, what that boy did. And Debbie says she saw that awful father staying behind with him after church this morning.'

Dolly grips the cart handle until she thinks her knucklebones might burst through the skin. Goddamn it, Sam, you said you were just going to talk to Noah. I said, Don't you take him to Ed Lewis, it's none of that man's business, and you said, No, we're just going to talk.

'Well, it sounds like you know already,' says Eleanor, 'so what can I possibly have to add?'

But she's just warming up to it, Dolly thinks – she can hear it in Eleanor's voice. Getting the crowd pumped like a little cheerleader before the touchdown.

'All I know,' Eleanor says, and Dolly notes she doesn't even have the decency to lower her voice, 'is that he was rude as anything to Ed. Called him a Fascist and a bigot.'

'You're *kidding*.'

'Luckily Ed's got a thicker skin than most people nowadays, but honestly, you never heard anything like it.'

'I can't believe that.'

Neither can I, thinks Dolly. She can't imagine slouchy, quiet Noah calling anybody a Fascist.

'You know what they say, Ann, blood will out. There's a lack of parenting there. Some kids today just aren't raised right.'

In the frozen-food aisle, Dolly feels as though a soccer ball has come out of the blue and hit her right in the head.

'Still,' says Ann, '*gay* – that's quite dramatic. I wonder what the father will have to say about that.'

'Oh, I doubt he'll say anything. My guess is he'll probably just beat the boy stupid, and I for one won't be sorry. Spare the rod, spoil the son, you know. Oh, the way he behaved with poor Ed.'

'Poor Ed,' Ann agrees.

'He was only doing his job – the Lord's work, at that. A sin is a sin, no matter what sort of times we live in. Someone has to take a stand.'

Dolly recalls what she said to Melissa that afternoon, *It's not that I don't love them, I'm just not good at it*, and decides that is quite enough. She rounds the corner into their aisle, standing up straight behind her shopping cart like she used to do, before Abigail disappeared. Out of the corner of her eye, she sees Ann Traxler open her mouth, but Dolly just says, 'Good evening, ladies,' and keeps on walking.

Behind her, Eleanor mutters, 'Now look, Ann. You shouldn't have been talking so loud.'

Noah pulls up at the trailer park with a tank of gasoline he stole from the back of his father's truck. He would have come sooner, but ever since the sheriff's station last weekend, he has felt Samuel's eyes on him whenever he so much as looked at the front door. After his encounter with Pastor Lewis this morning, though, Noah just doesn't care any more.

Although it is evening, there is no light coming from the RV, and he wonders at first if Rat is even in there, but when he moves closer, he can smell the cigarette smoke coming from inside. As he makes his way to the door, something crunches underfoot. Lifting his boot, he sees broken glass glinting in the moonlight.

'Hey, it's me. Are you there?'

The door swings open when he pushes it, releasing a strip of orange light, and it's then that he realizes the windows have been taped over. 'What happened here?'

Rat is sitting on the floor, cradling his grandmother's guitar. All of the furniture that wasn't nailed down has vanished, and almost everything that was on the ceiling – his postcards and poems, his maps of home – has gone too. The guitar's fretboard dangles loose like a broken limb, and he strokes one of the tuning keys with his thumb as he says, 'Some of your congregation paid me a visit last week. Didn't you hear?'

Noah goes to him, cupping his chin in his hand. Despite the fall night Rat's skin feels hot, his eyes red around the edges, like he's halfway between having cried before and being about to cry again.

'They took your stuff?'

'Broke it. I had to throw most of it away.'

'Jesus. You should have called me.'

'I already got you in enough trouble. It's fine, they let up after a while. I think they figured I wasn't home.'

Noah sits down beside him, suddenly exhausted by the adrenalin that's kept him going ever since he walked out of Pastor Lewis's office. 'I told you, man. You should have gotten out of town while you had the chance.'

Rat looks at the broken guitar. 'I was doing okay, actually, but then I sat down to play, and . . . This was everything I had, you know. Everything I had left from before.'

'Before you came to America, you mean?' Noah watches him carefully, feeling as though he's trying to coax some animal to eat out of his hand.

Rat shakes his head. 'I didn't get to thank you properly, did I? For showing up at the station, I mean.'

'Don't mention it.'

'Come on, Blake, I know it cost you.' He touches a finger to Noah's jaw, to the brownish bruise that Samuel left last weekend. 'I'm sorry.'

'In the end, I just figured . . .' Noah sighs. 'Man, you mess me up. You and your bluesy guitar fingers. The way you look at me sometimes, I feel like this whole other person, and, I don't know, maybe that's the person I'm supposed to be.'

'Blake.'

'Look, I don't know how to say what I'm trying to say, but I need you to understand that I'm trying to say it.'

'Hey, now, where's all this coming from?'

Noah can't tell him about what happened this morning, about Pastor Lewis. He doesn't think he can ever tell anybody about that. The word *therapy* still feels like an oily thing stuck to him that he can't get off. It is accompanied by vague images of needles and vomiting, and even though he senses that probably isn't what conversion therapy means any more, he can't make them go away. Not like this, anyway. He left the pastor's office feeling so angry it was as though someone was digging their nails hard into his scalp. He'd wanted to break everything he came into contact with, and as the day went on, far from cooling, the feeling became something sharp and certain until he knew exactly what it was he wanted to break.

'I'm sorry about your RV,' he says. 'There's something wrong with those people.'

'Yeah, well.' Rat reaches down and plucks one of the guitar strings. The note sounds so lonely, it makes Noah's chest swell.

'I can make it up to you for real.'

Rat sighs. 'Promises, promises, Blake.'

'No, I mean it. Do you want to burn down the church with me?'

The radio cuts in and out on the lonely stretches of road between the town and the lumber mill, fragments of voices from mismatched conversations drifting through the car. At one point there is a loud burst of static, and Emma and Hunter glance at one another as a muffled voice says: *'And thou shalt eat the fruit of thine own body, the flesh of thy sons and of thy daughters, which the Lord thy God hath given thee.'*

Steep rock faces make everything secret here, collecting the dusk shadows. Disused agricultural buildings bleed into the undergrowth, all broken wooden slats and rusted corrugated metal, with 'Jesus saves' painted ten feet tall on one side. It seems strange to Emma that a place like the mill, which provides so many jobs and drives most of the town's commerce, should be so far away. She has never really been out here before. As they drive past a dead coyote strung up on a fence by its tail, it occurs to her that nobody knows she is there, not even her mother, who is working late at the clinic.

If something happens, she thinks, it could be days before anyone finds me.

The mill is bathed in the greasy glow of nighttime industrial lighting. It's just the outside that's always lit, Hunter assures her. There won't be anyone inside. He parks behind a tree so that the car can't be seen from the road, and then the two of them hurry across the timber yard and in through the emergency exit.

They creep past the silent machinery, serrated blades glinting slyly in the beam of Hunter's flashlight. His father's office is at the top of a flight of stairs, overlooking the main saw room, and the door is locked.

'Hold this a minute,' he says, handing Emma the flashlight. He pulls out a set of keys and jingles them in front of her face. 'Dad didn't even notice.'

Emma frowns. 'Doesn't it bother you how easy this seems?'

'Would you rather it was harder?' He unlocks the door and motions for her to go in. 'You check the desk. I'll stand guard.'

'I thought you said there was no one here.'

'And you said it was too easy. I'm just spicing it up a bit for you.'

Emma rolls her eyes and presses the flashlight back into his hand, using the torch on her phone instead. It is not a large office and the desk takes up most of the far end, but her heart sinks as she roots through one accounts ledger after another. 'Hunter, it's just books. Books and numbers.'

'No, come on. There has to be more than that.' With a cursory glance down the stairs, he leaves his post and nudges her out of the way. 'Try the drawers. He was looking at something in there the other day, I'm telling you.'

'Come on, Hunter, there's nothing. Let's just go before someone finds us.'

'Relax, I told you, no one's here.' He wrenches the top drawer open with a sound that makes Emma wince.

'I don't want another run-in with your dad.'

Hunter pulls a face as he reaches further into the desk. 'Hold up.'

'What is it?'

He holds out his hand to reveal a little tube of strawberry Chapstick. 'Oh, man.' She can see Hunter's throat bob as he swallows. 'That's hers, isn't it?'

A light comes on downstairs, suddenly illuminating the office.

Emma grabs the Chapstick from Hunter and stuffs it back into the drawer. 'Hide,' she hisses, 'quick, behind the desk. Hunter, come *on*.'

She just manages to pull him down beside her when they hear footsteps on the stairs.

33

Dolly switches on the kettle and watches her husband stacking logs by the back door. Suddenly she imagines slinging the boiling kettle at him, catching him right in the head with the scalding metal.

'Wish you'd get a new one of those,' he says, not looking up. 'Hate the noise of that one.'

Yes, she thinks, catch him right in the head and maybe he'd explode, like one of the beer bottles he and Abigail used to shoot off the fence at the bottom of the yard. Break his skull the way he's broken her spirit. She can't get it out of her head, what they said at Safeway this evening, Ann Traxler and the pastor's wife: *There's a lack of parenting there.* Before now, she might have agreed. She might have settled into the understanding that she was a failed mother as easily as pulling on a familiar pair of boots, but there was something different about today. Today Melissa had come into her kitchen, stood where Samuel is crouching now, like he didn't scare her. Years ago, he had made it very clear – with the back of his hand and the buckle on his belt – that they were not to have any more guests in this house, that Dolly could only see who he said she could, yet today Melissa had walked in bold as anything. Samuel wasn't there, so in that moment he had been powerless to stop her. Now, the very idea of going against him makes Dolly feel reckless.

'Why did you do it?' she asks.

Samuel stands up, wiping his hands on his jeans, getting bits of bark all over the floor. 'Do what?'

'I told you last night I didn't want you taking Noah to see Ed Lewis, but I overheard Eleanor at Safeway, Sam. She was talking about it.'

Samuel rolls his eyes as he turns away. 'The women round here need to learn to stop running their mouths.'

'But why did you do it? I told you I—'

'A cripple and a queer, that's what you've given me, Dolly. Those are the boys I'm supposed to raise. Damn it, you can't blame me for wanting to fix them.'

'*I* gave you? You threw Jude down the stairs!'

'And you were totally blameless, were you? It had nothing to do with your parenting, the way things got out of control? You're always so soft with them, like nothing I say matters in this house. I'm only trying to show them what the Lord wants, Dolly. I'm thinking about eternity here – I'm thinking about their souls.'

'That's what you're doing, is it?'

'If you want them to join us in Heaven, Dolly, then you have to put the time in now.'

Dolly bites her lip. She had enjoyed the look on Ann Traxler's face when she walked past her in the grocery store earlier. She had enjoyed being on her son's side. 'What about your soul, Sam?' she says. 'If Heaven's full of men who beat their children, I'll take my chances elsewhere.'

'You—!'

It's been a while since he smacked her. The indents of his knuckles feel almost familiar, and she closes her eyes because it is just as much of a release for her now as it is for him.

There is some wild sensation bubbling up inside of her, and just for a moment, a very small voice that sounds like some younger version of herself whispers: Go on, smack me again, and maybe this time I'll smack you back.

'Mom?'

Jude stands in the doorway, leaning on his stick. His face is pale, and Dolly knows, from the way his eyes keep drifting to his father, that he saw everything.

'What is it?' she says, and Samuel huffs.

'Your mother and I are trying to have a conversation.'

'I . . . I know, but . . .'

'Spit it out, kid.'

Dolly can see her son's throat bob as he swallows, glancing at his mother's throbbing cheek, and then again at his father.

'Noah's not answering his phone. He's just . . . gone.'

Rat is dancing in the church. Noah pours gasoline over the chairs and the carpet and the podium where Pastor Lewis always stands, as Rat tosses his head back and shakes, like he's getting slain in the spirit. The gasoline fumes make Noah lightheaded and he says, 'Give me your lighter.'

Rat looks suddenly serious. 'You're not really going to burn it down, are you?'

'What did you think we were going to do?'

'I don't know, break in and trash the place a bit.'

'This isn't all for nothing. They deserve it. This whole town deserves to go up in flames.'

'They'll crucify you.'

Noah laughs but Rat tangles his fingers in his hair. 'They'll kill you this time, Blake, I mean it. Your dad and that bullshit preacher man. They'll kill you. It's not worth it.'

'So, what? We just do nothing?'

'So we pack up and go, Blake. Come on, run away with me.'

'You don't understand.' Noah presses their foreheads together. 'I have to. *They* have to know what it feels like.'

Rat's breath is warm against his mouth. 'There are other ways, *dragă*.'

When one thing smells like gasoline, everything smells like gasoline, Noah thinks, even Rat, who takes his face in both his hands and kisses him, swiftly, sweetly, whispering, 'Here – here,' and he kisses him again. 'This is how we burn it down.'

And while his mother feels the back of her husband's hand across her face, Noah runs his own hands over a body he has learned by heart, like a nursery rhyme in Braille, and in the red and blue pools of stained-glass light, he takes communion on his knees. His God knows his name and calls it at the top of his lungs, arms outstretched like Christ on the cross, while their affirmations echo in the empty room that smells of gasoline.

Samuel has taken Jude out to help him look for Noah, so it is Dolly who answers the phone to Sheriff Gains.

'I see,' she says.

'Dolly, I'm sorry.'

'No. Thank you. Goodnight, Sheriff.'

She is glad, then, that there is no one in the house to hear her as she collapses to the floor and wails.

Is it all her fault? She told Melissa she'd done a terrible thing once. Done a terrible thing to Abigail. But is this her God-given punishment – to have lost her only daughter? She wants to tear her hair out, leave chunks of bloody scalp all over the living-room floor for Samuel to find when he comes home. What part of this is God's plan? she will say. Why did God shoot our little girl?

Out loud she says, 'I've just about had it with You.'

In the hallway, the coloured stones on the cross wink at her, as if they know something she doesn't, the smug light dancing off each chintzy facet. Until Dolly picks up the kettle and smashes it right through the middle. Her arms move with a tireless anger, the ball of fury burning white-hot in her chest once again.

At last she drops the kettle, hears it clatter against the floorboards as she stands, panting, surrounded by flecks of stone. The hole in the wall looms like some dark throat leading to the recesses of the house. She has never looked behind the cross, not since the day she hung it up, but she is sure that ball of paper wasn't there all those years ago.

The flame in her chest is doused right out when she sees her daughter's handwriting. The long loops of the Gs and Ys, the heavy rightwards slant, the way she drew full little circles on top of the Is and Js – Oh, yes, yes, she thinks, pressing the pages to her lips before she's even read them. They even smell like her still, just a little. The pages are all ragged along one edge, as though they have been torn out, and Dolly knows at once that this is her daughter's diary.

Tell me, she begs as she begins to scan the lines, tell me your secrets, sweetheart.

Tell me what happened.

'Hunter, I know you're in here.'

Behind the desk, Hunter's eyes are wide and pale in the dark.

'I know it was you who took my keys,' his father says, taking another heavy step into the office. 'You really didn't think I'd notice?'

Emma puts her hand over her mouth to quiet her breathing. Hunter bites down on his lip.

'I don't know what possessed you to come snooping around

here at night.' The floorboards groan as Jerry makes his way further into the room. 'But just come on out, and we can talk about it like adults.'

Emma feels Hunter squeezing her hand and then he mouths, *Run*. She shakes her head. The office is too small and Jerry's a big guy: there is no way she'd get past him. Hunter looks at her like he understands, but before she can stop him, he stands up.

'There you are,' says Jerry. 'What do you think you're up to in here?'

'Dad, did you do something to Abigail Blake?'

'For God's sake, Hunter, she's irrelevant. I thought we'd been over this.'

'She was relevant enough for you to hang on to her Chapstick.'

'Ah. Look, Hunter, it's not what you think. Come on now, come with me. Your mother's worried about you.'

'Shit, Dad. The town's going to want your head when they find out.'

'Find out what? It's just a lipstick, it doesn't mean anything.'

'How can you keep saying things like that? How can you keep lying?'

'Oh, so now my son the drug dealer, the gun thief, is going to give me a lecture about honesty.'

At the mention of the gun, Emma gasps, and from behind the desk she feels the room go still.

'Is there someone else here, Hunter?'

'No.'

'Yes, there is, there's someone here.'

The floor creaks as Jerry elbows past his son and leans over the desk. Emma tries to push herself further underneath, but it's too late; he grabs hold of her wrist and hauls her up.

'Well, now, look at that, like father like daughter.' He squeezes her wrist so hard she thinks her hand might pop off like a champagne cork.

'Dad, let her go. She hasn't done anything.'

'You think you know something?' Jerry takes hold of Emma by the shoulder now, shaking her slightly. 'You think you know something about me? I can deal with you just like I dealt with your daddy, little girl, and don't think that I won't.'

Emma can't speak, can't even breathe.

'Come on, Dad, let her go. We won't tell anyone, I swear. Just put her down.'

'You stay out of this. These people have to learn someday.'

'Jesus, Dad,' Hunter says, and clocks him in the face.

Jerry lets go of her and Emma bolts for the door, not even stopping to check if Hunter is following. She bursts out of the emergency exit and runs until her chest hurts and her throat is so dry she can taste blood in the back of her mouth. Branches snag on her clothes and hair as she tears through the woods, her heart beating so fast she swears she can feel it thumping against her ribs, certain that any second now it's going to give out.

She knows she can't have run much more than half a mile – she can still see the mill chimney beyond the tops of the trees – but it feels like she's been pushing herself for hours by the time she stumbles out into the road, hands on her knees to steady herself as she gulps down air, and coming round the corner in his pick-up truck, Samuel Blake only just manages to slam on the brakes in time.

34

Then

Abigail, sitting with her bare legs dangling out of her bedroom window, feels sick with the hazy sameness of July. The sun going down over the mountains looks like God cracked an egg over the peaks and the yolky light is running down through the grooves left by glaciers long ago. A weak breeze stirs her father's bone wind chimes in the trees below, and Abigail digs her nails into her thighs.

At eight thirty, her mother comes in to say goodnight. 'School tomorrow, sweetheart. Don't stay up too late.'

'Goodnight, Mom.'

Her mother waggles her fingers at her as if she were saying goodbye to a baby. Abigail grits her teeth and grins.

A little while later, Noah stands in her doorway, stooped, like he isn't sure how to fill up the space. There is a big tender-looking mark just above his eye. He asks if he can borrow her foundation powder.

'What did you do?' They both know what she means is: What did you do to piss Dad off?

'I put all the leftovers in the same Tupperware box.'

'Rookie mistake,' says Abigail. Their father does not like

his food touching; but she knows this because she asked him once and he explained (something about a turkey dinner and a garbage can, a long time ago). She's never had the knowledge beaten into her.

Noah narrows his eyes. 'Are you going to give me the makeup or not? I can't go to work tomorrow with my face like this.'

'Hey,' she says, when she's given him the compact and he's turning to go. 'When did you start smoking?'

His cheeks colour as red as the budding bruise on his forehead. 'I don't smoke.'

'You smell like you do.' She gives him a look that she hopes is sympathetic. 'You should get one of those spray-on deodorants and just spray it all over. And always brush your teeth first thing when you get in. If they ask, just say you had one of Mom's Dunhills.'

Noah stares at her. 'I don't smoke,' he says again, and he doesn't close the door behind him.

She's glad he didn't ask her how she knew about covering it up like that.

At eleven she gets a text. *End of the road*, it says. She changes out of her pyjamas and puts on the little black velvet dress that she keeps at the back of her closet. She has to hitch it up over her hips as she shimmies down the trellis, but there's nobody around to see. That is always the first excitement of the night: it gives her a little thrill, being exposed like that in the dark.

Hunter is waiting for her at the end of Hickory Lane. He cuts a line of methadone on the dashboard of his car and they snort half each, then roll down the windows and howl like coyotes as they take off into the night.

'You haven't told me how it went,' she says, while they slip through miles of black forest.

'Kind of weird, I guess. I had to meet the guy on the third storey of some parking lot. And the light overhead was real glitchy, kept flickering on and off. It was like a horror movie.'

Abigail nods to say, *Yes, I expect it was, you're very brave,* because men need to be treated with kid gloves. She understands that now. 'Did you get it, though?'

'Oh, your boy got it, don't you worry.' He grins at her. 'Cleared out my allowance for the last few months, but it'll be worth it.'

Abigail doesn't feel sorry for him: he's probably the only kid in town who gets a hundred dollars in pocket money every month.

'Thirty grams of coke. Nobody can get that kind of shit up here. We're going to make all sorts of profit. We're laughing, Abi.'

We're laughing, he says, although neither of them does.

They drive on, past cabins and outbuildings slouched in the tall grass, like skeletons of long-dead animals, their lights flickering with a hum that Abigail swears she can hear even from inside the car.

After a while she asks, 'What was it like in Boulder?'

'You've been to Boulder.'

'Feels like years ago.' Maybe it was.

Hunter sighs. 'Yeah, I mean, it was Boulder, you know? I tried to order a muffin and it was gluten-free *and* sugar-free. I mean, come on. A sugar-free muffin. As if the world isn't disappointing enough already.'

Abigail smiles at that. Hunter can make her smile, sometimes, and that is enough. She wishes she had gone with him, but just the sight of a road sign to Denver might have made her want to take off then and there, and she knows they can't do that, knows they have to be smart about it.

She tries to imagine what it will be like when they cross

the state line. Last night she looked it up online, and she hopes it isn't true – that Kansas is just miles and miles of nothing, empty roads and rows of silent corn and rest stops that all appear the same. Is that really what freedom will look like? *At least it won't look like here.*

There are kids between the trees up at the Tall Bones. They drive each other wild, rutting up against one another like dogs in heat, snorting lines off each other's arms and stomachs and collarbones. Some of the boys smack each other about a bit, grinning with blood between their teeth.

Hunter gets out his Polaroid camera, takes pictures and, as always, no one offers to take any of him. When he gets bored – Abigail knows he's bored because he starts drinking – he sits on the trunk of his car and sells bumps of their new coke for twice as much as these kids could buy it down in Boulder. They'd probably smack him about too, if they knew he was scamming them like that, but then most of them have never been to Boulder. Most of them have never been anywhere.

Abigail prefers getting high to getting drunk. All these people ever have to drink is beer, and that makes them smell like her father. She likes it when she gets to snort something out of a rolled-up dollar bill. It makes her feel like what she is: Trash, she thinks. I'm as trashy as they come.

Two lines in and she gets up on top of Hunter's car and starts dancing, because this is where everyone is congregating to buy his cocaine, so this is where she will be seen. Cole and Luke Weaver holler at her to take off her dress. She hitches the skirt up a little higher and shakes her ass, tossing her hair back, running her hands over her body. Bryce Long yells that he loves her. Yes, she thinks, I'm beautiful. I'm trash and I'm beautiful and you all want me, but it's me, I'm in control, I can take it away just like that.

*

'Stop it,' she says. 'No, I don't – *stop it*.'

Bryce pins her against the tree with one arm and shoves his other hand up between her legs. 'Yes, you do,' he says. 'You don't dance like that if you don't want it, so just keep still now.'

She can see the lights of the party a little way off through the branches and she tries to scream, but he pushes his mouth down over hers and kisses her hard, swallowing the sound.

No, no, no, this isn't how it's supposed to go, she thinks frantically. You want me because I make you want me, but you don't get to *have* me, that's not how it's supposed to work, you're ruining it, you're ruining everything. She sinks her teeth into his tongue, and he jerks back with a cry.

'You *bitch*!'

She can taste his blood in her mouth. He swings his arm like he's going to hit her, but she drives her knee up between his legs and makes a break for it while he's still staggering around in the pine needles.

After that she locks herself in the car and curls up on the seat waiting for everyone else to go home. She stares at the dust collected in the grooves of the steering wheel, the dirty imprint of Hunter's hands at ten and two on the old white leather, and she feels as if Bryce's handprints are branded on her like that. Maybe that's how Noah feels when their father hits him. A little part of her wants her brother now, but in a much more real sense she wishes Emma was here, curled up with her, talking about what they will do for the rest of the summer. Drink lemonade with their feet in the river, perhaps, or drive up to Trail Ridge Road and enjoy the last of the season's snow on the peaks; wake up early to look for moose in the national park, or hire a boat over in Grand Lake. Maybe they could even head down to Boulder, go shopping or something. Whatever it is that normal girls do. She misses the gentleness of their youth. Emma only ever put her hands on Abigail to hold her.

The clock on the dashboard says it is nearly three in the morning when Hunter gets into the car. He looks at her hair all messed up and tangled with bits of bark, her bra strap hanging loose off her shoulder.

'Abi, what happened?'

Abigail draws her legs up, trying to make herself as compact as she can. 'I can't figure out if I want to fuck everyone or fight them.'

Hunter laughs, but then she looks at him and he stops. 'Sorry, I just . . . That's kind of funny.'

'No, it's not. I feel like I'm sinking. I'm so mad all the time. Do you know what it's like to be pissed off constantly?'

'Sometimes.'

She knows he does, a little bit, so she doesn't press the matter.

'How much did we make?'

'About a hundred and fifty dollars. Not a bad first night, huh?'

'Not bad,' she agrees.

'Hey, Abi.' He looks very grown-up and serious all of a sudden, and that makes her nervous. 'Are you going to tell Emma?'

She digs her nails into her knees. 'Leave Emma out of it. She's got enough to worry about.' I'm the one who's supposed to be looking out for her, she thinks, and I can't do that if I'm sinking. Besides, what would Emma think of her if she knew? What would anyone think? She could lose the only real friend she's ever had.

Hunter doesn't count. He is a means to an end.

'You know you can talk to me, though, right?' he says. 'I mean, do you want to talk about it?'

She looks up at him, and the fading bonfire light through the car window softens the squareness of his face, making him look almost handsome. When you talk like that, she thinks, I wish I could feel some kind of way about you.

'It's nothing you don't already know,' she says. But the truth is, as much as she appreciates the sentiment, she's sick to death of people asking if she's okay. She feels as if she's always trying to guess the reactions other people want from her, so conversations become exhausting, with her on a razor's edge every time. Sometimes she gets it wrong – laughs when she shouldn't, things like that – and then they know that she has been lying the whole time. That Abigail Blake, they must think, as they look into her young, grinning face, such a liar.

35

Now

EMMA DOES NOT say a word, shivering in the back of Samuel's truck with dirt and sweat streaking her face. Jude keeps turning around to look at her, but she just stares straight ahead.

'Dad, I think we should take her to a hospital.'

'You want me to drive all the way over to Estes?' Samuel glances over his shoulder. 'She'll be fine. Probably just high like the rest of those waster kids. This town's going to hell in a hand basket, Jude, you hear me?'

They drive to the top of Emma's street, at which point Samuel lets the engine idle and says, 'Go on, get out.' When Emma moves slowly to unbuckle her seatbelt, he yells, 'Get!' as if she were a dog.

'Dad, what about Noah?' Jude watches Emma grow smaller in the truck wing-mirror as they drive away.

His father grunts. 'He's made his bed, he can lie in it for the night. You lock the door when you get back home and don't let him in. He can sleep out in the yard. I'll deal with him tomorrow.'

'Yes, sir.' Then he adds, 'Aren't you coming home?'

'Is that any of your business, boy? I'll drop you back,

someone's got to keep an eye on your mom, but I've got someplace else I need to be.'

You don't need to be at O'Shannon's bar, Jude thinks. You need to help me find my brother. I can't lose him as well.

Emma sits in the shower, letting the hot water burn away the feeling of Jerry Maddox's hands on her wrists, of the body-odour reek of Samuel Blake's truck, and she tries not to think about what might have happened to Hunter, tries not to worry about him, because what was it his father had said? Hunter had stolen a gun.

Rat had told her about his gun. That afternoon at the trailer park, after the stones had come flying through the windows, she'd been so shaken up, and drunk on cheap liquor, she had demanded answers. His gun had gone missing months ago, he told her. He figured it was probably one of Hunter's friends messing around, but now Emma thinks she has a decent idea of who took it.

While Emma scrubs the dirt off her face, Jude Blake stands in the hallway full of scattered gemstones and tries calling his brother again, only to hear the automated voice telling him, for the fifth time, that this number is currently unavailable.

Dolly, lying on the couch with half a Valium circulating through her bloodstream, can hear her son sobbing faintly in the hall, but she has no inclination to go to him, or to move ever again. She holds Abigail's diary pages scrunched up in her hand and thinks she wouldn't get up now even if the whole house caught fire.

The Lewises, responding at last to an alert from the church alarm system, arrive at the First Baptist Church of Whistling Ridge to find it reeking of gasoline. Apart from that, the church is unharmed and nothing has been taken, the pastor is quite confident of that, but something has been left – a single earring shaped like a wolf's fang, discarded in haste on the carpet.

The trail road feels like the backbone of the world. To Noah, sitting in the darkness with his hands tucked into his armpits, it's hard to tell where the trees end and the mountains begin.

They slept for a little while in the truck, parked up at the side of a county road, leaning against one another. But when Noah woke, he could still smell the gasoline clinging to them, so they drove higher, following the road out past the Tall Bones and up towards the timberline. Now, perched together on the hood, they breathe in the sweet-cold air and the scent of woodsmoke, curling up from unseen cabins in the trees below.

Up here there are snow banks that never melt, as high as Noah's waist in some places, and they make everything silent. Rat says it reminds him of Transylvania.

'Is that where you lived?' Noah asks.

'Yeah, I lived in Dracula's castle. Just lay around draped in furs and went hunting with wolves every day.'

'You're such an ass about everything.'

'Transylvania's the arse-end of nowhere, but it does have some good forest. And it had my grandmother, and her guitar.'

Rat's fingers are turning red, so Noah takes them in his own and blows on them gently.

'Do you ever miss it – Romania, I mean?'

'Not really. I was a kid so it's all pretty blurry. England was more of a home.' Rat's breath makes clouds in the frigid air. 'Long church services, though, I remember those. You think the Baptists are bad, you've never been to an Orthodox mass.'

'I never knew you went to church.'

'Well, now you do.'

Rat clicks his tongue, smiling down at their hands, palm

pressed against palm. 'So, you know, I never really got a straight answer from you before. You want to run away with me, Noah Blake?'

Noah takes off Rat's rings and links their fingers together. 'Where would we go?'

'Anywhere you like, anywhere away from here – this town, these people, so pissed because Jesus won't turn them from water into wine.'

Noah feels as though he's about to pull the dustsheet off a piece of old furniture, something precious stored away in a room he hasn't entered in a very long time. 'I've always wanted to go to California.'

'Oh?' Rat holds up their hands between them. 'Could we do this in public in California?'

Noah's not sure about that. The word *public* makes the bruise on his jaw sting.

They sit a little while longer, hand in hand, until the sky is blue and yellow, and the wind shoos them back into the truck.

As they drive back down the mountain, Rat props his feet on the dashboard and says, 'I tell you something I do miss.'

'Yeah?'

'I never get to hear my own language unless I speak it myself.'

Noah looks sideways at him. 'Well, then, teach me something.'

'You want to learn Romanian.'

'Don't say it like that. Come on, teach me. If it's that important to you . . .'

The way Rat smiles at him then, it feels as if there are flowers budding inside his chest, and he doesn't hear his phone buzzing on the back seat with another missed call from his brother.

*

The house feels stale, and there are pieces of coloured stone here and there, fallen between the hallway floorboards. His grandmother's cross is gone, Noah notes, but someone has tacked a square of Christmas wrapping paper over the hole in the wall. He is grateful. The thought of seeing it again, even after all these years, shocks him in a way he did not expect.

'I thought you might not want to look at it,' Jude says, resting on his stick in the living-room doorway. 'Where were you? I've been calling all night.' He doesn't sound angry, but he doesn't sound like himself either – as if he has aged a year for every hour that Noah's been gone.

Noah doesn't like it. 'I was just out. Since when do you care?'

He makes to brush past him, but Jude plants his feet and blocks the way.

'Dad and I went out looking for you.'

'Well, that must have been nice for you, some father–son bonding time.'

'Where *were* you? He just left me here so he could go out drinking. I had to deal with Mom on my own.'

'What do you mean? What's wrong with Mom?'

'She . . . I don't know. I got home and she was just sitting in the hall. She'd pulled out a load of her hair.'

'Well, that's Mom for you. Supportive as ever in a crisis.'

'No, you don't get it, she wouldn't calm down. I had to give her some Valium.' Jude looks at his feet. 'I've never done anything like that before. It felt like she was a crazy person.'

'Maybe she is.' Noah leans against the doorframe too. 'You know one time I found her in the bath with all her clothes on? Like, a few months back, I came home from work and she was just sitting there, wearing all her clothes.'

'Oh, man.' Jude's face gets all pinched, like he's about to cry. 'What's going on? Why is this happening to us?'

'Don't say crap like that. You know how dumb you sound when you say that? You sound like a Pilgrim or something, like you're worried the harvest is going to fail.'

Jude swallows. 'God wouldn't—'

'This has nothing to do with God, you idiot. God doesn't do anything, He just whispers in people's ears that they're worth jack shit, and they pray and pray hoping He'll stop, but He doesn't, and in the end they just go crazy. That's all God does, He makes people go crazy, so get that into your head and grow up!'

Jude stares at him, his eyes growing red and watery around the edges, and Noah feels momentarily guilty. Or perhaps he has been feeling guilty the whole time, ever since a few photos on his computer resulted in his little brother being thrown down the stairs. Perhaps it hurt so much losing out on California that it was easier to be mad at Jude – the sight of him shuffling around on his stick reminding Noah every day that his indiscretion was at the root of all this – than to admit to what his brother has lost as well.

But then Jude presses something into Noah's hand. His voice is cold – strangely older again – when he says, 'You're the one who needs to grow up.'

Noah looks down at the Polaroid, at Rat all drunk-sweaty and nonchalant with his arm around Abigail in a dress he's never seen before, the pair of them looking bored at the camera, and for a second longer than he would ever admit, he thinks, Oh, God – why *is* this happening to us?

36

He remembers when he lost his fingers. Eli Gains had got his hand caught in a steel trap on a hunting trip with his brother, back when he still had a couple of people who called him Eli. The brother, Abel, was one of them, and he died of bowel cancer the following year. The other was wild Bonnie Harris, who only had to bat her eyes and he'd be skipping time at the police academy to smoke pot with her in her grungy Denver apartment. He'd proposed to her before the accident, but afterwards, when it came to picking out his ring, she'd said, *Well, I don't know what finger you're going to stick it on*, and it was like she'd slammed a door in his face. They broke up two months later. She'd screwed up her mouth every time he touched her with that hand.

Then one afternoon, many years later, he'd put that same hand on Abigail Blake's back, and she hadn't flinched. He doesn't regret it, even now. For a moment he'd felt himself again, *normal* for the first time in so long, and he remembers briefly thinking, There are still people out there to whom we are not merely the sum of the bad things that have happened to us.

'Chief, are you listening?'

Gains looks up. Pastor Lewis is tapping his fingers on the

back of a plastic church chair. 'Yes, sir. You were telling me about the gasoline.' He can smell the memory of it in the air.

'We'll have to have the whole place deep cleaned, of course.'

'And you have no idea who it could have been?'

'Oh, no, it's just one of those things, isn't it? One of those mysteries. But we thought it was best to report it, all the same.'

The pastor shakes his head, and it's probably a trick of the light – probably because Gains hasn't slept, thinking about Dolly Blake's miserable voice on the phone – but he thinks he sees Pastor Lewis's mouth curl up at the edges, like a smile that is trying not to be a smile. It makes Gains's skin feel cold.

'You boys are busy enough as it is, I'm sure – what with that missing-person case still open.' The pastor leans back and tucks his thumbs into his waistband. 'You made any headway with that lately, Chief? Only I hear a lot of folks' worries in my profession, and I can tell you that plenty of people round here are getting worried. Been over a month now, hasn't it, since that poor child disappeared?'

'That's correct, sir. But I'm not at liberty to discuss an ongoing investigation, you understand.'

'Oh, no, of course not. I wasn't trying to step on any toes. But – well, you know how people can get around here when they start itching to place blame. Poor old Miguel Alvarez, he certainly knew that, not that it did him much good in the end. People want this to be over, Chief, you can appreciate that, can't you? They just want to have someone to blame.'

Pastor Lewis is shorter than Gains but he raises his chin when he talks, as if he's attempting to stare down his nose at him. Gains tries to relax into his stance.

'Well, now, I'm not sure I understand you, Pastor.'

Ed Lewis just smiles. 'Eli, I think you do.'

'You look like bad news,' Rat says, jumping down from the roof of the RV.

Noah knocks the cigarette out of his hand. 'What did you do to my sister?'

'Your *sister*? Blake, what are you talking about?' Rat looks around, but there is no one to be seen between the rotted rows of metal and clapboard. 'Come on, Blake, I was barely even aware of your sister.'

'You're talking about her in the past tense.'

Everybody is, Noah knows that. Everybody started acting like she was already dead the moment those flyers went up. Just another no-good Blake kid, and if even the pastor couldn't bring himself to care what happened to them then why should anybody else? But Rat had cared – cared about Noah, at least – and now the thought that he might have been lying all along, that he might have had something to do with the blood they found all over his sister's cardigan, with his mother curled up like a dead thing on the couch this morning . . . He could have gone back to the Tall Bones that night, after Noah had left. It wasn't impossible. Noah feels as if his eyes are about to pop out of his head.

'Look,' says Rat, putting his hands on his hips, 'if you've got something to say to me, then come out and say it.'

Noah grits his teeth so hard his jaw hurts, but he can't get his words out, at least not anything clever – he's just the boy who pronounces it *carmel* – so instead he slaps the Polaroid against Rat's chest.

Rat looks down, eyes wide suddenly. 'I don't remember—'

'Oh, save it.'

'I swear on my grandmother's bones, Blake, I don't remember this.'

Noah can see now, in the daylight, the grey circles under his eyes.

'Hunter Maddox used to take photos like this. We hung out sometimes – all of us from the trailer park, and him, like he had nothing better to do. He'd take these photos. But I was always high as the fucking trees, Blake, I'm telling you. I remember, like, a third of those parties at best.'

'Why would you want to hang out with teenage girls anyway? I saw the liquor you bought for Emma Alvarez. What the hell kind of person are you?'

'The kind of person whose trailer gets trashed by half the town, Blake. I take whatever friends I can get.' Rat sticks out his lip. 'And for the record, there was never anything between me and Emma. She's a lonely kid, she just wanted some attention – and, you know, maybe she wasn't the only one.'

'You get everybody's attention, that's your whole problem!'

Rat presses his hand to his forehead. 'So, what, you think I was banging your sister? You think I murdered her? I was with you that night, remember? So exactly what are you getting at here?'

'I don't . . .' Noah sinks his teeth into his lip. 'Are you even gay?'

'What?'

'Maybe you want to hang around teenage girls so it's easier for you if . . . if nobody suspects you because they think you're gay. Was I just a convenient alibi?'

'Blake.' Rat sounds calm, but in that way people do when they've run out of anything else to say. 'I would like you to leave.'

Noah just stares at him, and Rat crosses his arms and cocks his head to one side.

'Am I speaking Romanian? I said get out of here, go on. Before I say something that really hurts your feelings.'

Then

Is it true, Dolly? What that boy told me, is it true? You good-for-nothing little slut—

Jude looks at his mother, who is asleep now, dried patches of blood matting her hair, and he remembers his father shouting that at her, the last night in March, when there was still snow on the ground. He probably wasn't supposed to hear it, since it was after lights out, and their parents tended to forget about their children then. There had been a muffled thud, the sound of many small things clattering to the floor, the slap of leather against bare skin, followed by a dull groan that he recognized as his mother's, because this was not the first time he'd heard it.

'You stupid, dumb bitch, Dolly. You really thought you could keep that from me?'

His father sounded like a big wolf panting, and Jude imagined froth and bloody spit swinging from his lips.

'Sam, I never, I swear—'

'For Christ sakes, don't look at me like that! You make me feel like shit when you look at me like that. Get up! You only ever make me feel like shit, Dolly.'

There was a creak on the floorboard just outside Jude's door and he sat up. The door opened and a thin strip of light filtered in from the landing, followed closely by Abigail.

'Jude? Jude, are you awake?'

He didn't dare switch on the lamp in case his father saw, but he felt Abigail's weight on the end of his mattress.

'I'm awake.'

'He's belting her. Can you hear it?'

Jude wondered why she'd come – surely not just to tell him that. It occurs to him now that maybe she felt guilty. Perhaps she knew it was about her.

'Are you scared?'

'No,' he lied.

'I'm scared,' she said, and he believed her. 'I keep thinking it's going to happen again. Like, he's just going to lose it again, you know?'

Jude felt his leg twitch under the covers. Yes, he said, he did know.

In the morning, their mother sat stiffly at the table. There was a big yellow-grey bruise on her jaw, and she poured orange juice over her cereal instead of milk. The Blake children looked at one another and knew – in the unspoken way that siblings simply know sometimes – that each of them felt this was the logical conclusion to their mother's life: that their father would finally drive her crazy. Jude knew, too, that he was probably the only one who cared if this happened or not.

Later, however, after Noah and Samuel had left for work, and Jude was waiting for his sister in the hallway, trying not to look at the big gemstone cross sparkling in the spring sunlight, he heard Abigail with their mother in the kitchen.

'Mom, I really need to talk to you about something.'

'Not now, sweetheart.'

He heard the clink of cutlery as the breakfast things were cleared away.

'I know, Mom, but . . .'

They spoke too low for him to make out the rest, but then he heard his mother cry out, and something smashed on the floor. A moment later, Abigail came striding into the hallway, her cheek smarting red.

'She smacked you?'

His sister slung her school backpack on to her shoulder and wrenched the front door open.

'Why did she do that? What did you want to talk to her about?'

'Let's just go.' Abigail wiped her face on her sleeve. 'I'll figure it out myself.'

37

Now

Jerry Maddox has his head in his hands when the phone on the desk rings. Lord, what a night. Hunter and that stupid girl sneaking in here, like this was all just some game and they were playing detective. What is it going to take, Jerry thinks, for his son to realize what's at stake? It's not often that he raises his hand to the boy. You kick a dog too often and one day it'll turn around and bite you, that's what Jerry's father used to say, but last night, when he saw Hunter standing by the open drawer, he'd panicked.

Abigail Blake's Chapstick is still there. He's checked. It should never have been there in the first place, he knows that now. He should have thrown it away.

The phone is still ringing, and he's half tempted to rip the cord out and throw the damn thing down the stairs. But then what? All the guys in the saw room would see, and how would that look? *Jerry's lost it,* they'd say, and he needs to appear in control, now more than ever.

'Maddox Lumber,' he answers, kneading his eyes. 'Jerry Maddox speaking.'

'Jerry, glad I caught you,' says Pastor Lewis, with far too

much energy for a Monday morning. 'You all right? You sound a little tired there.'

'It's nothing. Everything going okay?'

'Well, that's just it, Jerry. We have a situation on our hands.'

He listens to the pastor reel off details about security alarms, the price of deep cleaning a carpet, and something to do with an earring they found on the floor. Jerry leans on his elbow and tries not to zone out. What it all boils down to, eventually, is that there will be a special service tonight at the church. Why Ed Lewis couldn't have just come out and said that first is beyond him, but then the man does seem to enjoy the sound of his own voice.

'We are about the Lord's work, Jerry. This is going to be a big one. I need to know I can count on your support.'

Jerry sighs without meaning to. 'You've got it, Ed.'

'I hope you're taking this seriously. Something has to be done, just like with Miguel Alvarez. Every breach of trust shall come before God.' The pastor is using his church voice, loud and righteous and just a bit manic. 'I helped you out with Alvarez, Jerry. It's a simple case of tit for tat.'

Jerry drags a hand down his face. Alvarez is the last thing he wants to think about now. First Miguel's snooping little daughter and now Ed Lewis – why can't people just leave things in the past where they belong?

'There is something unholy among us,' the pastor continues. 'It's time to put an end to this whole mess. People in this town are frightened, as they should be. But they look up to you as much as me, Jerry. You're their boss, their landlord, you've got influence, and that's what I'm going to need tonight . . . Say, Jerry, are you still there? What's the matter with you today?'

Jerry's eyes travel to the desk drawer once again. It would probably be wise if Ed didn't find out about the Chapstick just yet. Better do as he says for now. After all, he thinks, you'll want him on your side if all this comes out.

Emma rolls down her sleeve to cover the bruising on her wrist. It's only faint, but she doesn't want anyone to catch sight of it as she walks through town. A part of her hopes that if she covers it up she can forget it's there: the finger marks from where Hunter's father squeezed like he wanted to snap her. She'd never been touched by a man like that before. A gesture with so much violence in it, the implication that he could do worse, if he felt so inclined. Even now it makes her hands unsteady as she reaches for the door of the Aurora diner.

'Emma.' Chrissy Dukes smiles at her, as the bell over the door chimes. 'Still off school, huh? Lucky you.'

Emma makes a noncommittal sound, glancing about, but it's a Monday morning and so far she is the only customer. 'Is Noah here?'

'Actually, he called in sick. He does that sometimes, you know, when he doesn't want us to see . . .' Chrissy taps the side of her face where, just the other day, Noah had been badly grazed. 'I don't like to bug him about it.'

Emma thinks she looks genuinely sad, and she wonders if Noah has any idea that there is somebody here who cares about him.

The bell over the door chimes again, and this time it's Hunter. He nods at Chrissy.

'Don't any of you go to school any more?' she says.

'Got more important stuff to do, haven't I?' Hunter winks, and she rolls her eyes.

Emma does not invite him to sit at her usual table – the one by the window, in full view of her mother at the clinic across the street – but slides into a booth near the back, its tall seats concealing them from the counter.

'She has a point, though,' Emma says. 'How come you're not in class?'

Hunter shrugs. 'I was, but then your text said you needed to talk.'

'Yeah, but I meant later. You didn't have to come now.'

'Maybe I was worried about you. You know, after last night.'

Emma rubs her wrist through her sweater. 'I'm fine.'

'It was my fault. We shouldn't have gone there. I just figured my dad was always so secretive about his office, maybe you'd find something there.'

'*You* found something.'

Hunter gives a weak laugh. 'Yeah, don't I know it.'

'Were you okay? I just ran – I didn't know if you were following or . . .' She notices for the first time that he isn't sitting at quite the right angle. 'Did he hurt you?'

Hunter grunts and lifts up the hem of his varsity basketball hoodie to reveal a smattering of red that will likely bruise. Jerry Maddox is no Samuel Blake – this isn't something that's going to put him in the hospital – but Emma winces all the same.

'Jeez, Hunter, I'm so sorry.'

'Whatever. Better he does it to me than you, right?'

Better he does it to no one. She wants to reach across the table and place her hands on him. Abigail said that's what they used to do at church sometimes, when somebody needed to imbibe the strength of the whole congregation. I want to put my bruises on your bruises, she thinks. She imagines his skin would feel warm.

'So, what was it you needed to talk about?'

'Oh, I . . .' She wasn't expecting him to show up with these battle wounds, this vivid reminder that he'd put himself in harm's way for her. 'It's nothing.'

'Come on, what's up?'

She won't mention the gun, she decides. Not yet. It wouldn't be fair to accuse him of something right after he's taken a beating for her. Besides, even if he did steal Rat's gun, that doesn't mean he fired it. *He wouldn't be helping me if he had. Right?*

'Maybe we're looking at this the wrong way,' she says instead. 'Like, maybe we should be focusing on what Abi did, rather than what somebody else did to her.'

'Meaning what? Why would my dad have her Chapstick if he hadn't taken it from her? It's all messed up, man.'

'I agree, but that probably won't be enough for the sheriff. I mean, she might just have dropped it, and he might have picked it up. We need something more convincing.' She rubs at her wrist. 'We should stick to Abi, figure out what her last movements were. Maybe that'll help. What happened with you two after you went into the woods? You gave her some coke, and then what?'

Hunter scratches the back of his hand with one finger. 'I don't know, I was pretty high. At some point I guess we split up. I went home and watched the end of the Buffaloes game.'

'So you have no idea where she might have gone afterwards?'

'She always liked being up at the Tall Bones. Maybe she just stayed there. She used to say it was the skeleton of some big old creature, that before there were ever people in the forest, it was full of—'

'Giant animals. Yeah.' Emma smiles. 'She used to say that to me too. Gains said they've combed that whole area, but I guess it wouldn't hurt to look again. I mean, if we know we're looking for something to do with your dad, it puts us ahead of the police, at least.'

Hunter scratches his hand a little harder. 'You want me to come with you? More likely to find something if there's two of us looking.'

'You really want to do that?'

For a moment she thinks of Rat, how he'd smashed a whiskey bottle and said, Stay out of the woods, *drăguţă*, just so he could keep his own secrets. But Hunter wants to help – hell, he's actually offering, even though it would be just as easy for him to turn his nose up at her the way the other boys in town do. It seems strange now that she once thought he was just the same.

'Sure,' he says. 'We're a team.' He leans his elbows on the table and smiles at her.

The gun. *You need to ask him about the gun*. But she likes the way they're pressing their bruises together – the same shared bruise of Abigail's absence. Emma is only seventeen, after all, and she has never known a boy to smile at her the way Hunter Maddox is smiling at her now.

Then

'Mom, I really need to talk to you about something.'

Dolly remembers her daughter standing in the kitchen, that first morning in April, and she thought Abigail was wearing more makeup than usual. It didn't occur to her then that she might have been trying to mask something.

'Not now, sweetheart.' The imprint of Samuel's belt on Dolly's back still stung, and the bruise on her jaw was making her whole face ache. Everything, from the morning light to the clink of the breakfast crockery, only made it worse.

'I know, Mom, but . . .' Abigail lowered her voice, casting a wary glance towards the hallway as she leaned across the table. 'Mom, can you take me to the clinic?'

Dolly paused, a stack of dirty bowls in her hands, a clump of soggy cereal nudging up against her thumb. 'The clinic? What do you need to go there for?'

'I need . . .' Abigail wouldn't look her in the eye. 'I think I have to . . .'

'Abi, what's the matter?'

She remembers how she could actually see the colour leaving her daughter's face. The morning-after pill, she'd said. And Dolly had smacked her.

She thinks now that it was the aftermath of her husband's rage that made her do it. The morning-after *what*? While Dolly was being beaten, her little girl was sneaking out and getting herself into trouble. Is that what this was? Dolly couldn't take it. Stupid, stupid child. Samuel would never forgive her if he found out: he was *weird* about sex, which meant that God was weird about sex, which made it everyone's problem. Samuel wouldn't beat Abigail, not his precious Abi, but Dolly on the other hand . . . He would say the child was *her* responsibility, and he would be right. But how could Abigail have been so thoughtless? Did she really care so little about what happened to her mother?

Dolly had watched her daughter hurry out into the hallway where Jude was waiting. She didn't hear what they said to one another, could barely concentrate on anything except the way her hand was smarting suddenly. It would take two cigarettes for her to forget about the pain, and another to soothe her anger at her daughter, and while she was smoking, Dolly thought, This must be how Samuel feels all the time.

Months later, she couldn't tell the police that she'd hit her own daughter. Couldn't stomach the idea of people knowing she was in any way like her husband, so Sheriff Gains never knew about the pill either.

That will be the thing that stays with her down the years. The terrible thing. If Dolly had only said something, if she had asked Abigail instead of wallowing in her own self-pity, everything might have been different.

38

Then

By the end of April, it is warm enough for the students of Whistling Ridge High School to sit outside during their lunch period. It is on one of these afternoons, with her legs swinging over the edge of the bleachers, a notebook in her lap, that Hunter finds Abigail.

'You writing something?' he says, and she knows it's him before he's even spoken – knows him by the looming breadth of his shadow and the locker-room stink of him.

Emma says it's best just to ignore boys like him, but Emma is home, sick, today, and Abigail has two too many brothers to be afraid of boys, so she raises her hand and flips him off.

Hunter clicks his tongue and laughs. 'That wasn't very friendly. I thought you were a nice little church girl.'

Don't try and be cool with me, she thinks. We go to the same church. Everybody round here does. But she is suddenly very aware of the dewy red patches on her knees, and she tries to reposition her notebook to cover them. The movement must catch Hunter's eye, and he leans over and swipes the book out of her hands.

'Hey!'

'What are you writing here? A goddamn novel? Let's have a read of this Pulitzer Prize shit.'

He starts flipping through the pages, and Abigail feels like she's trying to scream in a dream, but instead of a shriek that conveys the full depth of her terror, she's waking up to find herself rasping alone in the dark. 'Give it back. Give it back *now.*'

But he has found the page. She knows he has because she can hear his breathing, and his eyes dart back and forth as though he's rereading those lines over and over, just as she does.

Give it back, she begs silently, but she knows it's no good. He's already seen it. He already knows. The realization of what that means makes her eyes hot and wet. He's going to tell everyone what I wrote, she thinks, and then he's going to tell them I cried.

It's been hard, this whole business of lying. She's been carrying it around with her like a weight, a heaviness hanging between her hips, or else a chain dragging behind her foot. A lie like this is nothing but a burden, and she doesn't want to give it to anyone else, least of all someone she loves. But she knows she won't be able to hide it for ever. She wants to cry because, in its own way, it is a relief that now someone else knows. Even if that someone is Hunter Maddox.

She is not expecting what comes next. Hunter sets the diary next to her on the warm metal of the bleachers and then, with a deep breath, sits himself down too. He sticks his legs over the side like hers, and the two of them sway there for a while in the soft spring breeze, fresh with the clean scent of meltwater from up in the Rockies. In the parking lot, the asphalt is white with shredded mountain ash blossom, pressed into it by so many footprints and tyre tracks. Grackles pick at the remains of dining-hall fries in discarded styrofoam, and the sound of cheer practice can be heard floating through the open gym windows. Abigail is glad that Hunter has nothing to say because she knows otherwise he'd just say something dumb, and she wants to let these sounds and smells soak in while they still can.

Everything is going to change now, she realizes. Everything is going to change because somebody else knows what happened to her.

Now

Eventually, the vibration of her cellphone wakes Dolly. What had Jude given her again? All the colours in the bedroom seem too loud. And the house – the house seems too silent. It's as if, while she was sleeping, God had picked it up and placed it on top of a mountain. There is nothing – not the sound of birds outside, or the blue spruce tapping on the windows, or wind whistling through the gap under the door. Dolly feels like she's in the eye of a storm.

But that damned phone won't stop buzzing. She scrabbles around the folds of the duvet until she finds it, but her fingers are lagging behind what her brain wants to do, so she ends up pressing 'answer' rather than 'decline'. She nearly says, *Oh, shit,* but then she's very glad she didn't, because it is Ann Traxler's tinny voice on the other end.

'Dolly, hey, are you there? It's Ann, from church.'

'Yes, I know.'

'Oh, you sound half asleep. Were you napping? I sometimes like to take a nap in the middle of the day. I didn't wake you, did I?'

Dolly chews the inside of her cheek. 'Did you need something?'

'I just didn't know if anyone else had called, is all. But I thought you ought to know, there's going to be a special service this evening. At about six, I think Eleanor said. Real important stuff, you know. Everyone's going to be there.'

'Oh.'

It seems strange that the rest of the world still thinks she is the same person she was yesterday. They have no idea. Ann Traxler, who yesterday in Safeway said, *It's all over the station, what that boy did* – Ann has no idea. She's just called Dolly up as though everything is hunky-dory. (And, really, who is she to be talking about Dolly's Noah like that, as if Austin Traxler wasn't a little shit who used to toilet paper their house in the seventh grade?)

She thinks Ann is probably the way she is because of that woman who died in her hair salon a few years back. Just upped and died while she was having her hair washed, and Ann said she didn't even realize until after she'd rinsed out the conditioner. Dolly remembers thinking at the time that there was definitely something quite grotesque about washing a dead woman's hair, and she understood that Ann had wanted to talk about it with anyone who would listen, to try to make some sense of it. But since then she has talked about everything, anything, as if that woman dying on her broke some sort of dam in her throat.

'So, will we see you there?' Ann asks. 'It'd be real nice to see you, Dolly.'

'I don't know. I don't think so.'

'Listen, Dolly, about what you might have heard at Safeway, me and Eleanor didn't—'

Dolly ends the call and stuffs the cellphone under her pillow. For the first time, she thinks it can't have been much fun for that lady who died either, what with Ann Traxler's reedy little voice being the last thing she ever heard.

She heaves herself up off the bed and realizes – with a sense of horror that she is certain belongs to her mother – that she is still wearing yesterday's clothes. Nobody should go to bed with their socks on. That is for people with gout, or something like that. It makes her feel old-fashioned, then just plain old.

With a sigh, she goes to press her head against the window-pane, watching her breath slowly fogging up the glass. Noah and Jude are out in the yard. She is vaguely aware that today is Monday, and Jude ought to be in school and Noah at work, but she can't find the energy to care about it too much. Noah is raking leaves outside the shed at the bottom of the yard, its timber so weathered and sagging it seems to be relaxing into the earth. Jude is sitting on the bare ground, staring at the shed door as it swings in the breeze.

He has a dark look on his face, her patient little Jude. Both boys do. For an awful moment she wonders if they know. But then she puts her hand into her pocket and feels the crumpled paper of her daughter's diary pages, and she is reassured: no, they cannot know. Only I have read this.

She is quite certain now that Abigail is dead. Even if Sheriff Gains hadn't told her about the blood on her cardigan last night. *We still can't be sure if the shot was fatal*, he'd said. *Without a body we can't be sure of anything*. But if what's written on these pages is true, that hardly matters. If it's true, then Abigail was dead long before she went missing that night.

Such a dark, hollow word: dead. The sort of word that clubs you over the back of the head if you let it, but Dolly knows she mustn't, not yet. She will open herself up to it later, after she has figured out what to do with these scraps of her daughter's diary. Until then, she must wrap these feelings up tight and put them in a box for later. The boys are such strange creatures, tougher than her in many ways, but so fragile in others. They will need her to be strong now.

This is not the sort of mother she had imagined she would be when the midwife first put Noah into her arms. Her fear of her husband, of his knuckles and his howling, has made her prioritize his happiness over her own and that of her children, but what sort of love is it if you must be threatened for it first? And what's wrong with Samuel that he would want to be loved in that way? What a wretched creature she has become as his wife. She feels like love is a very distant concept, and one she doesn't deserve to reach. But she can see now that it wasn't Samuel who put down the phone on Melissa Alvarez so many times, who dropped out of the women's church committee, who turned the comfort of her body away from her sons. It was Dolly all along. He has made her so ashamed that she has isolated herself of her own accord.

And now, she thinks, because of this, her daughter is probably dead. She must tell her sons. She will have to tell everyone at some point, so that nobody can sneak up on her at Safeway and ask, off the cuff, 'Hey, Dolly, any news about Abigail?' But how do you tell other people that your child is dead? She can imagine it already: they will want her to be unhappy because that is what they expect, so that is what will make them most comfortable. If she tries to be anything else, it will throw people off, and they won't be sympathetic. The problem is, Dolly doesn't even know how she feels yet.

There should be a service, she thinks, watching her sons silently in the yard, not really looking each other in the eye. A service that does this sort of thing for you. A number you can ring, and they will tell everyone on your behalf that you have a dead child so, please, no further questions.

Emma sways her hips a little as she heads back down Main Street. Watching her outside from the diner, Hunter doesn't know what he was so anxious about. When he saw her text earlier, he got this awful sick feeling in his stomach: Emma asks so many questions, and it's cute, really, she's got a lot of energy he never noticed before, but she doesn't always give him time to come up with the answers. And he needs time for some of the things she asks.

His phone buzzes in his hand. Unknown caller, it says, but he picks it up anyway – he still gets a few people from school or the trailer park calling about the coke.

'Go for Hunter,' he says.

The line is quiet.

'Hello?'

Nothing.

Hunter swallows. He looks around but the street is fairly empty. He cups his hand around his mouth and whispers, 'Abi?'

He does not recognize the voice that answers. It could be a man, but it sounds distant, like somebody speaking through a cushion.

'You know what I can do to you.'

'Who is this?'

'You know what I can do to you if you tell.'

Hunter freezes. His throat is painfully dry, but he forces himself to say, 'I haven't told anyone. I swear.'

'Don't go talking to the Alvarez girl again. You know what I can do to her as well.'

39

JUDE WISHES HE had never shown Noah that photograph. His brother is stamping around the yard in his steel-toed boots, cast-offs of their father's, glaring at the logs and dead leaves, his face as dark as the sky overhead is searing and white. It is a headachy kind of afternoon, when the light seems to get in around the edges of your eyeballs and poke at your brain. Jude wants to go inside. It's cold sitting on the ground, but he doesn't like the thought of leaving Noah alone when he's like this.

It was probably nothing, Abi and the Romanian boy. That guy really liked Noah: Jude could tell by the way he had stood there and stared after him at the grocery store that time, looking like Noah had just punched him in the gut. But that's how Jude had felt too, when his brother came home this morning, and said, *You idiot, God doesn't do anything. Get that into your head and grow up.* Noah doesn't hit like their father does, but he still has his way of knocking people down.

If anyone slaps you on the right cheek, turn to him the other also. Jude tugs some grass up and watches the wind sweep it out of his palm. He hopes he won't stop believing in God. God is like this stick he leans on. In his physio sessions they tell him maybe one day he'll be able to stand up without it, and that day feels almost frightening in its distance, even though he longs for it too. But if someone took his stick away now, he would fall down. Perhaps he should look forward to a day when he can stand up without God as well, but for now that seems like a much further distance to fall.

The wind picks up, dismantling Noah's pile of leaves, and he yells something at the sky, just as the shed door bangs shut. The sound makes Jude sit up straight. He has never liked that shed. Their father keeps old bodies in there – raccoons, skunks, sometimes deer, sells their fur to some of the stores in town, saves their bones for decoration – but Jude has liked it even less these last few months. The shed was where he saw it, one night when there was still snow on the ground: a bad thing that he can't find the words for. The wind dies down now, the door swings open, and Jude has to look away, in case he sees the bad thing again.

His stomach mutters, and he realizes he's hungry. He had a piece of toast for breakfast (tried to take some to his mother too, but she was still sleeping off the Valium) but lunchtime has come and gone, and he's pretty certain Noah hasn't eaten anything all day.

'We should go to the store,' he says.

Noah leans on his rake and runs a hand through his hair. 'I suppose you want me to drive you.'

'I can try and make you a grilled cheese, if you like.' Jude has watched his brother make them enough times, on nights when their parents were too busy or too angry to feed their children. It had almost felt normal then, the three of them sitting on the balding living-room carpet, drinking sweet tea and laughing over long strings of melted cheese. Often their father would bang on the ceiling overhead and tell them to shut their mouths, then Noah would turn stony-faced again and retreat to his room. But for a while, now and again, they had played at being just like everyone else.

Noah sighs and presses his forehead against the top of the rake handle, like he wants to bore a hole right through himself. 'Yeah, fine,' he says at last. 'Go get in the truck.'

Jude pulls himself up with his cane, but he lingers a moment, watching his brother wipe his face on his sleeve. Has he been crying? Jude hadn't realized. He wants Noah to know he's sorry. Sorry for showing him the photograph, or perhaps just sorry that the photograph exists at all. Maybe it reminds him of other photos, years ago now, and all the trouble they caused. *God doesn't hate you for it,* Jude thinks, hoping his brother can absorb his thoughts from the air. God doesn't hate anyone: that's His whole thing.

But then Noah says, 'I told you to get in the truck. Do you want to go to the store or not?' and Jude realizes his brother hasn't heard what he was thinking at all.

Just for a moment, as he turns to go, he thinks he sees their mother's face at the upstairs window. He wants to talk to her, but it seems she's always watching from some unreachable distance. Jude ducks his head and limps quickly across the yard without looking up again. He can't be sure, but he thinks she was looking at the shed too.

Please, Lord, he thinks, what do I do? What do I do when I know something I shouldn't?

Emma hasn't had a drink for a week. Seven whole days. It doesn't really occur to her, until she and Melissa pass the beer and wine section in Safeway, and the want is still there, a kind of hunger lurking in her gut, but it feels softer around the edges, fuzzy, like a memory she has half forgotten.

She isn't kidding herself that it's over. She had been naive enough to think that last week, until Rat's trailer and Noah handing her the bottle of peach schnapps. The hunger had flared up again then, gnawing at her until she wanted to tear out her own stomach. When those people came and threw rocks at the windows, and Rat held her under the table, it had all felt so surreal that it was only the very physical sensation of glass breaking under her feet as she walked back across the trailer park that made her certain it had happened. After that, she had just wanted to rid herself of the memory. She had thrown up, downed as much water as her throat could handle, then slept all the way through until morning.

When she'd woken up, Emma had felt that some line had been crossed, that somehow what had happened at Rat's RV could have been prevented had she been sober. She hadn't drunk anything that day – but had gone to speak to Hunter, and he had given her things to think about, so she didn't drink the next day either, or the one after that, and now a whole week has passed. Hunter is good like that. He doesn't fill her up with liquor and tell her not to ask questions, not like Rat did. Hunter is different. He wants to help her.

'What's that smile for?' Melissa nudges her gently as they meander through the bakery section.

'I'm just having a good day.'

Emma slings her arm around her mother's waist and hugs her, breathing in her soap-and-onion smell. It feels as though someone is inflating balloons inside her ribcage and at any moment she might take off.

Then Melissa says, 'Oh, it's Dolly's boys,' and Emma has to float back down. The melancholy of the Blake brothers always seems to have its own orbit, but this afternoon they look especially grim.

'Noah,' says Melissa, 'how's your mom? She seemed a little on edge yesterday when I called round.'

Emma thinks her mother is being very polite. Dolly Blake is always on edge.

Noah is clutching a bag of sliced bread – *perfect for toasting*, it says on the side – like it's a lifesaving ring in the middle of a lake, and when Melissa mentions his mother, he grips it harder.

'Mom's just been tired lately,' he says. 'All this stuff with Abi. It's been nearly a month now.'

'One month and one day,' Jude adds. 'Seven hundred and forty-four hours.'

Emma thinks that sounds too few.

'Your poor mom. I can't imagine,' Melissa says. 'You know, if she's having trouble sleeping or anything, you just send her over to the clinic. We've got a new—'

'No,' says Noah. 'She's not having any trouble sleeping. Thanks.'

Jude has wandered over to a table display of Bundt cakes, but he's staring at Emma. She leaves her mother, who is smiling awkwardly at Noah, and approaches him the way you would a deer in the forest. 'Hey, are you okay?'

Jude taps his fingernails on the handle of his cane. 'What were you doing in the road last night?'

'Oh.' She's managed not to think about it since she left Hunter at the diner, but now she feels the memory settling over her like a net. 'I was just looking for something.'

'Something to do with Abi?'

'What makes you say that?'

'Aren't you trying to figure it out? I don't think the police are trying very hard. They barely call any more. Won't even tell us what they think happened to her. Sheriff Gains said she was a *missing person*, but . . .' Jude has his mother's slightly wild look in his eyes. He folds his lips together and taps on his cane, but he doesn't stop staring at her.

'Jude, do you know something?'

He stops tapping.

'What is it?'

Jude is looking over her shoulder now, at his brother squeezing the bag of sliced bread. Noah says, not unkindly, 'Come on, kid, we're going,' and Jude limps away, returning his gaze to anywhere but Emma.

'Those poor boys,' her mother says, as they watch the brothers disappear around the corner. 'Weird as all hell, don't get me wrong, but still. What they must be going through.'

'Yeah.' Emma nods. 'Weird.'

Talking to Jude has brought everything back, so when they get home, Emma tries to call Hunter.

Gun thief – that's what his father had said. Jerry Maddox had cornered them in his office and called him a gun thief.

Emma doesn't know any more about bullets and ballistics than she's seen on TV, but she figures the police probably wouldn't have rounded up Rat if his gun wasn't a match for that shell casing they found. She knows Rat had nothing to do with it because he was busy getting it on with Noah Blake, but somebody fired a gun that night. Somebody spattered that blood across Abigail's cardigan, but it can't have been Hunter. It can't. After all, he's been helping her. He took a beating from his dad for her. There's something else going on here, she's certain of it. She just needs to talk to him.

But Hunter doesn't pick up. Not the first time, or the second. It goes to voicemail every time, and Hunter, sitting alone in his room with a cigarette shaking in his fingers, keeps watching it ring, not daring to answer.

40

Then

'WE MAY BE strangers to ourselves, yet God sees us,' Pastor Lewis declares. Gripping his Bible, he is a dark, faceless figure, backlit by the summer light streaming through the window behind him. 'The Lord knows each and every one of your hearts. He sees the sin, but He also sees the conscious choice that all of you have made to be here today, in His house, to give worship to His glory, and when the time comes to separate the sheep from the goats those who have been righteous in the name of the Lord will be righteous still. God *sees* us, my brothers, and thus He *knows* us – but do you know Him?'

Abigail wonders.

The Blakes are always the first to leave church because they sit closest to the door, at the back, and everybody seems to agree that this is where they belong. Even the Blakes themselves have never tried to sit anywhere else. Now, dabbing at her dewy forehead as they file out into the parking lot, Abigail's mother says, 'I'd like to go to the store before we head back.'

Her father shakes his head. 'Woman, you were just at the store yesterday. I'm not made of money.'

Abigail shifts her weight from one foot to the other,

feeling the heat of the concrete through her thin-soled shoes. 'I'll come with you, Mom.'

'Sam, do you want anything?'

Samuel glances at his wife and daughter, then spits on the ground. 'Six-pack of Lone Star.'

Dolly begins shepherding Abigail and Jude across the parking lot, while the other members of the congregation emerge from the church, blinking in the midday light as if they have just awoken from a long sleep.

'Noah, are you coming?' their mother calls over her shoulder.

'I'm going for a drive.'

Abigail watches him slouch off in the other direction, his shoulders held high, hands shoved deep in his pockets. Almost arrogant in his secrecy. He is going to the woods. She knows because she has followed him there before.

Among the ruins of the old Winslow house, Noah crowds Rat up against the crumbling stonework and kisses him with his teeth against his throat. He fucks him until he stops speaking English, and then they collapse back amid the soft ferns while the mountain breeze blows over them, cooling the sweat on their chests. In this moment they are not just two relative strangers lying in the earth, they are something infinitely softer: ancient love letters, Oscar Wilde's poetry, lips pressed gently against the back of a hand – they are lovers. Rat's shoulder feels waxy against Noah's cheek, and he knows if he were to move his lips just so, he could kiss him there.

Instead he says, 'I think I'm doing this wrong.'

'Trust me, church boy, you're doing it just fine.'

'Don't call me that. And you know that's not what I meant.'

Rat props himself up on one elbow, grinning his half-moon grin, the aspen branches above framing his face like some pagan crown.

'Come on then, Blake, tell me what you mean.'

'I don't . . .' Noah chews his lip impatiently, frustrated that the words aren't coming out like he wants them to. 'I'm not like you. I don't know how to do this. I'm not part of "the community" like you are.'

'Who says I am?' Rat snorts. 'Look, Blake, if you're talking about the gay community or whatever, it's not some sort of exclusive club you have to join in order to validate the way you feel.' He huffs and tucks his hair behind his ear. 'Like, I assume you don't go to every potluck dinner or middle-school play or moose-petting apple-bobbing square dance that happens in Whistling Ridge, but you're still a part of this dumb town, aren't you? A community is there if you need the support of your own people, but that's all. It's not an obligation.'

'I don't think I have my own people.'

'Sure you do,' he says, running his thumb along the broken line of Noah's nose. 'You've got me, haven't you?'

Noah lets Rat lean down and kiss him. He thinks, *We may be strangers to ourselves, and yet God sees us.* The afternoon sun bathes Rat in warm green light, and when Noah looks him in the eye, he looks right back.

In Safeway, Abigail and Jude stand in the fresh produce section in order to catch some of the water from the mister as it sprays the vegetables. It doesn't do much to cool them down, but it makes Jude laugh and Abigail loves him for that, for laughing. Nobody else at home seems able to.

'You two stop that,' their mother says. 'You're going to ruin your church clothes.'

The store is full of tourists. Abigail can't see their eyes behind their big sunglasses; as a child she used to wonder if they had eyes at all. She hates them because they will not help her. So many times since the night her father put the hole in the wall, she has longed to run to one of them and say, 'Please, please help me, take me away, there is something wicked happening here,' but she never does. They would think she was crazy, and maybe they would be right.

'Abi, sweetie, do you want strawberries?' Her mother holds up a carton and Abigail can see the fruit is already on the turn, too red and soft, like blood and guts.

'No thanks, Mom. They'll be rotten by the time we get home.'

'They're not expensive.'

'We won't be able to eat them. They'll just go to waste.'

Dolly shrugs and puts the carton in the shopping cart anyway.

'No, Mom, really.'

'You might change your mind later.'

Suddenly Abigail wants to scream, wants to smash her knuckles against the shopping-cart handle until all her fingers are as red and sticky as that fruit. No, she thinks. Mom, I said NO. Why won't you listen to me? Why does nobody ever listen?

Jude puts his hand on her arm. 'Abi, are you okay?'

'I need to go to the restroom.'

As she walks quickly across the store, she can hear Pastor Lewis saying, *The Lord knows each and every one of your hearts. He sees the sin*. In the cubicle, she pulls out reams and reams of toilet paper and stuffs it up her skirt between her bare thighs until she can no longer feel any space there. *He sees the sin.* She lets her head fall slack against the cool bathroom tiles, taking deep, shaky breaths of muggy disinfectant air.

No. She said *no*. When did that word lose its meaning?

Now

When Noah and Jude get home from the store, their mother has propped herself up against the kitchen counter and is smoking studiously. The house has always reeked of cigarettes, but today is the first time Noah can remember really disliking the smell. Perhaps it reminds him too much of someone else. Perhaps. All he knows is he has to get out of here, so he goes into the backyard to finish sweeping up the leaves he'd left earlier.

He thinks maybe he gets it now – his mom wanting to have something to do with her hands, with any of her limbs, really. Since that meeting in Pastor Lewis's office, Noah feels like a marionette who, finding himself suddenly cut free from his strings, has just upped and walked away. Except now, without Rat, Noah doesn't know where to put himself. Doesn't know how to be.

He gets out his phone. A message on the screen tells him he has a missed voicemail, and he is glad he cannot see his own face while he plays it back.

'Hey, Blake, it's me. Listen, I'm getting out of here. It'll take me a little while to fix up the RV, but I should be ready to go by six. I wasn't lying, you know, about the photograph, or anything else. I'll wait for you. One hour. And if you don't show . . . Well, I hope you do, Noah.'

41

'BEWARE OF FALSE prophets, who come to you in sheep's clothing.' Pastor Lewis thrusts his Bible into the air. 'They are but ravening wolves.'

Dalton Lewis stands shoulder to shoulder with Bryce Long and Cole Weaver, and the other straight-up-and-down boys from the basketball team, as he watches his father preaching from his little podium. He can still smell the gasoline, a lingering undercurrent now to the stuffy scent of people after a full day's work. His mother had had him down on his knees after school, scrubbing at the carpet until his knuckles were raw, and now, he thinks, flexing his red fingers, he's glad that the gypsy boy left his earring behind. Oh, he's glad.

'This stranger comes to town with his loud motorcycle and his long hair, and some of us are taken in by his slick talk, his so-called liberal idealism, and some of us offer him hospitality in good faith, inviting him to be a part of our cherished community, and yet behind our backs, he corrupts our children with drugs and homosexual deviancy.'

When Dalton's father mentions *hospitality in good faith*, big Jerry Maddox nods vigorously, turning expectantly to those standing around him until they begin nodding too.

'In the Bible, when Matthew talks about a wolf in sheep's

clothing, he's talking about exactly this kind of smooth operator, but you will know, my brothers, exactly when you are being led astray, because these people are not faithful to the teachings of Jesus Christ. No, it should be clear to us all that no good Christian man would seduce a member of *this very congregation* to commit the sin of sodomy. No good Christian man would try to intoxicate minors with illegal addictive substances. And no good Christian man would attempt to *burn down* a place of Godly worship!'

There are several gasps from the pews, the crowd fidgeting now as if they are a nest of ants that Dalton's father has ripped apart, exposing them to the daylight.

'But I,' Pastor Lewis shakes his head, hand over his heart, affecting a look of such deep sorrow that Dalton almost believes it too, 'I have to take some responsibility here, as we all do. Only when we are truly following the word of God, when we are living and breathing and preaching God's message at every turn – only then can we truly spot a wolf when he sits in our company. And, oh, my brothers, my sisters, what a wolf we have allowed!'

Here, Dalton's father reaches into his pocket and produces the gypsy boy's earring, holding it aloft so that the fang glints wickedly in the yellow light.

'These days they call us intolerant when we try to defend our rights as moral citizens of the world and, most importantly, as Christians. Well, I say we have been about as tolerant as we can be, don't you think? In the Book of Exodus, it clearly states if there is harm then you shall pay, life for life, eye for eye, tooth for tooth, hand for hand, foot for foot – burn for burn, my brothers, *burn for burn*!'

And it is this chant that the congregation carries with them as they pour out of the church, pile into their cars and pick-ups, and travel in convoy up the mountain towards the trailer park. Dalton goes with the other boys from the basketball team to buy garden torches from the Home section of Safeway. He hollers about justice and morality at the self-checkout, and then a couple of the guys from the deli counter tag along with them when they leave. Dalton imagines, just for a moment, that this is what his father must feel like when he stands up in front of the congregation, and Dalton likes it. Raising their young voices, like a pack of wild dogs, they wave their makeshift firebrands in the face of the oncoming night.

Dolly shivers and shrinks down into her coat. The electric sign for the clinic is on – fritzing a bit, but still joining the chorus of hums that make up urban America at night – and yet there is nobody inside. She scolds herself for not having come earlier, when Melissa would surely still have been on shift. Melissa would have known what to do about those diary pages; she would have been able to help. But now the whole of 17th is strangely empty. The wet ground is awash with reflected neon light, and there is the distant, familiar sound of O'Shannon's *Best of Irish Fiddle* CD from the next block over, but there are no people. Even for a Monday night, Dolly feels there is something not quite right about that.

She jumps when she hears footsteps in the alleyway across the street. But they are too fast and light to be a man's, and when little Chrissy Dukes emerges on to the sidewalk, Dolly sighs, relieved. She raises a hand to wave, but Chrissy hurries to the door of the Aurora diner, panting as though she ran all the way here, and after a brief battle with her keys, she ends up hammering the flat of her hand against the glass.

'Dad! Hey, Dad!' She steps back, calling up to the second-floor window. 'Dad, you've got to come quick. It's Beau, he's taken the truck!'

But there are no lights on and nobody answers.

Dolly waves again. 'Hello? Is everything all right?'

'Oh, Mrs Blake!' Chrissy clutches a hand to her chest. 'You scared the crap out of me.'

The girl is too short, her chest sticks out too much, and her hair is too straight for her to be Abigail, but Dolly surprises herself by saying gently, 'What's the matter, sweetie?'

'It's my brother, he went to that stupid sermon. God, Mrs Blake, I swear they've all gone off to lynch that poor guy.'

'Which guy?'

'You know, that guy! The one they're all saying . . .' She looks down at Dolly's shoes for a moment, and when she looks up again, her cheeks seem very pink. 'He used to come in sometimes. I just know Noah really liked him, is all.'

'Hold on, the gypsy boy?'

Chrissy bites her lip and nods. 'I'm so worried about Beau – you know my brother? Those boys he hangs out with can be so mean, and he gets swept up in stuff so easily. I don't want him to do something he'll regret.'

A nice girl, Dolly thinks, to worry about her brother like that. 'You listen to me, sweetie, we'll go to the station together and tell the sheriff.'

'Oh, no, we can't! There were cops at the service, Mrs Blake – I saw them. They're just going to let it happen, I know it.'

Dolly watches the cloud of steam growing from each of Chrissy's nervous little breaths, and she tries to think, but the only thing she can seem to summon to mind is the gypsy boy's face. She remembers him standing there in the police station with the curler in his hair, the way he'd just gazed at Noah.

It's only now neither of them is talking that she realizes

she can no longer hear the music from O'Shannon's. The two women lean into the night, and Dolly isn't sure what she's listening for, but she is almost certain she can hear the distant sound of many engines headed towards the mountain road.

42

Then

'You don't go into the woods to find yourself,' Samuel tells his daughter, when she is thirteen. 'You go to lose yourself, and you must, or the forest will know you don't belong, and it'll carry you off in its jaws.'

They are hiking along the memory of an old trail, now cluttered with the grey bodies of fallen trees. Somewhere up ahead, Samuel can hear a waterfall, but sound carries differently in the forest and it's difficult to judge the distance yet. He explains this to Abigail, and she nods, her patient face shining with sweat.

'You ever get lost out here, you find the river,' he says. 'Big Thompson flows east and goes through town, so you can find your way by that.'

'I'm not going to get lost, though, am I? I have you.' She elbows him lightly, and he elbows her back.

'Well, sure, baby girl, I won't let anything happen to you if I can help it. But that's the thing about the wild – you can't always help it.'

They come upon the remains of an old fence, green with moss and half sunk into the earth. Climbing over, Abigail catches her foot on a piece of barbed wire and it tears across the back of her ankle.

'All right, all right.' Samuel sits her down among the springy pine needles and takes off his vest, bunching it up against the wound to staunch the blood. 'Here, hold this tight. Hey, Abi, listen to me, listen, you got to do as I say.'

He can see his daughter blinking hard, staring at the fabric around her ankle as patches of deep red begin to soak through.

'What do I always tell your brother – what do you get if you cry?'

'A busted lip.'

'That's right. Now hold on tight, press real hard, and it'll stop, okay?'

He puts a hand on the top of her head and her hair is soft and warm. For a moment he is back in the jungle, his hand buried deep in Alex Major's hair to keep him still as he twitches on the sun-baked ground, bleeding out no matter how hard Samuel presses on the hole in his gut.

'Tell my mom I couldn't help it,' Alex had said. He was like Samuel, only eighteen. 'Dying in a place like this.'

Samuel watches his daughter now, barely flinching as she presses on the wound, setting her jaw like she knows she has a job to do and she'll get on with it without complaint. 'Atta-girl,' he says. Whenever he can teach her something, it gives the rest some meaning.

With his bloody vest tied tight around Abigail's ankle, they press on to the waterfall. He can tell that it's midday because their shadows have been sawn off, so they lie out on the boulders beside the river, eat the energy bars that Dolly packed for them, and listen to the water.

'I always like that sound the best,' Abigail tells him. 'Helps me tune everything else out.'

'I know what you mean, baby girl.' The sun beats down on the rocks under his hands, and he tries not to picture young Alex Major.

He would have been fifty-eight this summer, if he'd lived. The same as Samuel. That was no way to die, Samuel thinks, but sometimes he gets to wondering if this is any way to live. His joints ache and click all the time, these days; sometimes he thrills at the sound of gunshot, at others the slightest noise makes him want to rip off his ears. And when he closes his eyes, even now, sitting out in Colorado on a sunny day, the jungle shadows are always there, the body of poor Hoa who ran from him always with him, as if someone had soldered her shape on to the back of his eyelids.

But when he opens them now, there is Abigail, stretched out on the boulder, her slender, freckled arms tucked under her head, her red hair shining like a beacon. That is what she is to him. When he gets himself lost in those low, dark memories, he can always find his way back to her, his guiding light. She is easier to find than God sometimes, although he would never admit that to anyone.

The water froths and jumps like it's alive. Samuel thinks, In the fall, I will take her downstream to fish the kokanee salmon as they make their run. I'll show her how to twist her own lures, and we'll catch us some dinner, cook it up right there under the stars. He cannot imagine, sitting here among the quiet trees with his daughter, listening to the river, that this will be their last visit to the woods together. Two weeks from now he will beat her brother bloody because of some pictures on his computer, and then Abigail, his Abigail, won't like to be alone with him any more.

For now, he just smiles at her and says, 'Hey, baby girl, take off your shoes. I'm going to teach you something new today.'

Abigail does as she's told, frowning as she peels off the sticky fabric around her ankle. 'I think it's stopped bleeding.'

'Told you it would. Now come over here. You remember me telling you about how sometimes we had to hide from Charlie by getting under the water?'

She squints at him in the sunlight. 'What are we doing?'

Samuel looks at the river roiling under the relentless pummel of the falls. 'You're going to learn how to hold your breath.'

Now

'Where's your mother?'

Samuel stands in the hallway, staring at the space on the wall where the gemstone cross used to be. The outline is still there, where the paint has faded around it, but now the hole is covered with a piece of Christmas wrapping paper, which Jude is eyeing regretfully. The way the glued-on glitter winks as it catches the lamplight seems to be taunting them both.

'I said, where's your mother?'

'She just went out earlier, didn't say where. Dad, she's been weird all day. I tried to call you, but—'

'I was at the mill, wasn't I? Was out last night and then I've been working all day, which is more than I can say for you, boy. Why did I get a call saying you weren't at school today?'

'I had to stay with Mom.'

'Your brother should have seen to that. Where is he?'

'He said he was going to get some gas.' His son glances at the clock, tapping his finger on his cane.

Samuel nods at the Christmas paper. 'When did this happen?'

'I don't know, sir. I mean, I put the paper up, but the cross was already gone when I got back last night.'

'And your mom didn't say anything about it?'

'No, sir. She had a Valium, then just slept all day.'

Samuel nods again and eases some of the tension in his back. 'Your mother, she gets sort of crazy sometimes. You know that, don't you? Not quite right in the head.'

Jude looks at the patch on the wall again and folds his lips together.

'I should go look for her,' says Samuel. 'Not good for a woman to be out running around at night when she's not in her right mind.'

'Yes, sir.'

Samuel rubs his eyes, and as he shoulders past his son, he surprises himself by thinking: He's a good boy, Jude.

In the kitchen, he pours himself a glass of water and leans against the sink, listening to the tap of his son's cane on the floorboards as the boy approaches the kitchen door. If it weren't for the stick, he thinks, perhaps he might have been able to make something out of this one. Jude lacks Abi's fire, but he takes orders well enough, like a little soldier. It's a shame, really. There are too many years between them now – fifty, if he's counting – and that's more of a lifetime than most of his friends got. It occurs to him that maybe he should tell his son this, or something to that tune, or at least say: You're all right, kid. But what would be the point in that now?

Samuel raises his arms over his head and pulls on his elbow to crack his shoulder, groaning loudly as he does so. From the doorway, Jude is looking at him very strangely, as if he is only just recognizing him.

Emma's phone goes just as she is sitting down to dinner with her mother.

'Aren't you going to answer that?'

'Mom, we never get to eat together. They'll call again or text me if it's important.'

'Well, who is it?'

Emma glances at the screen. 'Oh, that's weird, it's Jude.'

'Jude Blake? You should probably answer it then. It could be about his mom.'

'Emma?' Jude's voice sounds very close but slightly echoey, as if he is cupping his hands around the receiver while he speaks. 'Hey, Emma, can you talk? I need to tell you something.'

'What's wrong?'

'I can't get through to my mom or Noah, but you have to . . . It's just, if you really are trying to find out what happened to Abi, there's something you need to know. It was right back at the end of March, I think I saw—'

There is a clunk, and then the line goes dead.

43

By the time Noah arrives, the RV is already on fire. He feels the heat on his face as he climbs out of his truck, sees the smoke rising above the trees before he sees the actual flames, but, somehow, he already knows what they're burning.

It was half past six when Noah left the house. He said, 'The truck was looking a little low earlier. I'm going to the gas station. Tell Mom when she gets back.'

Jude said, 'Can you pick up a new thing of toothpaste? I forgot to get some earlier,' and Noah said that he would, and then he put his suitcase in the back of the truck and left his father's house. I'll wait for you, Rat had said. An hour. Noah thought about the way Rat had looked at him that afternoon in the woods so many months ago, and he thought about the way Rat looked when he told him to get out, only that morning, and in his truck Noah put his foot on the gas.

Now he runs across the trailer park, past the residents standing on their roofs to watch, over the deep, muddy scores in the grass where a chaos of cars and pick-ups have parked, through the throng of folks, all eerily smart in their church clothes, as they holler like a pack of coyotes.

A fire of this scale has no real shape. It is just one great mass of flame and smoke, bulging out of the broken windows, vividly orange against the night sky. The door peels away, black and burning, as the whole vehicle begins to sag in the middle. Any view of the inside is blocked by a wall of thick smoke that stinks of burning metal, leaving a strange sweet taste in the back of the mouth.

The heat is like something solid that he has to prise apart with his bare hands, and somebody grabs him from behind and tries to hold him back. In his periphery, he catches sight of Pastor Lewis, ghostly pale in the dark, flickering around the edges as the heat distorts Noah's vision.

'Fire is the Lord's cleansing instrument,' the pastor cries, arms raised. 'Harm shall be repaid, burn for burn!'

Noah won't remember what he says then, if he says anything at all, because that is when the screaming starts. There are boys in the crowd – boys he has known all his life – who start to cheer, waving blazing garden torches above their streaky faces. People, it turns out, don't burn in any special way. Burning people scream like animals, and neither the cheering boys, nor the ranting preacher man, nor the fire itself, thundering like the engine of an eighteen-wheeler, can drown out the sound completely.

Noah kicks back hard against the sweating body holding him and feels it buckle, then breaks free, elbowing another man in the teeth as he tries to grab hold of him from the side. Somebody hits him with something solid across the shoulders, and Noah staggers but he doesn't go down. He doesn't go down because his father taught him that, at least.

He thinks, at the last minute, above the howls of the men and women, above the blaze, that he can hear his mother calling his name. But Rat cries out again, and then there is only the fire.

*

Dolly, arriving in time to see Noah disappear into the blazing RV, remembers that morning, eighteen years ago, when she came home and found her son in the bedroom closet. *You smell disgusting*, she had said, to a little boy who'd only stood there wanting someone to hold him, and she thinks now, Is this what I have pushed him to?

Dolly screams his name until her vocal cords are raw, and the pastor's wife has to hold her back from running into the fire after him.

'Is he dead?' someone asks.

Dolly watches her son stagger out of the RV and drop that poor boy's body in the grass, before he collapses to his knees beside him, retching up lungfuls of smoke.

She stumbles towards them. 'Noah!'

There is movement in the crowd, some people running away to their cars, others pushing forward to get a closer look.

'What's going on?'

'What happened to the Blake boy?'

Then somebody shouts, 'Get the fire department before the whole forest burns down!'

Noah's blackened face twists as he looks down at the figure slumped in his arms. 'Wake up. Rat, please wake up . . .'

He sounds so small and young again. Dolly says, 'Don't worry, I'm here.'

She crouches in the dirt beside him and presses her fingers to the base of Rat's neck. The texture of the skin feels wrong. His head rolls to the side, but he doesn't move.

'Hell, Ed, I think he's actually dead,' someone says.

'Jesus Christ.'

Ann Traxler is close enough that Dolly can hear her familiar voice directed at the pastor: 'You let this get way out of hand.'

'An ambulance!' Dolly cries. 'Somebody call an ambulance, he's got a pulse.'

It is Ann who eventually phones the emergency services, although Dolly will not find this out until later, and they will look at each other differently then.

Noah, his cheeks streaked with tear tracks, is trying to wipe the grime off Rat's face, his fingers rubbing frantically as he murmurs, 'Please, please . . .' Dolly closes her hands over her son's. She can tell from the way Rat's skin feels, all gnarled, like a tangle of ropes, that Noah won't want to see what's underneath.

Behind her, she hears Pastor Lewis say, 'Let him be. This is God's will.' He extends a hand, which seems to shine so clean in the firelight. 'Come back to town with us, Noah, and we'll get you cleaned up. Come back to God's path.'

Dolly pushes his hand away as she gets to her feet. *All these years of looking at the bruises on my son's face and now you care about cleaning him up?*

'You stay the hell away from Noah.'

'Come on now.' The flames snap, engines rev into the distance, and the RV groans as it melts, yet the pastor still sounds so very calm. 'The Lord makes it clear to us in the Book of Exodus, Dolly. If there is harm then you shall pay, life for life, eye for eye, and this boy intended harm upon our church.'

'But,' Dolly settles into her stance, and some faraway part of her mind laughs bitterly because at least she knows she can take a punch if someone starts swinging, 'what about the Sermon on the Mount? What about that? *You have heard an eye for an eye and a tooth for a tooth, but I say to you – if anyone slaps you on the right cheek, turn to him the other also.* What about *that*? You step back right now, or so help me, Ed Lewis, I will slap you anyway, and I will make it hurt.'

See how you like praying on that.

By the time the emergency services arrive, the heat of the fire has dimmed, and Rat's skin feels cold as Dolly holds one of his blistered hands. She takes Noah's too, and the three of them hold on to one another in some semblance of prayer, until the paramedics load Rat into the back of the ambulance. Then Dolly feels the weight of her son as he sinks against her, almost chokes on the smell of gasoline and burned fabric that clings to his clothes and his skin, but finally, as he sobs into her hair, she puts her arms around him.

'Oh,' she says, rubbing the back of his head. 'Oh, my boy.'

44

'THEY WON'T LET me see my face.'

Rat lies slumped on his side, staring blankly at Noah with his one visible eye. The whole right side of his face is covered with two large squares of gauze, and Noah hadn't wanted to hear the words the doctors said last night, had pushed them to the back of his mind, quietly certain that they must be making some mistake. Words like *serious upper body burns, temporary blindness, permanent scarring* – those couldn't apply to someone you actually knew. They just couldn't.

Noah rolls his neck, trying to ease some of the stiffness from having slept upright in a chair. 'It's probably just until you get the vision back in that eye.'

Rat's doctor had said he had something called an acute angle-closure glaucoma, caused by too much sudden pressure, and had told him to quit smoking.

Soon after they'd arrived at the medical centre over the mountain in Estes Park, Noah was taken into a small room by a different doctor. She'd made him take off his shirt so that she could listen to his lungs with a cold stethoscope. She bandaged the minor burns on his forearms, then gave him a washcloth and told him he could use her sink to clean up his face. The simple kindness of this stranger in the middle of the night had made his eyes water.

His mother had been waiting for him when he emerged. She put a cool hand against his forehead, the way she used to when he was a child and would play sick so he could stay home from school. 'They think he's going to make it,' she told him, and he wondered if she was playing with him then.

She's gone now: she had a bunch of missed calls from Jude. Noah is glad, in a sense, because he's worried that if she stayed much longer then the sudden affection she'd found for him would start to wear off. He still doesn't really know what to make of that, but he has decided he'll deal with it later. Rat needs him to be present, even if he won't say so.

Noah looks at him lying in the hospital bed, and the word *hanging* comes to mind. Something about Rat reminds him of the wind chimes that his father makes out of animal bones, just dangling there on a day with no breeze, uncertain of their purpose.

Rat's hands are heavily bandaged, with only the tips of his fingers visible. They took the worst of the damage, the doctor said. He was probably trying to put out the flames. Noah wants to press his mouth to them and say: They will heal and toughen, and I will buy you a new guitar to help you grow new calluses, and new books whose pages you can learn to feel again. He wants to lean forward right now and tell Rat this, and kiss him and kiss him, but when he looks again, his stomach turns. He can't help it: Rat has no fingernails.

'I'm sorry,' Noah whispers, and Rat looks away.

'I'm ugly.'

'You're not.'

'I wish you hadn't . . .' His voice is faint, gravelly. He raises one of his hands, turns it one way and then the other, and they both stare at his gummy fingertips. The hand, too, just seems to hang there, before Rat lets it fall heavily to his side again.

Around mid-morning, a nurse comes in to check his face. She lifts up the gauze with a pair of tweezers, and Noah catches a glimpse of the skin underneath, all red and peeling.

'Try and think positive,' the nurse says, before she goes, and Noah isn't sure which one of them she's talking to. He puts his hands into his pockets – it feels wrong to have them on display.

'Hey.' He speaks softly, afraid that somehow his voice might take up too much space and push Rat away. 'Is there anyone I should call for you? I mean, do your parents know where you are?'

'My parents?'

'Yeah, or a relative or something. I don't know. Don't you have anyone?'

Rat stares straight at the floor. 'No.'

Noah doesn't know what to say then, so he just sinks his teeth into his bottom lip and tries to think of some way he could be useful. Just sitting here makes him want to rip out his fingernails too. There has to be someone else in town who cares about Rat, someone else who'd give a damn that half his face has been burned off. Noah looks at him, one bandaged hand over his mouth, his eyes screwed up, like he doesn't want anyone to know he's crying. He thinks, I cannot be the only one who loves the way your lips turn up at one side more than the other when you smile, or the routes of the veins in your wrists, or the sight of your wet footprints on the floor after a shower. He doubts the kids at the trailer park are that cut up about it: some of those *friends* were there last night, waving their firebrands around. But Emma Alvarez – she cared about him once, not so long ago. Didn't she?

'I'm just going to run down to the lobby to make a call,' Noah says. 'I'll be right back, okay?'

He pulls the big blue curtain around the bed as he leaves, so that Rat can cry without anyone looking at him.

Grief is tidal. This occurs to Noah as he strides down to the lobby. One minute he can sit there and say that everything is going to be all right and *believe* it, and the fact that Rat needs him to say it gives him the confidence to do so, but then all of a sudden he's drenched in the awfulness of it all. What the *hell*? What a thing for a group of people to do to another human being. These people he has known his whole life, they just set fire to somebody, like they were getting together for a potluck dinner.

'Don't expect the police to do anything about this,' his mother had said last night. 'Some of the deputies were there and they didn't lift a finger. We can't trust them, Noah. We can't trust anybody but each other now, you understand?'

But Noah could tell from the way she had looked at him, with her big wild eyes, that this was about more than just the fire.

Dolly pulls over on 17th and kills the engine, leaning back against the headrest for a moment as she tries to gather her thoughts. It was an effort just to keep her eyes open on the drive home from Estes, but she still has to figure out what to do about these pages from Abigail's diary.

The police have given up looking for her daughter, she can sense it. When was the last time she heard about them interviewing a witness? The blood on the cardigan was encouragement enough for them to hang up their hats on a case that was proving too tough. Even the town will have lost interest now, after what happened last night. She wouldn't take the diary to the police anyhow – especially after she saw those deputies standing in the crowd all shameless in their uniforms as the RV burned – but she has to show it to someone. Someone who can help her decide what she should do next.

Dolly looks out of the car window at the clinic. Melissa is sensible; she's a good mother. Always had the measure of things, back in the day, when she still came around. Always sensed Dolly's unhappiness and Samuel's black presence in the house, even if she knew better than to try to do anything about it. And Melissa understands – that's the most important thing, the diary being what it is. She understands the mistakes that mothers can make. She will know the right thing to do.

A sudden knock on the glass makes Dolly start. Ann Traxler is out on the sidewalk, scrunching up her face as she peers inside the car.

Dolly rolls down the window. 'Can I help you?'

'Dolly,' she says, 'you will not believe what happened to me this morning. I've never known anything like it.'

'Can this wait? I have to speak to the doctor.'

'I'm sure you do, but just listen to this, Dolly Blake. Your husband has a lot to answer for!'

Dolly swallows. 'What's he done now?'

'Only nearly blew my head off! I wanted to ask about the gypsy boy, you see, wanted to know what happened to him, so there I was calling by your place, only obviously you weren't there, you were at the hospital, except that didn't occur to me until I noticed your car wasn't there, but by that point I'd already rung the bell and then your husband opens the door with a *rifle* pointed in my face, demands to know where the *heck* you are, says he's going to blow me away if I don't tell him—'

Ann has to stop to take a breath, but Dolly has already turned the engine back on.

'Did you tell him I was at the hospital?'

'Of course I did.'

'Oh, hell, Ann. Did you see Jude?'

'What?'

'While you were at the house, did you see if Jude was there?'

'Believe it or not, Dolly, I was more concerned about the gun in my face. Really, there is something very wrong with that man of yours.'

Don't I know it, Dolly thinks, and she hits the gas.

There is no sign of Samuel or Jude when she gets home. Dolly feels an awful sense of déjà vu as she moves through the house, calling for her son, and this time she checks all the closets, all the storage spaces, but her youngest is nowhere to be found.

She runs out into the front yard, calling his name until the wind pushes the air back down her throat. Then, as she stands there, digging her nails into her scalp, she hears a dull banging, something hard striking against wood. She follows the sound, hurrying around the side of the house, and there is the shed, the door jumping in its frame as though being battered from the inside.

'Jude! Jude, it's me!'

'Mom!'

The door is fastened with a thick padlock and there is no sign of the key. She circles around the shed to see if there are any tools outside, something she could use to cut the lock, but there are only splinters of bone and antler discarded in the long grass.

'Can you hear me, Jude?' She presses her fingers to the sliver of space between the door and the frame. 'I don't know what to do.'

She feels his fingertips cold against hers.

'I thought he was going to kill you, Mom. He had his old gun and he was waiting by the door. I thought he was going to shoot you.'

'Are you okay? Did he hurt you?'

Her son goes quiet then, but in the absence of his voice an idea comes to her.

'Did he take the rifle with him?'

'I don't know. He put me in here, so I couldn't see. I just heard him take off in the truck.'

'Right.' Dolly squares her shoulders. 'You hold on in there. I'll be right back.'

She finds Samuel's old M-16 in the hallway, propped up between their winter coats to conceal it. She had feared he might have taken it with him to the hospital, but he is angry, not stupid: he wouldn't risk bringing a gun into a building with armed security guards – they would shoot him on sight. There's a box of cartridges too, but the rifle is already loaded. He really wasn't bluffing about shooting Ann Traxler, she thinks. *Or shooting me.*

At first Dolly tries hammering the lock with the rifle butt, but she hasn't got the kind of brute strength her husband has, and it barely even makes a dent in the metal.

'All right.' It's been a long time since she fired a gun. Samuel tried to teach her a couple of times, before they were married, but she never had the same knack for it that he had, or their daughter. 'All right, Jude, stay as far back from the door as you can.'

'What are you doing?'

'Just do as I say.'

It takes her five messy shots to shatter the padlock enough for Jude to push the door open. He is on his hands and knees, his cane snapped in two in the corner behind him; she doesn't need to ask who's responsible, as she kneels down in the grass and puts her arms around her son. He feels sort of stiff, but that could be her too. It will take them time to find the way they're supposed to go together.

'Jude, I'm so sorry I left you alone with him. Noah was in trouble – I just didn't think. I was trying to help your brother, but . . . I can't seem to help any of you, can I?' She squeezes him tighter. 'Christ, I couldn't help any of you.'

'Mom.' Jude pulls back, and his face seems suddenly older. 'Do you know?'

'Do I know what?'

He glances back at the shadowy recess of the shed, just as the door bangs shut.

'Do you *know*?'

45

WHILE DOLLY IS still talking to Ann Traxler on the street, Emma arrives at the Estes Park medical centre. Her hand hesitates on the big blue curtain around the bed, afraid she will have the wrong reaction to the person on the other side. She has never seen anyone all burned up before. 'He's real sensitive about how he looks,' Noah had told her on the phone. 'I mean, obviously he's cut up about everything, but you know what he's like. He could do with a friend.' Great, in theory, but what if she's grossed out and just makes it worse?

Noah pulls the curtain back before she has the chance to turn around and walk back the way she came.

'Hey, Rat, look who it is.'

The figure sitting in the bed raises a hand that looks like part of a child's Halloween costume, all wrapped in white. He has only half of Rat's face, only one of those sharp blue eyes, and the rest is hidden beneath gauze. What skin she can see below the neck is patterned with thick red welts, and everything in between is puckered, like newly plucked chicken flesh.

'*Drăguță*,' he says, very faintly, but the word gets its hook in her, and she feels on the verge of tearing up.

'How's it going?' Emma sits down on the edge of the bed.

Her instinct is to put her arms around Rat, but she's worried part of him might peel off and come away with her. The burning had nothing to do with her, she knows that, but looking at him she can't help this feeling of guilt, like a hot cloth over her cheeks. *We're your friends and this happened on our watch*. Just like Abi.

'Been better,' Rat replies.

'Well, you look great. I mean, I'd still date you, if you weren't gay. And a drug dealer.'

Emma grins and the corner of Rat's mouth twitches.

The three of them sit together for a while, trying to forget there is any more to the world than the space contained by this big curtain pulled around them. Rat, she learns, gets tired easily from the pain medication, and eventually he drifts off. Emma watches Noah watching him, and asks, 'What do the doctors say? Is he going to be all right?'

Noah nods, still looking at Rat. 'They're talking about doing a skin graft on his arms. It sounds horrible, but apparently it only takes a few weeks to heal. They reckon he'll be out of here within a month.'

'Noah, what you said on the phone, about what those people did, I'm so sorry.'

'Did you know it was my mom who . . . ?' He rubs his eyes. 'She drove behind the ambulance the whole way here. My mom. Can you believe that? She's been so weird and nice, said she was even going to call our insurance people, try and sort something out for Rat. I got kind of mad at her about it.'

It has never occurred to Emma until now that Noah might dislike his mother as much as he does his father. She has always seen Dolly Blake from the perspective of a woman and has felt sorry for her for marrying that kind of man. She's never really thought about what it must be like for the boys, to have your father treat you that way, and for your mother to just stand there watching it happen.

'I think it's okay to be mad at her, a little bit.'

Noah shakes his head. 'Nothing good ever comes of me getting mad at her. Either I get hurt or she gets hurt, or we both do, and then . . . I don't know. It's no good.'

'What do you mean?'

'Like, I used to try and make Dad angry with her. I thought maybe if she knew what it felt like then she'd do something about it. This one time . . .' He looks up at her suddenly.

'Go on?'

'No, never mind.' He bites his lip. 'Jude was telling me yesterday how you've been trying to figure out what happened to Abi.'

Emma picks at a thread unravelling on her denim jacket. 'To be honest, I'm more confused about the whole thing now than when I started.'

'Yeah, well, that's Abi for you.'

'It's funny you mention your brother, though – I got the weirdest call from him last night. He said he had something to tell me, about Abi, and then the line just went dead.'

Noah frowns. 'Did you try calling him back?'

'Sure, but it just went to voicemail. That's been happening to me a lot these last couple of days, though, so I don't know. Boys, right?'

Then

On the last day of March, the snow still lies thick over the Rockies, and the people of Whistling Ridge are up early to shovel it from their driveways and grit the roads and sidewalks after yesterday's slush has frozen.

Noah and his father are clearing Hickory Lane, since nobody else will do it. The rising sun makes the snow a sort of peachy colour and Noah remembers how, when they were all much younger, he used to carve it out with an ice-cream scoop and serve it to his brother and sister. This summer it will be four years since the hole in the wall. Sometimes he misses Jude, the way they used to be together. He is so much younger, Noah used to pretend, just to himself, that Jude was his son, and he would take great pride in looking after him better than their dad did. It's different with Abigail, though. Perhaps they'll outgrow this grudge – Noah sort of hopes they will: it is exhausting sometimes, being angry. But it is difficult to really miss somebody when they're forever being shoved in your face.

'I should get your sister out here,' his father says. 'She'd clear this faster than you.'

Then why don't you? Noah thinks. He wants to curl back up in bed, where his hands and feet will be warm, and he can bury himself in a book until he forgets about his sister, his father, all of them.

'How's that make you feel, boy? Knowing a girl could do a man's job better than you?'

'She's not even yours,' he mutters.

Samuel stops, and looks at him with surprise. 'What'd you say?'

Emboldened by his father's hesitance, Noah says, louder, 'Abi isn't even your daughter. Mom had an affair.'

'You watch what you're saying about your mother.'

'All those years ago, when she ran away to Longmont.'

'Shut your mouth.'

Noah takes a step back, out of reach of his father's hands. 'She told me.'

'You're lying . . . You're lying to me, boy, and he that speaketh lies shall not go unpunished.'

Noah adjusts his grip on his shovel, possessed by the short-lived notion of clubbing his father. Then Samuel, heavy breath white and cloudy in the air, makes a sudden lunge for him, and Noah drops the shovel and takes off running up the lane, his father's cries muted by the snow.

To this day, he doesn't really know why he said it. He'd wanted to hurt the man, but why that particular line? His mother had run off to Longmont once, that was true. Back when she was drinking gin by the pint, trying very hard not to be pregnant with Jude, she had told Noah all sorts of strange stories like that. She said there had been a nice man who'd helped her with her suitcase, who'd bought her a drink at a nearby bar, but nobody who'd taken her to bed. Noah remembers because, moments later, he'd had to hold her hair back while she vomited, and he'd thought any man would be crazy to want to be around his mother.

But that morning, shovelling snow on Hickory Lane, it was the worst thing Noah could think of saying – because Samuel Blake took such pride in his daughter, even more than he took pride in his service in Vietnam, or in crying 'Hallelujah' louder than anyone else in church, and because Noah was not permitted to take pride in anything.

His father was right, of course: neither Noah nor his mother would go unpunished. Samuel took off his belt and beat them with the buckle, which left deep welts across their shoulders. The sad thing was hearing his mother admit to it – at least the part about staying in a motel in Longmont – like she thought maybe that would make him stop, even as the buckle swung around and caught her jaw. She lost a tooth that evening, but she never demanded any explanation from Noah, and he thought she was probably embarrassed that he remembered the motel story and holding back her hair.

Their punishment was a given. Noah had known that the

moment he opened his mouth, but the need to hit back at his father had been too strong. He never imagined Abigail might be punished for it too.

Now

Emma, leaving the hospital, barely registers Samuel Blake standing in the lobby, until he calls her name.

'Hey, you,' he says, beckoning her over. 'Why is it every time I turn around, I run into you?'

Emma never much likes the look of him but this morning he appears especially rough, like he's been sleeping inside out on the floor for the past couple of days.

'I'm talking to you, girl. Have you seen Dolly? Is she here?'

'I think she went home.'

Emma doesn't want to look him in the eye, so she stares at his hands instead as he picks at his cuticles, like it's some nervous tic. It is then that she notices the bracelet. It's nothing special, just a few tarnished shell casings threaded on a leather thong, exactly the sort of thing Emma can imagine Samuel wearing, except that the loop is far too small and it strains around his wrist, carving a red groove into his skin.

Samuel looks at her, and then at the bracelet, and then he turns around and strides out of the hospital.

'Hey, wait, where did you—?'

He moves fast on his long legs, much faster than her, and Emma only reaches the front doors in time to see his pick-up tearing out of the parking lot, almost swerving into another truck at the exit.

As she hurries to her own car, she tries calling Hunter again. He doesn't answer, and in the end, she just leaves him a message.

'Listen, do you still have those photos from that night at the Tall Bones? That one of me and Abi? I'm coming over. There's something I need to check.'

She can't help feeling she has seen that bracelet before.

46

Then

After spitting out her tooth in a mouthful of blood into the bathroom sink, Jude's mother takes half a Valium and goes to bed. Jude creeps out to the bathroom and stares at the tooth for what feels like a long time, marvelling at the way the blood slowly slips towards the plughole, red against the white porcelain, like a candy cane. Eventually Noah shoulders him out of the way to get some painkillers from the cabinet, and then they both retreat to their rooms.

As Jude lies awake, listening to the sounds of the house settling down, he thinks he feels like that blood in the sink – slipping away towards something.

At a quarter past midnight, he is woken by the sound of feet descending the stairs. When he hears the back door, he scrambles to the end of his bed to look out of the window. Everything is lit up by the moon gleaming off the snow and he can clearly see his father hauling his sister across the yard, his hand over her mouth as she struggles.

Jude doesn't understand: Dad never hurts Abigail. He doesn't know what it is he thinks he can do by going down there, but for some reason Jude feels he must. He couldn't help Noah or his mother, but maybe this time . . . Edging his way down the stairs and out through the kitchen, he tells himself that the right moment will come, that he will step in and stop it.

There is a light in the shed, bleeding out into the night from between the clapboards, and Jude creeps closer and peers through one of the gaps. He sees his father take off his belt – one quick, sharp motion – and the fear on his sister's face as she shrinks back against the opposite wall. Jude remembers how his father beat Noah and their mother with that same belt earlier that evening, how his mother had looked that same shade of frightened, how the buckle had left wet red scores across his brother's back. And Jude is only twelve, so he puts his knuckles into his mouth and limps back towards the house because he doesn't want to see that again.

But as he goes, he does not hear the sound of leather on skin. Instead he hears his sister cry out suddenly, and an odd, pained sound from his father. It isn't until that day in the woods, months later, when he watches Noah take off his belt with that same fluid motion, that he realizes what it was he really witnessed.

Now

Emma loses sight of Samuel's pick-up on the way back to Whistling Ridge. Perhaps he takes some back road to avoid the traffic, or maybe he really is driving that fast, but by the time the familiar church spire comes into view between the trees, there is no knowing where he might be.

She tries Hunter's phone again but there's still no answer. When she pulls up at the Maddox house, only his car is parked outside, there is no sign of his parents, and yet the front door is wide open.

She approaches slowly, clearing her throat. 'Hello?'

There is a red handprint on the doorframe. Emma feels the hairs on her arms standing up as if they were hundreds of little hooks in her skin trying to pull it right off her bones. Her instinct is to run back to her car, but she takes a deep breath, and then a voice from inside, faint but familiar, calls: 'Hello . . . is someone there? Please—'

'Hunter?'

She finds him in the hallway, lying on his back, the blood on his hands and clothes slowly seeping into the carpet around him. His shirt has been torn open. The wound in his gut looks like a second mouth, and when he tries to move it opens up, spilling more blood on to Emma's hands as she tries to touch him.

'Oh, God, oh, Jesus, Hunter! What happened?'

His head lolls to one side. 'He stabbed me . . . I went to the door and he just stabbed me.'

'Who? Who stabbed you?'

'After what he did to her . . . what he did to Abi, I had to help her . . .' Hunter's eyelids flutter as if he can't keep them open.

'Oh, no, no, please just look at me.' Emma takes hold of his face, shaking him as much as she dares. 'Hunter, come on, just keep looking at me, keep looking.'

Something to stem the blood flow, that's what she needs. That's what they always do on TV.

'Just hold on, I'll be right back.'

'No, don't leave me . . .'

'You're going to be okay, you're going to be just fine. You know what they say, it takes ages to die from a stomach wound.' She laughs, only because she needs some way to let the pressure out, and it's either that or bursting into tears.

In the kitchen there is a hand towel with little woodpeckers on it, so she takes it back to the hall and presses it against the wound, trying to apply as much pressure as she can, although she's worried she's hurting him even more.

'Hey, Hunter, do you have those photographs? That one of me and Abi at the Tall Bones?'

He blinks heavily, rolling his head to the side again.

'I know, Hunter, but this is really important, it's important for Abi.'

'Upstairs . . . the drawer . . .'

'I'm going to go get it, okay? But I need you to . . . Here.' She takes his hands and puts them on top of the towel. 'Jesus . . . You need to keep holding this as hard as you can, okay? I'll be right back.'

Emma has never had to dial 911 before and it takes her several tries because her fingers are so bloody. It is such a surreal experience, and there's a little part of her that is almost excited as she dials the number while taking the stairs two at a time to Hunter's room, her cellphone tucked between her shoulder and chin.

The man at the other end sounds too calm, Emma thinks. He takes her address and tells her to sit tight. They'll send someone as fast as they can, he says, but it's a difficult drive from Estes to that part of town: those mountain roads are pretty tough for an ambulance.

'What about the police?' she says, kneeling down at Hunter's bedside table and wrenching out the drawer. 'My friend was stabbed. Shouldn't they be here too?'

'Ma'am, do you believe the assailant is still on the premises?'

'No, but I—' She looks down at the Polaroid in her hand, at her and Abi's faces now covered with the bloody whorls of her fingerprints. Abigail's arm is around her shoulders, her hand dangling right at the edge of the frame – and there on her wrist is that same bracelet made of old bullets.

'I know who he is.'

He knows these woods better than anyone. He could have taken some secret back way from the hospital and she would never have seen him.

'Please, you need to contact Sheriff Gains at the Whistling Ridge Sheriff's Department. Tell him . . . tell him we know what happened to Abigail Blake.'

Just like TV, she keeps telling herself, and perhaps it is the adrenalin that makes her so certain of what she must do next.

Downstairs, she presses the towel firmly against Hunter's stomach, trying to ignore the warmth of the blood between her fingers, the taste of it in the air, like she's been holding a coin in her mouth.

'I'll wait until the ambulance comes.'

'Emma, don't leave . . .'

'I'm staying right here until it comes, I promise. Just hold on, okay? But then I have to warn Abi's family. I can't let him do this to them too.'

47

Then

It is a small-town sort of night – the last that Whistling Ridge will see for many years to come, although nobody knows this yet.

Noah Blake tries not to look at the mud-stains on his jeans as he peels out from the dirt road near the Winslow place. His face feels hot as he watches Rat, high cheekbones illuminated by the spark from his cigarette lighter, retreating in his wing-mirror.

Dolly sits at the bottom of the stairs, staring at the cross on the wall, wondering if this is the night. Maybe tonight her son simply won't come home, and what will she say then?

In their big wooden house, Jerry Maddox exchanges an anxious glance with his wife as he tapes up twenty grams of cocaine in an old Safeway carrier bag.

On the edge of the woods, Emma Alvarez shrugs and says, 'See you tomorrow, I guess,' and picks her way back through the shadows of the Tall Bones. Abigail watches her friend until she is out of sight, and her heart hurts as though somebody is sitting on her chest. The bonfire crackles and the trailer-park kids holler at the moon. Across the field, Rat emerges, dragging on his cigarette, in time to see Abigail turn into the trees.

'Are you sure?'

Hunter lowers his flashlight so that it isn't shining directly in Abigail's face, but he can still make out the way her eyebrows furrow when she says, 'Last week he tore the pages out of my diary – I know it was him. He didn't say anything, but he put the book back like he wanted me to find it. He knows everything, Hunter. And he knows I was supposed to meet you tonight. We're out of time, we have to go now.'

'But what about the money? My parents found the coke.'

'Look, you don't have to come if you don't want to, but I'm not going back.'

The forest creaks around them, brittle pines bending in the wind. Hunter reaches for her in the dark, feels the veins raised on the back of her hand. She does not meet his eyes, but eventually she grips back.

'Come on,' she says. 'If we go against the river, we'll know we're going the right way.'

'What about Emma? Did you say goodbye?'

'I told you, Emma has enough to deal with.' Abigail leads the way, tugging him behind her. The branches paw at them as though trying to hold them back. 'It's better like this.'

Hunter can't see her face, but he can hear it in her voice: she does not believe that.

'If we stay on course, we can be in Estes before sunrise and catch the first bus to Denver. No car, no trace, no nothing.' She adds, 'Did you bring the gun, at least? The one you took from Rat's place?'

He tries to ignore the little sting of *at least*, and tells her, yes, of course he did. 'I don't know about it, though. I've never shot a pistol before. I don't see why we couldn't just take one of my dad's hunting rifles.'

'He'd notice it was missing.'

'I guess.'

'You'd better let me have it. You're a lousy shot.'

'You don't really think we're going to need it, though, do you?'

In the beam of the flashlight, he catches the look on her face as he hands her the gun.

'Hunter, we're in the wild now.'

Samuel parks the truck among the trees, shutting off the lights and laying fallen branches over the windshield to prevent any reflective glare from the bonfire across the field. Kids are dancing among the stones that reach up out of the earth, like the devil's fingers. He sees Abigail, her red hair brilliant in the firelight as she melts into the forest, and then, keeping to the trees, he slips around the Tall Bones to follow. The ground is still damp from the evening's rain, and he presses his fingers into the instep of one of Abigail's footprints. It isn't the first time Samuel has had to track without being seen, and it's easy enough to fall back into the old rhythm.

They come to a halt where trees give way to rocks at the edge of a steep drop, ten feet or so, where the river has worn away the earth. Even without the Maddox boy's flashlight, Samuel can tell there are rapids below, the thundering rush filling up the gorge and pouring out into the woods. He watches from among the pines as the two kids lean up against a large boulder, stopping to catch their breath. The boy just seems tired, but Samuel recognizes in Abigail the kind of weariness that comes with hyper-vigilance. She twitches at every sound the forest makes. A bird taking off from a nearby tree makes her jump, and Hunter puts his arm around her. She is stiff for a moment, but eventually she relaxes against him.

'You're not saving me, you know that, right?' she says. 'You're not saving me, you're helping. There's a difference.'

Samuel emerges then, while her defences are down, striding into the clearing with his teeth bared. Abigail falters, her face white as the moon, grappling for something in her purse. The Maddox boy stands in front of her, arms raised, but there's no conviction in his fists: he misses the first punch he tries to throw, and then Samuel grabs him by the shirtfront and thrusts him aside, kicking the boy's ankles so that he falls on his face.

'Abigail!'

She has pulled out a gun, but Samuel grips her by the wrist and wrenches it from her, tearing off her shell-casing bracelet as he does so.

'Stop this, Abi, you hear me? Come on now, come home.'

She squirms in his grip, and then she tosses her head back and spits in his face. He lets go, only for a second, to wipe his eyes, but Abigail takes off towards the rocks.

'Don't you run from me, girl! Don't you dare turn your back on me!'

And in that moment he is no longer in the Colorado woods, but back in that clearing in Sơn Tịnh, rifle in hand, the laughter from the bar filtering into the night. He can see the whites of Hoa's eyes as she pulls away from him and runs, bare feet crushing dead leaves. 'Hey,' he yells, 'don't you run from me!' In that last second before he pulls the trigger, she looks over her shoulder and the fear he sees there is so certain he swears he can actually taste it: bitter, tangy on the back of the tongue, like licking a lemon with a cut in your mouth. The way she falls, the way she lies in the dust, he can still see those eyes. In support groups down the years, he will hear men say that they could not bear the eyes: the eyes always seemed to say something to them afterwards. Samuel had no such epiphany – there was nothing in Hoa's still, silent gaze: no anger, no blame, no forgiveness. But God forgave him, didn't He? God understood. Samuel had to get rid of the evidence, he had to – what would his mother have said . . . ?

When he looks again, the Vietnamese woman is gone, but Abigail is clutching her shoulder, a dark stain spreading under her hand.

Samuel makes a sound as though someone has punctured his lungs. Abigail looks from him to the Maddox boy, her eyes frighteningly wide, but in that last moment, when she turns back to him again, Samuel thinks he catches the hint of a smile pulling at the corner of her mouth. Maybe it is just a trick of the moonlight. A second later she is gone, over the edge of the rocks, lost to the thrashing water below.

He doesn't know how long he crouches there on those rocks, the cold air from the river down below hitting his face as he calls her name to the water. It feels like a long time. His knees seem to think so, the way they click as he stands up at last. When he turns around, the Maddox boy is still there, sitting with his back against the foot of a pine tree, his legs drawn up to his chest, staring at the spot where Abigail had been, either too shaken or too stupid to move.

Samuel takes a slow breath, weighing up his options. He could shoot the boy as well. He could certainly do that. But that would also make Samuel the only real suspect the police could place here. That's assuming they even get that far – bunch of inbred mountain folk in the Sheriff's Department – but still. It never hurts to have a fallback plan, and this kid, he's an easy read for Samuel.

He empties the remaining bullets into the river, wipes the

empty gun down with his sleeve, and tosses it into Hunter's lap on his way past. 'There. Now you shot her.'

Hunter sits bolt upright as if Samuel has just handed him a live grenade, gripping the pistol and staring at him open-mouthed. 'But I didn't shoot her, I would never . . .'

'I'm the only other person who knows that.'

The kid just gapes at him again, and Samuel thinks if this weren't his boss's son, he would have slammed that square jaw shut by now, knocked all of those too-straight teeth out.

'You want to get out of this town, don't you, boy? You want to go to college? Can't do that if you're stuck in a cell somewhere, and I know what happens to boys like you in prison. Believe me, no amount of Daddy's money's going to help you in there.'

Hunter scrapes his hair back flat against his scalp. 'Oh, God . . . Oh, shit.'

'You breathe a word of this to anyone, and you'll be learning how to make shivs out of your own toothbrushes for the next sixteen years.'

'But what about this? What do I do?' Hunter holds the gun up, fingers curled around the trigger, like he still almost thinks he could shoot it. He seems, to Samuel, like a man holding his own flaccid dick.

'You brought it. Not my problem.'

'No, you have to—'

'I don't have to do anything, boy. But if you do as I say and keep your mouth shut, then maybe I'll keep mine shut too.'

48

Now

Dolly almost shoots Noah as he comes through the front door.

'Mom, Jesus Christ!'

She lowers the rifle, her whole body sagging with relief. She had been so certain when she heard the truck in the driveway that it was Samuel arriving home.

'What are you doing here? I tried your cell, but I thought you were at the hospital.'

'I was.' Noah is still eyeing the gun. 'Then Emma told me about some weird phone call she got from Jude, and I started thinking . . . Hey, where is Jude? Is he okay?'

It's been a long time since Noah got that kind of worry in his voice about his brother. Dolly might even be glad, if these were any other circumstances.

'He's in the living room. Your dad broke his stick.'

'Where's Dad now?'

She clutches the rifle to her chest, like some treasured keepsake. 'I expect he'll be here soon.'

In the living room Jude, sitting awkwardly on the couch, says, 'You're not really going to shoot him, are you?'

Dolly thinks about what he'd told her, about the things that happened in her own tool shed, in her own backyard. About what Abigail wrote on those torn-out pages.

'Mom, we should call the police.'

'With what evidence? A few scraps of a diary? What you thought you saw when it was dark?'

'I *did* see it.'

'That won't matter much to them, not without . . .' Without her body. Abigail's poor body. It won't be enough that she wrote it all out by hand (her dear little hands!), they won't be satisfied unless they have a body to slice open and prod around inside.

'I don't think the cops round here give a damn,' says Noah, and when Dolly looks at him, there is a real coldness about him that shouldn't startle her, not after what he's been through, but it does all the same. She has always said that, when he gets that hard look in his eye, he resembles his father.

Dolly clenches her jaw. *Oh, my children, what have I made of you?* But this is no time for self-pity. For now, she must steady herself with the cold-steel clarity that fury brings.

Samuel arrives not long after. They wait for him in the living room, and he walks in holding his buck knife and wearing the blood on his hands like a pair of red gloves.

'Well, now, feels like I've been running around this whole mountain range looking for you, and here you all are.'

'Put down the knife,' Dolly says, gesturing with the rifle muzzle.

Noah is staring at his father's hands. 'Whose blood is that?'

Samuel looks down as if only just noticing it, but then he turns to Dolly instead, and she tightens her grip on the rifle.

'You haven't earned the right to carry that,' he says. 'Put it down before you break something.'

'You don't get to speak to me like that, not any more.'

'You're angry, Dolly, I can see that.'

'I'm past angry. Now put the knife down, Samuel.'

He gets a strange look on his face, almost as if he's smiling at her, and in an exaggerated gesture, he places the knife at his feet and holds his hands up.

Take him outside. That is what she has decided. Take him outside so the boys don't have to see. They have been witness to enough.

'Your dad and I are going to go out back now,' she says, not taking her eyes off Samuel. 'There are some things I need to talk to him about.'

'Mom,' says Jude, 'I don't think—'

'I want you and your brother to stay inside, you understand? Stay right here in this room until I say so.'

It could not be called a march, how they make their way through the kitchen and out into the yard, she moving slowly with the rifle poised, the butt resting on her hip, while he glances over his shoulder with that wry sort of look that makes her fingers itch. She takes care to keep her distance: she has no doubt he knows how to disarm someone if they're close enough.

Outside, she points the gun barrel at the shed. 'Tell me what happened with Abigail, in the shed,' she says. 'I have to hear you say it first.'

'First?' Samuel snorts. 'What's second? You're really going to shoot me?'

Dolly grits her teeth. 'You've benefited from your children's silence long enough. If Jude had to go through the horror of repeating it to me then so do you.'

'Dolly, you don't understand.'

'She was your *daughter*, Sam.'

'No, *no* – she was yours. You whored yourself out to some stranger, and then you brought that cuckoo into my nest.'

'She had your hair, Sam, the shape of your fingernails – she had your spite, too. Were you so angry with me you couldn't even see that? I didn't *do* anything in Longmont. I only wanted to get away from you, just like Abi did.' Dolly squeezes the rifle butt under her arm. 'Where is she? I know you killed her. I knew it as soon as I read what she'd written. Where's our daughter's body?'

'She's gone. The river carried her away.'

'I don't believe you. Christ, Sam, you . . . Your own child! At least let her have the dignity of a coffin and a headstone.'

Samuel shakes his head, his face reddening. 'No. I had to save her. She was growing away from me and I couldn't understand why, not until Noah told me what you'd done, and then it all made sense. That girl was all I had, Dolly. She was the only good thing I'd ever had a hand in, but then she wasn't even mine? I had to bring her back into the family, don't you see that? Don't you see that, Dolly? No, of course you don't. You've never understood a thing about me, but Abi, she was the only one who ever made it better, Dolly. Abi forgave me, she always did.'

'Abigail was a real person, Sam! She wasn't something your mother wheeled out to get you to do as you're told, she didn't exist just to ease your guilty conscience. She was our daughter, our only daughter, and she can't forgive you, Sam, because she's dead. Because you killed her.'

Samuel turns up his hands, palms open to her. 'God forgives me, Dolly.' A fly settles on his wrist where the blood is drying and begins rubbing its legs together. 'I am the way the Lord made me. He understands why I've done the things I've done. And if He can grant me forgiveness, then so can you.'

'Don't pull that one on me.' Dolly raises the rifle. 'God is always on hand to forgive men the things they do to women. But the women still have to go through those things first.'

'What's done is done, Dolly. It's done, and now all I ask is that my wife does her God-given duty and keeps her mouth shut.' Samuel scratches at his chin, leaving a smear of blood across his jaw. 'Come on now, woman. Put the gun down, before you hurt yourself.'

At first Noah and Jude do not react. The sound is a lot like the fall of their father's axe when he's out chopping wood. Then Jude says, 'Oh my God,' and Noah helps him stumble to the kitchen window. Their mother is standing there with the rifle, her whole body one stiff line, unmoving. Their father is lying on the ground with a hole in his face. Without really thinking about it, Noah pulls his brother against his chest so that Jude won't have to see.

There has always been some small part of him that, seeing his father shouting at the sky and waving his Bible around, had assumed Samuel Blake was God Himself. What Samuel hated God also hated because they were one and the same; the certainty with which his father punished them could surely only be the Lord's own wrath. Now, looking at the blood and the meat that is left, Noah understands.

My father was just a man all along.

49

Emma leans against her car in the gravel driveway, her sleeves still gummy with Hunter Maddox's blood. She watches the lights of the emergency vehicles washing the Blake house in blue and red, more vivid now in the gathering dusk, as the sheriff's deputies mill about the yard.

The Blakes are standing out front. Dolly has a blanket around her shoulders. It is supposed to help with shock; the people in the ambulance tried to give one to Emma when they were taking Hunter away. Now she wishes she'd accepted it.

'He came at me with the knife,' Dolly is telling Sheriff Gains. 'I was just lucky I could get my hands on the rifle in time. I didn't mean to shoot him, honest to God, but I panicked and it just went off.'

Gains gives her a slow nod, writing it all down in his notebook. 'And your sons, they saw this happen?'

Dolly looks up then, stark-faced, and Emma is certain she is looking at her.

Noah says, 'Yes, sir.'

'Jesus,' says Gains, and he repeats this several times, reading a handful of crumpled pieces of paper that Dolly has given him. Then he says something about sending someone round later in the week to speak to Jude, and Dolly just stares at the ground all the while. The sheriff touches her briefly on the arm and says, 'I'm very sorry for your loss, Mrs Blake.'

Emma watches Noah clap Jude on the shoulder. Then he breaks away from his family and walks over to her. His bottom lip looks well chewed, but there is a kind of weary grace about him.

'God, Noah.'

'Yeah.'

'I don't know what to say.'

She thinks about the things Hunter murmured to her as he lay there bleeding out on his parents' rug before the ambulance arrived. The things he'd whispered about what had happened in the woods.

'Did your dad say anything about Abi before he . . .? Sorry, that's probably really insensitive.'

Noah glances over to where the sheriff is talking with one of his deputies. Lowering his voice, he says, 'I'm going to send you something. Abi wrote some stuff down, and I managed to get some photos on my phone before Mom noticed. It's real messed up, and I don't know if it'll answer any of your questions, but Jude and I agreed, if you want, you should probably see what she wrote. You know, since you're the only person who cared enough to ask questions in the first place.'

Emma reaches for her phone, still patterned with bloody fingerprints, but Noah puts his hand over hers. 'Not here. Read it when you're alone sometime.'

'Is it true what they're saying? Your dad attacked you?'

Noah looks as though he is trying to swallow something large. 'Plenty of times.'

Over by the door, Dolly puts her arm around Jude, and he closes his eyes and leans up against her. Both look as though they have finally let go of some deep breath. Gains tips his hat and says, 'We'll be in touch.' Emma tucks her phone back into her jacket, and does not say anything.

Three days later, Emma drives over to Estes to visit Hunter in hospital.

'They had to give me a blood transfusion,' he says. 'It was so metal.'

'How're you feeling?'

'Oh, like I want to die, for sure. I'm living on a diet of bananas and toast right now – you know, while my stomach heals up – and the doctor said I can't have any nicotine or coffee. Zero out of ten. I would not recommend getting shanked in the gut.'

Emma smiles and sits down on the edge of the bed. 'I was going to text you, but then I realized you didn't have your phone. Did you hear what happened to Samuel?'

The watery sun dips behind a cloud, and without the sheer brightness, Emma can now see that Hunter's face is quite grey.

'Heard he got himself shot.' He adds: 'My parents were here yesterday. They told the police some story about how Samuel was mad at my dad because of work or whatever, and that's why he came over to the house and carved me up. It avoids any awkward questions about Abi, and it makes Dad look good. *Jerry Maddox, intended victim of brutal stabbing, sheds tears for innocent son clinging to life in intensive care.*'

'Catchy.'

'You know it.' He lets out a deep sigh and rocks his head back against the big pillow propped up behind him. 'At least he's dead, I guess. Am I allowed to say that? I'm saying it. I'm glad he got his face blown off.'

'Yeah,' says Emma. Then after a little silence, which seems to know it is on the brink of something, she asks, 'Why did you help me? I mean, you knew it was Samuel who shot her, so why did you help me go after your dad?'

'Jeez, my dad.' Hunter groans. 'I wasn't lying about that, I really did see him in the woods that night. But I mean, he kept her Chapstick, for Christ sakes. He was real weird with Abi, and then you said that thing about her cardigan, and I knew she'd been wearing it when she . . . I guess I figured maybe she'd made it, and then my dad had come along and, you know . . . finished her off.' He punches his mattress weakly. 'I don't know. It's all so screwed up, what happened to her. I was just trying to help.'

Emma fiddles with the zipper on her jacket. She thinks about the pictures Noah sent her of gently crinkled pages, how after she'd finished reading them, she'd dug out their last high-school yearbook and filled it with all the photographs and keepsakes of Abigail she had left, pressing them between the pages as if they were wildflowers, before placing the book under her bed. A little funeral that nobody else attended. The only coffin Abigail would ever know.

'I wish she'd told me what was going on.'

'Abi worried about you all the time. She said you had enough crap to put up with already. You know.'

Hunter looks her up and down, and Emma is suddenly uncomfortable with herself in a way she cannot fully articulate.

'I didn't ask her to be some kind of saviour.'

'I don't think she meant it like that. She was just trying to look out for you.'

'But I was her friend – I should have been looking out for *her*. Jesus, how come she could trust you but not me?'

'Honestly, Emma, I think it was shame. She didn't want anyone looking at her differently, especially not you. She loved you. And in her defence, she didn't trust me – not at first anyway. I was just some asshole who'd read her diary.' He sighs and flicks idly at the tube snaking out of his arm. 'She did trust you, I promise; she just figured you had enough to deal with and didn't want to drag you into her mess.'

Emma thinks about the things the pastor's son said to her at junior prom, about the way Andie Maddox looked at her that night at Hunter's house, about Jerry setting up his 'AMERICANS ONLY' sign outside the trailer park. A little lifetime of words and glances that have made her feel sometimes as though she were trapped like a spider under a glass, watching Abigail on the outside living fearlessly. But it's one thing to think about yourself like that. It's something else entirely to realize that others may have seen you that way as well. If Abigail had chosen to suffer in silence because she thought her best friend was just too busy being bullied, it feels like pity. And Emma feels like it's her fault all over again.

Would I have to have been somebody else, Emma thinks, in order to have saved her?

She catches the strap of her purse on the door handle as she's leaving the hospital, and it jerks her back sharply. Perhaps if she hadn't sworn so loudly, the people at the front desk wouldn't have looked up, and perhaps Jerry Maddox wouldn't have noticed her.

'What are you doing here?' He strides across the lobby, turning a few heads as if they can see his anger hovering around him. 'Haven't you caused my son enough trouble?'

Emma takes a deep breath as she tries to unhook her purse from the door. Not now, she thinks, please not now, not when Abi is— But her strap is all tangled and she can't get it free.

'It's your antics that landed Hunter in here, I hope you know that,' Jerry says. 'Now he's going to be benched for state play-offs, and he may never be able to play— Are you even listening to me?'

Emma feels as though her scalp is suddenly too small for her head.

'You leave my son alone, Miss Alvarez, or you'll end up just like your father.'

She looks up at him then, looks him right in the eye, and there is something almost gleeful there that makes her want to run. 'What did you do to my dad?'

'I just pointed out what can happen to people like you when you stick your nose in my business. But, you know, maybe you should ask your mother about that. I always did wonder where he disappeared to.'

Jerry rolls his shoulders and suddenly he seems to take up twice as much room. *Run!* Emma thinks.

'I don't want to catch you lurking around my son again. You've ruined his life, do you understand? I see you here again, I'll—'

Run! So she does, tearing the strap of her purse clean off as she makes a break for the parking lot.

Dolly is in the front yard when Melissa pulls up. She has her arms full of things from her husband's shed, and is tossing them on to a bonfire at the far end of the driveway.

'Are you burning Jesus as well?' Melissa says.

'It's all got to go.'

Plastic Jesus's mouth stretches wider and wider as the flames gather Him up.

'I never liked that one anyway.' Dolly wipes her hands on her thighs. 'Come to see where it all happened? Half the town must have driven by these last few days.'

The look Melissa gives her is almost fond. 'I've come to see you, of course,' she says. 'How're you holding up?'

'I don't know. I think I should know, but I don't.'

'Are you sleeping okay?'

'Are you here as my doctor?'

'No. My friend just shot her own husband in self-defence. I'm worried about her, is all.'

Dolly nods. 'How's Emma? I heard about what happened, her and that Maddox boy. And then she was here, you know, after Samuel. That's a lot for her in one day.'

Emma had had blood all over her sleeves, Dolly recalls, and she remembers thinking it was particularly striking because the girl's hands were mostly clean. The paramedics had probably wiped them off in the ambulance, but there was nothing anyone could do about the stains on the fabric. She imagines Melissa trying to scrub it out, the way she'd once had to scrub her sons' blood from the hallway floorboards, the night they found those pictures on Noah's computer. Even if they live, she thinks, we all end up with our children's blood on our hands, one way or another.

Melissa says, 'Emma's okay, I think,' and Dolly feels sorry for her, because that is what she says when people ask her about the boys.

Dolly rubs her eyes. 'It's the fire,' she says. Burning plastic makes her eyes water. She knows she should probably invite Melissa inside, but the house is a giant article of clothing that doesn't fit right, and she can't make up her mind how she wants to be in it yet. It feels important to get it right with Melissa, if she doesn't want her friend to slip away again.

'I enjoyed it,' she says at last. 'Shooting him, I mean.'

'God, Dolly.'

'God's got nothing to do with it.'

Melissa laughs, short and sudden, and Dolly joins her, both glad of some way of releasing the tension in their throats.

Then Melissa says, 'I've heard what people are saying about Abigail. A little, anyway. About what . . . he did.'

It must have been one of the sheriff's deputies who started it, Dolly figures. It wouldn't surprise her, after they'd seen what Abigail had written. Who could look at that and not have something to say? Or maybe it was Bill Tucker's wife Maggie, who does the department's catering. All of them gossiping like they did when Noah showed up to give Rat an alibi. Perhaps they don't even mean to be unkind. If you're far enough removed from an event, it just becomes a story, and stories make things easier sometimes, Dolly understands that.

'What are people saying?' she asks.

'That he . . .' Melissa swallows. 'And then he shot her. Up there in the woods, where they found the shell casing.'

Dolly nods.

'It's not your fault. Oh, Dolly. You couldn't have known.'

'Abi tried to tell me once. I think that's what she was doing. One morning she asked me to help her get the morning-after pill, and I . . . That's the terrible thing, I didn't want to hear about it so I smacked her.'

Dolly did not mean to tell her. Melissa looks uncomfortable, and Dolly can feel that discomfort beginning to take shape between them, something solid that will drive them apart again, but she can't seem to stop herself now that she's started. Just like Ann Traxler with the dead woman in her chair.

'Noah hates me. He's been so good about all of this, but he hates me. Do you know what he said to me at the hospital yesterday? I told him I'd sorted out the insurance for his boyfriend, and he said, "Where was all this when Dad tried to take me to *conversion therapy*?"' She shudders. 'Oh, it was horrible,

Melissa. He said it like that, right in front of the nurse. And then I tried to say I didn't know about that – because I *didn't* – and he said, "You always knew exactly what he was going to do and you just sat back and let him do it."'

'Well, I don't think he should have said those things.'

'But he was right!'

That's what she's really upset about. Until yesterday, until Noah had yelled at her in front of that nurse and that poor burned-up boy, she had thought that what she'd done with Samuel would be enough. That they could all agree on a clean slate now. But she was the one who'd fired the gun, she'd got to blast all her pent-up anger into Samuel Blake's face, not either of her sons. And anger has to go somewhere.

'I've ruined my children, Mel. All this time, things were happening to them and I knew, or I didn't know, or I didn't want to know, but it makes no difference. They still got hurt. I still did nothing.'

They stand there looking at each other for a moment, Dolly trying to figure out what Melissa is thinking about her.

Eventually Melissa says, 'I'm so sorry for what happened to Abigail. But Noah's still here, you know, and so is Jude. Recovering, it's like digging up bodies, except some of them aren't even your bodies. I think, with the father they had, your sons probably have a little cemetery of their own. You might have to walk through it every once in a while – sometimes they might even drag you through it – but that doesn't mean things are ruined for ever. Ruined sounds so final. Dolly, as long as your boys know they have someone to stand in that cemetery with them, I don't think you should worry about things being over just yet.'

Dolly lets out a sigh and tips her head back, staring up at

the sky, which is a washed-out shade of blue. 'I've been going to church long enough to know guilt when I hear it. Whose body have you been digging up?'

She cracks a smile, but when she looks, Melissa is staring at the fire and her face seems much older than Dolly can ever remember it being.

'My husband's,' she says.

50

EMMA DOESN'T CARE that she's drunk when her mother gets home. She braces herself against the back of the armchair and levels a bottle of whiskey at Melissa that she managed to take from Mr Wen's liquor store, with more success this time. All the colours in the room can't seem to stand still, but her mother does, just stands there with her hands folded awkwardly in front of her, like a loose attempt at prayer.

'Abi's dead.'

Her mother, whose friends are still alive, says, 'I know. I'm sorry.'

'She didn't want to tell me what was going on with her because apparently I had too many of *my own* problems. Did you know that, Mom? Did you know about all my problems?'

Melissa presses her lips together for a moment, and Emma doesn't trust how quiet she's being. She thinks, I stole this liquor, Mom. I lied to you. If I were you, I would be so mad, I'd want to scream.

But her mother says, 'I think Abigail was going through something none of us could really have understood.' Then she adds, 'Give me the bottle, please, Em. We don't have to talk about where you got it right now, but please give me the bottle.'

Oh, Emma thinks, she's trying to be gentle, like I'm crazy or something. It makes her want to be ungentle in return.

'I know you know something about Dad and you're not telling me.'

'Not this again, Em. I thought we were done with this.'

'I'm tired of people not telling me things. It's all right for you, you got to be someone before my dad, but all I've ever had is the lack of him!'

'Emma—'

'My whole life people in this town have treated me different because I'm Latina, and the one person who could have explained that to me, who could have helped me, he just disappeared. I know something happened to him. Something happened and you won't tell me.'

Melissa rubs her elbow. 'I *have* told you, Emma. He left.'

'People don't just . . . They can't just keep leaving me. That's not *fair*. What happened to him that night, Mom? What did Jerry Maddox do to him? What did *you* do?'

When Emma says that, her mother sits down. She actually sits down, as if Emma had walked across the room and pushed her on to the couch.

'Em . . .' Melissa puts her head into her hands. 'It wasn't meant to be like this. I thought I was helping . . . I never meant to hurt you.' Her mother stares at some distant spot on the carpet, her hands splayed out over her knees as she takes a deep breath. 'He was bleeding when he came home, your dad. They'd cut him up so bad, Jerry Maddox and the others. He still had bits of glass in his hands, and I had to pull them out with my eyebrow tweezers.'

'Mom.'

Emma sits down at her feet. She feels very much like a child, looking up at her mother's face, but the pale creases there remind her that they are both older now, so she puts her hands over Melissa's white knuckles.

'Your dad, he worked at the mill, and business was bad then. A lot of people were unhappy since they'd had to take a pay cut, and they got this rumour going that Jerry Maddox was skimming money. But Miguel took it seriously, started poking around. I think he must have found something, too, because he got Sheriff Gains involved – although he wasn't the sheriff back then, just some deputy – and Gains went and told his boss. Sheriff Ringer, as it was back then, he spilled it all to Jerry Maddox because the man offered to give him a leg up. Got him working for City Hall down in Denver, last I heard. Gains probably thought he was doing the right thing, I guess, but he should have known better in a town like this. If he hadn't said anything . . .'

Melissa sucks in her breath, and Emma isn't sure she likes the way her mother's looking at her.

'You know what they did to that Romanian boy? See, Jerry's always been pally with the pastor and he had him saying the most awful things in church back then. People listened to Ed Lewis every Sunday, and eventually they got it into their heads that migrant workers were the real reason they weren't making as much money as before. Miguel wasn't even a migrant worker, he was from Albuquerque, for Christ sakes, but these people couldn't tell the difference, or maybe they didn't care. One night, your father came home all bloody, said a bunch of guys from the mill had jumped him and . . .'

Melissa's eyes begin to water, although she is not crying properly, not yet.

'He wanted us to go. Wanted us to take off just like that in the middle of the night, said it'd never be safe for him here. But, you see, I'd just got my qualification. I'd worked so hard and spent so much money, and I was going to be a doctor, that was *my* thing, I'd earned that all by myself, and I wasn't about to give it up. We got married so young, and God, Emma . . . Your dad, he wanted to take you with him. He didn't want to leave his little girl behind. He said it didn't matter how white I was, you would never have it easy here. But you heard us shouting and you came down and saw him like that, with the blood on his hands, and you were so frightened. Oh, Em, you were so scared, you didn't want to go with him, you just held on to me and cried, and I held you right back and wouldn't let you go.'

Emma stares at her. Her mother's mascara is running.

'I loved your dad, I really did, just . . . I thought . . .' Her voice breaks and she paws at her eyes. 'I thought, if I could keep it a secret, what those bastards did to Miguel, you wouldn't have to grow up knowing that some people can be so hateful. I just figured they would leave you alone, if you had me. And I was ashamed of what I'd done, letting him go like that when he had nobody else. I let myself think I was helping you, but in the end all that's happened is you've grown up thinking your father never loved you, that *people* never loved you, and that's not true, Em, it's never been true.'

Melissa covers her face with her hands, sloping forwards in a way that feels like a landslide to Emma kneeling at her feet. Emma puts her arms around her mother, pulling her as close as she can like she's trying to contain her.

'Oh, God, Em, I'm so sorry.'

Emma has said *sorry* herself so many times this last month, she knows what it is her mother needs to hear.

'It's okay.' She says it for both of them. 'It's not your fault.'

After a bland dinner of soda crackers and banana, Hunter looks up to see his father standing at the foot of his bed. He has recently dyed over the strands of grey in his hair and he is wearing a tie.

'You didn't have to get all dressed up for me, Dad.'

Jerry Maddox smooths out a non-existent crease in his shirt. 'There's a journalist from Boulder, wants to do a story about the stabbing. It's dramatic stuff, Hunter. Your mother and I had our photo taken.'

'Cool, I guess. Do they want a photo of me?'

'They already got one while you were sleeping off the anaesthetic. Apparently you look more sympathetic unconscious.'

Hunter gives a low whistle and flops back against his pillow. 'So I take it you're still mad at me for breaking into your office?'

'Can I sit?'

He feels the weight of his father settling on the far end of his bed. Jerry appears to be attempting to cross his legs, but seems to think better of it.

'Hunter, I'm concerned you might have gotten the wrong impression the other night. That lipstick, or whatever it is – I wasn't keeping that because I . . . She dropped it, see. It was ages ago now, but the Blake girl was all strung out on something, so I gave her some water and we talked a little, and then she dropped that lipstick when she was walking away. Now,' Jerry holds up his hands, 'I'll admit that I shouldn't have hung on to it, that was just plain dumb, but I need you to understand: I never laid a hand on her. It was nothing. Just an appreciation of a pretty girl. You can understand that, can't you?'

'Does Mom know about your appreciation of pretty girls?'

'Come on now, don't be difficult.'

'Well, someone has to be.'

'You know, Hunter, I can't figure you out. Samuel Blake didn't come round and rip your guts out for nothing. If you were mixed up with the Blake girl, you could have told me. I would have helped you. I'm doing everything I can to keep your name out of it – hell, what do you think the journalist is for? But now you've lost out on the state championships, you can kiss goodbye to ever playing competitive sports again with an injury like that, and you don't even seem to care.'

'Because I *don't*. Dad, you're the one who wanted me to play basketball, because that's what you did in high school, but nobody's ever asked me what I want.'

'Well, what do you want?'

Hunter sighs and turns his face away. 'I don't want to end up like you.'

He feels the mattress shift as his father stands. 'This journalist that's come up to talk to us, if she does pay you a visit, I would appreciate it if none of this business with the lipstick came out. You know how they are down in Boulder. She's got very liberal sensibilities.' At the door his father pauses. 'And your mother. Don't mention it to her either.'

Hunter closes his eyes and nods. *Whatever you want, like always, Dad.* Maybe he owes his father that much. He had been so desperate to believe that Abigail might have survived that fall – to believe what happened to her in the end might have been somebody else's fault – he was prepared to accuse his own father, because of, what, an overheard conversation behind the Tysons' trailer? Because Hunter had seen him in the woods as he trudged home that night?

It was probably the rough waters of the river that had pulled her cardigan off, he thinks. And yet, when he squeezes his eyes shut now, he remembers the strange curve of Abigail's mouth as she disappeared over the rocks. How she'd said, *You're not saving me, you're helping. There's a difference.*

*

Jerry drives home with the radio on to keep him from thinking too much. He only slows the truck when he sees the journalist's car turning out of Elkstone Bend, and he pulls over to flag her down.

'You get everything you need?' he says, rolling down the window.

'Oh, yes.' She smiles. 'It's going to be a great story, Mr Maddox.'

He sighs with relief and doesn't care if she sees it. 'You take care now,' he calls, waving as she speeds off towards town, although she does not wave back. Women today, he thinks. This new-wave feminism is not a replacement for simple manners.

He parks in the staccato of late-afternoon shadows stretching across the yard, but he keeps his hands on the wheel a moment longer, even after he's killed the engine. I am not a bad husband, he thinks. Not a bad father. I am a man, and the Lord would not have made me this way if He had such a problem with it.

Sitting there, he can see that some of the aspens near the porch need pruning back: he'll have to get on that before winter sets in. The tarp over the garage roof has come loose, flapping in a wind that smells deeply of woodsmoke. That will need fixing too, and the loose board on the deck that Andie's always nagging him about. He leans back in the driver's seat and closes his eyes. Life will go on. Hunter will come around.

It's only when he climbs out of the truck that Jerry sees the writing on the front door. For one horrible moment he thinks it might be blood, and he gags, remembering the great hole in Hunter's abdomen when they first brought him to the hospital. Looking closer, he sees it is only red spray paint, but he thinks he wouldn't have minded so much whatever the hell it was written with, if only that journalist hadn't seen, in big block capitals: 'RACIST JERRY LIKES TEENAGE GIRLS.'

Melissa holds her daughter's hair back while she throws up Jack Daniel's.

'Mom.' Emma's voice has a slight echo in the toilet bowl. 'I think I need help.'

'Can I get you some water or something?'

'No, I mean, like . . . I mean professional help.'

It strikes Melissa cold for a moment, that word, 'professional'. As if what she has to give isn't good enough. As if what she's been giving all this time has never been good enough and that is how they've ended up here. If her daughter needs professional help, what will people think of her as a mother?

But this makes her think of Dolly – poor Dolly who had said the same thing. For an awful moment she pictures Abigail lying pale and silent in the dirt, her lips blue, her eyes glassy, sodden leaves tangled in her brilliant hair. Then suddenly it is Emma lying there instead.

Melissa shakes her head and rubs her daughter's shoulders, to reassure herself that her little girl is still there. 'Whatever you need,' she says. 'We'll figure this out.'

When the phone rings, they are curled up together on the couch. Emma has her head in her mother's lap while Melissa strokes her hair. It smells mildly of vomit, but that hardly seems to matter when her daughter is alive.

Emma's cellphone continues vibrating in her purse, and eventually, tired of the sound, Melissa picks the bag up off the floor, rummaging between scrunchies and tampons and a can of red spray paint. She doesn't recognize the number, but she answers anyway, thinking it could be Emma's friend from the hospital. At first she can't hear anything, but then, faintly, comes the sound of someone breathing.

'Who is this?' she asks. 'Do you want to talk to Emma?'

The breathing stops and there is just the faint crackle of static.

'Hello?'

The line goes dead.

51

THE DAY AFTER Halloween, when pumpkins still sit grinning from every porch and loose candy wrappers rattle down the sidewalks in the mountain wind, a crowd gathers outside the Whistling Ridge cemetery to watch the Blake family put Samuel into the ground.

They tug on their scarves and stamp the cold out of their feet, whispering. There is Dolly all in black, the heels on her best shoes still worn down unevenly, but she stands straighter now, one arm around her younger son, who holds his head up, daring anyone to look at them for too long. And there is Noah, his lips still chapped, his nose still broken, but beside him, Rat takes off a pair of big dark glasses, tilting his head up slightly to feel the bleary sunlight on the puckered side of his face.

People are looking at Rat. They are looking at Pastor Lewis too, as he reads the burial service. There is a sense of resentment in the air, Dolly thinks, as she watches a Hershey's wrapper alight on the edge of her husband's coffin. Folks resent Ed Lewis for inciting them to do what they did that night at the trailer park. They feel guilty, but they can't all blame themselves, so they will blame him instead. A week later, people will begin asking when the last time was anybody saw the Lewis family.

'In the sweat of your face you shall eat bread until you return to the ground, for out of it you were taken; for dust you are, and to dust you shall return.'

Dolly isn't sure what she's expecting – a sense of closure, maybe, at seeing Samuel lowered into the earth. It's not as simple as that, she knows. Closure comes with understanding, and she will never really understand why he was the way he was. There will be people down the years who nod knowingly and say it was because of Vietnam, or because Samuel was a 'something-o-path' or a 'something-ist', and she will say, 'Yes, maybe you're right,' but it won't make things any clearer. In that sense, Abigail is not the only thing he has denied her burying.

As it is, she can only burn his plastic angels and his bone wind chimes and have someone plaster over the hole in the wall, and that will have to be enough for now.

After the service, Noah says, 'You go on, Mom. I'll see you back at the house.' He stands by the grave with his hands tucked up under his armpits, while everyone else files out slowly, as if there is still some part of them that doesn't quite want this to be over yet. He understands that. Transitional moments like these give the impression that things will be different next time around, but what if nothing's really changed?

Rat leans on a nearby headstone and pulls out a carton of cigarettes so scrunched up that Noah doesn't even realize what they are until he hears the click of the lighter.

'Hey, stop that.'

'Blake, you're killing me here. Just one. I won't tell if you don't.'

'You know what the doctor said about your eye.'

'My eye's fine.' Rat lowers his sunglasses and waggles his one remaining eyebrow.

Noah sticks out his leg and taps the toe of his boot against the little plastic cross currently marking his father's burial plot.

Rat says, 'Come on. Let's go for a walk.'

The cemetery is empty now so the two of them meander among the graves, arm in arm, while the winter wind catches up their hair and makes their jackets flap.

'Do you talk to your parents at all?' Noah asks.

'I haven't spoken to them since I was . . . eighteen, I think?'

'Is it better that way?'

'Oh, I see. This is about your mother, isn't it?'

Noah nudges him. 'Don't change the subject.'

Rat nudges back. 'You're upset because she won't have a proper row with you. I think you're just going to have to accept that she's sorry.'

'Right, but it's not that simple. I mean, she screwed up, you think she should just get away with it?'

Rat frowns, which always makes him look more severe than he means, these days, the one side of his face crinkled like old newspaper. 'You think that's how the world gets fixed,' he says, 'people just getting mad and staying mad? I know we've all got that fantasy of telling the people who hurt us just how much it hurt, but most of the time they're not even sorry, and then what? You're just going to be pissed off for the rest of your life?'

'But aren't you still mad? About the fire, I mean?'

'Now who's changing the subject.' Rat turns his face away so that Noah can see only the unburned side.

They have slowed to a stop, and Rat stomps on the dead leaves collecting by his feet, getting mulch all over the pointy patent boots that Dolly bought for him, perplexingly, when he got out of hospital.

Noah says, 'You never talk about your mom.'

'I was living in an RV on a whole other continent. I imagined that spoke for itself.'

'Right.'

'Look, Blake, take it from someone who has literally nothing: one day you're going to want a mother. Accepting her apology doesn't mean you think that what she did was okay, it just means things get to change now. Isn't that what you want?' Noah watches him rearrange his hair to conceal his disfigured ear. 'And for the record, of course I'm still mad about the fire. But who does that benefit? Can't go on being ugly *and* miserable, or even you'll get sick of me.'

He starts to walk away, but Noah grabs him by the elbow, cupping his scarred jaw in the palm of his hand. 'Don't talk like that.'

'It is what it is, Blake.'

'None of this – you and me – ever happened because I looked at a boy and thought he was beautiful. It happened because when I looked you looked back. You saw me. I felt like no one had ever really seen me before, and now I see you too, just like this. And I'm still looking back at you.'

Noah kisses the top of his head, and he thinks he likes the way Rat smells more like shampoo than cigarettes now. He wraps an arm around his shoulders. 'You won't ever have *nothing*. Just by the way.'

It isn't a wake so much as a handful of people who didn't want the family to be alone. Melissa brings a casserole. Ann Traxler brings a dish full of chocolate brownies that she baked herself. 'They're not *funny* brownies,' she keeps saying, and Dolly thinks that is the most absurd thing she can imagine, Ann baking pot brownies, but also more's the pity. Samuel would have hated it.

When she hears the rumble of Rat's motorcycle in the

driveway, sees Noah climbing off the back, she has the strongest feeling that some guillotine blade has just come down between them. His returning here for the wake is only performative: in his mind a decision has been made, she can tell. He is already far away.

There is so much she wants to tell him, but in the end, all she can do is push his bright hair back from his face and say, 'California's a long way. I'll miss you.'

Noah nods, looking at his boots. 'Jude can finally teach you how to video call.'

'Oh, sure.'

It's not just him leaving, it's all of it: the memory of the weight of that rifle in her hands, the nightmares where she rolls over to find Samuel still lying beside her, and the fact – the awful, weary fact – that her daughter really is dead.

'Mom . . .'

He hesitates, and for a moment she's not sure if he's going to do it. Then suddenly he has her in his arms, and how big they are now, how small she feels pressed close against him. He is no longer that baby who made her husband hate her. He hasn't been for some time.

'Promise you'll call,' she says. 'Only when you have time. But promise.'

She lets go of him and looks over to where Rat is letting Emma Alvarez try on his sunglasses. 'He's nice.'

'Yeah, he is.'

Noah says this carefully, as though he suspects it might be a trick, and Dolly can't help thinking: I did that to him. That thought will keep coming back to her, every now and again, throughout the lives of both her sons. There will be drunken phone calls at strange hours of the night, angry calls, and calls that end with tearful I-love-yous. There will be one Thanksgiving when Noah storms out and smashes a bottle on his father's grave; there will be many more that do not end this way, but then a Valentine's Day when Jude announces he is getting a divorce, and a Christmas when Noah refuses to come home at all. Every time, Dolly will think, *Yes, I did this to them*. But although neither of them ever says it aloud, it will never be her that Jude and Noah blame.

Evening stealing over the mountains finds Emma and Hunter at the Tall Bones, sitting on the trunk of her car while the season's first snow settles thin and tentative over their hair and shoulders. At the edge of the trees, the scrubby ground where Emma last saw Abigail has already disappeared beneath the white.

She's always thought they were eerie, these tall, pale rocks, but now they seem to her like a mirror of all things: half buried in the earth, half reaching towards the sky, they are the meeting place between two worlds – the fixed and the possible, the past and the future.

She could stay. She could wait for the grass to grow up around her ankles and fix her here too. There will always be a part of her – she understands this now – that will remain here, where her mother is, where Abigail was. But then somewhere out there is her father. For the first time since she was four years old, she can feel herself reaching towards him.

It's strange, the liminal sense this place gives her. She imagines she can see them all – her friends, and what a word that is – their lives stretching upwards as though each of them were a stone in this circle. One day (and she is sure of this, although she cannot say why), driving back from California, Noah and Rat will stop at some lonesome gas station on the other side of the Rockies. And Rat, waiting in line to buy nicotine patches, will see a red-haired woman, who smiles at him like she half remembers him from another place, another life. Out in the dusty daylight, the smell of pine resin in the air beckoning them home, he will watch this woman climb into a car with a man who kisses the top of her head, with children who tug on her red hair and make her laugh. And when Noah, who no longer chews his lip or walks with his shoulders hunched, says, 'Who's that?' Rat will simply watch the car drive away, leaving insect-shaped offerings all along the blacktop. He will wait for the dust to settle before he replies, 'Nobody, *dragă*,' and who's to say that won't be true?

'Em, you're shivering. Here.' Hunter takes off his coat, holding it out to her awkwardly.

Emma smiles and shakes her head. The coat smells musty, and reminds her too much of Rat's jacket, which he once gave to her here, at the Tall Bones, when they were all different people. Instead she takes Hunter's hand, stroking her thumb gently over his knuckles, because she wants to tell him, wants him to know that she knows: We *are* different people now.

'We can head back,' he says, 'you know, if you're cold.'

'In a minute. Just a minute.'

She has always loved the way snow falls, so soft and noiseless, filling up the hollows of the landscape. That is what they need now, she thinks, this moment of quiet, just for themselves, before they continue.

Acknowledgements

I'd like to thank my editors, Kirsty Dunseath in the UK and Kaitlin Olson in the US, for their commitment to this novel and for being such a joy to work with. Thank you to Alison Barrow for promoting this book so passionately, and to everyone at Transworld who worked so hard to make it happen. I am beyond grateful for my wonderful agent Alice Lutyens for all her astute advice, whether on writing or life, and for Sophia MacAskill at Curtis Brown for reading *Tall Bones* in the first place.

Thanks to Anna Davis and Jack Hadley at Curtis Brown Creative; to everyone on CBC's online novel-writing course for their wise words; and to my tutor Lisa O'Donnell for giving me confidence in my writing.

Thank you to Aude Claret for all her insight and fierce encouragement. To Lucy and John for their patience and enthusiasm. And to Jane Bailey for her unwavering support, without which this novel would not have been written at all.

Lastly, my thanks to all the people between Texas and Colorado who shared their stories with me in a country so divided. Your nation is richer for having you in it.

Anna Bailey was born in 1995 and grew up in Gloucestershire, before going on to study Creative Writing at Bath Spa University. She lived in Texas and Colorado before returning to the UK and enrolling on a course with Curtis Brown Creative, where she wrote her first novel, *Tall Bones*, inspired by her experience of small-town America

Twitter: @annafbailey
Instagram: @annabaileywrites